To Amy

ESCAPE FROM
paradise

— ✦ —

GWENDOLYN
FIELD

XOXO
Gwen.
Field

DEDICATION

To all the women out there struggling to do it *all*.
You are amazing, and this is for you.

CHAPTER ONE

Full blown guilt didn't hit me until I stepped off the plane into Mexico's heat.

Crap...If Mom and Dad find out I went to Cancun for spring break behind their backs—

"*Wooo!* We're in Meh-hee-co, baby!" Sabrina, one of the three sorority sisters I'd come with from Texas, screamed right in my ear. She was ready to go with her sunglasses and floppy sunhat covering her red curls. "Cheer up, girl." She linked her arm through my elbow and pulled me tighter. "Nobody's gonna find out. What happens in Cancun stays in Cancun." She bumped her hip to mine and I tried to smile.

"God, Angela, I hope you don't whine about your parents the whole three days we're here," said Caryn from behind us.

And just like that my smile disappeared.

"Chill, Caryn." Sabrina shot the warning over her shoulder, squeezing my arm.

Caryn decided to come at the last minute, much to my

disappointment. We used to get along great, and even joke about being twins with our straight, blonde hair. But she had this weird competitive jealousy toward me ever since we were pledging last semester. Rumor had gotten around that her boyfriend left her to try and hook up with me. He never attempted to talk to me, probably because rumor also got around that I wanted nothing to do with him. I was newly single after an emotional breakup with my high school boyfriend, so the last thing I wanted was drama. But the damage was done, and Caryn had been bipolar toward me ever since.

"Everything's gonna be great, guys." Megan slid on her sunglasses and tugged my ponytail. I loved Megan, our resident peacemaker, always positive and as boy crazy as could be. Her dark spirals bounced on her shoulders as she pulled Caryn up and linked arms with the rest of us. The four of us—Caryn, Megan, Sabrina, then me—set off from the airport together.

I did all the talking with the cab driver and hotel personnel. Even though most of them spoke English, I enjoyed the opportunity to practice my Spanish skills. It was one of the main reasons I'd wanted to come so badly. I was majoring in Spanish and minoring in Communications. Nothing beat real life conversation. Plus, the locals seemed happily surprised when this little blonde American girl spoke the native language, and I liked crushing some of those stereotypes about how most of us spoke nothing but English. Even though the stereotype was true.

The concierge was so pleased with my efforts that he sent four rum punches to our room. We cheered when we saw the beautiful glasses with cherries, lime wedges, and little umbrellas.

"Cheers to Angela and her mad Español skills," Caryn said in one of her kind moments. I felt myself warm to her when she smiled at me. When she was nice like this it made me miss her.

"Cheers," we all said, clinking glasses.

I took a tentative sip and coughed.

"Damn!" Sabrina laughed.

"This has to be local rum." Megan took another drink and smacked her lips, raising her eyebrows. "We're not in Texas anymore girls!"

I wasn't a huge drinker. The girls had come to count on me as their designated driver, and that worked for me because alcohol made me puke every time.

But I drank half of the strong punch before handing it to Sabrina. She rewarded me with a loud kiss on the cheek. Caryn and Megan went out on our tiny balcony and made cat calls to guys walking by.

I reached for my phone, checking for missed messages from my parents. Sabrina took it from my hand and tossed it to my bag.

"They think we're camping somewhere with no reception, remember?" Sabrina whispered, "We made a pact not to post any pictures. They'll never find out. Now get your suit on and let's have some fun."

I nodded. It wasn't that I'd never lied to my parents before. I'd snuck out back in high school, and forged notes to skip class, but this was different. They'd specifically told me "Absolutely not" when I asked to go to Cancun. Yes, they were overprotective of their only daughter, even though I was a sophomore in college now, and that was annoying. But they trusted me and I'd used that to manipulate them.

After that, when I'd approached them with Sabrina's fake plan for a camping trip on her grandparent's land, they thought it was a great idea. They gave me way too much money to buy supplies and food. Their money coupled with money I'd earned over Christmas break was just enough to cover my flight and hotel.

If I'd have known the guilt would be this bad I wouldn't have gone. But now I was here for three nights, and there was nothing I could do to take it back. So I reached for my bathing suit and told myself I'd use the experience to hone my language skills for when I was a translator someday. Everything was going to be fine.

It was easier to let the guilt slip away when my toes dug into the soft, hot sand and I was peering out at crystal blue water. Texas beaches were nice, but nothing like this. The sand here was white, and the atmosphere up and down the beach was like a huge party. Most of the people were U.S. college kids on Spring break, but some were from other countries, and then there were the local hotties with their dark tanned bodies. I had to admit it was kind of awesome.

"I *so* need a guy," Megan said, eyeing the group playing volleyball near where we sat on our towels.

"So does Angela," Sabrina said. She tried to hand me her margarita.

"No thanks." I was still slightly lightheaded from half a freaking drink. "And I don't *need* a guy."

"Need, want, whatever," Megan said, flipping her dark curls at a six-pack who walked by. She giggled when he grinned at her.

"How long has it been?" Sabrina asked me. "A year?"

My face warmed and it had nothing to do with the blazing sun.

"Ten months," I mumbled.

All three of them snorted as they tried to hold back laughter, even Caryn, though she looked asleep as she lay on her back, soaking rays on her flat belly.

"Bitches," I said, falling back on my towel and closing my eyes. When they laughed harder I cracked a smile too. "It's not like I never hook up."

"She's a relationship kind of girl," Megan offered.

It was true. I liked the comfort of being committed if I was going to have sex, and I'd only had that with one person in my life. Too bad our love hadn't been strong enough to last through the long distance.

Sabrina scoffed and leaned on her elbows. "We're all hookin' up in Cancun."

The three of them raised their margaritas and I raised my lame bottle of water.

"Cheers to boys," Megan said.

"*Hot* boys," Caryn corrected, and we all drank to that.

When I was finally relaxed enough to let go of the guilt, I came alive. The first two days flew by in a blur of late nights and waking hours soaking up sun. I was open to meeting a guy, but when that didn't happen I was happy to keep an eye on my three friends and make sure we all made it back to the room safely each night. During the days the other three might sneak off with guys they'd met, but at night we all came home together—no sketchy hotel flings. When Megan had asked to stay out longer the night before, and the guy she was with offered to walk her back to our room, we shot them down and dragged her back, ignoring her drunken pleas.

She was still bitter when we all woke at ten the next morning.

"He was the cutest guy I've met here! What if I can't find him again? It's our last day!"

"There's tons of guys here, Meg," Sabrina grumbled from her hungover fetal position on our bed.

Megan flung her forearm over her eyes. "You guys are evil. Seriously. Spawns of the horned one."

We smiled at that, because we knew she loved us.

"He could've been a serial killer using his baby face as a disguise," I told her. I was the only one up and about, moving around the room getting ready.

"Or some guy on a mission to knock-up as many girls as possible," Caryn said from her spot next to Meg.

"Or a herpes and HIV carrier with a vengeance against women," Sabrina chimed from her fetal position.

"Ugh!" Megan flopped onto her belly and groaned into her pillow.

I leaned forward and smacked her butt, making her jump. "Come on. Last day on the beach. Let's go!"

"Geez, someone's all hot to trot after moping the whole first day," Caryn said. She was looking just as groggy as Megan.

"I didn't mope the *whole* time." I grabbed my brush and ran it through my shoulder-length layers. "Just the first couple hours."

"I need some fucking coffee," Sabrina said, rubbing her temples. "But I can't move."

I sighed. "You guys suck. How about I go get us some coffees and those pastry things? But when I get back you have to get your little asses out of bed. Deal?"

They grumbled their agreement, and Sabrina pointed to her purse with the money. I took what I needed and headed out.

We'd discovered an amazing cafe and restaurant near the hotel the day before. I smiled at the aproned woman behind the counter.

"Quatro cafe con leches, por favor," I said.

She brightened at my use of Spanish and said, "Ah, bueno" as she got to work.

The bell to the door chimed as I hovered over the pastry counter, staring in at the mouth-watering delicacies. I bit my lip, trying to decide between the little strawberry shortcakes or fruit-filled pastries. The rolls also looked heavenly.

"It's hard to decide, no?" said a rich male voice from behind me.

I turned and my insides swooped at the sight of the gorgeous Hispanic guy. Definitely a local with his smooth, accented English, tanned skin, and black wavy hair. But he was dressed in expensive-looking clothes—crisp dark jeans that fit perfectly and an unwrinkled button down shirt.

A fierce blush rose to my cheeks when I realized I'd been staring. I smiled a little and glanced back at the case, saying, "Yes...everything looks so good."

The guy stepped closer. I couldn't get a read on how old he might be. Most likely older than me, probably mid-twenties.

"It is all good, trust me. But my favorite is the chicken soup."

"Chicken soup?"

He stood next to me again.

"Sí. The arroz con pollo. It's delicious." Rice with chicken. He smiled with straight, white teeth, and my tummy wobbled with excited nerves.

"That sounds...good." I would have never bought chicken soup by choice, but with this guy recommending it I wanted to buy the whole pot.

"My name is Fernando."

He stuck out a warm, firm hand and I shook it, glad when he didn't let go right away.

"I'm Angela."

"Angela." The way he said my name in his accented English, giving the "g" an "h" sound made me shiver.

Dude. This guy was...wow.

The cafe matron slid my four coffees across the counter in a beverage carrier. She shot a misgiving frown at Fernando before smiling at me.

"Anything else, bonita?"

"Um, yes." Since she'd asked me in English, and I was flustered by Fernando's presence, I found myself slipping back into English myself. "Four arroz con pollos, and four rolls to go, please."

Again she shot a glare that I couldn't read toward Fernando, but when he stared back at her she quickly dropped her eyes and began ladling soup into containers. She handed me a large bag after I paid, and we exchanged smiles. Her eyes darted to Fernando for a fraction of a second. I couldn't understand why he made her nervous.

"Thank you so much," I said.

"Enjoy, Miss. And be safe." She didn't look toward Fernando again, even to ask what he wanted, and he didn't try to order. It was all very strange.

But Fernando beamed at me, so I suppose I'd misread the awkwardness. Or maybe there was some history there. Small town family drama or something.

"Your hands are very full, Angela. May I help you?"

"Oh, you don't have to do that."

"Please. Let me."

I handed him the bag of food while I held the coffees. "Thanks."

"De nada," he said, then laughed. "I mean, you're welcome."

I laughed too, because oh my gosh, he was too cute. The girls were never going to believe I'd picked up a sexy local on a coffee run.

Outside in the sunshine I started to feel bad. It was only a couple blocks to the hotel, but I was sure he probably had stuff to do. I mean, he went in the cafe and didn't even get anything.

"You really don't have to walk me all the way to the

hotel," I said.

"Don't you worry. My destination is farther. However, if you wish to repay me I have a request."

My heart jumped a little. "Oh? And what's that?"

"That you come to this club tonight." He adjusted the bag to one arm and pulled a business card from his back pocket, holding it up between his fingers for me to see before slipping it into the bag.

"I'll talk to my friends, but I'm sure we can swing it." And what I really meant by that was that I would beg, scream, and kill to get to the club if I had to.

"I would be very sad not to see you again, Angela." He was smooth. Probably too smooth. The kind of guy I'd normally veer from, but he'd already ensnared me and there was no turning back now.

"I'll be at the beach all day today," I said, embarrassed by the hope in my voice.

"That would be a beautiful sight. However I have much work to do."

We stopped in front of the high rise, moving to the side next to a palm tree to let people pass. I balanced the coffee carrier on one outstretched hand and reached for the bag of food. He handed it over with a grin and gave me a bow of his head.

"Until tonight, then."

"Yeah. Tonight. Thank you."

I bit my lip to hold back my enthusiasm, and turned to enter the hotel. As soon as I was inside the smile overtook my face. I was still geeking out when I got to our room. The girls were in bed, but they were at least sitting up now.

"What the hell are you smiling about?" Sabrina asked, but seeing me had caused her to break into a grin, too.

"Hottest guy ever." I set down the food and drinks and

flopped onto the bed on my back.

All three of them pounced.

"Who?" "Where?" "What's his name?"

I told them the whole story, leaving out the weirdness about the cafe lady, and they fawned with me. Megan grabbed a pillow, crushing her hips against it and said, "Oh, yes, Fernando!" I swatted her hip.

"Ew, hussie. Get your crotch off my pillow!" Sabrina snatched it away.

"This looks legit," Caryn said, reading the business card for the club. "We should definitely check it out."

That made me sit up and clap my hands. I might have even kicked my heels in the air a little. We were all in good moods now. They didn't even complain about the chicken and rice soup, which, by the way, was as delicious as Fernando'd promised—light and flavorful—definitely the healthiest thing we'd eaten since we got there.

After we ate and got our caffeine fixes, we put on our suits and headed out for our last rays of Mexico sun. The day was amazing. My skin was as dark and beautiful as it had ever been. We made friends with some of the other people in the hotel, and played games of volleyball. Megan found her guy from the night before, promptly attaching her mouth to his for the duration of the afternoon.

The giddy excited feeling Fernando had given me stayed with me all day. I couldn't stop thinking about the gorgeous, dark-eyed guy, and how nice he'd been. It had been a long time since I felt excited about a guy. Trevor and I stuck it out through our freshman year of college before admitting to ourselves that it didn't feel right anymore. After that I made out with a few guys at parties, but never felt any connections. Nobody had turned me on enough to make me think about sex again. Until now.

My nerves were still jumping that night when we

showed the business card and got free admission into the darkened dance club. My eyes started scanning before they were adjusted to the lack of light. I didn't bother trying not to look eager. It didn't seem necessary since he was the one who'd pursued me.

In the end, Fernando was the one who found us.

"Hola, Angela," he said into my ear. I could feel the heat of him behind me, and I saw my three friends as they practically licked him up and down with their eyes.

I turned and hugged him, surprising myself, but he only chuckled and hugged me back. I pulled away, motioning to the girls.

"Fernando, this is Caryn, Sabrina, and Megan. Girls, this is Fernando."

"It is a pleasure to meet Angela's beautiful friends."

When he smiled they all melted into giggles, and I wanted to shout, "I told you! Hottest guy ever!"

Fernando knocked on the bar behind him, and a handsome older man raised his eyebrows.

"Anything these four women want tonight is on me, sí?"

"Sí, Señor." He looked at us girls. "What are we having tonight, eh? Something fresh and fruity?"

I stepped back with Fernando while the girls moved to the bar and proceeded to laugh at everything the bartender said.

"Are you working?" I asked.

He tweaked my chin. "My work is done for today. Now I can enjoy. Do you dance?"

An unfamiliar song was blaring through the club, but it had a good beat.

"Sure." I took his hand and tapped Sabrina's shoulder. When she looked, I pointed to the dance floor to let her know where I'd be and she winked.

Fernando led me into the swarm of people under flashing lights, and within moments our bodies were pressed together, my hands on his shoulders and his hands on my hips. He had the moves. I could feel his toned body under his clothes, and I loved the spicy scent of his cologne—especially the fact that he'd used it sparingly. I was feeling him, everything about him, and when I looked up into his dark eyes I let it be known.

His arms slipped behind my back as my arms went around his neck and he tugged me until our mouths met. His lips and tongue worked mine in a perfect balance of harmony. I'd never been kissed like that. Never had a kiss affect my whole body, making me weak and hyper at the same time.

His hands slid down over my bottom and squeezed hard, making me gasp against his mouth. He laughed and moved his hands back to my waist before looking in my eyes.

"So fucking beautiful."

I needed to catch my breath. I was feeling reckless...thinking thoughts that were not me. Wishing he'd push me up against the wall and feel me up in public. The thought both shamed and thrilled me. He was a total stranger. But this was my last night in Cancun—on the trip that only happened because I'd been rebellious—and I wanted to be wild and carefree, just this once.

I felt like all these thoughts were plastered across my face as Fernando looked down on me, studying me, moving strands of hair from my face with his nimble fingers.

A new song started and he turned me around, pulling me against his chest, and grabbing my hips to grind his sexy self into the back of my skirt. I arched my back, lifting my butt for better leverage, and he nipped my ear.

"Bad little girl."

Sounds of my friends' laughter and voices trailed to us

as they entered the dance floor, drinks held above their heads.

"Oh, my gawd," Sabrina hissed in my ear. "He is hot as shit."

I tried not to giggle like an idiot as Megan and Caryn waggled their eyebrows and made lewd gestures when Fernando turned to say something to some guys who'd walked up.

The guys surrounded us and each took a girl. They were all good-looking, but nothing like Fernando. We danced until we were tired and sweating lightly.

"Let's get a drink," Fernando shouted.

The eight of us made our way back to the bar.

"What would you like, beautiful?" Fernando asked me.

"Just a soda, please."

He cocked his head as if curious, but nodded and turned to the bartender.

"Una cerveza y una coca-cola, por favor. Hagala especial."

A special coke?

The bartender stiffened and raked me with his eyes before looking back at Fernando. "Una niña Americana— estas seguro?" *An American girl—are you sure?* What was that supposed to mean? Did he have something against Americans?

"No te metas en mis asuntos." Fernando snapped. *Get out of my business.*

"What's wrong?" I asked Fernando.

His eyes were dark. "You like cherries, yes?"

"Um...yeah?" I watched the bartender's back as he turned to make my drink. He didn't pour any alcohol, so at least I knew it wasn't some spiked special, not that I thought Fernando would do that. When the man turned back around he plunked two fat cherries on top with grenadine syrup and slid it to me. Ah...the "especial" cola had cherries.

"Thank you." I smiled at the bartender, but he only scowled down at the bar, refusing to look at us. Fernando smiled and the awkwardness between he and the bartender slipped away. I took a big drink and felt refreshed after all that dancing.

I was happy when Sabrina and Megan came over. Caryn was deep in conversation with one of Fernando's friends.

"We're going in the next room to play pool," Sabrina said. "Wanna come?"

I looked to Fernando, who shook his head.

"Not yet. One more dance," he said. His smile melted me. Who could resist that kind of charm?

"Come over when you're done!" Megan flung her arms around me for a hug before practically bouncing away. Sabrina squeezed my hand and gave me a meaningful look, like she was happy for me, and then she left to catch up with Meg. I smiled in their wake.

Fernando clinked his beer bottle to my glass and we both drank. When mine was almost done he said, "I want to see you eat your cherries."

Now who was being bad? I'd never thought myself good at the whole seduction thing, but he made me want to give it a try.

I fished one out, licking the drop of coke and watching him as I took it into my mouth. He seemed to approve. I tried to feed him the other one, but he laughed and reverted the fruit toward my mouth. I dropped it on my tongue and closing my mouth. I'd never been so flirtatious with a guy.

"Angela..." Fernando trailed the back of his fingers up and down my arm. "Would you be very mad if I lied to your friends?"

"About what?" I asked.

14

"I do not wish to dance again. I want a few minutes alone before you leave me."

I bit my lip as my heart sped up. "Where would we go? I don't want my friends to worry."

He leaned down to speak right in my ear, making me shiver. "My car is outside. In back where it's private. We won't be gone very long."

When I looked up at him and nodded, I felt shy all of a sudden. I let him take my hand. We made our way through the people to an exit door, and into a small dirt lot behind the building. A handful of cars were there, along with nearby shanty houses with dirt yards. I thought I heard the low cluck of hens as Fernando opened the back door of a sedan with heavily tinted windows. He waved a hand for me to get in. A momentary pang of apprehension shot through me until I looked into his smiling face.

I climbed in and he slid beside me, closing the door and encasing us in darkness. It was a full moon, but there weren't any street lamps. The car smelled like new leather. I looked down and could barely make out my tanned knees.

Fernando pushed my hair aside and kissed my neck. "How do you feel, Angela?"

"Nervous," I whispered, immediately getting turned on again by the feel and smell of him.

"Are you a virgin?" He trailed kisses down my neck to my naked shoulder, exposed in the black halter top.

"No, but..." It was a little disconcerting that he'd ask such a personal question first thing. It showed he had sex on the mind. Of course he did—he was a guy. Even I'd had sex on my mind all day. But I still wasn't sure if I planned to let it go that far. I wasn't against it, but I also didn't want it to be an assumed thing.

Fernando's mouth found mine and his body pressed me back until I was laying with his weight on me. His hands pushed my skirt up and grabbed my knee, hiking it so he was between my legs. As nervous as I was I couldn't help but be aroused from his confident control and the way he moved against me. Even through our clothes I could tell he would be an amazing lover. I pushed my fingers into his hair and he surprised me by reaching up, grabbing my wrists, and thrusting them over my head before he continued to kiss me more passionately than I'd ever been kissed.

Nobody had ever pinned my hands over my head before, and it did crazy things to me. I bucked my hips, trying to grind closer. He readjusted my wrists so that they were both held together in one of his strong hands, and his other hand trailed down my body, between my legs. He pushed aside my panties and slid two fingers inside me.

I moaned and pushed my hips against his hand.

"You are so wet for me, Angela. My beautiful little slut."

I tensed and froze at what he'd called me, but his hands kept working.

"What is wrong?" he asked, pushing deeper. I could have sworn there was amusement in his voice. His fingers pushed slowly in and out, and I wished he would stop for a second. I was pissed off that he'd ruined our awesome moment. Maybe it was just a slip. A cultural misunderstanding. I needed to relax.

"Nothing's wrong. I just...I don't like that word," I whispered. That was an understatement. I hated the word.

"It's only a word."

"I know. But where I'm from it's...offensive." I was ready to drop the subject. "Look, no big deal, okay?" I wanted him to kiss me again. Turn me on again.

"There are two kinds of women." His voice seemed to get colder. "Prudes and sluts. I can tell you are a slut, though you don't like to admit it."

16

What. The. Hell.

The apprehension I experienced earlier had nothing on the sick sensation going through me now. I felt him trying to slip a third finger inside me, and I pushed with my shoulders, attempting to sit up. His hand tightened on my wrists and his body felt heavier as his breathing picked up.

"Fernando…*stop*." I rocked my hips and turned to the side, knocking him slightly off balance.

He pulled his fingers out of me and slapped my face hard, making me yelp.

Holy shit. In the dimness I saw the white of his smile. That's when panic set in and I really began to struggle. The more I fought and the louder I yelled, the harder I felt him get between my legs.

This could not be happening. My friends didn't know where I was! Why was he doing this? Everything had been going fine. I started feeling woozy.

"Angela." His voice was so smooth. So sickening. "Relax. You are angry over nothing. Be still and you will enjoy this."

I blinked, my eyes feeling heavy, but my mind still angry.

"What alternate fucking reality do you live in where women enjoy being raped?" I spat the words, panting and verging on tears. A very small part of me still clung to the hope that he would see reason and stop.

"American girls. Always so quick to cry rape. Where you are from, women wish to rule the men. Where I am from, women know their place. And they enjoy submitting. You should try it, Angela. I'm told it is *freeing*."

He was a psycho. How could I have so horribly misread him?

All I knew was that if Fernando raped me, he would not get away with it. My parents would nail his ass to the wall, using any means necessary. They were hard asses in the Texas legal world.

"My parents are lawyerrsss..." Damn. All the struggling I'd done had made me so tired. My words were slurring. I felt heavy.

Fernando ran a finger down my cheek.

"That's it," he murmured. "You're feeling good now, eh?"

No. His words. Oh, God. No. The special drink.

In one last hurrah, I fought, bucking and clawing and thrashing with all the energy I had left. Fernando laughed. He fucking laughed. And then he flipped me over onto my stomach and tore my panties down. My tears soaked the leather seat where my face was pressed. A spinning sensation began. Fernando placed gentle kisses all over the side of my face, neck, and ear, while his hand worked to push my thighs apart.

The last thing I felt before my world went black was Fernando forcing himself inside me.

CHAPTER TWO

Colin Douglas

Twelve Years Earlier...

———— ·◆· ┊ ◆ ┊ ·◆· ————

Sixteen-year-old Scottish boy Conall McCray was rudely awoken far too early with a punch to his chest. He came to bleary-eyed with a hangover from alcohol and whatever white stuff he'd inhaled. He stared up into the eyes of his best mate, who was looking quite irate. Perhaps he was mad at Conall for passing out on his bed last night. The thought made Conall want to smile as he ran a hand through his wavy brown hair. He always took what he wanted.

"Of all the lassies at my party you have to shag my own sister?" his friend hollered.

Ah, yes. His sister, home from uni. She'd tried to fuck him. What was he to do? Conall relaxed back onto the bed.

"We didn't fuck, ya knob," Conall told him. Actually, she'd given him a head job in the bathroom.

His friend looked prepared to hit him again, but when Conall leveled his eyes at him in warning, the other lad settled a bit.

It was true that Conall could have landed any girl at his friend's party. He was the oldest son to one of Scotland's wealthiest families—generations of men who pioneered the country's finance and banking system. On the outside he was the handsome, well-educated, artistically talented son of a billionaire, while privately he nurtured his rebellious nature by living a double-life.

Conall McCray was never satisfied with the fake kind of respect money could buy. Watching his father kiss corporate arse made him ill. He learned in his hidden life that true power, control, and respect came from being feared. So he watched and learned, hoping that one day when he took his father's place he'd be as powerful as he was rich. He craved control. Control of his life and circumstances. Control of how people viewed him.

Control to make the people he loved love him back.

An irritating, persistent string of knocking began on his mate's front door. His friend growled and went to answer, allowing Conall to close his eyes and drift off again. Sure, his friend was angry, but he'd get over it, just like usual. He always let Conall do whatever he wanted.

Loud adult voices sounded from the hall, men, and then the trampling of hard footsteps down the hall into the bedroom. Conall sat up, ready to fight.

Two uniformed officers with pinched faces surveyed him.

"Conall McCray?"

"Aye. What do you want?" he asked. Had someone snitched on him about the drug sales? He'd gladly kick their arses. His father would get him out of any charges, but it was the bitching from his parents he hated. He wanted to punch something. Or someone.

"Lad, have you any clue what's happened at your estate?"

A bitter heaviness settled itself low in Conall's abdomen. "What are you on about?"

He stood now, wishing he wore something more than tight boxers. He grabbed for his shirt and pulled it on. The two men looked at him with pity.

"I'm sorry to tell you this," one of them said softly. "But we must work quickly. Your parents have been murdered and your brother's gone missing. We're taking you into custody for your own protection. Do you ken what I'm telling you, son?"

Conall's world tilted off its axis. He had a floating thought that if he could just reach his jeans and put them on, pretending he hadn't just heard what he'd heard, it would all go away. But when he reached for the jeans he caught the ashen face of his best mate in the doorway, and the words hit home.

Graham, his wee ten-year-old brother, was out there somewhere with psychopaths. Graham, who Conall cannae have been bothered to give an ounce of attention to over the past year because he'd been too damn busy partying. Graham, with his mop of curls, who looked up to Conall like some sort of god.

Conall bent and spewed his sick on the carpets. He puked and gagged and heaved until his head cleared, then he tried to force his way out of the room. He had to find his brother.

Arms grabbed him. He managed a hit to one of their jaws and a kick to the knee. The men were shouting and cursing for him to stay still. Then a sting punctuated his shoulder. Conall felt the effects immediately, his legs going weak, and then blackness.

He came to that afternoon on a couch in a small office. He jolted upright, fighting the urge to be sick again. A man with a badge knelt in front of him at eye-level. Two men with holstered guns stood behind him.

The man stared into his eyes. "We will find your brother." He'd said the one thing that could keep Conall from jumping off the couch and fighting to get free. "But we need your cooperation. You are the heir to your father's estate, but we are sending you into hiding. The estate and lands will be sold and liquidated, and put into a fund for when you become twenty-two. This was your father's wish, stated in his will as to what should happen if his life was taken by force. Do you understand?"

Conall swallowed bile and nodded. He understood he was homeless. Without a family. Or money.

"I have an aunt," Conall told him.

The man's eyes were sad. "She's a bit shaken by all that's happened, and she prefers to distance herself from the events."

So his one living relative wouldn't take him in? His own mother's sister? Fucking cow.

"Where am I to stay?" he asked.

"We're working to find you a home, but your life will be much different now. Whoever takes you in is not likely to be wealthy. This will help to keep you out of the public eye and under the radar. Your name will change. From now on you're Colin Douglas. You'll be homeschooled—"

"Fuck that!" This city was his home. It was all he knew. He couldn't lose all his friends and his identity, too.

Conall tried to stand, but the man grasped his forearm. "It's just a few years. And in the meantime we're working alongside the SIS to search for your brother. Airports and all avenues of travel are being scouted as we speak. We will find him, and justice will be served for your parents."

He felt the weight of it all forcing its way down on him, and for the first time since he was a wee bairn his eyes stung. He couldn't hold back the sobs as they came, and he didn't have the strength to push the man away when he took

Conall's neck and pulled it to his shoulder, roughly rubbing his back.

Every ounce of control he prided himself on slipped away, and he realized it was all a ruse—a childish facade. His family's wealth had always backed him up, and knowing his parents would always be there for him had given him the safety net to live his life like a selfish prick. Now he had none of that, and it hurt. Who was he, really? He dappled on the dark side, equating those minor dangers with power, but he saw now it'd all been shite. Out there in the world was real danger. Fucked up people with no conscience.

How badly had the people he loved suffered at the hands of brutal madmen? Could he have fought and saved any of his family if he'd been there? Had his father fought? Somehow Conall couldn't imagine that, which made him feel a moment of irrational anger toward his father, followed by guilt.

When Conall pulled himself together he said in a choked voice, "Tell me everything."

Their Edinburgh estate had been methodically broken into. The overseer of the lands was taken captive and forced to disarm the alarms before being killed. Conall's parents were not supposed to be home. They should have left for an event in Dublin; however, technical issues with their private jet caused a delay.

The thieves were taken off guard to find the owners home. Reports showed that a struggle had taken place. An antique vase in the foyer was broken, and Conall's mother was found with flesh under her nails. His father had abrasions on his hands. Both his parents and the nanny were murdered, and the perpetrators left with the one thing they'd come for: his brother, Graham.

The authorities called it a kidnapping-for-ransom gone

bad. They'd only expected the nanny and Graham to be home. And all the while Conall had been partying, just like every weekend. He couldn't have been arsed to check-in with a fucking nanny.

Conall shook his head back and forth as an angry vengeance and self-loathing soaked into his blood. His future as he'd known it had been seized and choked. He knew he'd never be the same, because all his aspirations changed in that moment. He would never be the respectable business man his father had been. His one and only thought was to get his brother back, and then do whatever he had to do to find the people who'd done this to his family and destroy them.

"We'll find these bastards, young McCray," the officer told him.

And if you don't, Conall thought to himself, *I will.*

CHAPTER THREE

I had a secret fantasy. Something I'd never told anybody because it was too shameful. For years I'd fantasized about being taken against my will—Stockholm Syndrome kind of stuff—rape fantasies. I imagined big, sexy men busting down my door, overcome with the desire to have me. In those visions I somehow knew they meant me no bodily harm. It was lust. They just wanted to momentarily own me. Those imaginings had been so hot. Being overpowered. Being brought reluctantly to orgasm.

But in real life there was nothing sexy about rape.

I felt the soft foundation underneath me rocking and heard the faint whir of an engine when I woke. My hands were tied behind my back, and my ankles were bound. A dull, distinct pain was present between my legs. My first instinct was to scream, but I stamped down the urge, forcing myself to sit up and take in my surroundings.

I was in a small, clean room on a twin bed. Through the rectangular window on the wall I could see the dim morning sky, or at least I assumed it was morning.

And I saw water. Lots of water.

My stomach turned and I heaved, leaning my head over the bed. Nothing came out, but my gut continued to convulse.

When I heard footsteps and murmured voices, I quickly laid down on my side, curling into a ball and letting my hair fall over my face. The door opened, and although I was panicking inside, my body went into some crazy, shocked self-preservation mode of calmness.

"She's still passed out," I heard Fernando say in Spanish. My stomach clenched.

A string of cuss words came from the mouth of a deeper-voiced man.

"Idiot! Why would you bring her to my boat?" the man yelled in Spanish.

"It wasn't my plan. I was going to fuck her and dump her somewhere before we left this morning, but she said her parents were lawyers!"

"This is why you do not drug Americans! This is why I have told you time and time again, foolish asshole, not to fuck American girls!"

"I know! I'm sorry! I wasn't thinking clearly."

The man sounded irate. "You were thinking with your cock! When will you learn self-control?"

The sound of rapid blows and Fernando hollering in pain made me ball up tighter. I hated Fernando, but the sounds of violence, even against him, made me ill.

"How many people saw you with her, son, eh?" he yelled.

"Only the people at your club, Papa!"

"She was alone?"

"She had...friends with her. But they were drunk!"

Another bestial sound of anger came from the man,

presumably Fernando's father.

"Did they see you leave with her?"

"No. They were in the pool room. No one was paying attention."

"The girls have probably gone to the authorities by now. Their parents will be on the next plane to Mexico, and reporters will be crawling all over my club! People saw you together! This is the last straw, Fernando. When we stop to refuel in Cuba I'm sending you away. I am done with you."

"Sending me where?" Fernando sounded like a pathetic little kid next to his father's angry voice.

"I don't know yet. Asia, maybe."

"Asia! I don't want to go to Asia!"

"And I don't want this girl! Nor do I want a fucking police investigation. What I want is to have you out of my sight where you can't cause me anymore trouble."

Fernando didn't argue. A beat of silence passed before the man spoke again, sounding closer, as if he were standing over me.

"What am I to do with her, Fernando? American captives do not make good slaves. They are too hard to break—too willful and entitled."

"Men will pay good money to have her fight against them."

"Stupid boy." His father's tone was scary calm. "Most men do not share your particular *tastes*. My patrons seek submissive women who enjoy sex, not women who scream and cry in terror when they're fucked!"

Slaves? His patrons? Oh, my God. These guys were into sketchier shit than I first feared.

"I said I'm sorry!" Fernando sounded out of patience. "I'll kill her and throw her overboard if you want."

I whimpered involuntarily, and then held my breath.

"Does she know Spanish?" his father asked in a whisper.

"No."

I realized this was in my favor. They had no idea I could understand every word of their conversation. I jolted when I felt a warm hand move the hair from my face.

"Are you awake?" the man whispered in English.

I thought he probably knew I was, so I slowly blinked my eyes open to see the man crouched next to me. He was an older, more distinguished version of Fernando, but he had a black mustache. He smiled at me.

"Tu sabes Español, nina linda?" *Do you know Spanish, pretty girl?*

I didn't respond, only stared up at him with big, frightened eyes.

"It's okay," he said in accented English. "I will speak your language. Tell me, pretty girl. What is your name?"

I tried to talk, but my throat was so dry nothing came out but a rasp. The man turned his head to Fernando and barked, "Agua!" Fernando left, returning a minute later with a bottle of water. I couldn't look at Fernando. Just thinking about him made me want to dry heave again.

The man held the bottle to my lips and I drank three gulps to satisfy him. When he pulled the bottle away I whispered, "Angela."

Something about his self-controlled kindness terrified me. Maybe the fact that he was not the kind of man you could try to bargain with or trick. He seemed too smart and cunning for that.

"Ah." He smiled. "*The angel.* My name is Marco. I am sorry for what Fernando has done to you."

He seemed so sincere that I couldn't hold back a whimpered plea, and then I began to babble in desperation. "Please...please let me go. I swear I won't tell anyone. I *swear*. I'll say I wandered off and passed out or something. I just want to go home."

He sighed. "I am afraid that is not possible, Angel. Are you hungry?"

I was, but I didn't think I could actually eat, so I shook my head as tears began to fall and panic set in. "Please, let me go home. Please."

"I know this is difficult, but it does not have to be bad. You must come to terms, pretty girl, with the knowledge that your life will never be the same. You will never return home. You belong to me now, and I will treat you well. But if I cannot trust you, I will have to dispose of you. Do you understand?"

Oh, God. I felt edgy, panicky, because I understood perfectly. He'd kill me in a heartbeat. Why   was   this happening? How could this be my life?

The tears continued to stream. "Please don't kill me. I'll be good. I promise."

I made the mistake of looking over at Fernando then. From the bulge in his pants I could see he was enjoying my crying, begging, tied-up scenario. Marco noticed, too.

"Fuera de aqui!" Marco shouted.

Fernando scowled at me and stomped out, slamming the door.

Marco shook his head and began untying my arms. Hope sprouted in my chest, until he pulled out a pair of handcuffs and handcuffed one of my wrists to the headboard.

"Please." It came out as a sob, desperation flooding me. "I'll do anything. Please let me go."

He grasped my chin, making me to look into his dark, hard eyes. He spoke more forcefully than he had before. "I told you. That is not an option. You would do well to make the best of this situation."

"What do you want me to do?" I couldn't keep from

whining.

"I want you to relax, and learn to trust me. And stop crying." He reached down and wiped both my cheeks dry. "I will require your complete obedience at all times, or you will be punished. You will refer to me as Sir, and when the time is right you will refer to me as Master. Do you understand?"

Master? Appalled, I nodded.

"Answer me with words."

"I understand...Sir," I rasped.

"Good girl. I have things to take care of. Try to rest. I will have Perla bring you food soon."

He left and I heard the door click when it locked from the outside.

I scrambled up to my knees, as high as I could to see out the window, but I couldn't reach it.

Water. We were definitely out at sea. *Fuck!* Where were we going? Cuba? I started breathing hard. Okay. Time for a plan. When we stopped, I would cause a scene and get rescued. It could be my only chance. Who knew where we'd end up next?

The headboard was sturdy, but I gave it a hard yank and shake anyway. I pulled, grunting as I tried to squeeze my hand through the cuff. My wrists were thin, so he'd closed it as tight as it would go. My fingers started turning purple from the effort and I pushed my hand back down, panting and crying with frustration.

I was dealing with rich, foreign, hardened criminals here. Powerful people. I didn't think Marco wanted to hurt me, but his earlier talk about slaves, fucking, and patrons made it all too clear. I'd seen a special on television about sex slavery. I'd felt sad and horrified for those victims, but also distanced from them. Those girls and boys had mostly been from Europe, Asia, or South America—people who were sold or stolen out of already rough life scenarios that I couldn't fully relate to except in compassion. It was terrible and wrong, but so far from my life.

This was not happening to me.

I couldn't understand. I was a good girl. Mostly. Not perfect, but I worked hard at everything I did, and I looked forward to my future. We weren't filthy rich by our nation's standards, but my family did well. This was not how my life was going to end up. There was just no way. My parents would find me. They were probably on their way to Mexico right now, ready to raise hell, just like Marco said. They knew people in high places. They were resourceful. This boat could be tracked and they'd meet us in Cuba and save me!

My parents. My stomach clenched and I trembled. They would find out I'd lied. Oh, no. I was so sorry. So ashamed. They didn't deserved to be lied to, and then to have their worst fears come true—the very reason they'd refused to let me go to Cancun in the first place. Why hadn't I listened? Why did I give in to my friends, and why had I been willing to sneak off with a guy I didn't know?

People were right about Karma—she was a bitch, because only a bitch would be this cruel. My punishment far outweighed my crime. So much so, that I could barely wrap my mind around it. This couldn't be my reality. I was meant to be on a plane flying home right now!

Sobbing cries racked my body at the thought of the pain and disappointment and terror my mom and dad were probably feeling. And what about my friends? Were they feeling guilty, like it was their fault for leaving me with Fernando? Had they panicked and searched for me? I didn't want them to feel bad. I wanted to tell them it wasn't their fault. We'd all been fooled.

The door opened, and I screamed. The young, Latina woman standing in the doorway with a tray jumped slightly, and her dark brown eyes widened. She came in and set the tray on the nightstand next to me. She wore spike heels and a minuscule strapless black dress with her black hair down around her. And a small black, leather collar.

"I am Perla. You are Angel?" she asked. She said it like Marco did: Ahn-hel. It was pretty, but it wasn't my name.

"Angela."

"Ah…" She seemed to be searching for the words in English. "Forgive me. If Master say you Angel, I call you Angel. Sí?"

Master. She really called him that.

"Are you, like, an employee of his?" I asked.

She seemed to toy with the word "employee" in her mind before answering, "No. I am his slave. Same as you. But he treat you well, y you be polite, y you work hard."

My heart rate tripled when she called me a slave. I needed her to confirm or deny my worst suspicions, even though the thought of her answer terrified me to the core.

"What do you have to do as his slave? Just…clean and cook and stuff?"

She seemed too calm and wise as she regarded me.

"I do whatever he say."

"Like what, though?" I pushed. I needed to hear it.

"I pleasing to him. I pleasing to his patrons. I sometimes help to clean, but no much."

My heart had not slowed. "How do you please him? And his patrons?"

"In many way. Men have many need. You will learn." She smiled, as if to encourage me.

No. *Please, no.* I stared at her, appalled. Her calm expression melted into one of pity.

"I feed you now." She lifted the silver lid off the plate, revealing eggs and chorizo sausage with bread. It looked good, and I cursed my stomach for wanting to be fed at a time like this.

"I'm not hungry."

"You need food." She took a forkful and raised it toward me, but I slunk back on the bed and shook my head.

I couldn't imagine being fed like this. Like a baby or an invalid. "Please. Can't you unlock these so I can just feed myself? It's not like I can go anywhere."

"No, Angel. Only I feed you."

I wasn't allowed to hold a fork? I shook my head again and whispered, "I don't want any."

She gave me the sad expression again.

Perla took a piece of bread and placed it in my free hand. I took it, because she was offering me the civility of feeding my own self. Then she left me, locking the door again.

I couldn't look at the bread in my hand. All I could do was cry big, ugly, wailing tears as my life capsized, forcing me into unknown waters where sharks and other nefarious creatures were surely waiting to eat me alive.

CHAPTER FOUR

Colin Douglas

Six Years Ago...

❖ ┆ ❖ ┆ ❖

Colin Douglas was no longer recognizable as the rich youth he'd once been. Gone were his posh wardrobe and stylish hair. He kept his head shaved and a touch of scruff on his face. His clothing was dark and durable, and underneath them were scars from fights and tattoos. Colin's Scottish accent had been tamped down by time spent traveling other parts of the UK, primarily London. His steely gray-blue eyes gave away nothing about his past.

As soon as he'd been brought to live with foster parents in the city of Glasgow, he'd begun the double life once again. He eventually became a university student, studying art, while in his free time he made his company with the less savory undercurrent of the city.

He'd long since lost hope that authorities would find Graham. He knew the task would fall on his own shoulders, and he took up the responsibility with quiet zeal. In his years without money he'd earned respect the old way—inciting fear. In order to infiltrate the crime world, he'd had to become a criminal.

Colin's paintings began to garner attention with their passion and edge. As he sold them in his early twenties, making a name for himself among elite artistic circles, he used the funds to quell his taste for high-end drugs. Women of all classes flocked to him, sensing the dangerous undertones in his unsmiling eyes—the man whose hands could bring a canvas to life, taking one's breath away with a perfectly placed streak of color. And he was happy to show them what else his hands could do.

Colin worked out his extra aggression in the weight room. His physique was lean, not allowing him to put on massive amounts of muscle; however, the muscle he did have was well-defined and allowed him to move quickly in a fight.

By the time Colin was twenty-two, his ruthless temperament had earned him the respect of seasoned thugs. He'd worked his way through the worlds of crime, beginning with drug rings, and moving to the more serious circles of human trafficking. He was smart, unlike many of the uneducated idiots on the streets. He kept under the radar of the authorities, and knew how to use polite properness at necessary times. With his estate money now available, Colin's power was complete.

Within a year of gathering his inheritance, Colin's manipulation of his criminal counterparts came full circle. He rented out nightclubs and took people on spontaneous flights to the Caymens. They believed he'd earned his money through illegal activities, which worked in his favor. Colin learned names of the most elusive kidnappers in UK crime rings, and he heard rumored places where captives were held.

At twenty-three Colin ventured to London on a lead. He hadn't the slightest clue if his brother was dead or alive—could find no information about him at all, but he refused to give up. The house in London made Colin feel diseased just walking through it. He was brought in as a potential buyer and taken to see the slaves.

A strung out seventeen-year-old boy sat against the wall, sunken McCray eyes looking up at him through a mess of tangled curls—a shell of the brother Colin had once known, and it made him unable to breathe. The sight of Graham struck Colin with immense relief and shock. He was alive, and would soon be safe.

Graham registered no response to his older brother. Colin knew that he himself had changed greatly in the past seven years, but it killed him that Graham didn't recognize him at all. He knew better than to expect a happy reunion, but he'd never imagined his brother would be so lifeless.

Hiding his fury of emotions, Colin paid cash to the fuck-faces and they seemed glad to be getting rid of Graham, even smug, as if they'd pulled one over on Colin. He memorized their faces so he could kill them in the future, but at that moment all he could think about was getting his brother the fuck away from there.

On the private jet, flying back to Scotland, Colin couldn't get Graham to speak. His brother cowered in a seat by the window with his arms around his stomach, eyes dead, unresponsive.

Colin couldn't take Graham's catatonic state anymore. He went to him, grabbed him by the shoulders and shouted, "For fuck's sake, Graham, wake up!"

The boy skittered out of Colin's hands with a whimper and fell to his knees on the cabin floor, fumbling to undo the belt at Colin's waist.

"What are you…? Oh, shit." He grabbed Graham's hands and wrenched them away. His own brother was trying to give him a blowjob. The realization of his diminished mental state made Colin want to cry for the first time since he was sixteen. Those fuckers had stolen his little brother's life—his childhood and innocence, and who knew if he'd ever be able to live a normal life now?

Colin fell to his knees and took Graham's face, forcing him look at him. "It's *me,* Graham. Your brother, Conall."

Graham's eyes glazed and he began trembling. With each passing second of witnessing Graham's agony, Colin's hatred and vengeance grew, morphing into a strong beast inside his chest. He spoke through gritted teeth, trying not to scare his brother with his angry passion.

"You're free now, and I swear to God I'll kill them if they come near you again."

Colin had no idea if Graham comprehended what he'd told him. All he knew was that the boy needed serious help. He watched in horror as his brother began to cry and shake, curling up and rocking, pulling his hair like he was going mad.

That's when Colin knew saving his brother from captivity was not enough. They'd ruined the boy's life, maybe permanently. He would bring the fuckers down, and spend the rest of his days finding people like them, and making them pay. Somehow.

His opportunity soon came in a different form than he'd expected...a *legal* form.

One thing Colin and the authorities agreed on was not to make Graham McCray's rescue public, especially since he'd been found by Colin and not the government.

Colin was grilled for information, and the local police brought in MI-6 agents, personnel of the Secret Intelligence Service. They wanted to know every step of his process, starting from the moment he'd been put into foster care, but Colin was no fool.

"I need a legal statement that you won't hold this information against me. Informant protection. And I want protection and help for Graham."

The agents pawed through his record, no doubt seeing

his plethora of misdemeanors, fighting and drugs, nothing to earn himself prison time. They agreed to his terms and he told them everything, hoping they'd fucking learn something from it.

He saw their eyes lighting up, and their hands speed-writing information as he gave years' worth of illegal knowledge. The agents often shared knowing glances and nods, as if Colin's information were confirming certain suspicions.

"We tried last year to take down this group in Dublin, but they'd moved by the time we got there."

"That's the problem with government shite," Colin said. "You spend too much time talking, and mucking about waiting for permissions. You give them time to catch wind and escape."

"Our success rates are actually quite high," one of the agents told him.

"You didn't find my brother in the seven years he was missing, so fuck your success rates."

The room of officers and agents stilled as they watched his gunpowder eyes, and not one of them had a retort.

The door swung open and a man with a serious, lined face walked in. His dark hair and the scruffy partial beard on his face were graying. The others stood, which signaled to Colin that this was a high-ranking official. The man cocked his head toward the door and said, "I'll take over from here."

Everyone filed out and the man took a seat across from Colin, leaning his elbows on the table.

"Agent Abernathy," he said as way of introduction. He motioned toward a mirrored window. "I've been listening, and I'm damned impressed by what I've heard, Mr. Douglas. We failed you."

Colin didn't respond. He sat back, legs out straight with his hands linked across his flat stomach. The Agent stood and opened a wall panel, hitting all switches, and then pulled a screen down over the mirrored panel.

"There. Nobody can see or hear our conversation, and we are not being recorded. Everything said now will stay between the two of us."

Colin gave a single nod, wondering about the sudden secrecy.

"I've no right to ask anything of you," Agent Abernathy continued. "But I'd like to make you an offer. A very rare sort of offer. Many laws were broken while you pursued your vigilante ways, and we're washing your record clean of those, but I'm wondering if you'd be interested in getting paid to use your...unique skills."

This peaked Colin's interest. Without moving or changing his expression he said, "Go on."

"I'm offering you the opportunity to become an undercover agent with MI-6."

Colin laughed, but Abernathy ignored him and kept talking.

"We have an elite unit of personnel, unknown even among our own ranks. You've made quite a name for yourself, so you'd continue to work under the name Colin Douglas with your art as your cover story. But you would be an informant for us. It's increasingly difficult and time consuming for our agents to infiltrate themselves the way you've done. They're expected to abide by the law and follow certain protocol—all of which would not be expected of you."

"Why would I do this for you?" Colin asked. "I don't need the money."

"I think we have the same agenda when it comes down to it, Mr. Douglas: justice. As one of our undercover elite there's certain protocols you'll have to adhere to, but you'll have freedoms regular agents do not. You'll be thoroughly trained in weapons and defense, but you'll report to me and only me. Few will know of your involvement, and you'll be paid in cash. Under the table. Aye?"

Colin probably should have asked for time to think about it, but he was good at reading people, and he knew Abernathy wasn't blowing smoke up his arse. His offer filled Colin with visions of James Bond scenarios, which he knew was ridiculous, but it gave him a jolt of excitement nonetheless. In essence, he was being given permission to do the exact thing he planned to do anyhow—destroy the types of people who took Graham. But in this case he'd have training and additional resources at his disposal.

"Aye. And if we try this and decide it doesn't work for us?" Colin asked.

"Then we go our separate ways. We're not the mafia. You won't work against your will, and nobody will attempt to take you out if you quit. But while you're with us, we do require complete loyalty, and for the rest of your life we require the upmost secrecy. We have no leniency for traitors."

Especially traitors not on the payroll, Colin thought, understanding the threat clearly.

Colin half-grinned. Abernathy half-grinned. And together the men struck a deal.

CHAPTER FIVE

I'm not sure how long it took me to break down and eat the bread but it was pathetically short. An hour maybe. I hated myself for giving in, even though that made no sense. How was I hurting anyone other than myself by not eating? I needed to choose my battles better. My body was weak from being drugged, and I really could have used that meal. I stared at the cold plate now with regret, out of hand's reach.

My heart accelerated when I heard footsteps and male voices nearing. I sat up straighter, wary.

Marco entered with another nicely-tailored middle aged gentleman, also of Latin descent. They both looked me over and I dropped my eyes. Then they began conversing in Spanish, talking about me like an object of property.

"Attractive," the other man said. "A blonde American would be an excellent asset if you can get her to cooperate."

Marco grunted his agreement. "I'm afraid my son has ruined her. She may not be worth the effort. If I cannot get her to cooperate, I will need your assistance. You know that is not my particular area of expertise. I will pay kindly to have this burden removed swiftly and silently."

My stomach sunk as the men shared a knowing look,

and I struggled not to show emotion on my face. Then the other man chuckled and spoke.

"Always a lover, not a fighter." He clapped Marco on the shoulder. "When have I ever denied you services, friend? Eh? If the girl is unusable, she will disappear and never be found."

Terror slid like a cool knife down my spine.

I was glad I hadn't eaten the full meal because I might have lost it then. This man was obviously some sort of criminal business partner who did the dirty work for Marco. The way they spoke so callously of ending my life left no doubt that they'd kill me without reservation. I worked hard not to react. To control my breathing and facial expressions as the men looked me over.

The nameless man said, "You should test her out. Don't let her get too comfortable. The sooner you begin training her, the better."

Marco ran his thumb over his lips in thought, then nodded, calling out, "Luis!"

A moment later a slightly younger man with longer hair entered the room.

"Sí, Señor Ruiz?" His voice was eager, and when he glanced over and saw me he stilled, a look of interest in his eyes.

"I need you to test out this girl so I may see if she's trainable," Marco explained in Spanish. "Be careful. Fernando fucked her last night. And she only speaks English."

Luis nodded and wet his lips, stepping toward me, popping open the button on his pants.

No. Oh, God, no. This was not happening. Luis's body language became seductive as he moved toward me, and I couldn't help but pull my legs toward my body.

He sat on the edge of the bed next to me and spoke

gently.

"You are very pretty." His dark eyes roamed my face. He wasn't bad looking, but I was still repulsed by his touch. Looks meant nothing to me after falling for Fernando's ruse. When Luis reached out to touch my cheek I went stiff and forced myself not to pull away. I would not react to any of his touches.

"That's it," he said with false gentleness. "You be good, an' I make you feel good, yeah?" He spoke softly and sweetly, but it wasn't real. It was like someone trying to lure an animal who might bite.

I had a choice to make. Failing this test would mean death. Passing would mean sexual slavery. Both options were inconceivable. If I fought against this, how would they choose to kill me? How long would it take? I'd never been good with pain. The very idea of that man attempting to take the life from my body filled me with an almost paralyzing fear. I wanted to be the tough kind of person who could choose death, but everything inside me screamed to live. So when Luis gently pulled my ankle, I let him.

He straightened both my legs and grasped my waist, lowering my body to a laying position with my hand outstretched above my head, still cuffed to the headboard. I tried to drape my other arm over my eyes, but Luis lifted it and stretched it up alongside the bound arm. He murmured sweet things, which he probably thought were very soothing, as he unbuttoned my skirt and pulled it down my legs along with my underwear. I pressed my knees together.

My heart was working overtime now, and my breaths were too short.

"Muéstranos las tetas," Marco's partner said. *Show us her tits.*

Remaining gentle, Luis pushed my shirt up. I had on a strapless bra, so he slid his hands behind my back and easily unclasped it. I whimpered and turned my face to the wall

43

when I was exposed to the men.

"Too small," the man said in Spanish. "She'll need implants."

Luis took my breasts in both his hands and kneaded them.

"Demasiado pequeño?" *Too small?* Marco asked.

Luis answered in Spanish, his voice lower than before. "Nah. A nice little palmful. Firm."

I was a full B-cup, and I couldn't help but feel resentful as they picked apart my appearance like a farm animal for sale.

"We have big-breasted women," Marco explained. "Might be nice to have a natural, smaller girl."

The other man laughed. "Put her in some pigtails and a school girl uniform and you'll have a best seller."

They both chuckled, but as Luis leaned down and took one of my nipples in his mouth, making me accidentally gasp with surprise, they quieted. I refused to enjoy the feel of his mouth on me. No matter how kind he was being, knowing those men were watching made me tense and sick. I couldn't relax.

When I felt Luis's weight lift off the bed I made the mistake of looking to see what was going on. He was stripping. Naked. Hard.

Marco stood with his arms crossed, watching critically, while his friend leered. I wished so much they would leave. Especially my would-be murderer.

Luis's weight dipped the bed once again and I began to pant with fear. I couldn't seem to control it. I pulled at the cuffs, whimpering.

Calm down, Angela, I scolded myself.

"Shh." Luis bent and kissed my neck, taking my breast in his hand again. He pulled away long enough to wet two fingers with his saliva and bring them down to my center. "Open your legs," he said softly.

In that moment, as I gave in to save my life, I felt far more broken than I had in my drug-induced state when Fernando forced me. Because I had fought him. And now I was allowing it. I'd never been more disgusted with myself than I was when I let my knees fall open and Luis touch me with his wet fingers. He climbed on top of me, seeming pleased with my cooperation. But even with the moisture from his fingers I was too dry.

He pushed in and I bit my lips against a cry. Tears fell as he worked his way in and out, shushing me quietly, until I was finally wet enough for him to really move.

"Ah, pretty girl," he said, wiping my tears as he moved above me. "Why you cry when a man make love to you?"

I closed my eyes. This was not making love. I was being raped for the second time in a day's span, and even though the physical pain had mostly passed, there were layers upon layers of mental anguish in its place.

I didn't cry anymore. I wanted him to get this over with. He enjoyed my body, running his hand from my wrist down to my waist, then bending to suck my nipple again. In other circumstances I might have enjoyed his ministrations, but here, like this, they made me ill.

"Bueno," I heard Marco say. Apparently he was happy with my cooperation. Asshole.

My eyes stayed closed. *Please hurry*, I silently begged.

Then Marco's evil friend said in Spanish, "Let's see how she reacts to the back trap."

Back trap? What the hell was that? My eyes opened and Luis was looking right at me. He was sweating a little now.

"I gonna make you feel good," he said. "Okay?"

I was too uneasy to respond. Staying inside me, he hiked up one of my knees and reached around, squeezing my ass.

Then he lifted that hand and stuck his middle finger in his mouth, wetting it. Reaching around again I felt his fingers roam down to the crack of my body and press against my anus. The tip of his middle finger slipped in and I cried out, bucking upward. Nobody had ever touched me there, and it felt like the worst kind of violation.

The disgusting man by the door laughed at my reaction.

"Shh," Luis murmured. "You relax, baby, and feel good."

"No," I whispered. It was horrible and demeaning, but he didn't seem to be able to push his finger any deeper from that angle so I stopped fighting.

With his finger half inside my ass, he began moving faster, breathing harder, getting closer. A single thought crossed my mind, and I couldn't help but say it.

"I'm not on birth control!"

"Don't worry," Marco said. "He will pull out."

Less than two minutes later he did. I was so relieved when Luis finally came on my stomach that I wanted to cry again. He gave me a smile, as if to say "good job" and I felt an overwhelming gratefulness toward him. I was experiencing genuine gratitude toward a man for not being violent when he violated me...how fucked up was that?

Luis dressed and left the room with a nod from Marco. I didn't like the way the other man was staring at me now. Or the fact that he was obviously hard inside his slacks, and not afraid to rub himself in front of others.

"Perla!" Marco called.

She must have been nearby because she came at once, bowing her head to him and saying, "Sí, Amo." The word surprised me. It was almost a loving, worshipful way of saying "Owner."

"Take señor Hernandez to the Atlantic room and see to his needs," he said in Spanish.

Perla, beautiful with her bronzed skin and shiny black hair, led Mr. Hernandez away with a sway of her hips. He gave me one last lascivious glance before leaving. How was Perla not afraid of him?

When Marco came to my side I was trembling from the aftereffects of the encounter. He unlocked my handcuff and said, "It's time to clean you up."

I pulled my shirt down over my breasts. Taking me by the wrist, Marco led me to the bathroom inside the room and let me go, but he made no move to leave. He gave the toilet a pointed look. I unwound toilet paper and cleaned off my stomach, then flushed it and looked at Marco again.

"You must need to relieve yourself," he said.

I did, actually. Really bad. I hadn't gone since last night and it was at least ten in the morning by now. I must have been dehydrated.

Was he going to stand there and watch?

"Go," he commanded. Well, that answered my question.

I sat reluctantly on the toilet and stared down at my hands, feeling his eyes on me. It's not like I'd never peed in front of anyone before, but going in front of my girlfriends, or a serious boyfriend, was different than in front of this strange man who proclaimed to own me and just ordered my rape. It was just another exertion of his power over me and my loss of personal freedom. Another reason for me to hate him.

I finished and he led me back to the bed where he cuffed me again.

"When we dock to refuel, it will be time for your shower. I will have clothing brought to you. And food. You will not waste food again."

"Yes, Sir," I said, feeling chafed and hungry. I was ready for him to leave because I desperately needed some alone time to gather my strength.

He got up to leave, and on second thought came back to the bed and sat, lifting my shirt. I drew my legs up to my body and held my breath. *No, no, no.* I couldn't handle having sex again so soon. I would lose it. But he only seemed to want to inspect my boobs for himself. Pushing my legs aside, he gathered my breasts in his hands and squeezed, then cupped their light weight. He ran his thumbs slowly around my nipples until they both puckered into tight knots. His thumbs brushed over their tips and I sucked in a breath, feeling light headed.

With a satisfied nod he pulled my shirt back down and left me with my dark thoughts.

CHAPTER SIX

I felt the boat slowing as we neared the Cuban port. My heart rate jacked up and I craned my neck to see out the window. My view was not good. When we stopped, could I chance a bloodcurdling scream for help? Would anyone outside care enough to report it? And the bigger question was, would anyone dare to go against a man like Marco Ruiz?

Aside from the heated moment where he'd shouted at Fernando, Marco had seemed nothing but distinguished and controlled—the sort of wealthy and refined man who oozed confidence and control over his surroundings. His mustached smile was warm, but his eyes missed nothing. He was rich, and if necessary, ruthless.

No. With a sinking feeling I acknowledged that screaming would get me nothing but a bed at the bottom of the ocean.

As the engines cut off, sounds of bustling around and raised voices came from around the boat. My door opened and I jumped, immediately tensing. I'd have felt more comfortable if I at least had on underwear.

A guy walked in carrying some clothes, and closed the door behind himself. He had a soft half-grin on his face, and stood relaxed in his lanky, toned body. He had brown hair down to his chin, and he dressed stylishly like Fernando. His face was beautiful—pretty even—pronounced cheekbones, full lips, and dark lashes that made his eyes look weepy and lined. But he didn't move with the confidence and bravado that Fernando or the other men on this boat moved like. He moved with the same unhurried ease as Perla. And like her, he wore a black collar around his neck.

"Hello, Angel." Even his voice was pretty, a light tenor with soft Spanish tones.

"Hi," I said, wishing it hadn't come out quite so timid.

He sat on the bed next to me and I scooted away. He was unperturbed, studying me in a different way than Marco and the other men had. This guy seemed...curious.

"I am Josef." He smiled and I smiled and it was a little awkward. He didn't seem threatening, but after Fernando I didn't know if I could trust my instincts anymore.

"You are sore?" he asked, nodding down my body.

"Oh...um...a little."

His casual attitude about my post-rape condition rattled me a bit. I didn't want to be casual about it. I didn't want to pretend any part of this was normal or okay.

"I bring ointment in case you need. You take shower now, sí?"

This is not normal. It's not okay. This is all so wrong.

He reached across me to unlock my cuff and I got a whiff of the same cologne Fernando wore. A moment of terrified panic consumed me and I let out a scream, scrunching away from him as my heart pounded.

"Whoa. Relax, Angel pequeño, I no hurt you." He took off the cuff and rubbed my wrist. My eyes stung.

"You smell like him," I whispered. I shouldn't have said it.

Josef cocked his head to the side. "Who? Oh...sí. Cologne. His son choose it para me."

I was confused. Fernando recommended for Marco's henchmen to wear cologne?

"I am slave," Josef explained. "Like you."

My eyes widened. I looked at my uncuffed hands, and the fact that this other slave was in charge of me. Before I could concoct any brave plans, Josef spoke again.

"I am loyal to Master, Angel. He trust. Do not make problem for us, por favor."

He held out a hand and I placed mine inside it, letting him lead me to the bathroom. When we got inside he closed the door behind us and turned on the shower.

"You need toilet?" he asked.

I shook my head. At his prompting I climbed into the shower. He peeked in a few times, I assumed to make sure I wasn't poisoning myself by drinking the shampoo or something. Afterward I dried and put on a white cotton pullover dress that landed just above my knees. It was a low cut V-neck, sleeveless. No underwear. I hated not wearing underwear.

When we entered the room again Josef sat me on the bed and handcuffed me to the headboard again. Then he surprised me by sitting behind me and brushing my wet hair. It felt nice. I shivered and almost fell asleep. With a jolt I wondered if I had any business feeling this comfortable with a man who was loyal to Marco. Then I wondered.

"Josef...are you gay?"

I didn't turn, but I thought I heard a smile in his voice when he said, "I pleasure men y women."

"Oh."

When he was done he said, "Time for lunch."

Someone had brought in a tray while I showered. Josef

lifted the lid and revealed a sandwich. At that moment Marco opened the door. Josef slid to his knees on the floor and dropped his head in reverence.

I stared up at Marco.

"Angel?" he said.

"Yes, Sir."

"Do you see how Josef kneels and lowers his head and eyes when I approach?"

Uh-oh. I didn't like where this was going.

"Yes, Sir," I whispered.

In a calm voice he said, "I would like you to begin practicing that same behavior. You will no longer meet my eyes unless you are instructed. You will also not speak to me until I initiate conversation with you. If you break these rules you will be punished. Do you understand?"

Nervously, I dropped my head and said, "Yes, Sir."

"Bien. Josef, you may feed her."

"Gracias, Amo," he said.

I raised my head when I felt Josef touch my chin. I opened my mouth, hungry despite the churning anxiety and discomfort of having Marco watching. Being fed took some getting used to, but my hunger overcame my pride. I ate every bite.

Marco made Josef brush my teeth on the bed, having me spit in a paper cup, which I thought was ridiculous. I didn't understand why I couldn't be allowed to walk to the bathroom and brush my own teeth. Josef left and Marco took his place at my side on the bed.

I kept my eyes down, my heartbeat ratcheting up. Would this be when he'd want to have sex with me?

"You are a natural submissive, Angel. That is in your favor. I think we can make this work and we will both benefit."

Anger burned like acid inside me. Being called a submissive felt like being called weak, and I hated the truth in that. I hated that I felt so weak. And how the hell did he figure I'd benefit from being his slave? I let my anger simmer, too afraid to lash out and face any of his mysterious aforementioned punishments.

My skin crawled as Marco patted my knee. Rubbed it. Pushed my skirt up and ran his hand the length of my outer thigh to my bottom. And just as he'd done with my breasts, he watched his hands on me, eyed my limbs and skin with interest and care, like the upholstery of a fine new car.

"You will like your new home, Angel. Many have called it Paradise."

I gave a small nod.

The boat began to move and I realized with a grasping, frightened feeling we were leaving the Cuban port already. I swallowed hard.

"I have sent Fernando away, Angel. You will never have to see him again. He has put us both in quite a predicament, yes? But we will make the best of this arrangement." He thought for a moment, seeming pleased. "Perhaps it was meant to be."

Meant to be? Oh, so now he was feeling glad about his new acquisition? Now that he knew I wouldn't fight? I didn't want to be his object! I didn't belong to him, and this was not fucking *meant to be!* How dare he?

Hot anger churned inside my clenched abdomen, running down my arms and legs, making my feet and hands tingle. I clamped my jaw down hard, grinding my teeth together. With a last pat on my knee Marco left me again. And this time I was too filled with rage to cry.

CHAPTER SEVEN

Throughout the next few days I overheard conversations about pushing the yacht—raising the knots to its maximum speed to get us at our destination faster. I knew this was because of me. Marco seemed extremely tense about what he'd find waiting for him at his villa in Spain, which brought me immense hope.

During the quick stop in Cuba someone had purchased hair dye for me. Perla colored my dirty blonde hair a chestnut brown, and she'd given me a spray tan to make me even darker. I looked like a strange, exotic version of myself.

My stomach had begun to hurt as we entered the Mediterranean, and it had nothing to do with nerves. I hadn't gone to the bathroom during our entire four days on the boat. When I was younger I suffered constipation whenever we traveled from home. I'd forgotten the discomfort of it—the hardness in my abdomen and stiffness in my lower back.

But how was I supposed to relieve myself with someone always watching? It would be the ultimate shame and embarrassment. I could only hope I wouldn't need a constant babysitter when we got to this so-called paradise, and I could have a little privacy in the bathroom. Surely I'd earned that.

I'd been quiet and cooperative the entire four days. Nobody came to hurt me or rape me again. My days were monotonous, and though my fears had slightly waned for the moment, I knew things were bound to get bad again when we arrived and I was expected to "please Marco's patrons."

My stomach turned violently each time I thought about it.

As we arrived at our destination, my curtains were closed and I was told to wait in the room with Josef. There was talk of unknown boats nearby, which made my heart bang with exhilaration. Maybe my parents had hired someone to track Marco, or the FBI was on his tail. If they saw me get off the boat I'd be rescued!

I must have had a look of hope on my face because Josef slowly shook his head, strands of brown hair brushing against the line of his chin.

"Master will no allow you to be seen, Angel. He have hidden entry for...ah...discretion. Y, nobody in Spain dare to attack. Master give very much to important men. Money y service."

My jaw went slack and the elation I'd felt seeped out of me. How had Josef known what I'd been thinking and the exact horrible thing to say to deflate me?

He smoothed his long fingers over the top of my hair, which Perla had fashioned into an elaborate bun.

"I don't like this brown," he said, looking at my hair. "You be blonde soon."

I didn't care about my hair. "I'm scared," I whispered.

"Sí," he said softly.

We waited there in the room until nightfall. Everything was so quiet.

"How many of us are there?" I whispered.

"Slaves? Three female y myself. Five now, with you."

I shuddered. I could not include myself in those numbers. It was only a matter of time before the U.S. found a way to bust me out. They would trace my disappearance to Marco.

They *had* to.

When it was pitch black outside, Marco came for us. He blindfolded me and they each held one of my arms, which were cuffed in front of me. My ears and nose became sensitive. The boat smelled like new leather as we walked through it, and for a quick moment I felt warm night air on my skin and the smell of salt sea in my nose. Then it was quiet and echoey, like a tunnel. Damp. We took steps down and I smelled damp earth. Underground. Complete silence.

"Stay here with her tonight," Marco told Josef in Spanish. "We will get you out tomorrow when the perimeter has been checked."

"Sí, Amo."

A puffy *thwunk* sounded beside us on the floor and I felt a rush of air on my legs. Then the door shut and clicked locked. Josef removed my blindfold.

We were in a tiny room without windows or vents. I wasn't claustrophobic, but this room messed with my head, seeming to close in on us. It was lit by a single lightbulb in the ceiling, next to a small black dome which I supposed was a video camera. In the corner was a gray bucket. Was this some sort of holding cell or prison? My breathing hitched, and Josef took me by the shoulders.

"Relax, Angel. We no stay here long. You rest."

A pile of blankets was at our feet. Josef bent and arranged them into a pallet. He pulled me down to lay on my side, and he spooned behind me.

"Close you eyes," he said, pulling the bun from my hair and running his fingers through the strands.

My stomach cramped and I curled myself tight.

"What's wrong?" he asked.

"My stomach hurts."

I didn't have the urge to go, which made it even worse, like my bowels had hardened. This was not good.

"You need the toilet? The bucket es there."

"I...can't," I whispered.

"You can't? Why?"

I didn't respond.

"Ah...you afraid to shit in front of me?" He sounded amused. I cringed, horrified. Boys were so open about their bodily functions. I did not want to talk about crapping with anyone, much less do it in front of them.

"It's gross," I said. The smells, the sounds, all of it. Yuck.

He laughed. "Angel, you must get past this. We slaves have no secrets. No...what you say? Ah, privacy. We eat, we drink, we fuck, we shit where all can see."

Emotion wracked my body and my chin began to quiver. How could he talk so nonchalantly and callously about things so serious? I couldn't accept those words as my fate. As tears slid down my face, Josef shushed me.

"You no cry in front of Master, little Angel. He does not like."

Well, the *Master* wasn't there, so I let the tears fall, and the sobs heave in my chest, and I cried myself to sleep with Josef curled behind me.

———— ✦ ————

Despite our location, I must have gotten a decent amount of sleep because I felt rested when I woke. I straightened, on my side, stretching, then relaxed. Josef muttered sleepily behind me and his arm came around my waist, hand splaying across my stomach. His face nuzzled into the crook of my neck and shoulder, and he pressed the rock hard length of himself against my ass.

"Josef!" I whisper-hissed.

He rubbed against me, gripping my thigh. I pushed back with my shoulder and elbow, making him snort and come awake.

"Ah, fuck," he groaned, grabbing himself through his pants and rolling to his back. His forehead creased and he shut his eyes. I had to admit, yesterday he'd seemed kind of young and boyish to me, but this morning, with that hard-on and the serious look on his face, he was an attractive guy.

I rolled back over, feeling bad for some reason. With my back to him I said, "You can, you know, take care of yourself if you need to. I won't care." I'd never seen a guy do that, or been in the same room with someone masturbating, so the thought made my heart beat faster with nervousness.

"I cannot," he said. "No without permission."

"You need permission to masturbate?" I rolled toward him and he nodded. What was the point of a rule like that?

His breathing had become steadier, and his pants had gone down. I felt my cheeks heat when he caught me staring at his crotch.

"Don't look, little Angel," he teased. "You bring him to life again."

I bit my lip and looked away, trying not to smile from my embarrassment. It was beyond strange to have the urge to smile or to think sexy, joking thoughts at a time like this. I felt guilty. Josef was so nice, and he felt safe to me, but I couldn't get in the habit of letting my guard down.

"Where are you from?" I asked.

His eyes shot up to the camera then back to me.

"I come from a fishing village in Honduras. My parents, they die when I am thirteen, y Master save me from bad men who buy me at orphanage."

Bile rose in my throat. In my book, Marco was a "bad man," but Josef obviously cared for him. I'd hate to know how "bad" the other men must have been for Josef to see Marco as a savior.

"So how old are you?" I asked.

"Twenty-three. Y tu? Ah, and you?"

"I just turned twenty."

I sat up as Josef stood and went to the bucket. I looked away as he peed, throwing back his head for a loud yawn.

"Now you," he said.

I stood with my bound hands in front of me and he lifted my dress until I was squatting over the bucket. I peed, and when I tried to stand he held my shoulders down.

"You try to go," he said.

I shook my head and felt my cheeks warm. "I can't." I stood again, hating the wet feeling left behind when I couldn't wipe.

"Maybe I shit first, y you won't feel bad."

Surely he was kidding. He smiled, completely at ease and serious.

"Aw, Josef, come on. Can't you hold it?"

"Why? Es no good to hold."

"This is such a small room..." Dear God, it would smell awful in here, especially since we couldn't flush it away.

"Angel..." He became serious. "Our bodies...no es *dirty*. We are animals. It's natural." He pulled his pants down and I lay on the blankets, rolling with my back to him to try and block it all out. Thankfully he didn't take long.

"Now you," he said afterward.

I heard him pull up his pants, but I stayed where I was, not looking at him.

"No. No way."

"Just try."

"I can't. I don't need to."

He sat next to me. "I can help. I massage you."

Massage me? Oh, heck no. I sat up, leaning against the wall, and pulling my legs up. The room stank, and Josef's face was as adorable as ever. I realized then that I liked him. Not like *that,* but as a person. He was cute and genuine.

"Thank you," I said. "But I'm okay."

He sighed, clearly not believing me.

Footsteps sounded from outside the door and a key turned in the lock. Familiar panic rose inside me, and I shrunk back into the wall. Josef went to his knees, lowering his face to the floor and placing his palms face down on his thighs. My instinct was to stare at the door and see who came through it, but I forced my eyes down as it opened.

"Look at me," Marco said.

We both lifted our faces and did as he said.

"We have guests arriving at lunch. Josef, you, Jin, and Perla will provide the entertainment after our meal." Josef nodded. "Angel, you will stay at my side and remain silent. Is that clear?"

"Yes, Sir," I said.

"Bueno. Time to get ready."

He blindfolded me, once again, and took my arm, leading me down the hall and up a set of stairs. Then, all at once, a mix of gorgeous sensations hit me—a warm breeze, the sounds of the sea, birds calling, and the strong fragrance of tropical flowers. Too quickly it was over and we were indoors again.

"Introduce her to the others and show her the slave quarters," Marco told Josef in Spanish, all business. "Dress her in a black shift. She is a non-worker tonight and until she's fully trained."

"Sí, Amo."

I felt Marco release me, and then we were winding through the house, sounds of people working—pans clanging, water running, a vacuum somewhere. My bare feet felt carpet, then textured tile as we went from room to room.

The air was crisp and tendrils of foreign scents hit me as we walked: cumin and jalapeños from a kitchen, strong flowers on a warm breeze, probably drifting in from an open window or door.

We entered a quieter area and stopped. Luis removed my blindfold and uncuffed me, then closed the door. I heard a lock click from the outside. I rubbed my tender wrists and rolled them around with a grateful sigh.

"This es our room." Josef took off his collar and set it on a corner table next to another, smaller one.

My eyes searched the large, multi-level room. Three things struck me at once. In all of the beautiful, arched doorways, there were no doors except the one which locked us in. Those black half-globes with video cameras were in every room on the ceiling. And there were no windows.

To my right was a kitchenette area, the counter laden with fruits and rolls. Perla sat at a round table with a breakfast plate in front of her. She was stark naked. A quick glance at her boobs told me they were not real—too high and firm for their size, but she wore them well with perfect posture. I wondered how old she was. Maybe late twenties.

Perla gave me a warm smile. "Buenos díaz."

I was about to answer her when she said, "That mean 'good morning.'"

Crap, I'd almost forgotten I wasn't supposed to understand Spanish. My heart sped as I dropped my eyes and nodded. I needed to be more careful.

"Um, good morning…buenos díaz."

Josef took my elbow and steered me left to an archway

leading into a communal bathroom with multicolored stone walls. Two commodes and four shower heads lined the walls. All out in the open. My insides began to shake. Josef hadn't been joking or exaggerating.

Moving forward through a larger stone archway and down two steps was a long room lined with five comfortable looking floor shifts. We would all be sleeping on the floor. Josef led me down to the second to last one.

"This es yours. Mine es next to you." He pointed to the last one by the wall. I gave a small nod.

"Where are the others?" I asked.

"Es early still. They finish with the patrons."

My hands began to shake.

"Did they…stay the night with them?" I asked.

"Sometime we stay. Sometime we give wake-up call. But no always."

Ew. I swallowed hard. I didn't want to stay the night with strange men or go to them in the mornings.

"Es no so bad," he whispered, seeming as easy-going as always.

For a moment I tried to imagine him having sex with a man, then a woman, and I felt myself blush. I cleared my throat.

"Time for breakfast y then shower," he said.

On our way to the kitchenette I saw the entry to a large, walk-in closet full of clothes and shoes. A lot of black and red. Beside the closet door was a long vanity area—a counter with appliances for hair, manicure sets, and mirrors.

I sat in the kitchen area with Josef and Perla, but only picked at my food, not wanting to put too much more in my body. Plus, it was strange and distracting sitting across the table from Perla's boobs. I kept glancing at Josef, whose eyes would casually drop to her chest now and then, but for the most part he seemed accustomed to the sight, and it certainly didn't hinder his appetite.

Afterward they led me into the showers. Perla turned one on for me, then herself, and climbed under the water, motioning me to do the same. My heart beat harder. Josef began to strip next to me, kicking his clothes toward the wall. Then he came up to me, naked, and grabbed the bottom of my dress, lifting it up. I gasped and considered backing away, but what was the use? I let him pull it over my head and toss it to the wall with his clothes. He smiled at me, nonchalant, and gave me a once over. I crossed my arms over my chest and pressed my legs together, but he didn't try to stare. He went to his shower head, so I went to mine.

I felt awkward and stiff showering in front of two other people, though they didn't care at all. Just washed themselves and paid no attention to me. I washed my hair and peeked glances at Perla's perfect body. Thin and sculpted. No cellulite in sight. I wondered if they made her workout. Or if constant sex was her workout.

I shivered under the hot water. I felt chubby next to her. I was shorter, so every pound I gained or lost showed. I'd put on ten pounds since high school. Compared to Perla my body was soft and untoned. Trying not to look at her anymore, I turned toward Josef, who had his eyes closed and his face upturned to the water, his hands running back over his long, dark hair.

And, yes. I couldn't help myself...I looked down. He was *long*. In his unaroused state, he was almost as long as my ex-boyfriend got when he was hard. Maybe it was my imagination, but Josef seemed to be growing at that moment. I looked up and caught his dark eyes watching me with a half-grin.

"He come awake if you look at him."

Perla laughed next to us, shaking her head as she shut off the water. My face was burning hot. I stuck my head under the water to rinse, embarrassed beyond belief.

We dried off with the fluffy towels, and while they hung theirs up and opted to walk naked, I wrapped mine tightly around myself.

Low feminine voices sounded from the entrance to our rooms and a door shut. Two women stood in the archway to the bathroom and stared at me. I stared back. They were as different as can be—one a tall, stunning European looking woman with a brunette bob and icy blue eyes, the other a petite Asian girl with silky black hair that went down to her waist. The taller woman wore fishnet stockings, knee-high black stiletto boots, and a tight, black leather dress which spilled massive amounts of natural cleavage. Very dominatrix.

The tiny girl was in a purple mini skirt and a black lace bra. She looked like she'd had implants like Perla because they were too gigantic for her small frame.

Both of them wore the black collars. The taller woman gave me a sly smile as she looked me over.

"A new one? And shy, too, no?" Yes, her accent was definitely something European, but not very strong. She had to be at least thirty, which meant she'd probably been with Marco a while.

The other girl glared at me with something like contempt, and I felt myself shrinking from her. She was about my age, maybe even younger. I didn't want to make any enemies, so I dropped my eyes, trying to show respect. Josef stayed at my side. I felt the warmth of his arm next to mine.

"Sea amable..." Perla warned the girl as she passed her. *You be nice.*

"Jin," said Josef. "This es Angel. She speak only Inglés." He nudged me and I looked up, nodding at her. "Angel, this es Jin, y this es Mia. We make her feel welcome, yes?"

Mia nodded, and Jin rolled her eyes. She actually rolled her eyes! What was her problem? Her immediate attitude toward me made me want to lash out. I didn't want to be here and I didn't deserve to be treated like shit from another slave. It wasn't right. None of this was right.

"Angel," called Perla from the bedroom area. "Ven aquí...come here, por favor."

I passed the two girls, giving them plenty of space, and heard them enter the bathroom for showers. I went to Perla in the closet area while Josef fell naked onto his mattress for a rest.

Perla dressed me in a long-sleeved cotton dress that went to my ankles. It scooped low on my chest and back. She made a face at my chest.

"I tell Master you need bra. To lift." She cupped her hands under my boobs and pushed them upward and inward, smiling at the small bit of cleavage that appeared. I fought the urge to move away or cover myself. She let them drop and pushed me onto a stool to do my hair—again in an elaborate, sophisticated bun. She powdered me and blushed me and painted my lips red, then looked at my fingers. One of my nails had been bitten off and was jagged. She filed it, giving me a gentle admonishment.

"You no bite."

"Okay," I whispered. It felt nice to let her take care of me, even if her boobs were swinging in my face half the time. I felt the overwhelming urge to hug her, but I didn't.

She painted my fingernails and toenails red, just like hers. While I waited for them to dry, the door to our quarters opened and Luis stood there. My stomach dropped and my heart rate spiked. He was looking right at me.

"Angel," he called. "You come with me."

Perla quickly slipped my feet into a pair of open-toed

black high heels and handed me a beautiful black masquerade mask lined with black feathers.

"You wear at lunch. Okay?"

"Thank you," I told her, then walked up the step to meet Luis. I accidentally flinched away when he reached out and he shook his head, *tsk*ing.

"You must wear always except in this room." He took a thin, black leather collar and put it around my neck. As he secured the buckle my eyes watered. I felt constricted, like I couldn't breathe, though I knew it was only in my head. But fuck! I was being collared like a dog!

Luis reached for my arm and I pulled away, panicking.

Would they make me have sex with him again? Or someone else? Please not Marco. My stomach clenched and my feet wanted to dig into the floor to keep myself planted. Then my eye went to the gun holstered at Luis's side, and a too-familiar sense of weakness washed over me, doing crippling things to my mind and will.

When he reached for my arm again I let him take it.

CHAPTER EIGHT

I wasn't blindfolded or cuffed as we left the slave quarters, which brought me great relief, even if Luis did hold my arm in a vise grip. As if I could possibly outrun him or his gun.

I soaked in every detail of the house as he led me through it, and for a moment my terrible circumstances were not at the forefront of my mind. Calling the villa a house wasn't really accurate. It was too massive and elaborate for that—more like a Mediterranean mansion or resort. Rooms that faced the ocean had floor to ceiling glass walls on one side. Some areas felt cozy and warm with tiled floors and seating areas, while other parts were wide open with grand ceilings and art of every assortment: paintings, sculptures, and hanging tapestries. Vibrant colors sprung from every direction.

I was taken to a small room that looked like a clinic or nurse's station. Sterile. Medical stuff was lined on the counter. Luis led me to a paper covered exam table and I climbed up, sitting with a shudder. What was I doing here?

An older man in a suit entered and looked me over briefly before going to cabinets and doing something with his back to me. My pulse quickened as he pulled on rubber gloves with a snap and turned to me.

"Español?" he asked in a no-nonsense voice.

I shook my head. "No."

"I give you exam." He pushed my shoulder until I was laying, hesitant and unsure. I tried not to pull away or fight him as he lowered the front of my dress and prodded my breasts, or lifted the fabric and nudged open my legs. He felt around, and though one spot stung a little, it didn't feel too bad.

"You are good," he said.

He listened to my heart and did all the checks: throat, eyes, nose, and ears before turning and grasping a syringe. I shrunk back.

"You get shot. Every three month. No baby."

At first I thought he was telling me not to be a baby, but then I realized he was talking about a birth control shot.

Birth control. Because I'd be having unprotected sex with strange men. My stomach rolled and I fought a bout of nausea. This was really happening. It all came crashing down at that moment and I clutched the edge of the examination table. If I let myself imagine the possible things to come, I would be snowed under by fear and panic. I had to breathe and take everything one moment at a time.

As much as I hated to let them have this kind of control over my body, I really didn't want to get knocked up by some rapist sleazeball either. So I stayed still when he injected my arm. Then he took two vials of my blood.

When he was done, Luis was nice enough to take me by the other arm to lead me through the house. We ended up in a rectangular dining room with workers bustling around to set the two long parallel tables. A large gap was between the tables with an oriental rug, almost like a staged area. Luis stopped me.

"This es your Master's seat, yes?" He pointed to the

chair at the end of the table. "You stay on your knees and you don't leave his side." I nodded and he kept going. "You don't speak. You do *nothing* unless he say. Understand?"

"Yes." But I felt jittery. What would happen if I messed up?

"Lunch es soon," he said. "You stay here."

He led me to the wall behind us, which I hadn't seen when we first came in. It had a line of ten lightweight chains attached to the wall. Luis motioned me to my knees, and then to my horror pulled one of the chains and attached it to the collar around my neck. I reached up instinctively and grasped his wrist as he was securing it.

"It won't hurt," he said, securing the collar lock with a key.

I sucked in a breath, and reached up to feel how tight it was. I could push my fingers between the leather and my neck—snug, but not strangling. Still, this wasn't safe. What if there was a fire or something? I almost laughed at myself and my stupid thoughts about safety. As if anything in the entire place was "safe."

"Hands down," Luis said. I dropped my hands to my thighs.

Two of the worker women glanced at me, then whispered to one another, making me self-conscious. I couldn't believe I'd be sitting there, chained like a dog as people came in to eat. I swallowed another lump in my throat.

"Put on the mask," Luis said.

I'd been holding the mask this whole time. I brought it to my eyes and tied the ribbons behind my head. Being partially hidden brought me a measure of comfort as people began filing in, chatting and laughing as if a chained woman against the wall was okay. I kept my head down, kneeling in the position Luis showed me. After a few minutes I felt a warm, dry hand against the back of my neck and the clinking of a key unlocking my collar.

In a low voice Marco said to me, "You will crawl by my side and remain there silently the duration of the meal. Do not meet the eyes of my patrons. Try to relax and enjoy the entertainment."

Crawl? I hesitated for one moment as he walked to the table, then I followed behind him on my hands and knees, feeling the eyes of the people around him as their conversations hushed. I knelt at his side with my head down.

"Una nueva chica?" asked a man with a deep voice. *A new girl?*

"Sí, sí," answered Marco, sounding almost bored as he spoke in Spanish. "It was time. I'm still breaking her."

"Is she very green?" the man asked. He seemed too excited about the prospect.

"Sí," Marco answered. "Muy verde."

"A virgin?"

"No." Marco sighed, though I couldn't get a read on his mood. It was beyond disconcerting to have two men talking about my sexuality in front of me, so crudely, and not be allowed to say a word.

I found myself inching closer to Marco, the devil I knew. He reached down and smoothed a hand across the top of my head, a sensation that made me feel oddly safe and claimed in the room full of scary people. I kept my head down as I'd been instructed, too afraid to look up even if I were allowed.

The meal began with a clinking of glasses and silverware against plates. A well-mannered crowd, it seemed, until you listened in on their conversations about *buying people*. I'd never been more nauseated as they regaled one another about their recent trades and sales, how one slave's ass had widened too much with age, so she was

70

replaced with a fifteen-year old from Mongolia who was as tight as a sailor's knot. Laughter and appreciative murmurs followed. Marco managed to dodge questions about where he'd acquired me, turning the conversations back to other guests with ease.

Not everyone present was a slave owner. Some of them were there to "vacation" and enjoy the luxuries Marco had to offer. I'd never heard a group of people kiss someone's ass the way this group did to Marco, complimenting everything from his suit to the view to the food to the beauty of his slaves, as if they feared him or craved his approval. His powerful position became more and more clear to me throughout lunch, filling me with dread.

Marco wasn't the only one in the room with a slave at his side. There were two other slave girls kneeling next to their owners, men even older than Marco. Both girls were naked, making me grateful for my dress.

When Marco touched my chin and lifted it to meet his eyes I was not feeling well. He held a morsel of steak on his fork. The thought of eating disgusted me, but my fear overrode it. I opened my mouth and the meat practically melted. He fed me two more equally delicious bites and I prayed he would stop.

A group of workers bustled in, looking crisp in their black and white uniforms, and cleared off all the plates. They set out desserts and coffee, then disappeared once again. A spattering of excited whispers rose up, and without meaning to, I looked around. At the edge of the oriental rug were three people kneeling in slave positions. It took a moment for me to recognize Josef, Perla, and Jin because they were in costumes—a wolf, a grandmother, and Little Red Riding Hood. I think the other guests figured it out at the same time as me, because a few laughed with delight.

Marco gave someone in the corner a nod and Perla crawled to the middle of the floor. She wore a long, billowing white nightgown of lightweight material and a gray curly-headed wig. At first it was comical to see her in it because you could tell it was a beautiful body underneath the old lady getup, but then I felt disgusted by the spectacle they were making of her. She curled up in the middle of the floor and pretended to sleep. Music started overhead.

It began as a lullaby. And then the music sped up and darkened to alert us viewers of danger on its way. Josef prowled onto the scene on his hands and knees, moving with slow sureness. He wore a wolf-skin over top of his body. It looked authentic. The fur was strapped onto his arms, waist and thighs, and he was naked underneath. The frightening head with all its teeth came down over Josef's own head. I got a chill as he slowly crept toward the sleeping figure and the music quickened.

He circled Perla, sniffing her, then nudging her nightgown up with his nose until his face was between her legs. Aroused chuckling sounded across the crowd. Josef lapped at her slowly and she raised her hips, still sleeping and peaceful as if dreaming. Then Josef threw back his head as a howl sounded in the music. His cock was hard and long. Perla's eyes popped open and she saw the wolf above her. She mimicked screaming and tried to escape, but he grabbed her and held her down.

The show was pantomimed—they made no sounds, and their movements were slow, magnified, practiced.

They struggled. He overtook her, flipping her to her hands and knees and ramming into her from behind, grasping around her waist like an animal. A few people clapped and smiles shone around the room. Josef's strokes were long, rocking Perla forward with each thrust, her face looking pained and scared. I was ashamed of the throbbing that began between my legs, despite my total revulsion at the whole thing.

My stomach couldn't take much more. We were

watching a live porn. It felt wrong. The worst part was the way the people in the room watched them. The lust. The crotch rubbing. The crazed eyes. One of the men at our table unzipped his pants and pulled his slave girl's head to his lap, all but choking her as he surged deeply into her mouth. I shuddered and looked away, swallowing bile.

Jin skipped onto the scene in her mini dress and mini red cape, hood up, carrying a basket. When she entered the room and saw her grandmother being ravaged, the music screeched and her basket went flying. She tried to escape, but the wolf ditched the grandmother to catch the girl and pull her back, kicking and screaming. Her hood fell, revealing two long black braids and red lips. The grandmother hobbled over, trying to protect Little Red, but the wolf backhanded her, sending her sprawling. He held the girl down on her back with her hands over her head. She grabbed on to the chair legs of one of the patrons, jostling the man, and everyone laughed. Josef dislodged her hands, held them to the carpet, and pushed himself deep into her.

Jin's face was so expressive as she arched her back. She looked blissful in her state of fear.

If only. Rape was nothing like that. Tears welled behind my eyes for the lies and injustice all around me.

The show went on, a display of fighting and fucking, back and forth between the grandmother and girl, until they were able to overpower him with a bash to the head. He fell to his back and the two females decided to give him a piece of his own medicine by using him instead. Little Red climbed onto his hips and lowered herself onto his dick. She crouched above him, moving her hips all the way up and down for the crowd to see. The grandmother lifted her skirt to her waist and straddled the wolf's face. He grabbed her thighs and lapped voraciously at the offering.

As the music crescendoed, all three seemed to come at once, heads lolling, eyes closed, hips bucking. The room cheered, laughing and praising their performance to one another.

Marco looked down at me, a smile on his face, and all at once it disappeared. His eyes roamed my face angrily and I realized the tears I'd felt welling had spilled over and were running down my cheeks from underneath the mask. Before I could lift my hands to wipe them, Marco wrenched me to my feet and was shoving me toward the door.

My breathing went ragged. I knew I was in big trouble, and all I could do was frantically whisper, "I'm sorry. I'm sorry!"

Marco pushed me toward Luis at the doorway and said in Spanish, "Prepare her for punishment. I will be in momentarily."

My silent tears turned to sobs as Luis gripped my arm and yanked me from the room.

CHAPTER NINE

I would come to think of this day as the worst day of my life. The day my true brokenness began. The day I learned I'd do just about anything to avoid pain. The day I stopped thinking of my body as my own and gave in to the fate of my new life. I think that's the part I hated most…how easily I gave in, and what a relief it had been. I'd only been there a day. I was weak, and I hated myself for it.

It felt like Luis was dragging me clear across the villa. I mumbled pathetically, "No, please. I'm sorry." He shushed me and led me through a set of black, ominous doors into a darkened room. My eyes adjusted and an icy fear leaked into my blood.

It was a room of sexual torture. A rack table with wrist and ankle cuffs, chains hanging from the ceiling and walls. A frightening layout of whips and dildos. I shut my eyes against it all, as if that could make this long nightmare go away. I would open my eyes and be home again, and I could tell my friends about the horrible, vivid dream I'd had. I wouldn't even care if they laughed and call me a freaky perv for dreaming it, because I'd be home and safe, and I could laugh with them.

But that didn't happen.

Luis pulled me to a rounded piece of equipment that looked like a vault or horse, covered in brown leather.

"Take this off." He motioned to the dress.

I grasped my shoulders, crossing my arms over my chest, and scrunched inward. "Please, Luis. I didn't mean to cry. I won't do it again!"

He actually looked a little sorry for me.

"Please," I whispered.

"You must never upset your Master, 'specially in front of patrons. Never cry."

I nodded. "Okay. I understand. I won't—"

"You must be punished. Take off the clothing."

I held back another round of tears. I wanted to fight back, wanted to fight so hard, but I was scared. Fear and fury dripped like a numbing solution through my system.

My hands shook as I slowly pulled the stretchy dress over my head. Luis took it from my hands and tossed it toward the wall. Then he gave my back a push until I was bent over the rounded table. My whole body trembled uncontrollably now as he raised chains from the floor and bound my wrists. I felt him to the same to my ankles, tightening everything so I couldn't move. I whimpered, feelings of panic rising.

"Oh, God," I called out, trying and failing to get any wiggle room.

"Don't move," Luis said. He took a black cloth from his pocket, maybe a bandana, and wound it through my mouth, tying it behind my head. I bit down on it to keep my teeth from chattering. I heard him move to stand by the door.

Then the wait began. Every few minutes panic and

terror would set in, rolling through my body like a maniacal wave. I panted and made frantic noises, but I didn't cry. If tears were the thing that got me in this position, I never wanted to cry again.

I stilled when low voices and footsteps sounded from the doorway behind me. My heartbeats seemed to stop as a chill of apprehension seeped through my bones. Nobody spoke, but I could hear the shuffle of feet and wondered how many were in the room, looking at my naked backside. What were they going to do to me?

When a hand pressed against my back I let out a small scream through my clenched teeth.

Marco's voice was measured and calm when he said, "Silencio." His hand went slowly over the bulb of my bottom, rubbing down my thighs and back up, his fingertips grazing the crease of my ass. "You disappointed me, Angel. I do not tolerate tears. I will not allow you to upset my guests."

I wanted to apologize—to swear I'd never do it again, but I couldn't with the gag. My body was tensed, on high alert, waiting.

A hard smack landed on one of my ass cheeks. I gasped and clenched my muscles until the resounding sting waned.

He came around to stand in front of me, hands behind his back, a disappointed look on his face. I tried to plead with my eyes, but he wasn't having any of it. He smacked me across the face and it hurt on several levels. Besides the ringing in my ears and watering of my eyes it caused, being struck on the face was a shameful feeling.

"Lower your eyes," he demanded, and I did.

Another man came to stand at his side, also in a suit.

In Spanish he said, "Thank you for asking me to oversee her first punishment, Señor Ruiz." I recognized the deep voice of the man at the table who'd been so interested in me.

"You know how I enjoy a good whipping."

"Of course," Marco replied.

Whipping. The word echoed in my head, morphing into a pounding headache.

"Cinturón," Marco said. *Belt.*

My heart seized. *God! Please help me...*

From behind me I heard the *clink* and *whir* of a belt being unbuckled and pulled from its loops around someone's waist. My breathing quickened.

Two seconds later a loud *thwap* followed by a vicious stinging rose up across my butt and I cried out. The pain of it was stunning. Before I could process it another landed a bit higher. I took jagged breaths, the kind you'd take during a sobbing fit.

"Don't you dare cry," Marco whispered.

Thwap.

I screamed with each strike against my flesh. My ass was on fire, but I was too terrified to cry. I tried to focus my eyes, only to see the man next to Marco adjusting the growing bulge in his pants. So I shut my eyes and lost count of the stinging hits. I'd never been in pain like this. I lost control of my body as I tried desperately not to cry. I shook all over, and a childlike babbling rose up from my throat—a begging sound.

"Enough," Marco finally whispered.

I felt my heartbeat in the wounds across my lower back, butt, and thighs. I flinched against the bouts of throbbing pain. And like a dog I panted through it.

Marco walked to my side making soothing noises and running a gentle hand over my arms and upper back. I heard something plastic opening, and then Marco was rubbing a cooling salve against the welts.

"This is your reward for not crying, pretty girl."

My head hung limply, and I was grateful for my reward.

"Jesús y María, I need to fuck her," said the man in front of me.

"Not yet," said Marco evenly. "Tonight. I have something else I need to do with her before then, but you will be my first patron to have her. She is too green to be trusted, so she must stay gagged and bound."

"Fine by me."

I couldn't work up the necessary disgust and fear warranted by the man's lascivious chuckle. I was too relieved that Marco wasn't letting him have me now. How sad that I'd come to a point where I was thankful for any small reprieve, even when I knew something vile awaited me later.

"Shall I send Jin to care for you in the meantime?" Marco asked the man.

"No." I could feel his eyes on me, hear the dark lust in his voice. "I will wait for this one."

"Bueno," Marco said. "Enjoy your afternoon, Señor Feliz."

The deep-voiced man left the room and silence pervaded for many minutes as Marco cared for my wounds. The wounds he'd ordered. I couldn't even muster the deserved contempt for him at that moment. He was messing with my head, hurting me then caring for me. And I was falling for it, actually feeling thankful for his tenderness. What was wrong with me?

He commanded for me to be unchained, so Luis swiftly undid the clasps, leading me by the waist down to the floor where I held myself up on all fours. Marco crouched next to me.

I was so tired.

"Don't move," he said. He removed his suit jacket and handed it off. Then I felt his fingertip slowly circling the bud of my anus with lubricant.

I tried to say, "No," but it came out as a low moan with the gag in my mouth. I shook my head. He landed a warning smack to the side of my hip, a spot that hadn't been harmed by the belt. I bit down hard and stilled, fighting back the stinging behind my eyes. Marco's voice was clear and matter-of-fact.

"Never tell me no. I will do with you what I please, and you will take it. If you're smart you'll also learn to enjoy it."

His finger pushed in halfway and I sucked in a breath at the stretching invasion. He gave a low hiss and whispered in Spanish. "So tight…"

To me, in English, he said in a stern voice, "You are compacted, Angel. You must take better care of your body. Do you understand?"

I nodded, but I loathed that he was bringing up my personal business, prodding me like he'd palpate an animal.

"I know all that happens in my home, Angel. All that goes on with my slaves." He turned his head and called, "Perla. The enema."

Enema?!

I hadn't known Perla was in the room. She came to my side and gently pushed my shoulders down as Marco removed his finger.

"To your elbows," she said, molding me so that my upper body was close to the floor and my bottom stuck up in the air. "You feel better after."

Something plastic touched my butt hole and I dropped my hips with a whimper, clenching my muscles. Perla and Marco both grabbed for my hips, pulling them back up.

"Don't move," Perla gently warned. The plastic piece pressed in, and to my relief it was small, a thin nozzle. Then a cold, rushing feeling entered my bowels, causing an almost immediate bout of cramping inside me. I groaned and curled my body tighter as my stomach contracted. They were going to force me to shit. In front of them. This was the ultimate gross shame. I moaned, wanting to die and disappear. Perla rubbed my upper back, but Marco stopped her, speaking in Spanish.

"Don't comfort her. She must learn."

After another minute of the cold solution coursing into me, a horrible overwhelming need to use the restroom overcame me. I raised my head, breathing faster and making urgent little sounds.

"Here," Perla said. She motioned to a bucket against the wall.

The dreaded fucking bucket.

My momentary horror was overridden by another painful stomach cramp. I crawled in a rush to the container. Perla dropped her eyes, but Marco, Luis, and another of Marco's gigantic lackeys watched me as by body expunged its contents.

It was the most awful, degrading moment of my life. The skin on my backside shouted its anger, so I tried to hold myself up, grasping the sides of the bucket. Another wave of cramping came and I squeezed my eyes shut, cursing myself when I felt a tear slip from my eye. Without hesitation, Marco's big man whacked the side of my face with his open palm, effectively drying my tears and nearly throwing me off the bucket.

Everything I thought I knew about myself and life, all of my views, shifted and changed in that room on that day. Ideas of privacy and entitlement and freedom slipped away. The meanings of strength and weakness morphed and failed to matter anymore. All that mattered was survival with minimal pain. Maybe pain made some people feel alive, but not me. Pain made me feel hated and ashamed, like a dog tucking its tail when its master kicked it. If survival without pain meant obeying, that's what I would do.

When I was finally done my arms shook from holding myself up.

"Stand," Marco said.

I pushed myself, wobbling and unable to stand straight from the leftover pain in my abdomen and backside. He pulled the bandana down from my mouth and caressed my jaw with his thumb.

"What would you like to say to me, Angel?"

Twenty-four hours ago I would have thought of all sorts of cutting things I'd like to say to him, but with the shape I was in all I felt was glad that my punishment was over, and a deep desire to be in his good graces. My answer was immediate. "I'm sorry I disappointed you...Master. I'm sorry I cried."

He gave me a brief, warm, affectionate smile.

"Take her back to the quarters and have her clean herself and the bucket," Marco said.

With Luis on one side of me and Perla on the other, I walked naked out of the room, holding the bucket, my head lowered in absolute humility.

When we entered the quarters I went straight to the bathroom, ignoring the stare from Josef and the malicious giggle from Jin when she whispered, "Mira el culo*!" Look at her ass!*

Why did she hate me?

"I remember yours looking like that once." Josef teased her in Spanish and Jin laughed.

I dumped the bucket in the toilet and flushed, then cleaned it in the sink, trying not to gag. Once I finished I turned the farthest shower on cold and stepped under it, wincing. I caught Josef leaning in the doorway, watching me with a worried expression. I dropped my eyes and when I looked back up he was gone.

Drying off was painful. A glimpse in the mirror showed

ugly welts, the edges of some with tiny red blood blisters. The old me only knew how to deal with pain and emotional distress by crying and popping Motrin. That was no longer an option. I didn't know how to deal now except to keep going.

Just keep going.

I wrapped the towel around myself and passed the others, going to my bed to lie down on my stomach and pass out until it was time for Mr. Creepy Voice to have his way with me. I couldn't even bring myself to worry about what was in store for myself with him. I could only handle one horrible event at a time and I was currently maxed out.

CHAPTER TEN

I was woken by Josef some time later. I immediately tried to get up from where I lay on my stomach, and sucked in a gasping breath from the plethora of pain splicing across my backside.

"Shh…" Josef stilled me with a hand to my upper back. He then touched my collar, which was still slightly damp from the shower. "You can take this off when you come to the room." He wasn't wearing his. I nodded. From now on I'd take it off immediately upon entering the slave quarters.

He reached down and gently nudged my face up, then brought his lips to mine. I froze with surprise, first at the fact that he was kissing me, opening my mouth with his, and second that he was pushing something into my mouth with his tongue. Just as quickly as the kiss began it ended, leaving behind a pill. I only hesitated a second before discreetly working it to the back of my throat and swallowing it. I had no idea what it was, but I didn't think Josef would try to hurt me or steer me wrong.

He left me, going to the closet. The three girls were over there, too, getting ready. My stomach spun and dropped. Tonight… That man with the deep voice who got off on me being beaten. *Oh, God.* I didn't want him to touch me.

Was this really going to be my life? Day after day of being raped by strange men? And even worse than rape because I would be expected to pretend to enjoy it. What if he expected me to be all sultry, like kissing down his body and giving him an elaborate blow job? The very idea of being an active participant made me want to puke.

I sat up, but my butt hurt too much, so I stood. Everything was sore now, and my head pounded. Perla called me over. I'd fallen asleep with the towel around me, so I adjusted it and went across the room.

Mia was sitting at the vanity dressed in her dominatrix ensemble, shiny black boots coming up to her thighs. Her brown hair was coifed in a perfect bob and she was applying make-up to stage perfection. She looked dangerously sexy with darkened eyes, the only splashes of color being across her high cheekbones and full lips. She saw me in the mirror and nodded. I nodded back, kind of intimidated by her awesomeness.

Jin came out of the closet wearing a black corset top and black mini skirt. She looked me up and down with a smirk and then lifted her hair, saying to Josef, "Lace me."

With deft fingers he made her tiny waist appear even tinier. She winced at the tightness, but said nothing. When he finished she grinned a seductive smile and thanked him. He nodded and went in the clothing room to get ready. Jin frowned when she saw my eyes follow him.

Ah. So that was it. Did they have something going on? Or was it just Jin who had feelings? I couldn't imagine them being allowed to have something, seeing as how we slaves weren't even allowed to masturbate. I guess they didn't want us wasting any of our valuable sexuality. *Blech.*

Perla, completely naked, pulled the towel off me and I let out a small sound, covering myself.

"No." She stood in front of me and put her hands on my wrists, slowly bringing them down. "Es beautiful, sí?" She ran the backs of her fingers from my collarbones down my chest and over my breasts, making my nipples pucker, then down my stomach. Mine looked so small compared to hers, and my tummy seemed too rounded next to her flat one. Perla bent, and to my horror stared right at my crotch, then ran her fingers over the small patch of hair there. I gasped and stepped back.

"Es no too long. Okay for tonight."

Out of curiosity I looked down and saw that she was smooth and hairless. Perla took my wrist and pulled me into the closet. I had a crazy urge to laugh at her openness, but I didn't. Had it really only been a few days ago that laughter felt appropriate and normal?

Josef was in the corner in a black leather thong, a black studded collar, and matching cuffs around his wrists and ankles. His loose hair look like it'd been lightly gelled to tame it. He gave us a wink and strode from the closet. Was that his whole outfit? Wow.

Perla dug through dressers of stuff until she found a pair of black lace thongs for me and a sheer black negligee that was just loose enough not to hurt my back. I put them on, being careful not to move too fast—I was afraid of one of the welts opening and bleeding. Next, Perla found some black high heels for me. She put her foot up to mine and we had a moment of camaraderie when we found we wore the same size. And just as it had happened with Josef, I experienced a tenderness when I realized I really liked her. In all this mess, I was grateful to have her and Josef—two people who didn't want to hurt me.

Perla put on a red bustier-styled negligee and red spike heels, then we did our hair. As I wound the fat curling iron around the brown strands of my hair I felt a wave of sad bitterness. Why should I try to make myself look pretty for this asshole?

Then I remembered the belt across my skin.

I would do my hair because Marco wanted me to. My arm suddenly felt too heavy, but I held it up until the last strand was curled.

I didn't think I could ever have feelings of acceptance about this situation, or be content with my lot the way the others seemed to be. But I could fake it, just to get me through until I was rescued, and then I'd put it all behind me. It couldn't be too much longer now…

—⋅✦⋅✦⋅—

When Luis came to get us, something strange happened. As each slave exited the quarters, they fell to their hands and knees and crawled. When it was my turn I did the same, feeling ridiculous as people stared when we passed. Some of the patrons stepped closer to examine each of us, like trying to decide which lobster to pick from the tank for dinner.

And then there were the humiliating titters regarding the state of my ass. I kept going, making eye contact with no one. *I can do this. Keep control.*

One good thing happened as we crawled across the house…whatever Josef had given me started to kick in. The stinging and heat on the back of my body seemed to sooth, and the burning against my knees as I crawled eased up. I felt almost buzzed, lightheaded, calmer.

I wished I could thank Josef and tell him that I freaking loved him.

Without fanfare we went our separate ways. I kept my head down, like I'd seen the others do, so I didn't know where they went or with whom, but Luis stayed by my side and I followed at his feet down a narrow hall until we got to a room.

"Up," Luis said.

He took me into a beautiful bedroom and my eyes went to the gigantic window as he led me around the four-poster bed. I hadn't been allowed near any windows since I'd been there. I craned my neck to see the sunset sky and sparkling ocean. I wondered how it smelled out there— the Mediterranean air. Freedom...

"On the bed," Luis said.

My nostalgia for the outdoors disappeared with a snap as I came back to reality, staring at the high bed. I started breathing harder. Luis nudged me. I crawled up and he climbed up, too, taking my wrists and telling me to lay down on my back. I did as he said, and though it stung and pulsated, I knew it wasn't half as bad as it would've been without that pill.

Luis pulled out a chain attached to the headboard and clamped both of my wrists in it. The door opened and I instinctively brought my knees up. Marco walked in, closing the door behind himself.

Unease curled in my belly. Had there been a change? After having me beaten, did Marco want the honors of screwing me himself? I didn't know which would be worse, him or Marco. And then I decided Marco would be worse. So far he hadn't done anything to me himself, and I wanted to keep it that way.

He pulled a hip up onto the bed and looked me over. He touched the edge of my hip where one whelp ended.

"Does it hurt?" he asked, seeming concerned.

"Yes, Sir," I whispered.

"Yes, *Master.*"

I paused only briefly, remembering that after I'd been whipped I called him Master on instinct. The memory of how broken I'd been in that room this afternoon humiliated me.

"Yes, Master," I said quietly.

88

Gwendolyn Field

He ran a hand over my arms, then my legs, speaking to me all the while.

"Your patron tonight is a very important man, Angel. Señor Feliz is a great supporter of my work and I don't wish to upset him. He has been told of his limitations with you, and he is being watched. You are safe."

My eyes darted around the room. The ceilings didn't have any of those video camera domes. Marco chuckled.

"I wish my patrons to have a sense of privacy, but I must also protect what's mine. Don't you worry. Everyone is being watched at all times. Never forget that. Trust me to take care of you."

He paused, watching me, so I said, "Yes, Master." Although his idea of "taking care of me" was far from my idea.

"Bueno. Now. My rules for you are this: Never tell a patron no. Allow him to do whatever he wishes. If they are breaking a rule my people will swiftly intervene. Try to enjoy yourself, and if you don't, pretend you do." His fingers brushed over my nipples in the gauzy material, making them pucker and my breath quicken. My nerves were on high alert. "Eventually you will learn to enjoy the ease of your life here, Angel. My patrons will see you as a goddess. They will worship you with their touches and you will grow to find pleasure as they do."

Bullshit.

I gritted my teeth and stared straight up at the ceiling. Marco pulled something out of his pocket. A blindfold.

"This will help relax you for your first time with a patron, yes?"

I nodded. I definitely liked the idea of not having to look at this man. I lifted my head and Marco slipped the velvety covering over my eyes. Then he kissed my forehead, which was oddly comforting. As soon as I thought that, a revolting sensation slid through me. I didn't want to feel anything positive toward Marco. He was fucking with my head, and I needed to be strong.

A plastic click sounded, like something opening, and a moment later Marco was urging my legs apart, pushing aside my panties. What was he doing? I felt a cool slickness at the entrance and he swirled lube around, pushing some inside me. He then fixed my underwear and straightened my negligee.

I heard both Luis and Marco leave. Then I waited.

That bastard made me wait forever. I was high strung, pissed off, and scared to death when the door opened and slow footsteps approached the bed. He was silent. I could hear my breath coming too fast. In and out. My knees pressed together. My muscles tensed.

A belt buckle clinked as it was being undone and I whimpered, remembering that sound only hours ago. Was he allowed to whip me?

Don't cry, Angela, I begged myself.

Something touched the side of my calf and ran up my leg. He *thwapped* it against my thigh and I realized it was the end of his belt. I stayed still, practically panting, as he gently whipped the piece of leather across my legs. Then he pulled my thigh to spread my legs. I whimpered again and he chuckled, giving me the chills. He pushed the lacy material of my thong aside and gave my clit a smack with the belt. I let out a small holler of surprise. It hadn't hurt, necessarily. But it made me throb down there. He did it again and I clenched my thigh muscles, gasping.

No, no no. I would *not* be turned on by him. Hell-fucking-no.

With no fanfare or warning he shoved two fingers inside me, curling them upward and rocking his hand back and forth. Hard. I bit my lip and pulled on my chains. Nobody had ever fingered me so roughly. I gritted my teeth and tried not to think about abrasions. As he manhandled me, a wet, sloshing sound began and he moaned. The sound was coming from me. I could feel a fullness building deep inside me. I realized with horror he was working my g-spot, which wouldn't make me come, but it would definitely make me sopping wet.

"Ah, sí, putita," he moaned. *Little whore.*

He pulled his fingers out and I heard clothing being yanked off. Moments later he was against my arm by my head. He whapped my mouth with his fucking cock and chuckled.

Yuck! I wanted to scream at him to get it away from my face.

"Suck me," he commanded.

He yanked me by the hair to face him and prodded open my mouth. My wrists burned in their cuffs above me as he pulled me closer. He shoved himself in, all the way to the back of my throat. Thankfully his penis wasn't long enough to gag me. I kept my lips tight around him, letting him control the speed, hoping he'd come fast and get it over with. But he didn't. After a while of grunting into my face he flipped me, twisting my wrists, and climbed onto the bed behind me. He grabbed my hips and pulled them up, shoving my head face down.

Over. I just wanted this to be over.

His hands roamed across my whelp marks and his breathing went raspy. He open-palm smacked my ass cheek and my head flew back from the stinging pain, a holler wrenching from my throat.

He smacked again, a growling laughter bubbling up when I yelled again. He seemed to love when I vocally responded to the pain, so I gave the sadistic bastard what he wanted. Five times he smacked my already-sensitive bottom and hips. Then he bit my ass cheek and I screamed. It wasn't a skin-breaking bite, but his sharp teeth hurt. He did it on the other side and then buried his face in my ass crack. I squirmed, wanting more than anything to scream for him to get his face off me, but it wasn't necessary. He was finally so worked up that he went up to his knees and pushed his dick into me.

"Ah, apretado!" He called me tight and began to thrust faster, smacking my hip every few seconds like he was riding a horse. I made a lot of noise for him, praying it would end soon. He reached down and grabbed a handful of my hair, wrenching my head back. Freaking-A, that hurt! He was fucking me super fast now and with a hard yank of my head his deep voice went up a few octaves and I felt him coming inside me.

I breathed, relieved it was over.

That hadn't lasted long. Maybe fifteen minutes. Fifteen *unpleasant* minutes.

I thought about the soft little mattress waiting for me in the slave quarters.

He pulled out of me slowly, and turned me to my back.

"Now for dessert," he said in Spanish.

My heart sunk. Why couldn't he just be happy with his orgasm and leave me the hell alone? My head spun—I was feeling loopy now and I wondered if it was from the drug or the day's experiences crashing down on me.

He pushed my thighs apart, holding them up with his hands and squeezing so hard I'd probably have fingertip bruises. I yelped when his face went to my crotch and he began lapping at my hole, at his own come. And then he latched on to the sensitive nub of my clit and sucked with abandon, flicking the tip of his tongue. Every nerve ending came to life and blood rushed between my thighs. I panted.

No. *No!*

I orgasmed violently, my hips bucking from the unexpectedness of it. It didn't last long, brief and intense, but my scream and obvious pleasure were enough to make him hard again. He raised my ankles to his shoulders and slid into me, pushing my legs toward my chest so he was close enough to grab my nipples and pinch them, twisting.

Hot shame and regret filled me. That orgasm had come out of nowhere—I rarely ever came, even during good sex. Maybe the drug had relaxed me too much. Whatever the reason, I was mad at myself for making him think this was all okay. I hated my stupid body for reacting. It hadn't been enjoyable in the ways that counted to me. In that moment I swore to myself I'd never come again for one of Marco's patrons. I might not be able to keep anything else from them, but that would be mine.

Round two lasted longer than round one, but by the end he was tired out and I was sore all over. Luis came to get me, shedding my blindfold as we exited the room. I crawled back to the slave quarters with remnants of my first patron seeping down my thighs. The crawl of shame.

I felt like I'd died and gone to hell.

This is not my life, I chanted in my head. *This will all be over soon.*

I had to keep saying it or I'd lose myself. The moment this all became my "norm" would be the end. I'd truly be Angel instead of Angela, and I could never let that happen. I couldn't fight the people here, couldn't control them, but I could fight my own mind and control it.

I had to.

CHAPTER ELEVEN

Something was going on the next morning. Something big.

Luis got me out of bed early, wrapping a bandana around my mouth to gag me and slipping a blindfold over my eyes. He didn't even make me put my collar on. I still wore the see-through negligee from the night before, seeing as how this place had no pajamas, but I wished I'd had time to put on underwear. Luis pulled me through the house, speed-walking. My heart pounded. Did I do something wrong? Had Marco's friend been unhappy with me? I ran through the night, trying to remember any "rules" I may have broken.

But then I realized it wasn't just me. The whole house had a nervous ring to it. The workers were all quieter than normal. I heard someone whisper in Spanish about policía and news reporters. At the sound of those words, I dug my bare heels against the floor, a rush of exalted longing to escape rushing through me. *Someone is here! They're here for me!* A scream ripped from me, its glory muffled by the cloth in my mouth. Luis grasped me harder and another man grabbed me from the other side. I went into full freakout mode.

The men lifted me by the arms and rushed forward despite my kicking and thrashing. I didn't care if I was punished; all I knew was this was my chance.

I heard some sort of latch creak open and then smelled dank damp air as we descended. I fought with renewed passion, knowing they were taking me back into the confinement room I'd been in with Josef. Underground. Probably soundproof. My fighting earned me a ringing slap on the side of the head. They threw me on the dirt floor and the door slammed. I ripped off my blindfold and gag.

In that moment I felt like a deranged animal. I attacked the door, yanking on the handle and yelling as loudly as I could. I kicked the door with my bare feet, punched it, clawed at it, beat it with everything I had, all the while screaming like a banshee. When my whole body was thrumming with self-inflicted injuries and my throat was hoarse, I dropped to the ground and cried deep, heaving sobs. Screw Marco and his no crying rule. I didn't care about belts or cuffs or anything except *who* was at the villa looking for me and what, if anything, they'd find.

Please, God... I prayed. I begged, pleaded, and tried to make deals with that invisible entity I'd never given much thought to before. *If you get me out of here I swear I'll be good. I won't even question why You let this happen. I'll do anything You want.*

I crawled to the door and pressed my ear to it. Nothing. Not a single sound.

"Hello?" I banged my open palm against it. "I'm down here!"

Silence. I sat down with my back against the door and closed my eyes.

It didn't take long for me to start to feel crazy in the compact room with no stimulation. With no way to mark the passage of time I just sat there and listened, my auditory sense becoming so acute in the silence I could hear my own heart beating and the movement of air into and out of my lungs, but nothing else.

Twice that day the door was opened. Each time I would scream and try to fight my way out, but all that got me were painfully ringing ears from smacks to the head, bruised appendages, and plates of spilled food at my feet.

"*Fuuuck!*" I screamed in frustration the second time and kicked my plate of grilled chicken and steamed vegetables. It splattered against the wall and I didn't care because I couldn't even think of eating. Nobody was going to find me down here. A bleak feeling of despair settled over me like nettles.

"Why?" I cried. "Why are you doing this to me?" I didn't even know who I was talking to. Marco. God. That bitch, Karma. All of them. Why?

Hours later I lay curled against the door and sheer exhaustion took me.

— ❖ —

The next day they brought me nothing. In my hunger I thought about eating the dirty food that I'd thrown, but angry pride kept me from it. And just to ensure I wouldn't give in and eat it, I picked up each piece and threw it in the crap bucket.

Okay, so I was cutting off my own nose to spite my face, as my mom used to say, but my mind had gone to a dark and cloudy place. The kind of place where, for the first time ever, death began to hold some appeal. I spent the day dreaming about the least painful ways I could go—begging Marco to drug me or gas me. I wasn't above using his guilt about Fernando as leverage.

But, no. In the end, I knew I wouldn't do it. Because even in that scary, shadowy place of my mind, a feather of hope floated along, stark white and bright.

Someone would save me. Someday.

— ✦✦ —

On the third day I lay on my back and began chanting the silly name song from when I was a kid.

"Marco, Marco, bo-barco, banana fana fo farco, e-i-o, -arco… *Marco!*"

I busted into giggles and did a round with everyone's name: Josef, Mia, Jin, Perla, and Luis. I ended with yelling, "I fuckin' love the banana fana song! Everybody sing!" More giggles.

After a long while of singing childhood songs the door opened. I looked up from my position on my back, expecting to see Luis, but it was Marco's stern face looking down at me. I knew at once that nobody was there to save me.

My body and mind moved in harmony without thought. I rolled to my stomach and pushed to my knees, kneeling with my head down, palms flat against my thighs, breathing hard.

Oh, my God. I was his slave. A prostitute. I wouldn't allow myself to acknowledge it until that moment when it felt very, very real. There was no more hiding from what my life had become. This man owned me.

My heart pounded. Was he mad at me for freaking out? For being stubborn and not eating?

"Bueno chica," he whispered. He bent enough to lift my chin. In his eyes I saw disappointment and I had to look down again. He *tsked.*

"Mírate…" *Look at yourself.*

My nails were broken. I was dirty all over. My knuckles were scabbed and scraped, my legs and arms covered in bruises.

What punishment was I in for? I started shaking from the inside.

"I'm sorry, Master."

"Shh." He patted my head. "Do you want to leave so badly, Angel? Is it so bad here for you?"

I bit my lip and kept my head down, not answering. He sounded so…sad. I didn't get it. Why did he care whether or not I wanted to be here? He knew he was forcing me against my will. Did he think I'd get here and be so smitten by the fanciness that I'd forget about my old life? Was he crazy, or just extremely out of touch with reality?

Luis came in, blindfolded me, and guided me to my feet. They walked me out, through the house, and back to the slave quarters where I was told to shower. I awaited my punishment with a strange numbness, but it never came.

Instead I was pampered the next three days. The other slaves were not allowed in the room during these times. I was so confused. Was Marco trying to buy my loyalty and happiness? Did he really think spa treatments and gifts would make me okay with a life of sexual slavery?

Women who spoke broken English were sent into the slave quarters to do my nails and hair—making me bright platinum. I'd never been quite so blonde, and it was a stunning difference. I admitted to myself with reluctance that I liked the new color and layered style.

Boxes of clothing in my size showed up. Expensive bras and sexy dresses. Skimpy bathing suits. Satin camisole sets and a white, silk robe.

I was given a laser hair removal treatment and told I'd have to have several treatments for the hair to stop growing. Never having to shave or wax again? That was kind of cool, but I couldn't help wondering when the bomb was going to drop. Why was Marco spoiling me? I tried to enjoy the kindness and not constantly worry, but it was hard. Marco was the kind of man whose every action had an ulterior motive.

He came in that afternoon and I dropped to my knees.

"Siéntate, Angel. Sit."

I sat at the table and he sat across from me. I tightened the robe around myself.

He looked me over admiringly, then pulled out a newspaper article and set it on the table.

I held my breath as I read the title: *Missing American Girl Thought To Be Dead.*

Dead? *No!*

My heart went wild as I scanned the article, which must've been cut from an American paper. It talked about how Fernando and I had left the club together and neither of us was seen again. Friends of Fernando saw us heading toward the boat docks, and Fernando's boat was found sunk the next day—structural integrity of the boat and its engine were being investigated. No signs of our bodies were found. Probably eaten by sharks, a local said. Señor Marco Ruiz, a respected business owner, was reported to be mourning his only son, and spending his own funds for a private investigation of the two young people. My stomach twisted.

Don't cry, Angela. Don't you dare cry.

Marco was celebrating his win—beautifying his latest acquisition. And by showing me this article he was making it clear I was his. Message received. Time to stop hoping. Stop fighting. To the world, I was dead.

I swallowed hard, and with a shaking hand pushed the article back toward him.

My parents...did they believe this? Did they have nightmares about me drowning or being eaten by a shark? Were there any other leads or was this it? Was *nobody* looking for me anymore?

No. No. I tried to reach for my feather of hope, but it drifted deeper and farther into that cloudy mess of my mind.

I knew Marco was waiting for a response, but all I could do was stare at the table and nod, biting the inside of my lip to keep from showing emotion. He reached over and patted my hand, leaving his on top of mine.

"What can I get you, Angel, hm? Te gusta...ah, you like books?"

I nodded. He patted my hand again and left me.

— ♦ ❧ ♦ —

The following day a box of American books arrived. Bestselling fiction and romances. Even a few books of how to learn other languages, which he probably thought was useful since he has so many international patrons. The sight of the books actually cheered me a little. I could lose myself in them, however briefly. When the other slaves came in that evening and Jin took a look at my box and my makeover with astonishment, I knew I'd been given a gift and a luxury. I felt kind of guilty.

Perla and Josef nosed through my new stuff and of course I let them, telling them they could borrow anything they wanted. I didn't really consider anything at the villa "mine." Perla was excited to see the new shoes. Even Mia walked over and checked me out. She felt my hair and said brusquely, "I like." Then went to remove her makeup.

I tried to smile at Jin, but she looked away. I hated the animosity there, so I made a vow to myself that I'd try to get to the bottom of it and not let it get any worse. The way I saw, it the five of us needed to have each other's backs, and not for purposes of knifing. These four people were all I had now.

I lay down and closed my eyes, thinking of my sorority sisters. My dorm room. My mom and dad and their constant love. My life that seemed like a distant dream now. Had it ever been real? Thinking of them hurt too much. Imagining the pain they were feeling...it wrecked me that I was putting them through that. But it was probably better that they thought I was dead as opposed to what my life had actually become.

I curled tighter and thought about crying. I could hide my face. Nobody would know. It could help relieve my stress if I allowed myself to mourn.

But when I tried to cry, Marco's face filled my mind, and the tears wouldn't come. Even my tear ducts were afraid of Marco. I was his now. Really and truly.

CHAPTER TWELVE

Mia couldn't have been more of my opposite, but we took to one another. I loved listening to her talk. She spoke Spanish with a European accent, an exotic sound. She sat me down one morning at our small table and said, "I teach you Español." It wasn't a question, or even an offer, it was a command. And being the submissive I was, I complied.

I felt guilty that she was going to waste her time teaching me something I already knew. Mia was nice and I didn't want to lie to her, but the cameras were always watching and listening. I expected her to start with the basics—the items around us like "table" and "chair," but she didn't.

"*Culo* is ass." She stared at me, matter-of-fact, as if she wanted me to repeat after her.

"Oh. Um, okay. *Culo*."

She nodded, then proceeded to teach me every dirty Spanish word and phrase in the book. She taught me a ton of words I didn't know, all the things patrons might say to me, or I could say to them. It was very helpful.

"You are fast learner, yes?"

I blushed. "Yeah...thank you. I mean, gracias."

"Ah, bueno mi putita hermosa." She called me her beautiful little whore, but she said it so nicely. Words ceased to offend me the way they did when I first met Fernando. Actions were all that mattered now.

—•❖•—

Time was a funny thing. Small changes over a long course of time could go easily unnoticed, until one day you look up and realize you're not the same person anymore. At all. And all those small changes added up to something big.

After six months in the villa I had changed. Others might call it "giving in" or "caving," but I called it adaptation. Survival. In my early weeks I mourned every small change I noticed in myself. It started with my body. For months I'd been hungry all the time. I longed for food almost obsessively.

Without pizza and fast food, eating only fruits, vegetables, and whatever small morsels fed to me at the table, I lost weight quickly. My stomach, thighs, and arms tightened. My hair grew. I looked different. Felt different. In my old life I would have loved to have this body, but the physical transformation was not my doing. It was Marco's, for his purposes, and so it was hard to love it.

And then there were the bigger changes—the mental changes. Like how comfortable I began to feel in my own skin, walking or crawling around naked. But it was worse than just feeling comfortable...I began to feel sexy, and I craved eyes on me. Marco was right when he said some patrons would treat me like a goddess. I still hated having sex with the strange men, and I hadn't had an orgasm since that first time, but I was aware of my body in a way I'd never been before. Every breeze that blew in from the veranda was a caress across my skin.

My clit was overly sensitive. I found myself in an

almost constant state of arousal, until it was time to have sex, and then my body felt cold and stiff all over. I'd gotten good at faking enjoyment. The other slaves often gave me pointers about what certain patrons liked, so I played it up. Even Jin was helpful. She'd warmed to me slightly after realizing Josef and I weren't after one another. I still hated my life there, but I kept going.

I had no freedom. I hadn't left the inside of the villa since I'd been there. I wasn't allowed near the windows, and I was the only slave not permitted at the outdoor pool. I took this to mean people were still searching for me. Anyone traveling by on a boat could zoom in with their cameras on certain parts of the villa. That aspect gnawed at me daily as I longed for the outdoors.

But as far as slavery went, I knew I had it good. Besides the obvious creature comforts, Marco seemed to treat my differently. Like his favorite puppy. Maybe he felt guilty still for Fernando's actions against me, leading to my acquisition. Whatever the reason, he generally only allowed his more docile patrons to have me. That's not to say they weren't freaks. I'd seen, done, and had done to me more strange things than I'd ever thought possible—there was no end to the fetishes—but I knew there were worst patrons, the sadists, who were handled by the others. And while anal sex seemed to be a hot commodity at the villa, Marco never allowed it for me. I'd been fingered there, but never fucked. Perhaps he knew how scared I was, or that all things regarding asses was sort of a taboo phobia of mine.

Or maybe he was saving my anal virginity for a special reason. That thought made me shiver as I knelt by the wall after lunch one fall afternoon.

There was discussion of a festival in one of the big cities, and Marco needing to tend to some business there with one of his nightclubs. He mentioned taking Perla away with him for the night. I got excited about the prospect of a night off, only to have Marco snap his fingers and say, "Angel, aquí."

Yes, he snapped his fingers at me like a dog all the time. I'd long since stopped being offended.

I crawled to his side. He tipped my chin up to look at him.

"Señor Acosta will oversee the villa tonight. You and Josef will care for him well, sí?"

Me...*and* Josef? As in together? At the same time? My mouth went dry, and I swallowed.

"Sí, Master."

Marco nodded toward Mr. Acosta, my signal to look at the man. He looked a few years younger and trimmer than Marco, his mustache flecked with more brown than gray. He gave me a lazy side grin, his eyes traveling down my naked body, and I smiled back politely before dropping my eyes.

"Bueno." Marco waved his hand sideways, my dismissal, and I crawled to the doorway where I met Luis. I was allowed to stand once we were out of the men's sight, and walk to the slave quarters.

I'd come to think of Luis as my personal escort. He took me to and from everywhere I went in the villa. And maybe it was wrong of me, but I sometimes taunted him. An "accidental" brush of my ass against his hand, or my fingers against his crotch. I never met his eye and he never said anything, but he'd sometimes growl and have to adjust himself. It was fun to fluster him when he had work to do and couldn't take care of his arousal. I considered it payback for when he raped me that first day on the boat.

When I got back to the quarters Jin was the only one gone. Perla was packing a bag, Josef was eating an apple, and Mia was reading one of my romance novels, her spike heels on the seat cushion across from her.

"Um, Josef?" I said.

He raised his eyebrows at me, his long hair fanning across his cheeks.

"You and I are supposed to entertain Mr. Acosta tonight?"

I let the question trail off.

He took a loud, crisp bite and waggled his eyebrows.

Oh, God. My stomach wobbled. Were we having a threesome? I'd never done that. And though I'd seen Josef with Jin, Perla, other slaves, and patrons, doing their business publicly, I'd never actually done anything with Josef myself.

My next question came out almost a whisper. "What do I have to do?"

It was a common question from me, and nobody was shy about answering. But at that moment Josef seemed keen on screwing with me. He crossed his arms and chewed thoughtfully before answering.

"You see, Señor Acosta will lay on the bed with his legs off the side, y you will straddle him, yes?"

I nodded, more frightened than I'd been in a while.

"And then I," he said, "Will stand between his legs on the side of the bed, you see, y I will fuck your ass from behind."

"What?!" My heart rate tripled and I was struggling for breaths.

Josef laughed at the look on my face and clutched his heart. "Es no so bad, I swear!"

"You are asshole." Mia smacked the back of Josef's head with the book. She looked up at me through her long fake eyelashes. "Señor Acosta like to have someone watch him when he fuck. Okay? He want Josef to watch and touch his self."

Relief washed through me and I threw myself at Josef,

punching his arms. "You big jerk!"

He laughed and made a half-hearted attempt to push me away.

And then I thought about Josef watching me being fucked and I flushed all over. I walked down to my bed, away from the others, so I could lay and mentally prepare myself.

I'd given head in the great room, which was basically an orgy all the time, and I'm sure Josef had seen, but I was always taken to a private room for sex. *It's not a big deal*, I told myself. And it really wasn't. It was just Josef, someone I trusted. It might be weird for a minute, but I was sure it would pass. If I could handle some of the things I'd done, I could do this.

I draped my forearm across my eyes and tried to nap. I never slept well at night. Too many weird dreams and nightmares and waking up with my crotch throbbing. I needed some relief. Sometimes when I showered I'd quickly work myself up while washing, and then squeeze my thighs together and give myself a mini-orgasm. It was dangerous, and I was careful not to vocalize during those too-brief moments.

Josef woke me when it was time to get ready. He chose my outfit—a black miniskirt with no panties and a slinky, purple blouse that dipped low in the back. I did my hair and make-up, then looked over at Josef to see if he was ready. He looked sharp in black slacks and a navy dress shirt. The top three buttons were undone to show his chest. I must have stared too long because he grinned and said, "You like, eh?"

I rolled my eyes. He knew he looked good.

A knock sounded on the door and my stomach went into a low dive of nervousness. I experienced that sensation every night, but it was especially powerful tonight. We put on our collars. Luis led us to the suite. Mr. Acosta greeted us and handed Josef and I glasses of champagne.

Ugh. This was kind of unusual. I forced down half the bubbly stuff, but when I tried to set down the glass Mr. Acosta motioned for me to drink it all. So I did, feeling the lightheaded effects almost immediately.

As soon as I finished it he pushed me up against the dresser right next to Josef and began to kiss me. I *hated* when they kissed me. I rubbed myself against his crotch as I unbuttoned his shirt and pushed it open, hoping he'd hurry and get to it. Mr. Acosta turned me and put my palms against the top of the dresser. He moved my hair aside and kissed my exposed back, pressing his cock against my ass through our clothes. I moaned, like I was supposed to, and let my mind fall into auto-mode. I was over feeling dirty and disgusted during these interludes. Now I just played my part as if it were all a show, hoping it would end quickly.

He pushed the material of my shirt down my shoulders until it fell over my hips to the floor, and he grabbed my breasts. He watched us in the mirror, my breathless expression as he kneaded me. I could see Josef's head turned to the side, watching us as well, making my heart beat harder.

Mr. Acosta turned me to face him again and pushed me down by my shoulders until I was on my knees. I unbuckled his belt and unclasped his pants, freeing his erection and immediately submersing it into my mouth. He let out a loud groan and grasped the back of my head, urging me to take him deeper. After a few minutes he pulled me up and motioned me to the bed, bending me over the side. He pulled down my skirt, getting me naked. His fingers found my pussy—I rarely needed lube anymore—and he commented about how wet I was for him. Actually I was wet all the time these days, but he could think whatever he wanted. I arched my back and circled my butt, pushing it out for him.

A show. It was all a show that I did on reflex now. There was no room for emotions when it was time to entertain.

Then I caught Josef's eye. His long cock was through the opening of his pants and he was stroking himself, watching me through those long strands of hair with his dark eyes. I held my breath as hot sensations zinged across my skin and I felt Mr. Acosta's hardness probing around my opening. He thrust himself into me and for a moment I closed my eyes and moaned, *"Oh, sí!"*

When my eyes opened again I caught Josef's hot stare and couldn't look away. His strokes matched the exact speed of my patron moving in and out of me from behind, as if imagining it was him inside me. My breathing came faster than normal as Mr. Acosta began to pound me. I felt wilder, bucking my hips backward and making him holler with the effort it was taking not to come. Sex was often accompanied with a sense of momentary power, but this was different, more primal and erotic than usual.

Mr. Acosta pulled out and smacked my butt cheek. "Get on the bed," he ordered in Spanish. He crawled up behind me and flipped me to my back. He pushed between my legs and fucked me at hyper speed, pushing us to the edge of the bed where my head hung off. I made plenty of noise for him. Josef had moved closer. He'd shed his pants and now kneaded his balls as he stroked, only two feet away from my face.

Our patron sat up and looked at Josef.

"Join us," he said in Spanish. "Touch her while you touch yourself. We will all three come together."

Josef was going to touch me, and that sounded way too nice. Maybe it would be okay for me to come, just this once. He climbed on the bed, on his knees next to me, and unbuttoned his shirt, letting it hang open. Mr. Acosta held out my knees and pushed his cock back into me. Josef took his own dick in one hand and pressed two fingers to my clitoris, circling while he pumped himself. His face was so serious.

Oh, shit. This was so hot. I felt an orgasm building. But then my eyes left Josef and I looked at our patron who stared down at me like a hungry, sweating animal. Big mistake. My orgasm deflated along with my excitement at finally getting some relief.

I would have to fake it. I closed my eyes and squeezed my boobs, making low moans that became faster and louder. As I gasped, crying out, Mr. Acosta pulled out and grabbed himself. Both men tensed and shook, spewing their combined semen all over my thighs and stomach, shooting it all the way up to my breasts and neck.

As the three of us tried to catch our breath, Josef looked down on me with something akin to disapproval mixed with confusion. It cooled me and I suddenly wanted to cover up. Why was he looking at me like that?

Mr. Acosta fell onto his back, his penis flaccid against his thigh, and said, "Leave me."

Josef and I quickly gathered our clothes and did just that.

Outside the door I was shaking as I wiped the come off my body with my shirt. Josef pulled his pants back on and we followed Luis to the slave quarters where he locked us in for the night.

We both took off our collars and went straight to the shower in silence, keeping our distance. I could feel him looking at me, but I didn't look back. We dried off and climbed into our beds. Mia and Jin were still gone. I'd never felt shy or embarrassed with Josef, at least not since those first days. I didn't like this sudden distance between us. I curled up under the one sheet I was allowed and finally looked at Josef. He had a knee up, one arm above his head, and he was staring at the ceiling, naked.

"Why did you fake it?" he asked without looking at me.

I was surprised. He really was upset about it. Part of me was nervous to discuss this because of the cameras, but Marco wasn't home and he was too busy a man to come home and watch hours of footage.

"We fake it all the time, Josef. Me and the other girls. I fake it *every* time."

"Did it not please you when I touched you?"

His voice was soft, and my heart squeezed for him. I couldn't believe we were having this conversation. I wanted to explain, but I was afraid to badmouth a patron.

"It *did* feel good. But...I just couldn't. I'm sorry. It wasn't you, I swear."

He pursed his lips together and rolled to the side, giving me his back.

Wow. I'd hurt his feelings. I'd never seen him get upset like this. I knew he took pride in being good at what he did—he could get any patron off, but I wasn't his patron and he didn't need to please me. Maybe he just *wanted* to. The thought made me pulse between my thighs.

Shit. I'd never be able to fall asleep now.

I tossed and turned for what felt like hours, wanting desperately to touch myself or stuff the pillow between my legs. When I finally began to doze I heard a small moan from Josef. I looked over at him in the darkness. His sheet was tented and I saw him place a firm hand down over his erection, pushing it to his stomach, but not stroking or doing anything to relieve himself.

Intense arousal shot through me and I trembled. We both had something the other wanted—*needed.* When I moved I could feel the pool of slickness between my thighs and I couldn't help but breathe harder.

"Josef?" I whispered.

His head shot over to me and his hand tightened over himself. "Don't talk to me right now, Angel." His voice was gritty with lust.

We were both in a weak and vulnerable state, made worse with the knowledge that Marco was gone for the night. Stubborn rebellion kicked up inside me, fueled by extreme need. It had been a long time since I wanted something bad enough to be willing to face punishment. I threw the sheet off me and slipped a hand between my legs, watching as the whites of his eyes grew larger in the dim room.

"Josef..." I breathed.

In the next heartbeat he was on top of me.

I'd never been so desperate to be filled. When I opened my legs and Josef slipped between them we didn't bother with gentleness or try to be quiet. He plunged his full length deep inside of me, the longest I'd ever taken, and we moaned together. I gripped his back and felt his muscles clench as he pumped into me.

I screamed, coming almost immediately. Oh, God, he felt so good. It was a glorious, delicious feeling to be having sex because I'd chosen it and wanted it. I ground myself against him, needing more as the feeling of pleasure waned and grew again.

"More," I said.

Josef stroked harder, slamming into me with his solid hips until my nerve endings were exploding again, and a grin shone on his sexy lips. His worries about not being able to make me feel good were being put to rest.

Josef leaned down and brushed his lips against mine. "Let me in your ass," he whispered.

"No way," I said said with a breathy laugh.

I flipped us so I was on top and I rode him, feeling him so deep. My third and final orgasm hit me with a violent shudder, my head falling back in abandon. He grasped my hips, his arms flexing. I felt him inside me, rocketing with his own pleasure release as the tendons in his neck stretched taut and he grunted. He was beautiful.

Our movements slowed and we were both panting. Fear and panic set in almost immediately as reality came crashing down.

"Oh, fuck!" I whisper-yelled, lifting off his softening cock and pushing him out of my bed. "What have we done? Shit. *Shit!"*

Josef fell into his bed like a lump. In the dark I could see his tired smile.

"It was worth it," he said.

I huffed a laugh through my nose and shook my head. I was too scared to joke. Six months of sexual tension had been relieved, and raging bulls couldn't have pulled me away from him during the ten minutes we'd been going at it. But now…now I was filled with fear.

In my mind, I ran through all sorts of scenarios. Marco and his staff had so much to take care of. Maybe nobody was manning the camera room right now. It was possible nobody would ever know.

I let out a deep breath. Nobody was breaking down the door to reprimand us, which was a good sign. Josef had already fallen asleep in his bed, breathing evenly and harder than normal in his peaceful state. He wasn't at all concerned about punishment. I was being paranoid. Again, I let out a breath.

Nobody would find out. Everything was going to be okay.

CHAPTER THIRTEEN

The next morning when Jin and Mia came back to the slave quarters our breakfast tray had not been delivered, which was strange. A couple hours passed and it was clear they'd forgotten to feed us with Marco being gone. Nobody said a word. We went about our business, Josef doing his light workout in the corner while the three of us girls did our own things—showering, reading, painting nails. Sounded much more glamorous than it was. We were bored.

Not to mention the awkwardness between Josef and I. We'd yet to look at one another. I felt guilty, like I'd taken advantage of him. Not that he'd seemed to mind, but that was besides the point.

When noontime arrived and nobody came to get us for lunch I started to feel sick, both from hunger and nerves.

I met Josef's eyes for one brief moment. I think we were both communicating the same thing: *They know.* He appeared resigned, while I began to panic. I forced myself to curl up on my mattress as if napping, and tried not to look guilty. My mind raced. Maybe we weren't caught. Maybe something had happened to Marco. The thought of him being killed sent me on a roller coaster of emotion. I was elated at the thought we might be freed, then I felt guilty for being glad he might be dead since he'd been so nice, then I was pissed at myself for referring to my *captor* as *nice*. What the hell was wrong with me? I refused to go Stockholmy on Marco. I would never fall in love with him. It was more of a paternal feeling, which was just as disturbing in a different way.

Those were the screwed up kinds of thoughts I was having when the door to our quarters finally opened. We all got up and moved toward the entrance. I was expecting to see Luis, but it was Marco standing there with a stern face, Perla behind him. The other four of us fell to our knees with our heads down. My heart pounded.

Please don't know, please don't know...

In his customary calm, level voice, Marco said, "Angel, venga conmigo." He was telling me to come with him. I was expected to recognize basic Spanish commands at that point, so I moved forward on my hands and knees.

I raised my eyes just enough to make sure I wouldn't run into anything, and I saw Perla pass me, going into the quarters with a tray of food. My stomach grumbled with a gnawing emptiness. I reached up and grabbed my collar from the table at the entrance, securing it around my neck with shaking hands. Wearing a pink silk and lace camisole and matching undies, I crawled through the villa behind Marco. He led me to a wing of the house where I'd never been. Two armed men guarded the hall. What was going on? I was so nervous. Where was he taking me?

He stopped in front of a door and I watched his shiny black shoes turn to face me. I sat back on my heels, placed my hands on my thighs and kept my head down.

"Angel...my golden trinket..." His voice was even softer and lower than normal, which filled me with dread. "Do you think there is anything that happens in my home I don't know about?"

My whole body became as heavy as lead and the breath I'd been inhaling got stuck in my lungs. A deep tremble began inside me, starting in my belly and radiating outward until my hands shook and my jaw chattered. I tried to clamp my teeth together. The hall was so quiet I could hear my breaths as they started back, practically hyperventilating through my nose.

"Yo sé que tu hablas español. Siempre lo he sabido." *I know you speak Spanish. I've always known.*

So lightheaded...I felt my weight dip to the side and I caught myself. My body wanted to pass out from fear overload.

He knew. Of course he knew. He'd probably read every article and seen every newscast about my disappearance. He would have read about my college major. I'd been playing stupid all along for no reason. A burning sensation shot through my sinuses, behind my eyes, making my nose want to run, and my throat need to swallow. My body was trying to cry.

No. No tears. I kept my head down and swallowed hard.

In Spanish Marco said, "We will no longer converse in English. You will speak only Spanish, even to the other slaves. Do you understand?"

"Sí, Master." The words tumbled out quickly. I was so terrified I would have done anything, agreed to anything he said.

"Come with me," he ordered in Spanish. "I have something to show you."

I heard buttons being pressed on a wall panel, and the door clicked open. I followed Marco into a high-tech room filled with a static ringing from hundreds of television monitors.

"You may look," Marco said, again in Spanish, and I knew that's all I'd hear from now on. I wondered if I'd ever hear or speak English again.

I looked up and held in a gasp. Every freaking corner of the villa was being watched. A man sat in front of the screens with an earpiece and a gun, watching every movement on the property.

"This room is never empty, Angel," Marco crooned. "Nothing escapes me."

"I'm sorry, Master," whispered, and my voice cracked. I knew I was speaking out of turn, so I wasn't surprised when Marco smacked me across the face.

I dropped my eyes and held my sore cheek. Marco put a gentle hand on top of my head.

"Watch with me," he said.

I slowly lifted my eyes. Marco nodded to the man, who pushed a button, and a blank screen came to life. It was mostly dark, but my eyes focused on the moving figures and I had to clasp a hand hard over my mouth. It was Josef and I fucking. He turned the volume up. We were *loud*. I couldn't believe that was me—primal, graceful, wild.

"Hmm…" Marco made a sound of interest when I came in the video for the third time. "You are beautiful when you take your pleasure, Angel. Why is it that you do not come for my patrons?"

I bit my lip and dropped my eyes. I couldn't tell him the truth…that I refused to enjoy them, even in the few instances when the sex was decent. I couldn't tell him that his patrons disgusted me, the way they looked through me, and used me. That I felt strangely sexy all the time, but not because of them.

"Do I treat you poorly?" he asked.

"No, Master."

He was thoughtful and quiet for a moment.

"I thought if I allowed you to keep your few, precious things…your language…your books, you might be more comfortable, but all it has done is made you hold on to the past. You must let it go, Angel. You will never leave my home. I have spoiled you. The others..." His voice trailed off, as if gathering his thoughts about the other slaves. "They came from poor circumstances. Terrible lives. They were grateful when I took them in—grateful to me. But with you..." He touched my head. "I wanted to win you over. For you to see how good life can be for you here. But you cling to your past and cannot see the beauty in front of you. What must I do to win your loyalty, Angel?"

I looked at him, and I swore his eyes held a sort of desperation, or maybe exasperation. I bit my lip, unable to respond because I had no answer to that question.

"Do you know what my business partners do in cases like this? They sell their slaves to rougher masters who can handle them. Shall I sell you?"

"No! Please!"

"Other masters drug their slaves. Make them rely on them to feed their addiction. Those slaves will do anything to make their masters happy. Is that what you want? Do I need to drug you?"

"No!" Panic flooded me at the thought of losing my mental facilities to an addiction. "Master, please. No drugs!"

"I fear you must learn the hard way."

A sound escaped the back of my throat. I wanted to speak out again, to apologize and beg, but I held my tongue as he continued.

"There is no reason why you should not enjoy the attentive men I choose for you. From now on, if you are too stubborn not to come for my patrons and you find yourself needing release in the evening hours, you must practice self-control. Or, if you're willing to swallow your leftover pride, you may call out to me and I will be notified. I will send someone of my choosing to pleasure you. How does that sound?"

Awful. Like it would never work.

"Bueno, Maestro." It was so strange to speak Spanish to him, but I did. "I will never, ever touch Josef or myself again. I swear—"

"Silencio." His voice. So soft. It sent a chill down my back because I knew what was next.

"It's time for your punishment."

He let the words settle over me, making my breathing ragged, tremors of sickening anticipation lancing through me.

"Vamos."

When he said let's go, I followed, crawling, terrified of what was to come. It would be worse than the belt, that much was certain. Would they cane me? Scar me?

All for three orgasms? Josef was wrong. It wasn't worth it. Not to me. I could never let myself get to that desperate state again.

When we got to the punishment room I felt numb and stiff all over. I don't know how I got myself to crawl inside the dark, creepy room with its black walls and gleaming instruments.

I sat at Marco's feet barely containing my urge to grab ahold of his ankle and beg for mercy.

"Are you ready, Angel?" he asked in Spanish. Always in Spanish now. I missed my mother tongue already.

I needed to answer, but all that came out was a strangled whimper as I shook my head.

"Look up, beautiful."

Slowly, warily, I raised my eyes and I nearly vomited. Two chains hung from the ceiling. In the chains was Josef. His arms were spread and he stood on the balls of his feet with his calf muscles flexed. Naked.

My eyes shot to Marco and he petted my head.

"Don't worry, Angel. You will feel no pain."

My head whipped back to Josef, his back to me, his head hanging, his muscles tensed. Yes, I would. I would feel pain, and Marco knew it.

"What do you think?" Marco asked me. "Ten lashes for every orgasm the two of you had? Forty total?"

"No, Master, please! I'm sorry!" I threw myself on his feet now, pressing my cheeks to his shoes, hugging around his ankles.

Luis pulled me off him and forced me back on my heels.

With a nod of his head, the giant, nameless man who I thought of as Brutus, stepped forward. The man who whipped me. The man who people only spoke to in nods. A big, scary, hairy bastard. He held a thin, leather riding crop in his hand, and with a *whizzing* sound he whacked Josef across the middle of his back with it. Josef hissed through his teeth and clenched his fists. I covered my mouth to hold back pleas to make it stop. I tried looking away, but Luis pushed my face back up to the horrid spectacle.

With each lash Josef's resolve weakened and his pain-filled noises grew louder. Red markings began to show, vivid across his smooth brown skin. Moisture filled my eyes, but didn't fall. The worst moment was when someone murmured "twenty" and I realized we were only half-way through. It felt like he'd been hit a hundred times already.

I wanted it to end more than I'd wanted my own whipping to end six months ago. This was all my fault. This is what my stubbornness had caused. Josef's knees gave out after the thirtieth hit and his holler was so sad, like a young boy. Brutus kept going, cracking Josef across the shoulder blades with a sickening sound.

I dry heaved into my hand, swallowing back down the small amount of burning bile that came up.

At forty strikes Marco whispered, "Done." And I swear, he sounded tired. He'd stood there with his hands behind his back the whole time, watching with that sad disappointment. It dawned on me that he didn't want us to have to be punished, but he had to keep order. The rules and punishments were meant to keep the hierarchy of his establishment running smoothly. I'd tried to derail his hierarchy, and had been fighting against it all along, and for what? It hadn't helped me get rescued. It had only caused me and my friend pain.

Marco went to Josef's side. "Do you wish to fuck the girl now?"

Josef could barely respond. "N-no, Amo."

"Bring him to the clinic and have the nurse care for him," Marco said to Brutus. "No pain medication."

Brutus nodded and uncuffed Josef, who fell in a panting heap, his face sweating and pinched. *Sweet Josef.* My heart broke, and I wondered if he'd ever be able to forgive me. Brutus half-carried him from the room.

I watched Marco's feet.

"Do you think I spoil you, Angel?" he asked gently.

I answered him with truth, speaking to him in Spanish just as he spoke to me. "Yes, Master. And I appreciate it. I'm so sorry. I will not disobey you again."

"Hm. You have not eaten today. Are you hungry? Remember, I require the truth from you in all things."

The last thing I wanted now was food, but my stomach gnawed with emptiness, despite the churning I still felt. "Yes, Master. I am hungry."

Marco gave a small nod to Luis. "Feed the girl," he told him.

Luis came and stood in front of me. I was thoroughly confused when he began unbuttoning his pants. And then I was presented with my "meal."

Holy. Shit.

Part of the hierarchy at the villa was that slaves were prized gifts for the patrons. Being made to pleasure one of Marco's men was demeaning. I batted away my pride and went up on my knees, taking Luis's cock in my hand first then my mouth. He grasped the back of my head and pulled me forward, being rough, probably because of how much I'd teased him over the months. Definitely wouldn't be doing that anymore.

When he spurted into the back of my throat, I swallowed, trying not to gag.

I kneeled again, waiting.

"Still hungry?" Marco asked.

"No, Master." And it was true. I wondered if I'd ever have an appetite again.

He was quiet a long time, and fear filled me, zinging around like a damned pinball. I had a feeling Marco still wanted to drive home a point with me.

His next words proved as much.

"Your anal virginity is highly prized, yes?"

Oh, dear God.

"Yes, Master," I whispered, voice shaking. I closed my eyes.

"Why do you fear it so?"

"I don't know, Master." Part of my reason used to be that anal sex was taboo. It's not something anyone I knew did—and my friends were pretty open about their sexuality. I knew one person who'd done it, as we learned in a drunken game of Never Have I Ever. But here it was the norm, so it wasn't much of an excuse anymore. "I think it will hurt." In truth, it was the last thing I had that was still mine.

"It may hurt at first, yes. But like all things, you can grow to enjoy it if you get past the barrier you put up in your mind about it."

I nodded, although deep down I wanted to beg not to let it happen. I knew it was only a matter of time.

"You are still not ready," he said. "Mentally. But someday you will be."

"Thank you, Master," I said, trembling with relief. I wasn't ready, and I was so grateful he saw that, and in his own strange way respected it.

He still spoiled me.

Marco petted my head and I leaned into his hand, wanting to be his good puppy.

"Today," he said, "we begin your mental preparation."

I stilled, heart accelerating.

Marco held out a hand and I took it with hesitation. His was hot; mine was freezing.

He led me to a leather-covered table with a bottle of lube and a strange looking black plastic thing. One end of it sparkled like a diamond. Marco had to tug my hand when I slowed. He patted the table.

"Lay on your side with your back to me."

I crawled up, eyeing the cone shaped "toy." I wanted to kick it away.

"This is a medium anal plug," Marco explained.

Oh, damn. That thing looked big. I made a whispered sound of fear and Marco hushed me, guiding me on my side. I lay how he told me to and closed my eyes. He pushed my panties down over my cheeks and I was so tense. His fingers were firm, but gentle as he applied a generous amount of lube. I clenched my glut muscles, my heart thundering, and Marco made a sound of disapproval.

"You must relax or it will hurt worse."

I tried to relax. I really did.

I felt the tip of the plug pushing in, and at first it was

like a finger. Then I began to feel fuller. As he pushed more there was a sudden sharp, stretching pain. I gasped, wanting to scream.

Again, Marco hushed me, running his hand down my hair. He kept the plug in me at that uncomfortably stretched point, but didn't push any farther. It was like he was letting my body get used to it. After a minute he pushed a bit more until I gasped again in pain. How did people have anal sex? This freaking hurt!

On and on it went until the thickest part of the bulb stretched me. I held my breath, prepared for him to push it all the way in, but instead he slowly pulled it out and pushed it back in. He stroked my ass with it, each time making me suck in a breath as it stretched me to the thickest point.

"You are very tight," Marco whispered. His hand lifted hair off my sweating forehead, and it felt good to have him pay attention to me like that. "Relax. Let yourself feel every movement."

I inhaled a big breath and exhaled, trying to relax. When he began to move the plug inside me again, a little faster now, in and out, I was shocked to find my breaths quickening. Okay. I didn't hate it. He took his time with me and I moved my hips to meet his thrusts. Now that the pain had subsided, it was...nice. Then he gave it a deep push and I cried out, feeling my asshole close tight around the thinnest point. I was panting. The diamond stuck out, nestled between my cheeks, and I felt so intensely full.

Marco leaned close to my ear. "Never make me punish you again, Angel. I promise I will never go easy again."

"Yes, Master," I breathed.

"You will wear this plug when you visit your patron tonight. And Angel?"

"Yes, Master?"

"Do try to enjoy it."

I nodded. Marco looked at Luis. "Take her to the slave quarters and bring me Perla."

Luis nodded and helped me down from the table as Marco walked out. I'm not sure, but I think Marco was turned on by the whole plug experience too. He never took any of the slaves except Perla and girls brought by other guests. He seemed to enjoy those little gifts, new girls in his bed, but when it came down to it Perla was the one he came back to. I didn't think it was love. Maybe more of a comfort thing. He definitely treated her like a slave, but behind closed doors...I wondered.

Out of Marco's site I was allowed to walk, but walking with a butt plug in was strange. It was impossible not to think about it—not to concentrate on the fullness, and how nerve endings inside me were being rubbed and nudged in the most satisfying way. By the time we made it back to slave quarters my inner thighs were wet.

Damn it.

Score for Marco. Because tonight, for the first time, I would go to a patron seeking release. I didn't know if I'd be able to find it once I got there, but I knew I'd never look elsewhere again. Despite what Josef said, it was not worth it. Not to me.

CHAPTER FOURTEEN

Colin Douglas

———— ◆ · I ◆ I · ◆ ————

In Colin's five years as an undercover agent he'd helped incriminate hundreds of underworld criminals, but it wasn't enough. For each thug arrested a new one would rise up in their place. There was a never-ending line of evil men feeding off innocents—taking what wasn't theirs—ruining lives for the sake of their personal gain.

Being submersed in that world was wearing against the structure of Colin's mind. Too often he found the lines blurred between them and himself. Too often he felt like one of them. He came home to his small, sparse apartment at odd hours, and lost himself in canvases. Colin painted shadowy people in black, grays, navy blue, and deep purple. He couldn't bring himself to use bright colors when the world was so dark.

The art world was fascinated by his dark collection, and began calling him "Shadow Man" and "The Dark Artist." He didn't give a flying fuck about any of that. He painted to release his demons. He painted to lose himself, close his mind off to the shit he saw and heard every day.

Now and then he met women at bars and took them to hotel rooms. In a life where everything around him was hardened, he enjoyed the softness of a woman—the way they gave themselves to be overpowered by him. But the women he'd met always wanted more from him. His worst mistake had been leaving with a stunning brunette from a gallery showing. She now showed at every function with hopeful eyes. He ignored her, because he could never be what she needed.

At twenty-eight Colin was already considering retirement. He had more money piled away than he knew what to do with, even after splitting half the inheritance with Graham, who was swiftly pissing it away on drugs. Therapists and counselors had made little leeway with his brother, and Colin was at a loss. He had no idea how to talk to the boy who used to look up to him, but now looked through him with glassy, bloodshot eyes. Visiting him was fucking depressing.

It'd been awhile since Colin heard from Agent Abernathy, and he was getting restless, so when he got the text that morning he was out the door in five minutes. Outside in the pale Glasgow sunshine, he groaned. He'd forgotten it was fucking Maydaze. The May Day Rally and Parade was taking place in the city, bringing out hundreds of families. Colin kept his head down and shoved his hands in his pockets as he shouldered his way through the smiling faces. The happy folk music clashed with the dark soundtrack of his life, playing in his head on repeat. He had to remind himself that these were the very people he lived his life secretly protecting.

But damn. Sometimes the ignorance and cluelessness of people pissed him off.

He was a right grump this morning.

Colin slipped into a back alley and made his way to the door of their meeting place. With a backward glance to be sure he wasn't being followed, he knocked three times, paused, then twice more. Abernathy let him in and locked the door behind them.

They met in a back office of an old steel mill, which was now used for lumber storage. Colin sat across the metal desk from Agent Abernathy and nodded.

"What've you got for me?"

Abernathy wasted no time. He pushed a newspaper and several pictures forward. Colin took the paper first, reading the headline where his boss tapped a finger. It was about the missing American girl, Angela Birch.

"Aye. Heard about this. Unlucky. They thought she was dead. I take it they're wrong, as usual?"

Abernathy sighed, sitting back. He was looking ragged these days, really showing his age.

"Her parents don't believe it, and I agree with them. Too much funny business with the Mexican police. The boy she went missing with, Fernando Ruiz? The FBI say he was spotted in Thailand. His father, Marco Ruiz, owns nightclubs in several Latin American cities and in Spain. We believe it's a cover for a drug ring and sex slavery."

Colin's stomach soured as he picked up the three photos of Angela Birch and studied them. She looked sweet. All-American smile. Happy brown eyes. A girl with a bright future and loving family, stolen. Colin rubbed his face. He hated this shite. It never fucking ended.

"How long's she been gone?"

"Seven months," Abernathy said, sliding another picture forward. "Ruiz has a Spanish villa on the Mediterranean sea. We believe if he has her that's where she'd be, but we can't get near it. He's got local authorities and even government officials in his pocket."

A familiar buzz began inside Colin as he looked at the gorgeous seaside estate. It was the feeling he got when an especially tough case was presented.

"Think you can work your way into this place? Won't

be easy, that."

Colin grinned. He loved a challenge. Taking risks was just about the only thing that got his blood pumping these days. And judging by the look of Marco Ruiz's stronghold, this would be his largest and most dangerous undertaking yet.

"Aye. I'm in."

Agent Abernathy didn't look at all surprised. Colin never turned down an assignment, but they both knew this was no ordinary job. This one was delicate, and would take time.

Colin studied the pictures while his brain worked, and he plotted out loud. "I'll contact the local galleries there, make it seem like I'm branching out with my trade. I've got drug contacts who know people in Spain. It could take months to earn a name for myself, but I can't rush it. What's the goal once I'm in?"

"Get her out. Alive. By any means you can. Her parents have raised over two million dollars. They've been on every news station and television talk show. They've got web pages dedicated to this search. They've spent nearly half the raised money on private investigators, who led them to us. They can't send an American agent in there—too suspicious."

Colin nodded. Even as a Scot it might take longer to earn their trust.

"And Douglas?" Abernathy raised an eyebrow. "If you get the lassie out, you can keep the reward money, because it will be your last mission with us. Once you've taken property from a man like Marco Ruiz, you'll need to disappear. If Angela Birch is alive, and if she's at this estate, she'll also need to go into hiding. Only her parents will know. We've warned them that they'll need to make new lives for themselves too, and they're willing. They'll do anything to get her back."

Colin let this news settle into his mind. This could be his last job with the agency. He could start a new life for himself. Become a new person.

If he survived this mission and could get the girl out alive.

"I understand," Colin said.

"Good. Here's a video compiled of the girl by her parents so you can get to know her a bit." Abernathy reached out a hand and they shook.

Back at his flat, Colin got to work, sliding the homemade DVD into the player.

It began with a surprise party for Angela Birch's eighteenth birthday in her senior year of high school, went through her graduation, and extended through her year and a half of college before she went to Cancun. Colin watched her laugh, sing, and interact with her parents and friends. She seemed responsible, mature, intelligent, and unaware of her own natural beauty. Unassuming. Innocent. The video tugged at parts of Colin he hadn't felt tugged in countless years—or maybe never.

The Birches were a family. A real, loving family, who deserved to be together. He wanted to make this happen. And he couldn't deny that a strange, deep, selfish part of him wanted to meet this Angela. How would this responsible, smiling girl have taken to the world of slavery? He couldn't imagine her filthy and drugged on the floor like Graham had been. The very idea made him want to thrash everything in his path to yank her out of whatever situation she might be in.

Disappointment filled him when the DVD ended, and he pushed Play again. He couldn't take his eyes off her. After hours of repeated footage he had her voice memorized. He knew her expressions of amusement and sentiment. He felt like he knew her, which was ridiculous, but he felt it nonetheless and couldn't bloody wait to get her the fuck out of captivity.

His head spun with possibilities as he envisioned himself inside the world of Marco Ruiz. He would have to put on his best show yet, submersing himself into that shady battle land where lines of right and wrong became skewed.

To enter a snake lair, Colin would have to become a snake.

CHAPTER FIFTEEN

The night of Josef's beating, for the first time, Marco allowed a patron to keep me until the morning. Until that point he'd been sheltering me, but I knew those days were over. Now, men could have me for more hours, waking me during the night if they wanted, pushing my head down to their crotch in the morning while they were still half asleep. Making me feel less and less like a human.

When Luis took me back to the slave quarters to shower the next morning, I was nervous to see Josef. My patron had paid to have me all day, so I'd be taken back to him once I was cleaned.

In the room my eyes darted around for Josef. I saw Perla first, sitting on her bed with her knees pulled up, naked. She gave me a sad look and her eyes drifted toward the wall. I rushed in and saw Josef lying on his stomach. My hand flew to my mouth.

His back.

I'd never seen so many bruises. He was purple and red in criss-crossing streaks. My eyes burned with moisture, but no tears fell. The memory of him hanging there flashed through my mind alongside an image of the grin he'd given me during sex. I wanted to run over and beg his forgiveness, but Perla's voice stopped me.

"Déjalo dormir." *Let him sleep.* She'd apparently gotten the memo from Marco to speak only Spanish to me now. She didn't sound mad, only sad.

I gazed at the sleeping Josef and hoped he'd had one of those pills for his own self yesterday. With reluctance I turned and went for my shower.

— ⋅ ❖ ⋅ —

My stomach was upset when my patron led me into the dining room for lunch that afternoon. I crawled at his side and he sat on the end next to Marco. I hadn't slept well the previous night, and my neck hurt. He'd made me sleep on the floor without a blanket. Granted, the temperature in the rooms are always perfect, and the carpets were lush, but I still hated it.

I reached up slowly to rub my neck when I saw one of Marco's men escorting Jin into the dining room on her hands and knees in a red, strapless dress. When she got within five feet of me she looked up just enough so that our eyes met. Her face contorted into a raging, feral expression.

Oh, shit.

Somehow she knew Josef's beating was because of me. And she must have added up the pieces and figured out we'd had sex. Jin was yet another aspect I hadn't taken into account when I seduced Josef. I felt horrid and my guilt was surely written across my face. Her feelings for Josef had to be off the charts because she launched herself forward, taking me completely by surprise.

My ears filled with ringing as we both screamed. She had handfuls of my hair, yanking as we rolled, kicking, kneeing, snarling. I'd never been in a fight before. It was scary to have someone attacking me, wanting to hurt me. I grabbed her wrists, trying to subdue her hands and protect myself by keeping distance between us, but she was a strong and vicious little thing. Her teeth cut into my shoulder and I screeched in pain, bringing my foot up and kicking her back. She came away on her knees with blonde strands between her fingers, panting.

Why the hell wasn't anyone stopping this? One quick glance around answered that for me. They were too busy watching and laughing, enjoying the cat fight. Marco sat stiffly, unamused, but made no move to end the fight.

Jin raised a hand to slap me and I caught her wrist, but then she swung the other one and clapped me hard across the ear, almost making me vomit. I threw myself at her, trying to wrestle her down with my heavier weight and hold all of her limbs down. She bucked when I straddled her and I brought my face down close to hers.

"Lo siento," I whispered fervently through my teeth as she thrashed underneath me. "Lo siento." *I'm sorry...*

The room cheered, thoroughly entertained at my domination over her.

Jin finally stilled, pressing her lips together and breathing hard through her nose. I watched the fire drain from her, replaced by fear as she realized what she'd done. I wondered if we'd both be punished. My shoulder and scalp were freaking stinging, but I couldn't be mad at her. I hadn't been beaten, and I felt like I deserved it.

Someone yelled in Spanish, "Kiss and make up!"

Oh, no.

The girl on girl scenario was yet another thing I hadn't had to do in my time at the villa. But Jin didn't hesitate, and I knew she was trying to save face. She pulled her hands from mine, and reached around to grab my ass, pulling me closer. She craned her neck up to me. When our lips met I was shocked by the softness of her mouth, so small. She tasted like strawberries. I relaxed into her, kissing her, my heart still pounding. Jin moved her hips and I met her rhythm, rocking against her. Her body was so tiny under mine. The whole thing felt weird, but not bad…just…very different.

"Angel," Marco called. I broke the kiss and looked over at him. He nodded to my patron, who was giving me "the eye." I climbed off Jin and crawled to him, sore all over now as I felt an array of scratches from her nails and teeth across my skin.

My patron pushed his chair back enough to show me his tented pants. Without question I went forward and took care of him.

I felt numb, like I was coming down from a high.

I didn't think about the people watching.

I didn't think about how he insensitively grabbed the hair on my head, bringing further pain to my tender scalp.

All I could think about was how much Jin cared for Josef, and how she'd shown more human emotion in that moment than I'd ever seen at the villa. And how strangely grateful I was to witness her beautiful burst of passion.

—◆—

Months passed. I'm not sure how many. In the early days I'd kept a mental calendar, but that all stopped after the Josef incident. Even though he was a total sweetheart and held nothing against me.

When we'd finally made eye contact for the first time after his beating, he stuck out his tongue at me and freaking winked, like a kid. The tension immediately fell away from my body and cool relief had filled me, but I'd always carry guilt about it. We never discussed it, and even Jin went back to being her normal distant self.

I think Marco kept me hidden from many of the people who visited the villa. No doubt my parents and those in the

U.S. had rewards out there for information about my whereabouts. They weren't the type to give up or give in. And Marco clearly did not trust all of the people who came through his doors.

Sometimes whispers would spread through the villa about a government official coming, or a westerner, and I'd be locked in the slave quarters for the duration of their visit. I wondered what would happen if someone did recognize me. Would they have the balls to blackmail Marco, or turn him in? I could see some of these skeevy, disloyal criminal, mafia types pulling something like that. I could also see Marco's men hunting them down and killing them while they slept.

There seemed to be something missing from the eyes of everyone who came to the villa. They lacked the basic human elements I'd grown up seeing in facial expressions— compassion, remorse, joy. The eyes I saw here were calculating and suspicious, greedy and selfish. When they smiled or laughed it was usually about something fucked up.

And of course there was lust in their eyes. Always.

I tried not to look in their eyes unless it was clear they wanted me to, but thankfully they were usually fine without eye contact. Except the ones who liked to inflict a little pain. They enjoyed seeing my eyes.

The average patron was middle aged. Very few of them were young or in shape. Those with nice bodies had cruel faces. But we were expected to stroke their gigantic egos and screw them as if they were gorgeous rockstars. There came a point where attractiveness meant nothing to me anymore. The best looking men to come through the villa were some of the most boring. The fat and old men who I assumed would be sweet were some of the meanest. The average looking men who I wouldn't have given a second glance to in my old life could go either way. They never ceased to shock me with their wild deSires or surprising gentleness.

Even with warnings or advice from the other slaves, I never knew what to expect when I walked in a bedroom.

I did, however, know what *not* to expect. I never expected consideration or conversation, unless you count the "You like that, don't you?" question, to which the answer always had to be, "Oh, yes."

I knew I was just a body. I was ever aware. The way eyes followed me with hunger, even Marco's men. My body was not mine. It belonged to whomever paid the high price to rent it. Or it was gifted to business partners of Marco's as a "thank you."

The villa gave off an aire of romance, but it was a facade. Romance meant love, and love meant joy.

But joy didn't live at the villa. Only temporary satisfaction resided here. And even I began to rely on those temporary moments to hold me over from one day to the next—whether it be a much-needed orgasm, a pet from Marco, or a laugh with the other slaves. Every little moment of comfort was something to savor. In the end, those things were like ghosts in my hand. No substance. Nothing to hold. Nothing to keep.

CHAPTER SIXTEEN

Colin

◆ · ┃ ◆ ┃ · ◆ ·

Over a year Colin had been in Spain. Fifteen fucking months. He'd never expected it to take this long. Hell, he'd never been on a mission for this long, period, and it was screwing with his head.

He knew the sordid underbelly of the Spanish Riviera about as well as the shitty streets of Glasgow now. He knew who to turn to and who to avoid. He'd picked up a bit of Spanish. After nearly nine months of gallery events he'd finally mingled with the "right" crowd—the rich connoisseurs of beauty who also enjoyed indulging in the darker side of society. And still, most people claimed not to know Marco Ruiz. Slippery bastard.

Colin Douglas could read lies in the single shift of someone's eyes. These crooks were all liars, and yet he had to suffer them. He snorted lines of coke with them, and banged the women who were practically tossed in his lap—setting aside all emotions. Once he'd earned the trust of the elite, they took a sort of protectiveness over him, as if he were their special, exotic artist. A source of entertainment. He fucking hated them.

And while he was making leeway, days and months

were slipping away. For the first time since he'd hunted his brother all those years ago, Colin began to feel anxious that he might fail. His painting was even suffering. He felt strangled. When one of the biggest drug lords on the Spanish coast came to him asking for a custom painting, Colin was hesitant to promise it.

"What is wrong?" Señor Acosta asked, speaking in English for him.

In a split-moment decision, Colin decided to try his luck from a different angle.

"I...seem to be having a bit of an issue finding inspiration. A muse, if you will."

Señor Acosta pulled a pack of cigarettes from the pocket of his gray suit jacket and offered one to Colin, who accepted. He then lit both their tips with a fancy zippo and grinned at Colin on an exhale.

"I see you with the beautiful women. Do they not inspire a good-looking young man such as yourself?"

Colin took a drag, holding the filter between his thumb and middle finger, and shook his head. "They try to hold me down. Bother me all the fucking time." That was actually true. He couldn't seem to escape the women he'd been with, even here in Spain. Being one of the only straight and single men in a gallery had its positives and negatives. It wasn't that he disrespected women—it's that he couldn't afford any emotional ties in his life, and no matter how clear he made his intentions, there was always someone pushing for more. Colin gave a cynical laugh. "I need a woman, but I don't want to have to listen to her after we fuck, aye?"

"Take a whore."

Colin made a face. "Believe me, I've thought about it. But I don't want any fucking diseases, and I have a reputation to keep. If there're any high class, discreet whores in the area, I've yet to find them." He exhaled a plume of smoke and prayed the man would take the bait.

Señor Acosta rolled his cigarette in his fingers and stared at the gallery wall mural in thought. Colin held his breath until the other man finally turned back to him, a shrewd wariness in his eyes.

"What if there were such a place, Señor Douglas? A private paradise where you could paint, and party, and fuck to your heart's desire?"

Bingo.

Colin's jaw clenched in an effort not to show his elation. "Aye, pal. If there were such a place, I'd pay any price."

Señor Acosta ran a tongue over his lips. Then he nodded. "Let me contact an acquaintance of mine. I will be in touch."

The man walked out without another word, and a familiar rush of victory flooded Colin's veins. He rubbed a hand over his short cropped hair and his hand shook.

Don't celebrate yet, he told himself. Getting inside those walls was just the beginning. After all this time, he didn't even know if the girl was still alive. If she was, she might not be at the villa. He tried not to let his thoughts linger down that road. He'd face that path if he came to it.

The call from Señor Acosta came two days later with detailed instructions about which boat to board. The Señor was having his man take Colin to the villa since it could only be entered by sea.

"The proprietor is a well-respected man named Marco Ruiz. He is doing me a favor, Señor Douglas. He does not always take kindly to Westerners and their ways. You are never to breathe a word about him or his home, or what takes place at the villa to anyone. If you do, he'll find out, and he's not a man to be fucked with. Comprende?"

"I understand. And you know I'm tight-lipped."

Colin had witnessed some of the largest drug deals of his life go down in that past year.

"Indeed. If I doubted you for a moment I wouldn't dream of referring you. The villa will be perfect for you."

"Thank God. I need a good fuck. If this holiday doesn't inspire creativity, nothing will."

"My friend, I am expecting the most God damned incredible painting of your life after this." The man laughed darkly, like someone with many secrets. Colin chuckled too, because he had a few secrets of his own. He was one step closer to stealing something valuable that this Marco prick never should have had in the first place.

Colin packed his easel, paints, and clothing, and set off immediately for the docks. He slid his sunglasses on as the sunshine hit him.

He didn't allow himself to relax as the boat sped over swells of the Mediterranean sea. For all he knew they could be onto him, planning to kill him at sea and dump his body. If that was the case he wasn't going down without a fight, and he wasn't going down alone. He trusted no one.

After twenty minutes, when they slowed to round the corner of a hulking cliff, lush with greenery, Colin could only stare. Not much in this world surprised him. He'd found loveliness in Scotland, and a whole different kind of beauty in Spain, but this villa built into the cliffside was like nothing he'd ever seen. The Spanish architecture with its stone steps, archways and stucco, nestled into the tropical landscape, was breathtaking.

Nobody in the world should be that bloody rich. Marco Ruiz must have been the boss of Señor Acosta—*all* the Señor Acostas in Spain, for that matter.

The motor slowed to a purr as they entered the no-wake zone and came to a dock. The crystal waters around them were deep blue in the shadow of the cliff.

A brute of a man with his long hair pulled back in a ponytail met them at the dock. He gave Colin a once-over, unsmiling. Colin eyed him right back, because he knew from years of experience that's how respect was earned among these types. The boatman hauled Colin's things to the dock, and Colin picked them all up, giving the boatman a nod before he tipped his hat and left him there.

"Weapons?" Marco's man asked brusquely.

"No." Colin wasn't a fool. And as a sign of good faith he set down his bags and stretched his arms out at his side. The man patted him down. Colin had him in height, but the brute was broader. Still, in a fight Colin was quick and confident. When the man stood and looked in his eyes he saw that Colin was a man who wouldn't take any shite or back down.

"Follow me."

When they got to the stone steps a smaller man rushed out of a hidden entrance and smiled at Colin, giving him a small bow.

"Por favor, Señor. I take?" He pointed to Colin's bags. Though Colin hated to have this older man doing something he was perfectly capable of doing himself, he knew it was the kind of luxury Marco's guests were expected to take advantage of. He also knew they'd go through his things, searching for anything suspicious, but they'd find nothing. Holding back a sigh, he handed over everything except the easel, which was heavy, and the canvases, which were large and awkward.

"I'll keep these. Thank you."

The man bowed again, disappearing through a side entrance that looked like a dark hall. The door quickly closed and Colin followed Marco's big man up the steps. The higher they ascended, the more breathtaking the view became. After nearly a year and a half of seeking entrance into this place, a jolt of anticipation shot through Colin's system.

At the top of the steps they came to an open air garden, and a fragrant breeze hit him. A middle-aged man in slacks and a black button up shirt met them at the top. He had a graying mustache and dark eyes that seemed to pierce Colin, searching him thoroughly, and filling him with a sour loathing.

"Señor Douglas? Soy Marco Ruiz."

"Sí," Colin answered, holding out his hand, which the man shook solidly. He decided to speak to Marco in English, since his Spanish left a lot to be deSired. "Señor Acosta had only amazing things to say about your home, and I can see he didn't exaggerate one bit. I thank you for allowing me to come, especially at such a short notice."

The bodyguard hung back, never taking his eyes off Colin.

Marco picked up on his English cue seamlessly, and Colin recognized the man was extending a courtesy. "Mm. Our mutual friend is quite keen about his art."

Colin chuckled. "That he is."

Marco eyed him one last time, as if memorizing him. Cops weren't the only ones who took in details. Seasoned criminals were especially good at it, as well. Marco may have stood there appearing to be a gentleman, but Colin knew better. He wished this mission was about more than simply retrieving the girl. He wished he could take this man down, but that could only be done by Spanish officials, and they wouldn't allow it.

Marco led him to a table on the veranda set with brunch foods: tropical fruit salad, Spanish omelets, and coffee. Colin sat, knowing this would be a "get to know you" session. He'd had one of these, in some form, with every stage of vagrant who'd ever considered letting him into their confidences. This, however, would be his first brunch. His childhood manners came out as he placed the napkin across his lap.

Marco sipped his coffee and his head cocked to the side, as if trying to figure Colin out. He knew he didn't look like your typical artist, whatever "typical" meant. His face was chiseled and often scruffy. His dark hair shaved. Eyes as blue-gray as the Mediterranean sky before a storm. His physique was strong. And he didn't give much of a shite about fashion, though he dressed to impress when he had to. It was all about looking the part.

"I believe for the first time ever my slaves might actually *fight* over a patron," Marco muttered.

Ah, that thought did nothing positive for him, but Colin chuckled and set down his water. "You flatter me, Sir."

"Tell me, Mr. Douglas. What are you looking to get out of your week here?"

"Peace and quiet. Beauty. I can see you have that in abundance."

"Mr. Acosta mentioned a muse?"

The side of Colin's mouth went up. "That would be helpful."

"And how do you envision this muse? A dominant woman? Submissive? Or perhaps a handsome man? I do have one."

Now Colin grinned in full. He knew Marco was baiting him for the old all-artists-are-gay-stereotype. "A submissive woman."

Marco seemed pleased by this. Both men took a bite of their meals, thinking, savoring.

"If I may be so bold, Mr. Douglas…what are your

fantasies?"

Shite. That was a personal question he'd never been asked before.

Colin felt himself warming as the sun crept high over the cliff and bathed the veranda. His fantasies? Well, fuck. He had a hunch Marco Ruiz could smell bullshit from miles away. It was unlike Colin to open up and expose himself in any way. The thought of talking about sex, in detail, with this stranger, was off putting. But it would be the fastest way to gain his trust. So, he'd be honest.

"Ah, well, let's see. Believe it or not, I've never tied a woman up…"

A hint of a smile crested Marco's lips and he nodded for Colin to go on.

"I like to be in control. To do anything I wish to a woman without complaint, and have her enjoy it as much as me. I've always held back when truly I want to push a woman to her limits of pain—see how far we can take it." He took a breath and pushed himself to keep going. "I like to fuck outdoors where we might be seen. I love a good blowjob, especially if she swallows. I'm always up for anal sex, though most women aren't, considering I don't want a relationship. And, aye, most of all I love the smell and taste of a woman…and I'm happy when they're keen to fuck me and then leave me the hell alone."

Damn, he'd never put it all out there like that before. And his pants seemed to be tightening. Marco glanced down, then back up with a look of approval. Everything Colin had said had probably been tame in comparison with what some of the people came here wanted, but he'd been honest and passionate, which was all he could do.

Again, they both took a bite. Colin was thankful when the swelling between his legs began to go down.

"Any particular look you prefer?" Marco asked.

"I ken it's hard to come by in these parts, but I prefer blondes." Colin swore Marco's eyes darkened a fraction, but he forged ahead. "I've enjoyed my time in Spain, and the women are gorgeous, but I admit I'm often homesick for light haired lassies."

"That's understandable," Marco said. "And as far as body type?"

Colin shrugged. "Fit. Natural."

Marco nodded. "I'll see what I can do to find you a muse, Mr. Douglas. We do what we can here to turn fantasy into reality. I assure you everything that happens at my estate stays here, and I mean that with the utmost seriousness. I hope you'll enjoy your stay and make yourself at home. My servant will show you to your room."

"Thank you. Gracias."

Both men stood and placed their napkins on the table. The small servant who'd taken his bags was standing nearby with his hands clasped. He nodded at Colin to follow.

The villa was immaculate down to the last detail of the light salsa music playing overhead. In his room he moved his sunglasses to the top of his head and stared at the four poster, tall King bed. It reminded him with a pang of the bedroom suit his parents shared. Except theirs hadn't had cuffs attached by chains at various places of the headboard and posts. Colin had to wonder what kind of kinky fuckery took place in this room's lifetime. If it weren't for the villa's unfortunate circumstances he could really get down with the idea.

He adjusted himself, feeling that familiar and unwelcome tightening in his boxer briefs again. To take his mind off it, he went to the windows and stretched the curtains wide, revealing a set of french doors. He opened them and stepped onto the columned balcony into the salted sea breeze. Colin closed his eyes and breathed.

He was in. Nearly a year and a half of undercover work had led to this one week. No doubt, this would be the most difficult assignment he'd ever been on. To get the girl from this stronghold, alive, would be no small feat. He'd have to play the unknown factors as they surfaced and come up with a detailed plan as the week progressed.

But one single thought plagued his mind. What would he have to do to keep up his charade here? After all the shite he'd seen—the dirty brothels and slave quarters around the world, and what his brother'd been through—Colin did not want to have sex with any slaves. The very idea of it set his teeth on edge. But his motto had always been to do as they do. When the drug dealers were sampling the goods to make sure it was pure, Colin sampled the shite with them. When they fought, he fought. When they got plastered in pubs and picked up manky women, he was right there, drinking slightly less, and doubling up on the condoms. He'd always done what he had to to gain the trust of the goons he was attempting to bag.

But this was different. He didn't want to take advantage of people stuck in slavery. It felt wrong to his very core. Marco could put a fancy face on it, disguising his brothel as a paradise, but Colin saw it for what it was. He wanted to torch the place and kill every cunt bastard who thought entrapping humans was acceptable.

He had no idea if he'd be able to get out of having sex while at the villa, and he had to prepare his mind for the possibility of anything. So many hidden variables, the largest being how the *fuck* he'd be able to escape this stronghold with a piece of their human property?

If she was even here.

CHAPTER SEVENTEEN

Colin

—◆—·—I—◆—I—·—◆—

Colin rubbed his scalp roughly before going back inside his room. He began setting up his easel, his eyes scanning the room at intervals, searching for cameras. There were none he could see on the high ceilings, but the room held many places where cameras could hide. He didn't want to be obvious, so when his items were put away he crossed his arms and pretended to give a shite about the art around the room. An Asian vase. A painting of sailboats that was missing so much proper shading he could hardly look at the damn thing.

In the base of an ornate lamp he saw a minuscule hole. There was one camera. He didn't doubt there were more. A minted man like Marco wasn't about to let anyone have absolute free reign and privacy under his roof.

A knock sounded on the door and Colin opened it. A thin, older man bustled in without invitation, carrying a small kit.

What the hell?

The man set everything on the oversized dark dresser and turned to Colin, bowing his head. "Hola, Señor Douglas. You speak Spanish?"

"Ah, only pequeño."

The man nodded. "Lo siento. My English no es very good. Señor Ruiz send me to all new patrons to make blood."

Shock rippled through Colin and he narrowed his dark eyebrows. "Excuse me?"

"We have clean establishment. No disease. No worry, yes?"

Colin glared at the needles and vials. After a moment of thought he wondered what it would hurt to let them have a small sample. He'd shed more blood than that for less important missions.

"Fine," he said.

After the blood draw, the doctor man bustled out as quickly as he'd come in. And then there was another knock at the door. This one softer.

For fuck's sake.

He opened it and found a wee petite Asian girl in a bikini with tits that didn't quite fit her body. She wore a collar around her neck. Her eyes widened as she took in the sight of him, and then she seemed to catch herself and look down.

"Hola, Señor. You are invited to the pool area for cocktails if you so wish."

"Thank you," he said. For an awkward moment he wondered if he was supposed to do something—how he was supposed to act toward her, but he made no move.

The girl's eyes skipped up his frame one last, quick time, then she turned in her platform heels and walked away, swaying her thin hips. The entire sight was so strange he couldn't be aroused by it. Was she a slave? She didn't fit his image of a slave. Graham's deadened eyes came to mind. His drugged, dirty state. Colin's hands fisted in revulsion.

But this place wasn't like that, was it? They took people's fucking blood for God's sake, and he was sure that if any diseased bastard came through those doors he wasn't getting any arse.

Colin decided he'd take Señor Ruiz up on his offer to make himself at home. He left his room to explore, and hopefully catch sight of Angela.

Armed men stood in every entrance and exit of the vast home. He met their stares with nods as he passed. Most of the rooms were empty until he came to an outdoor veranda where voices carried on the breeze. People were outside. He took one step out of the grand arched doorway and swiped his eyes across the scene, taking in every detail. All the exposed skin.

Ah, shite. He probably shouldn't have come out here, but he'd look like a pansy if he turned and left now.

Live music played next to a bar area. Two men with guitars harmonized a quick rhythm of Latin roots. Distant sounds of crashing waves drifted up from below.

The pool was surrounded by tropical flowers and a rock wall that spilled a waterfall into the depths. The end of the pool came up to the cliff's edge and seemed to drop right off. Surrounding the pool were lounging chairs and umbrellas. Half dressed women delivered drinks to paunchy men in speedos, sprawled out in comfort. Colin's heart spiked when he spotted a blonde head kneeling next to one of the men, rubbing oil on his legs. But her face was too round, and her eyes an icy blue instead of brown—she appeared of European decent.

Colin saw the pretty Asian girl who came to his room sitting on a bald man's lap and running a finger down his hairy chest. In the hot tub was an older couple with a younger man who wore a collar like the Asian girl. This must be the male slave Marco had mentioned. The older man watched as the slave kissed the woman, his hands and their bodies moving under the water. Colin couldn't imagine sharing one's wife and watching. Fuck, he couldn't even imagine having a wife.

He heard light footsteps coming out behind him and turned to see Marco and two collared women. One of them stayed close behind him at his shoulder. In a black string bikini with a floppy black sunhat and heels, she was the embodiment of Spanish perfection—all straight lines and curves in the right places, with dark caramel skin. The other woman had smooth straight hair and wore a black bodice, strung tightly, and thigh high boots. Her tits were spilling out. She carried a riding crop and passed Colin with a nod.

He nodded back. Not his type, but impressive all the same. He watched as she approached a man laying face down on a lounge chair. The man yelped when she smacked his arse with the crop and pointed to the toe of her boot. He scrambled to the ground, kissed her foot, and allowed himself to be leashed around the neck and led inside the house on his hands and knees.

Now, there's something you didn't see every day.

Marco chuckled and patted Colin's shoulder. "Come, Señor Douglas. Have a drink with me."

A warm breeze kicked up as Colin and Marco took their places under a wide umbrella. The slave woman knelt beside Marco with her hands on her knees. She looked healthy, if not a bit thin, and content. In fact, the villa had a way of making the taboo seem almost normal. Acceptable. Which might've been the case if slavery weren't involved. To each his own, and all that. But when unwilling participants were forced to comply, that was a different situation, no matter what kind of happy mask they wore.

A servant was immediately at their table, and Colin asked for a scotch on the rocks. Marco ordered the same.

"What do you think of my quaint villa, Señor Douglas?"

Quaint? Was he fucking kidding?

"I'm mesmerized by it, Señor Ruiz. Already feeling more relaxed." The second bit was a lie, but Marco seemed to buy it as their drinks were delivered and they clinked the lips of their glasses. Naturally, the scotch was top notch and smooth. Colin drank it all in one go, and another appeared thirty seconds later.

"Señor Douglas, I'd like you to meet Perla." Marco nodded his head to the slave on the ground by his side. She raised her eyes long enough to catch Colin's and nod, then dropped them again. "She's not blonde, but she's a master of her trade." He removed the woman's hat and set it on the table, her brown waves blowing away from her shoulders. She sat up taller, causing her full breasts to jut out further. Colin felt a stir of lust.

Fuck. *Fuck.*

"She's gorgeous," Colin said. "Not my fantasy, but she'd definitely do." He gave Marco a wink and drank half his second glass. He needed to make the man think he'd take her. And unfortunately, if he had to, he would. To reject such an offer from a man like Marco would only raise suspicion and distrust.

Marco's head cocked and he ran an index finger back and forth over his chin.

"One of my patrons owns a blonde girl." Marco inclined his head toward the European woman, whose mouth was now as busy as her hands. "I'm certain I could work a trade."

Bloody fucking hell. Was Angela truly not here, or was Marco hiding her because he was a Westerner who might've heard of her? Was Colin going to have to fuck one of these slaves to prove himself? The thought repulsed him, though his traitorous body was more than willing.

Colin forced a grin. "Aye, pal. That'd be brilliant."

Marco nodded, a half-smile on his lips. "I shall work out

an arrangement for this evening."

Colin stood. "Many thanks, Señor Ruiz. Until then I think I'll retire and paint my view from the balcony."

Marco stood also, and the men grasped hands. Colin finished his drink and set it down. The last thing he heard as he left the pool was the shout of feminine ecstasy rising up from the hot tub to a background of mariachi music.

❖ ❖ ❖

As much as the high priced whorehouse gave Colin the creeps, he had to admit the view was inspiring. Señor Acosta had requested a painting that incorporated the sea. Colin stood on the balcony with his paints. So many colors. But too much darkness stirred inside him. His brush went to the blue, dabbing in a bit of red, then black to make a deep navy color.

When his brush hit the canvas his mind swelled, blocking out all thought and letting the movement of the strokes take over. His hand moved with a ferocious speed as anger and sadness coursed down his arm. It was the only time he let his emotions surface. What they created was a dark image of a terrifying sea, its mysterious depths swelling, a wild wind blowing shadowed sea flowers sideways with powerful force.

He dropped his arm and realized the muscles were sore. What time was it? The sun was lowering, preparing to set. He lay down his paint brush and went in the room.

"Fuck me," he mumbled, running his palm over his barely-there hair. He'd been painting six hours. In the mirror, he caught sight of himself and a smudge of blue across his jawline. He brought the easel and painting inside the room, and then showered, dressing in khakis and a blue button up shirt. He rolled the sleeves up to his elbows, revealing the bottom of his tattoos, and left the top three buttons open to stay cool.

A light knock sounded and Colin found the male slave at his door, shoulder length hair tucked behind his ears, wearing only a pair of crisp, black trousers and that damned collar.

The guy openly eyed Colin before clearing his throat. Colin was used to men eyeballing him, so it made no difference.

"Ah, good evening, Señor Douglas. Dinner will soon be served and the Master would greatly enjoy your company."

The Master. Bloody hell.

"I'll be there."

The young man nodded and dropped his eyes, turning to leave.

◆ · ┃ ◆ ┃ · ◆

Dinner was mostly a pleasant affair with small talk about the Spanish economy. Colin tried not to stare as "Masters" around the table fed bites to their slaves. Still no sight of Angela. Colin was beginning to lose hope, and wondering if a whole week at the villa would be a waste of time.

"Mr. Douglas," Marco suddenly said. "And how did you fare this afternoon?"

Colin set down his fork and wiped his mouth with the cloth napkin. "Quite productive, actually. Thank you."

"I'd love to see what you're working on, unless of course you don't share works in progress."

Colin kept a neutral look on his face, knowing full well the bastard had probably already seen his painting on the cameras.

"It still needs a bit of work, but you're welcome to see it at any step of the process, Señor."

This seemed to make Marco happy. "Perhaps one of these walls can someday be adorned with a creation of yours."

"Aye. I would be honored to paint something for your home, Sir."

The guest who owned the European girl spoke up. "What style of painting do you do, Señor Douglas?"

The conversation steered into artistic territory as Colin explained his use of water color and style of Abstract Expressionism.

"And where did you attend school to learn your craft?" asked the wife he'd seen in the hot tub. Her dark hair, streaked with a few strands of gray, was pinned up and she wore a straight gown with spaghetti straps.

"I was self-taught in my youth, Señora, but I honed my skills at university in Glasgow." This earned Colin a round of raised eyebrows and impressed sounds.

As soon as the dinner dishes were cleared away, the man beside him broke out a silver box and set to cutting lines of cocaine.

"Anyone interested?" he offered.

The classical music that had been playing softly overhead changed to something modern with a faster tempo and louder volume.

Everyone but Marco partook of the cocaine. Colin did one line. Then he watched as the man wiped his finger across the remnants of powder and brought the fingertips to his slave girl's nose. She breathed it in and shuddered with bliss.

Colin felt the room going wonky. Sounds were off, getting quieter, then suddenly louder. He felt his heart rate jack up. He was accustomed to this feeling, and he knew one line wasn't enough to overtake his mind. He basked in the energy ricocheting underneath his skin.

"Señor Douglas," Marco said in a low voice. Colin looked at him. "I have a surprise for you."

Shite. Colin hated surprises. Especially the typ

criminals liked to spring.

Colin braced himself and followed Marco's stare toward the doorway where a head of light blonde hair was being led into the room, crawling, her shoulders and backside swaying with the movements. Colin held his breath, his heart accelerating, unable to tear his eyes from her as she came to Marco's side and stopped. She wore a gold and white bikini. Even with her head down, Colin recognized the oval face. The small nose and perfectly shaped lips of Angela Birch.

"This is Angel," Marco said. He was calling her a different name. Colin made note.

His mind swam with euphoric relief and excitement, but he kept a straight face. She was really fucking here. Marco had kept her hidden, but somehow he'd made enough of an impression to bring her out. He bit back a smile of triumph.

"Señor Douglas." Marco's voice was hard. "You look almost as if you recognize the girl."

Colin tore his eyes away and landed them on Mr. Ruiz. Armed men from around the room stepped closer at the deadly sound of Marco's voice. Colin's buzz increased, setting his entire being on edge.

This was a test. Lucky for him, Colin prided himself on acing tests.

"I do recognize her, Señor Ruiz," Colin said, his voice going husky. "From every fucking wet dream I had as a lad."

One person at the table began chuckling, and others joined, until finally Marco relaxed and smiled. He snapped his fingers and said, "Time for the dancing."

The lights dimmed and all of the slaves stood. A Spanish pop song with a rhythmic beat began and Colin felt his high cresting as the bodies began to move. When his gaze found Angela again, he couldn't look away. She was no longer the soft, happy, innocent girl from the photographs and video. She was a woman now, with haunted eyes, and a sexy fucking body. Acrid guilt spilled through him for thinking it, but he was a man with eyes, after all. And a cocaine high. He wanted to shake the dark thoughts away, but they clung.

Colin barely noticed when Marco inclined his head toward him, sending Angela dancing closer. She turned, moving perfectly with the beat, her gold-thonged arse close to his lap, and God help him. His cock sprung to life, pressing tight against the inside of his trousers from the sensuality overtaking the room.

Ah, fuck. This was the girl whose parents were helplessly searching for her. The girl he'd come to rescue from her captivity. He shouldn't have had a bloody fucking erection for her. Hot shame flamed inside his chest, but for the life of him he couldn't look away. He wanted to touch—to see if her skin was as smooth as it appeared, her hair as soft.

Blood whooshed inside his ears and he vaguely heard someone speak. Whatever Marco had said caused Angela to lower herself to her knees in front of Colin with her hands on his thighs, and for the first time their eyes collided. He felt as if hot irons were branding the inside of his flesh—heat spread through him. They both froze momentarily, staring.

Every curse word Colin had ever heard, and some made-up new ones tumbled end over end through his mind. He'd never been as stunned by anything as he was at that moment by the depths of her brown eyes, a well of sorrow and lost hope. And he swore her breath caught as she froze, captured by his gaze as well.

It's because I'm a westerner, he thought. That had to be why she was looking at him like that. And he was turned on because he was high. Stupid fucking drugs. That's all this was.

Then her hand slid up and squeezed his cock through his pants. Colin hissed, scooting lower in his seat.

"Yo cuidaré de ti," she said in a sweet, seductive voice. He turned the phrase over in his mind, breaking it down until he realized what she'd said. *I will care for you.*

He didn't stop her as she undid his belt and had his erection out in record time. Her small hand circled the base of him, but her fingers and thumb didn't come close to meeting. Her pink tongue ran up the slit of his head, gathering his precome before her hot mouth surrounded him.

"Bloody fucking hell," Colin whispered. His head fell back and he slunk lower. Then he raised his head again to watch her.

This was wrong. He should have tried to find a way out of it. She was doing this because she had to, not because she wanted to, and that made Colin want to kick his own self in the balls. But damn it all to hell...for the life of him he couldn't bring himself to stop her. And what reason would he give Marco for denying the girl he'd already admitted was his fantasy?

He was doing this to save her. That's what he'd tell himself. It was the sacrifice they'd both make for her freedom. He watched her, slipping his rough fingers into her hair, which did turn out to be just as soft as it appeared.

She'd been cute in the videos, however he'd never expected to have any desire to fuck her, or fuck her mouth, as it was. But cute wasn't at all how he'd describe her now. As her head bobbed up and down, perfect suction, tongue teasing his flesh, one hand stroking his base while the other slipped up his shirt to feel his stomach... she looked up at him, fire in her eyes. He felt her nails dig lightly against his abs.

Shite. He wasn't going to last long.

He grasped her chin and pushed her head slightly back, holding her mouth open as he grabbed ahold of his slick cock. A low, growl of a grunt came from him as he watched his load shoot into her mouth, spraying her tongue and back of her throat. She stuck out her tongue, catching it all until he was done, then swallowing. The moment he finished she licked the last drop from his tip and went into her kneeling position next to him, her hands on her thighs and head down.

And that's when reality struck, ugly and foul.

He was in a room full of people, a few of whom were now clapping. For him. Because he'd just received the best blowjob of his life. From a slave. Who he was being paid to rescue.

Colin swallowed, wanting to vomit. He stood and inclined his head toward Marco, who looked rather smug.

"Thank you, Señor. Exactly what I needed, that. I'll continue working now, if you don't mind."

Before Marco could answer, Colin turned and headed for his room.

He should have played it cooler, but he was freaking the fuck out. In his room his hands shook as he frantically opened his paints, looking for one particular color.

Gold.

He propped the canvas against the wall and painted on his knees. Gold rounded the flowers. Gold crested the tips of the wind-whipped waves. Gold flecked the moon.

What had he done? He'd never been so furious with himself, but at the same time, her image was stuck in his mind, spreading its golden softness, and he couldn't stop his hand.

She was fucking everywhere.

CHAPTER EIGHTEEN

Colin

---◆·┃◆┃·◆---

It'd been ages since Colin stayed up all night painting, but he did that night. He finished Señor Acosta's dark sea image, and started right in on a different one—this one a golden flower that almost seemed to be dancing, pulled to and fro by the wind. Its petals were open, inviting, the center of it like a soft mouth.

Damn it. Colin's head was in a fucked up place. He'd felt similar to this in the past when he pushed limits, but he'd crossed one tonight. And worst of all he'd enjoyed it. Knowing he'd had to do it made him feel no better. When he got her out of this place and returned her to her parents, would she think he'd taken advantage of her? Would she resent him? He wouldn't blame her, and he expected her father to want to kill him—to say he was no better than the thugs who held her captive.

Who cares? You did what you had to do, and you'll never have to see her again after this.

Colin groaned. He was tired, and his subconscious was trying to do battle in his mind. He shook his head, scrubbed his face with his palms. He couldn't sleep because he had to get the image transferred from his mind to the canvas before the spectacular surge of details disappeared.

Just a bit longer.

He finally crashed in the giant bed after eight in the morning and allowed the comfort to engulf him until nearly dinner time. He was hungry and groggy when he woke, his internal clock out of sync.

He perched on the end of the bed and caught sight of the golden, seductive flower. That quickly, it all came rushing back. Every sensuous curve of the stem, leaves, and petals. Every golden edge popped brilliantly against the black and gray streaks of background. It'd been a long time since he loved something he painted, and this was his favorite creation yet. When he looked at it he felt his chest constricting. But he could never keep this piece. In fact, he knew exactly what he needed to do with it.

Colin showered and dressed business casual. He probably should have shaved. The scruff on his face was as long as the shadow of hair on his head, but he hardly cared for his appearance at that moment. He rolled the sleeves of his shirt to his elbows to free his wrists and forearms from their cotton confines, picked up the gold flower painting, and headed for the dining room.

He was the first guest to arrive, and he slumped into the chair he'd occupied the previous night, hell bent on not remembering the erotic encounter. Kitchen staff bustled around him and he vaguely realized they weren't quite ready for guests. He closed his eyes, not caring, because his head was pounding as if he had a hangover.

Five minutes later Marco entered the room with one of his bodyguards. Colin stood to greet him, and the two of them shook hands before sitting. A staff woman brought two glasses filled with dark, thick port.

"Mr. Douglas." Marco raised his glass, so Colin took his up and they cheered. "Good to see you out. I hope your stay here has been pleasant so far."

"Aye, Señor, it certainly has. I've been more inspired these past two days than I have in years." He revealed this truth to Marco with reluctance, and the man grinned.

"Excellent." Marco sipped his port, his ankle resting on his knee.

"I have a gift for you, Señor. To thank you for allowing me to come to your home. You've been most hospitable."

Marco lowered his foot and sat up taller as Colin pulled the canvas around from his other side and held it for the man to see. The artist in him relished the look of awe in Marco's eyes as he absently set his port on the table and took the painting to view it closer.

"Stunning."

"Thank you, Señor. I hope you'll accept it."

"I will. With great pleasure. I'm not much of an art connoisseur—what you see around my home was all chosen by the interior designers—but it would be impossible not to appreciate the beauty of this."

Colin inclined his head in thanks. Marco snapped his fingers and a servant appeared at his side. In quick Spanish, Marco ordered for the painting to be framed and mounted in the dining room. He pointed to the centerpiece on the great wall, saying this painting would replace it. Pride and shame spun in Colin's chest, a wicked dance.

Other guests soon began to arrive, talking animatedly. Marco was in a jovial mood. Nearly every guest had a slave next to them. Marco had the woman Perla on one side, and then Angela came in and knelt between Marco and himself. Knowing Marco's eyes were on him, Colin allowed himself to take in the sight of the girl. She wore a vibrant purple dress, short and tight, with strappy black heels. Her hair was pulled into a loose braid over her shoulder, strands falling around her face. Gorgeous.

Guilt assaulted him again.

He turned his attention to dinner as it arrived: a paella of saffron rice with local shrimp and chorizo. As Colin ate, his awareness of the girl so close never left him. He noticed the guests feeding the slaves now and then, but not nearly enough. They were all too thin. With sour distaste, Colin also noticed that Marco fed Perla two bites for every one Angela received.

"Señor Ruiz," Colin said. When the man looked over Colin asked, "May I?" He held a shrimp, as if to feed Angela.

Marco's eyebrows went up. "Of course."

Colin felt strange, almost shaky inside, as he brought the piece of food to her mouth in his fingers. Her lips opened in acceptance, taking in the shrimp, and biting down at the edge of the tail. Her lips were soft and warm against his fingertips.

Do not react, he commanded his body. Colin thought about rugby—running and dodging. Anything not to let himself become aroused and have a repeat of the previous night.

Angela dropped her head and chewed in silence. He fed her several more bites before dinner was over, experiencing a small rush each time she accepted his offerings. He wondered how often she felt hungry. Her collarbones jutted out. The thought upset him. When his creme brule came he took two bites and proceeded to feed her the rest.

Marco chuckled next to him. "You're going to make her fat."

Was he blind? Or simply a fucking arsehole?

"Not possible," Colin said. He set the spoon down with a clink and looked at the man. "I've never...fed anyone before."

Marco smiled, seeming to understand the sensual empowerment that came from holding a lover's sustenance in your very fingers. To be so needed at the apex of one's existence. To control another person in such a way…damn it…Colin could see the allure of it for the first time in his life, and he didn't want to feel that way. He cleared his throat and pushed back from the table, setting his napkin beside his plate.

"I think I'll take a walk and then retire to work for the evening. The meal was lovely, Señor Ruiz."

Marco nodded, a small smile hiding under his mustache. "As was the company. Enjoy."

Colin didn't like that shit-eating grin, like Marco knew his internal struggles. He felt the eyes of Marco's men on him as he walked through the halls and breezeway onto the veranda. As always, he was poised to fight if it came to that. He passed the empty pool, listening to the rush of water and feeling the warm breeze against his skin. Colin went to the edge and stared over the side at the rocks and distant crash of waves below. His mind began devising routes of escape. He could scale these cliffs down, but he couldn't expect Angela to do the same. A jump from this high would lead to death or maiming.

With surveillance cameras surely covering the property, and armed men at every corner, Marco's villa was the perfect prison. Colin loved a good challenge, but only when his own life was on the line, not an innocent's. He had no clue how he'd get her out of here, and he didn't enjoy the unwelcome nervousness and doubt that rose up in his gut.

He shoved his hands into his pockets as more immediate concerns filled his mind. He couldn't feign "inspiration" the entire time he was here based on one instance of good head. He'd be expected to do something more during his time. But not tonight. He would worry about that tomorrow. Tonight he would force himself to start another painting. An image of soft, luscious lips curling around masculine fingertips came to mind and he had to adjust himself.

This place was already getting to his mind. The way it all seemed so damned...*normal.* Acceptable. He was grateful this would be his last mission, because he'd need a long break to find himself again after this.

—◆·|◆|·◆—

Something felt amiss as Colin walked through the empty great room toward his hall. He couldn't place where the threat stemmed from, but warning alarms went off in his head, his senses going on high alert. He'd always had a keen intuition for danger. He glanced behind him. Nothing. When he turned the corner he saw one of the guards standing in front of his door.

Colin's muscles were readied for action and his heart was thumping hard as he approached. He was prepared to strike first, if need be. The guard nodded and stepped aside, clearing his throat and speaking in broken English. He thought his name was Luis.

"Master Ruiz have one rule for his slaves. No permanent damage to the bodies. Sí?"

What the fuck? "Okay," Colin said evenly.

"For his slave Angel he have special rule. No anal sex. And she can no go outside."

Colin nodded, baffled. Luis opened the door for him.

All at once, the blood pumping hard through Colin's body flooded one particular area, because there, dangling from his bedpost like a creamy gift, was Angela.

A "thank you" from Marco for the painting, no doubt.

Colin, already forgetting the guard Luis, closed the door behind him and stared. Her arms were stretched tight over her head, wrists chained to the top of the post. She wore nothing but a blindfold, black lace underwear, and those strappy black heels, which barely touched the ground. Her chest moved rapidly with breaths, showing her nervousness.

She'd been a captive for two years. Was she always nervous like this? The idea of it made him want to crush something. Namely, every man who'd ever taken advantage of her in this kind of vulnerable scenario.

Like he was about to do.

He hated himself as he reached into his pants and pulled his cock higher, attempting a more comfortable place for the damned, out of control monster. As he prowled closer to the girl he felt his own breaths coming faster and harder, matching the rise and fall of her chest. Those pretty, dark pink nipples calling to him.

He had to touch her. It was expected of him. And he *had* to. He felt like he might explode if he didn't.

But a horrible thought occurred to him. She had no idea he was there to save her. To her, he was just another perverted john, wanting a piece of her. He wished he could explain to her. The thought that she might be repulsed by him was nearly enough to deflate every ounce of lust from his system.

A low groan came from his throat and she gasped, apparently realizing his nearness. Her breasts seemed to rise up, calling to him.

I'm sorry, he thought to himself. One day, he hoped to be able to apologize properly, and God willing she could forgive him...and he could forgive himself.

His hands slid around her waist to the small of her back and she arched toward him. His mouth came down around her sweet nipple and they both moaned.

She's acting, he told himself. But he couldn't think that way. He had to pretend she was enjoying it too, or he didn't know if he could go through with it.

He circled his tongue around her nipple, feeling it tighten and perk so he could suck it properly. Then he moved to the other side until both nipples were at attention.

He hadn't been lying when he told Marco he loved the scent and taste of a woman. Colin moved slowly to his knees, running his tongue over her ribs, kissing her belly button, and trailing his hands over her ass and the back of her toned thighs. Too thin, but so beautiful.

She was panting when he lowered her thong to her ankles and lifted her feet one at a time to step out of them. At her core was a thin strip of trimmed hair, light brown. The rest looked incredibly smooth. Silky. Grasping her hips, his mouth covered her and she cried out. Colin needed better access, so he lifted one of her legs and draped it over his shoulder, glad when he felt her put some weight onto him. He used his thumbs to gently open her, and he dove in, his tongue going wild at the sweet and salty taste of her.

She was so vocal. Under his hands and mouth she bucked her hips. His tongue dipped further, finding complete wetness at her opening, and he groaned again. He wanted to put a finger in and feel her, but all his concentration was centered on her clit. As his tongue went back to it, flicking rapidly, he swore he felt her tense. And then she was moaning, her thighs tightening around his face. He felt the undulations of her orgasm, the pumping of blood through her sex as he suckled. Her breathing and shouts came in short, feminine spurts.

It gave him immense relief to know he'd brought her pleasure, but he couldn't let it go to his head. She'd probably had to learn to enjoy all things sexual in her time of captivity. A wave of remorse pounded him as he stood and faced her. He didn't want to be a nameless, faceless man, and she deserved to see who touched her.

She sagged a bit in her chains, but when Colin pulled the blindfold off she straightened, her eyes going wide. They stood there staring at one another, both of them resuming another round of hard breathing. Without thought, Colin lowered his mouth to hers. The sound of surprise she let out shot a spike of fear through him.

Was he not supposed to kiss her?

In an instant she reacted, kissing him back as if her life depended on it, her mouth hungry for him. His arms went around her waist and he pressed his hard length against her stomach. Their lips moved in perfect harmony, their tongues exploring as if they were discovering the bliss of kissing for the first time.

His fears disappeared, replaced by golden stars that flooded his vision.

He would get this girl away from Marco's lair or die trying.

CHAPTER NINETEEN

How long had it been since someone kissed me? Truly kissed me, like this? Like they couldn't get enough of me. Like I was a nectar to their dying thirst.

Never.

My boyfriend's kisses had always been sweet. After him, there were drunken kisses at parties, and of course the lust-filled kisses from Fernando that I tried never to remember.

When Marco's patrons kissed me with sloppy, impassioned ownership, it was for their own pleasure, never mine.

Every now and then I'd get a patron who I knew wanted me to come, but even then, it always seemed to be for their own egotistical purposes. An outward show of their control over my body. Not because they cared.

This felt different. Strangely real. It was confusing and worrisome, but I couldn't stop the thoughts that came to me.

My mind went back to last night. The way he'd looked into my eyes like I was a woman, not an object. The way I'd sensed something like reluctance from him. I couldn't place it. All I knew was it felt different. Deep down, I knew he was probably the same as anyone else who came here, but I wanted to enjoy this moment. For however many days he spent at the villa, I wanted to pretend he was just a sexy, normal man, and that I was a normal girl choosing to be with him.

I must have looked starry-eyed when we returned to the slave quarters last night because Josef eyed me with complete seriousness and disapproval.

"Qué?" I'd snapped. *What?* Though I knew what. Having any emotions was dangerous around here.

He only shook his head slowly and whispered in Spanish, "Be careful, Angel. Guard your heart."

I loved him for caring, but I wasn't going to fall in love with a patron—I wasn't that stupid. However, I would take my kicks where I could get them, and this guy was seriously hot. Nobody who came here was ever hot, except that Latin pop star who preferred Josef.

When I'd first looked up at Mr. Douglas after dinner, a feeling I hadn't had since Cancun filled me. My first thought was, "Oh, my God. I can't wait to tell my friends about this guy!" By "friends" I meant my sorority sisters, not my fellow slaves.

It was such a strange, alien thought to have here at the villa, and my heart sunk the moment it crossed my mind. I would never be telling my friends about him, and as that realization struck me I was filled with an overflow of loss and sadness that I hadn't felt in a long time. Yes, I had to be careful. Guard my heart. And I would.

Under that sexy scruffiness, Mr. Douglas was a heartless criminal just like the rest of them. I had no business letting "old Angela" thoughts into Angel's life. Still…the way he'd looked at me…and then when I'd heard him speak. Hearing my native language in that roguish accent made something bloom to life inside me that had been long dead. I hadn't heard English in a year. The sound was a salve to my soul, though I knew I was foolish to feel that way.

When I'd heard there was a Scottish man at the villa I'd ignorantly imagined some big-bellied, bald man in a kilt. Then Jin came in that afternoon giddy. *Giddy.* Whispering about the Scottish patron.

Still, I couldn't imagine any patron being worthy of all that.

Until I saw him.

The way he'd watched with those deep eyes as I danced made me tingle all over. And then when I'd unbuttoned his pants and sprung free the most perfect cock in existence— thick girth thrumming under my hands—I actually didn't mind going down on him. That's something that rarely happened.

And now. Now he was kissing me with unadulterated passion. Men needed to put more stock in kissing, and less importance on the size of their balls. A good kiss could bring a woman to the brink and make her beg for more, just as I was feeling now, panting against his mouth, the pain in my wrists long forgotten.

I remembered his mouth between my legs. The feel of his five o'clock shadow gently scraping the inside of my thighs. Men went down on me all the time, but it was like the kissing thing—it was for them, not me. Why did this feel different? Was it all in my head, because I actually felt attracted to this man? Whatever the reason, I had to stop analyzing it and just enjoy. I pushed my hips against the hardness at his crotch.

I wanted sex. I actually wanted it, and it was liberating, because that above all was something I could want and actually get.

Mr. Douglas reached up and undid the straps around my wrists, bringing my numb hands to his belt. I was breathing hard. He watched my face as I unbuckled and unzipped.

Then he stepped back and undressed himself the rest of the way.

I could do nothing but stand there in his predatory sights, anticipating what was to come and knowing I'd probably relive it every day in my imagination, even envision him while I was with future patrons.

I dropped my stare to look at his crotch, just as impressive as the night before, so thick. And then his shirt came off.

Oh, yes, yes, yes. I'd felt his muscles last night, but seeing that six pack made me breathe harder. He had tattoos up the insides of his arms, but I couldn't make them out. He came at me, backing me against the tall the bed and kissing me again with abandon, his hands tangling inside my hair, pulling, his erection pressing against my stomach. He was impassioned, but not gentle. My hands were all over him, up his taut sides and over his muscled back, waist, then his hard ass. For once I was behaving with a patron the way Marco really wanted me to. I wondered if he was watching. If he was proud. But the thought was fleeting.

Mr. Douglas growled, grabbing underneath my butt to lift me onto the bed. I crawled backward as he loomed, coming at me. Just as I was about to reach for his cock, he surprised me, pulling back the blankets and pointing for me to climb under the sheet.

It wasn't my strangest request ever. I complied, as always, without question or hesitation. He climbed under with me, pulling the sheet up to his shoulder blades as he found his way between my legs and held his weight above me. His eyes bore into mine. He looked at me so much. It was highly unusual for a patron, and even more unusual for me to stare back, but his eyes were so beautiful—an expressive dark blue, saying things I couldn't understand.

Would I get in trouble for looking at him like this? Momentarily scared, I dropped my eyes and concentrated on his body. Up the inside of one of his arms was writing. The other arm had a design...a tree, maybe? When he began to lower himself I stopped trying to focus on his tatts.

I raised my hips, ready for him, but when he settled himself on top of me he pressed his cock inside the crook of my thigh and leaned forward, rocking his body seductively. He bent and placed his lips at my ear, whispering low.

"Pretend I'm talking dirty to you. Say, *Oh, yeah.*"

What? That was...weird.

Damn it. Disappointment rushed through me. He was a freak, just like all the others.

"Oh, sí, Señor Douglas," I moaned.

He began to move his strong hips in a delicious circular motion and thrusting his hips, making the bed rock.

Again he lowered his lips to my ear. "Pretend I'm fucking you."

Was he kidding me?

This was beyond strange. What the hell was going on here? The man was as hard as a rock. Why wasn't he having sex with me?

My thoughts were interrupted when his hips moved enough to shift his cock against the center of my slit. He found my wetness there and we both groaned as he slid up and down against me.

Okay, weird or not, that felt really good. I rocked up and back, meeting his strokes. He watched me, moving a strand of hair from my mouth.

"You're fucking beautiful, you are." His thumb moved over my cheek, down my chin, and he watched it trailing my skin. "A wee, golden flower."

My fingers gripped his muscular sides and my nails dug in just slightly as I felt another orgasm building. This was my lucky freaking night. I wanted him to keep talking. Keep looking at me like that. My breaths quickened. He pressed harder, moved faster, taking all of my body's hints.

"Fuck, yes," he whispered as I clung tight and came hard against him. I rubbed and rubbed against his wide shaft, pressing to release every tiny tremor, and then a deep rumble rang from his diaphragm. Men made all sorts of funny sounds when they came. Most went high-pitched, but not Mr. Douglas. When he orgasmed his voice lowered, like a growling beast of a man, and it was incredibly sexy. I wanted to hear that sound again and again, and I hoped I would in my dreams.

His voice lowered further and he sat up on his knees as if pulling out of me, grasping himself as the sheet flew back. He came, a thick stream shooting across my belly and breasts, up to my chin.

We were both breathing hard. He wouldn't look at me now, and I had to wonder…

What *was* that? The best non-sex of my life, yes, but why hadn't we done it? If he was gay he could have requested Josef. Nobody around here had any qualms about that, so I couldn't imagine he was hiding homosexuality. Did he think I was diseased? He'd obviously been blood-tested when he came, like all patrons to my knowledge, so he had to know I was clean.

Why didn't he want to have sex with me?

Unfounded hurt crept over me. I felt offended, though truly I was more baffled than anything. Part of me thought it was ironic that I'd be upset over a patron not wanting to fuck me. And even more ironic that I'd wanted to fuck him.

Mr. Douglas moved to the edge of the bed and I sucked in a gasp. He had a gorgeous Gaelic word tattooed across his upper back. I wished I knew what the word meant, but I didn't dare ask. He sat there, running a hand up and down the back of his shave head. The short hair gave him a dangerous, edgy look. I could see from the outline of the new growth that he wasn't balding or receding. He was an utter mystery.

He climbed down and reached for his undershirt, coming back to the bed and wiping his come from my skin. The thoughtful gesture suddenly made my eyes burn and I had to swallow hard. It wasn't unheard of for patrons to be kind or gentle, but it was rare. I believed Marco was gentle with Perla, and I'd always wished for that. I was starving for true kindness.

He tossed the soiled shirt to the ground and pulled on his boxer briefs. I prepared myself to say the words I always had to say if there was no prearranged agreement.

"Señor Douglas…Quieres que me quede?" *Do you want me to stay?*

He finally looked at me again, but the passion was gone now. He seemed guarded.

Please say yes, I silently begged. *Ask me to stay.*

"Do you only speak in Spanish?" he asked.

I paused, taken aback by the question, and then nodded.

"No," he whispered, and my stomach sunk. In a stronger voice he said, "You may go."

Dismissed.

Without looking at him I quickly climbed off the bed, picked up my panties from the floor, and left. Luis was waiting outside the door to escort me to the slave quarters.

Josef, Jin, and Perla were all surprisingly there, sitting at the table. The girls sat up straighter, smiles on their faces like they wanted details, though that wasn't something we normally did. Josef eyed me suspiciously and I felt exposed under his stare.

Not saying a word, I turned for the showers to wash myself as we were expected to do after every encounter with a patron.

Well, what do you know? All three of them freaking followed me in.

"So, chica?" Jin said in Spanish, a hand on her silk-clad waist. "Was he good?"

I had to be careful. Attraction was fine, but I couldn't imagine Marco would approve of me crushing on a patron. Emotions were off limits. But I could talk about the sex.

"Sí," I answered, closing my eyes to go under the spray of water. I heard Jin giggle with glee.

"But he didn't want you to stay the night," Josef said, getting right to the heart of it. Ouch. He was watching me with his arms crossed and I could practically feel the waves of disapproval coming off him.

Perla *tsked*. "He's an artist. He probably sent her away so he could paint." She smiled at me and left the bathrooms, pulling a grinning Jin alongside her.

I couldn't look at Josef, and after a minute of my silence he finally left me alone. Why did he have to know me so well? Tonight was my first time in all my days at the villa that I was sad to be let go by a patron, and Josef knew it. It was dumb of me. I shouldn't have felt that way for any man who came through these doors, but after so long of feeling nothing, I couldn't help but grab ahold of this sensation, letting it grow. I had so little. What would it hurt?

CHAPTER TWENTY

Colin

He couldn't even force himself to paint after the mind fuck that was his time with Angela. Sending her away had been a spontaneous decision that he regretted now. Colin climbed into the shower and wondered if Marco had another man for Angela to be with tonight since he hadn't asked her to stay. He shut his eyes tight and wanted to punch the tiled walls at the thought of her being forced into another bed after being with him.

Damn it all to hell. He should have told her to stay. But then…yeah. He'd be expected to take her again and again. And he'd want to. No doubt she thought he was a bloomin' tosser after the stunt he'd pulled under the sheets tonight.

Although she seemed to enjoy it.

Colin caught his cock in his hand under the stream of water and willed it not to get hard again at the thought of her orgasming beneath him—her nails digging into his lower back and how she rubbed herself, making all those gorgeous fucking sounds. If she'd thought he was strange for not fucking her, she rolled with it, using his body for her pleasure. Made Colin wonder what kind of crazy shite she'd seen…he stopped his thoughts right there.

He was going to get her out of here. That's all that mattered. And he'd do whatever it took to accomplish that.

Colin needed to earn the trust of Marco Ruiz. He was making good progress, but he wanted to completely win the man over.

He dressed in shorts and a Spanish style button up shirt, and left his room, hoping Marco would be out. Colin followed the scent of acrid cigar smoke out to the veranda where Marco sat with two other men in the open air, flanked by three bodyguards. They looked to be talking business, so Colin steered clear, deciding to take a walk through the warm night instead.

"Señor Douglas," he heard called behind him. "Won't you join us?"

Marco waved him over with a cigar in hand, so Colin went.

He sat in the offered chair and accepted the cigar Marco held out to him. A Cuban.

"Señor, I'd like you to meet two of my business associates, Juan and Franco."

Colin nodded to the men, who stared at him a moment before nodding back, unsmiling.

Ah, hard arses.

Marco poured him a shot from the Patron bottle on the table, and Colin thanked him, tequila in one hand, lit cigar in the other.

"We were just discussing the subject of recreational drugs, internationally, which makes me curious. Are the preferences much different in the UK than Spain?"

Colin sipped his drink and shook his head. "Same across the board, Señor. Biggest problem in the UK right now for sellers is all these wanker kids trying to make their own shite and sell it independently. So many chemicals available. Big dealers try to squash the wee lads as they come on the scene, and prices have gone down a bit to accommodate. But as far as the art world goes, the preference is the same there and here. Cocaine." He threw back the rest of his shot.

All three men nodded.

"And the human trade?" Marco asked, tapping his cigar on a stone tray. His voice sounded careful. Colin had opted for openness with the man so far, and it had benefited him, so he decided to keep to that route.

"To be honest, Señor, prostitution and sex slavery are extremely taboo in the UK, so they aren't spoken of often, even among the drug lords. I'm certain it's present, but I haven't been made privy."

Marco hadn't looked at him. The man kept his eyes trained on the cigar. Colin felt his two associates and the three bodyguards tensing, so he tensed as well, preparing himself for anything.

"So then, this is your first experience?" Marco asked.

"Aye." Colin rolled the cigar between his fingers and took a single puff, readying himself to play this game. He let the air fill his mouth before he blew it out slowly. "And I want to thank you for the gift. You're a generous man."

Marco looked at him now. "You enjoyed her?"

"Very much."

"And she's the first slave you've ever had?"

Colin nodded, cigar at his lips again.

"Fascinating. Tell me, Señor Douglas…how would you say this experience differs from being with free women?"

What was this? Was Colin on a fucking talk show? No, he knew what this was. He wanted Colin to admit how much better this was for him. He wanted to make sure Colin left the villa sold to the idea of slavery. And Colin would tell him exactly what he wanted, but his gut would hate it. Because the words would be far too close to the truth.

He was more like these men than he wanted to admit. This place had stirred up darkness in him. Darkness that felt good. Darkness that nobody had any business embracing, especially him.

"There is no comparison, Señor Ruiz. The past two evenings have been...beyond brilliant. The girl, Angel, was ideal in every way and she expected nothing of me afterward. It was a fucking relief to be able to tell her to leave and having her oblige without getting an earful or dealing with tears. I fucking hate tears."

Marco laughed and smacked his knee, cigar ash falling onto his dark trousered leg. He pointed a finger at Colin as if he'd hit the nail on the head. The other men laughed, as well. Fucking minions. He wondered what their job was for Marco. Drug pushers? Or did they buy and sell humans on the underground market? Colin smoked his cigar, his stomach churning.

Eventually Marco dismissed his two business associates and the two of them sat there together. Colin downed two more shots until his nerves settled, but he was still highly aware of his surroundings and where the bodyguards' hands and guns were at all times. Marco met him shot for shot, and even had another.

"It takes a strong man, Señor Douglas, to go against the puritanical rules of society. A man who knows what he wants and knows he deserves it." Marco crushed his cigar and folded his hands over his stomach. "People act as if slavery is a new concept, but it has been around as long as people have lived. It has always been a part of the natural hierarchy of life, just as men have ruled over women. It is the way of things, and our modern societies try to fight against that, making chaos out of something simple."

Colin nodded as if contemplating those primitive words. He poured both of them another drink, and they clinked the small glasses, both sipping.

"Mind you, I don't see eye to eye with every slave owner," Marco said. "I believe slaves should be maintained with the upmost care. They are a valuable commodity. A healthy, satisfied slave is a loyal slave."

"I commend you for your way of thinking."

"Gracias. I can see why the masses are against slavery. They've seen the very worst of it displayed in documentaries and news reports. But is there a documentary for how my slaves were saved from unfortunate circumstances? I've taken them in like strays on the brink of death, and given them good lives here."

Tequila had loosened Marco's tongue. His eyes were bright. Full of zeal. And Colin stared back with just as much ardor, because transitioning a human from a terrible life into a life of luxurious slavery did not make their lives "good." Not to mention the bastard forgot to account for the one slave who hadn't come from unfortunate circumstances.

Marco sat back, apparently realizing he'd gotten himself worked up, and chuckled. He ran a hand down his mustache.

"The world is so quick to judge. But send any man to my home and let him experience the natural rightness of it. Men come here with stresses and anxieties that the world piles on their backs, and when they leave they are as they should be: empowered. Relaxed. Self-assured."

"Exactly." Colin finished his last drink. He had a buzz now, so he wouldn't drink more.

Marco's head inclined toward Colin's forearm, where his tattoo showed:

Is fhearr fheuchainn na bhith san duil

"Do you mind if I ask what it says?"

"Not at all. It's a Scottish Gaelic proverb. *It is better to try than to hope.*"

"Ah, sí. A man of action rather than words. I like that." Marco grinned.

Colin snuffed out his cigar. "I owe you many thanks already, Señor, and my week has only just begun."

The two men stood and clasped hands.

"I hope you'll join us for breakfast in the morning, Señor Douglas. We'll eat right here, weather permitting. And if work calls your attention, I will have breakfast sent to your room."

"You are a Godsend," Colin said, inclining his head, and with that the two men parted for the night.

That went well, Colin thought. He couldn't say getting in the mind of a madman was a favorite past time, but he did feel accomplished that Marco Ruiz had confided in him. He'd moved his pawn one step closer, though how he'd get the girl out of this fucking place was still the question of the hour. And he'd sure as hell better figure it out soon.

CHAPTER TWENTY-ONE

I hadn't been outdoors in two years. Of all the things I'd been denied in my time at the villa, the right to be outside saddened me most. My body became accustomed to less food—I'd even stopped craving things I couldn't eat, such as pizza and Dove bars, because I knew I'd never have them again. I'd numbed myself to the sexual encounters, and took affection in the small, fleeting doses they came to me. My body and mind had adjusted to all circumstances out of necessity. But I hated not being able to go outside. Especially since I was the only one denied that simple privilege.

I craved sunshine and night sky. I longed for the wide, open world.

And that loss, more than anything, had become a symbol of my lost freedom. The outdoors became a metaphor for everything I'd once had. Things like family and holidays, friends and school. Driving. Flirting. Shopping. They were all fantasies to me now. Fairy tales. When I thought about the sky, a painful, heavy depression threatened to settle on my soul.

Being stuck in a windowless room most of my days

didn't help.

I sat on a throw rug of the tiled floor in the slave quarters doing stretches. Alone. I pushed myself, enjoying the burning sensations in my muscles. It was hard not to think about how all the others were outside at the pool. Sure, it was more work time, and I didn't envy that. But I would have done anything to be out there.

Marco was paranoid. Any sailboat floating by was assumed to be spying. He didn't care if they saw people screwing poolside, or snorting coke on his veranda. Just as long as they didn't spy his precious stolen American girl.

I was still kind of surprised he'd let the Scottish man see me. Mr. Douglas. Just thinking of him sent warmth shooting through me.

Was another slave servicing him right now? In the hot tub or pool? Did he enjoy them better? An acidic feeling sliced at me.

I bent until my nose was almost touching the floor, and hissed from the pain of the stretch up the back of my leg. Jealousy over a patron was stupid and ridiculous and unheard of. What was wrong with me?

I jumped to my feet at the sound of the door opening. Luis stood there.

"Ready yourself for lunch," he said in Spanish.

I nodded, feeling entirely too enthusiastic. Strange, strange, strange. Maybe Josef was right. Maybe I should be more careful. Tone down the excitement. Mr. Douglas wouldn't stay forever. Most patrons only stayed a couple nights. Some a few weeks, but that was uncommon. For all I knew the Scot could be long gone. And damned if that didn't send a flare of disappointment through me.

I rushed to the closet and put on a skimpy black, silk dress that drooped down one shoulder and stopped just below my ass. Then I fluffed my hair, which I'd put waves in that morning, and I reapplied my make-up. I usually went for pink lips, but today I grabbed the red.

Luis gave me the once-over as I approached, fitting the collar around my neck. He led me out until we neared the dining room, then I went to my knees the rest of the way. I sat against the wall with my head down, waiting to be called upon. In my peripheral vision I could see all the others lined against the wall, as well, in their bathing suits. I caught the scent of body oils and chlorine, which made the old longing surface like a swirl of hot sadness.

I was about to attempt a stealthy peek at the table when I heard his voice in the hall. That brogue rumble sent a shiver through me. He was walking with Marco, and they both laughed about something. Happiness and relief overflowed. He was still here.

The two men stopped near me in the doorway and I stilled, holding my breath. Marco was in his slacks, as always, but I could see Mr. Douglas's legs—the dark hair and tanned skin on his calves. His feet in sandals, which almost made me want to smile. He was wearing shorts like guys I used to know. The cargo kind. Another surge of emotion stirred inside me—emotion for old, familiar things.

Yeah...I definitely needed to be careful. This stranger made me feel way too many things. Things I'd stopped feeling long ago because they weren't good for me. Things I couldn't afford to feel.

"Ah, there you are, Señor Ruiz," said another patron approaching—a wealthy man from Italy. "I was hoping to propose a trade. My African beauty here for your blonde white girl. Just for the day."

No... I tensed.

"Actually, Sir, I've claimed her for the day," said Mr. Douglas.

My heart pounded at the sound of his declaration and

Marco's ensuing chuckle.

"Have you, Señor Douglas?" Marco asked.

"That is," Mr. Douglas amended in a dangerously calm, low voice. "I *wish* to claim her. With your permission, of course."

I couldn't breathe. I saw the other patron shift his feet and shuffle, maybe crossing his arms.

"My apologies, Señor Bellini. I had planned to offer her to Señor Douglas here. Perhaps tomorrow?"

"Tomorrow I leave," the man said gruffly.

"Ah. Pity." Marco's voice was cold, completely lacking said pity. I could tell he wasn't happy with the slight attitude Mr. Bellini gave him.

The Italian cleared his throat and said, "Very well. Perhaps next time." Then he went to his place at the table. He kicked his kneeling slave in the hip to make her move so he could sit without having to pull his chair out. I forced myself to look away from the dark-skinned girl and the way she trembled.

Marco bent and gave my collar a gentle tug, bringing me from my sitting position to my hands and knees.

"Angel, you will accompany Señor Douglas this afternoon and evening. Remain at his side."

My breaths began to return to normal.

I crawled between the men and followed them to the table, kneeling between them as they sat, and feeling entirely too relieved. My face must have appeared pleased because when I shifted and caught Josef's eye, he was glaring at me with disapproval through strands of hair, his head tilted down. I quickly looked away.

I wished I could reassure him. I would be careful.

Once again Mr. Douglas fed me more than I usually received. Eating from his hands was so sexy it was almost like foreplay for me. I could feel his eyes watching as his fingers lingered against my lips. And at the end of lunch I didn't experience my usual growl of hunger pain. I crawled at his side to the sitting room where everyone went to smoke cigarettes and cigars, the far windows open wide to let in a breeze and keep the room from becoming stifling with smoke.

Marco had arranged for entertainment to be brought in, something he often did. This time it was a group of five belly dancers. As they began, Marco motioned Perla to sit on his lap, and several patrons did the same with their slaves. When Mr. Douglas patted his lap I stood and sat between his spread, muscular legs. I put an arm around his neck and leaned into his chest. I sat on mens' laps all the time. It was an act of ownership for them, not to mention the sexiness of having a woman on their crotch. But like everything else with the Scot, this felt nice. Natural.

Mr. Douglas never looked at me. At one point during the seductive dance he shifted me right over his semi-hardness. His hand trailed up my hip, dipping under the silky material. It remained there, absently petting my skin, his thumb moving back and forth as he watched the women. My mind began to whirl with boyfriend/girlfriend thoughts, and I had to grit my teeth.

Even pretending such things secretly in my head was dangerous. This is what Josef was worried about. It was one thing to enjoy Mr. Douglas physically, and a whole other thing to allow any unsafe thoughts into the mix.

He feels good, I told myself. *That's all.*

When Mr. Douglas reached down and took a cigarette I picked up the lighter and lit the tip for him, something I'd been trained to do for patrons. That's when our eyes met.

Oh, my gosh. I needed to breathe. The intensity there was unlike anything I'd ever seen. It was startling. So much more than lust was going on behind those dark blue eyes. He looked away, dragging in a breath and blowing a plume of dark smoke to the side. My hand shook as I set the lighter on the table. The clanking caused Marco to look over at me and I gave him a quick, small smile of apology, dropping my eyes.

I needed to stop shaking. I focused on Mr. Douglas's hand, trying not to let the allure of the Middle Eastern music and my own crazy thoughts sweep me away. He held his cigarette in that sexy, manly way, between thumb and middle finger. His lips as they went around the filter made me tingle between my legs. I shifted and he gripped my hip as if to stop me from stimulating him further.

The dance ended and everyone clapped politely. One man got up, clearly aroused, and left with Jin. Another dance began, the music mournful and sultry. Mr. Douglas made no move to get up. He seemed happy to sit there song after song, touching my skin, kissing my neck, but mostly staring at the dancers with far-away eyes, as if lost in thought. I wondered if he was day dreaming about his next painting.

People came and went from the room, but Marco and Mr. Douglas remained. I couldn't help but notice the look of peace and contentment on Perla's face as she sat on Marco's lap, her long, slim legs crossed, and her fingers in the back of his hair.

Across the room the Italian man was sitting with his slave on her hands and knees next to him. He was fingering her roughly from behind. Her eyes were closed and her forehead creased with discomfort. My stomach churned and I looked away. Any second he'd be on his knees behind her. I was so thankful that wasn't me, but I couldn't help but empathize.

I snuggled even closer to Mr. Douglas and then wondered if I'd done wrong, because he abruptly stood, catching me around the waist. I dropped to the floor in kneeling position.

"I think I'll have a walk," Mr. Douglas said to Marco. "I thank you for allowing me such beautiful company. I'll see you at dinner."

"Until then," Marco said with an incline of his head.

"Come," Mr. Douglas said to me.

I crawled at his side as he strolled through the house. He stopped to admire every piece of artwork he passed. It started to feel like he was purposely wasting time. He'd chosen me, but he was making no rush to get me alone. In fact, so much time passed that we were back in the dining room for dinner without ever having made it to Mr. Douglas's bedroom.

Paranoia rose up inside me. Why wasn't he making use of me? This was unknown territory, and I didn't know how to take it. What was I doing wrong? I felt scared, like at any second he would change his mind and ask for a different slave. It's not like he wasn't a sexual man. So what was the problem?

I felt like I'd somehow failed to entice him enough. I wanted to be wanted by him, and that was a rare, overwhelming feeling. To be denied was a sting of rejection. My head hung low, and I accepted morsels of tender scallops and seared tuna without joy.

After dinner I followed him back to his room.

"Make yourself comfortable on the bed," he said to me.

As I climbed up into the downy comfort he went on his balcony for a cigarette. I lay in the middle on my back with one knee up. When he entered the room he didn't even look at me; just strode right past into the bathroom. I heard the shower come on and I felt completely dejected.

Were all artistic people this confusing?

I lay where I was without moving until he came back in the room. My head turned and my breath caught at the sight of the towel around his waist, and the fact that it was slowly rising as the hardening length of his arousal became apparent.

I made the mistake of looking in his eyes again. Why did he seem so at odds? Almost...pissed off?

I desperately wanted to wipe the menacing look from his face. I slipped from the bed onto my knees and crawled forward, stopping in front of him to give him full access to me, but letting him have the first move, as always. *Please want me.*

He gave the towel around his waist a tug and let it fall to the floor alongside my fears, because it was pretty safe to say he wanted me.

"Señor," I whispered, staring at the solid beauty of his body.

"Stand up," he commanded. I lifted myself to stand in front of him, staring at his chest.

He moved forward and pulled the silky material down my shoulder, placing his hot mouth against my neck. I cried out and reached down, wrapping my hand as far around his cock as I could. The sound of his deep groan gave me shivers. He grasped my wrists and pinned them behind my back, devouring the skin at my neck and shoulder, nipping my collarbone, running his warm tongue down the trail of my jaw. My chest rose and fell rapidly.

In a quick motion he was on the bed, grabbing me around the waist, lifting me, and pulling me to straddle his face. He shoved the material of my dress up and held it around my hips.

Oh, yes. His tongue delved into my core, all hot softness, and he squeezed my thighs as I moved against him. I circled my hips so that I felt the scruff of his chin against my most tender parts, then the sensitive nub of my clit. When I vocalized my pleasure, he lifted my hips and spun me to face the rest of his body in a sixty-nine position. The dress pooled silkily around my waist.

I immediately went down, taking as much of him as possible in my hands and mouth. He groaned loudly against my thighs and raised his hips to meet the bobbing of my head. Then his attention went back to his mouth on me. I squirmed a little when he reached up and kissed the bud of my anus, flicking his tongue against that dreaded hole, and shocking me by sending a delicious throb up into my belly.

His mouth ventured back down and attached over my clit, sucking and flicking at the button of nerves as I moaned, taking him deeper, pushing his head to slide against the back of my throat as I kept my hands squeezing and pumping at his base. All at once we were both crying out, tensing, pleasure rippling through our joined bodies. His hot come shot into my mouth and I swallowed the waves as they came.

I was so sensitive, quivering deep inside in a way that told me I could come again and again if he were to be inside me. But he made no attempt. His body went lax beneath me.

I climbed off him and kept my distance. It wasn't unheard of for a patron to want to cuddle, or fall against me like a pillow, but most of them didn't want to be touched afterward. I prepared myself to ask the dreaded question of whether I should stay or go, but Mr. Douglas spoke first.

He lay there breathing hard, his eyes closed, hands on his abdomen. "You will stay with me tonight. Aye?"

"Sí, Señor," I whispered. Inside I was jubilant. I allowed myself to lay back, momentarily spent, and closed my eyes.

A moment later I heard him say, "Don't move."

I stayed still, but cracked my eyelids. He was staring down at me, a sort of wild look in his eyes. His gaze raked me up and down, and he slid quickly off the bed, rushing to his easel and propping up a blank canvas.

Was he going to paint me? Goose bumps sprang to life across my skin. The thought of his artistic eyes all over me…immortalizing me. Shit. It made me want to cry. Standing there naked, he practically fumbled the paints in his hurry to get them open, as if the sight of me would somehow disappear. I tried to imagine myself. My hips were twisted, one knee falling across the other. The loose silk of my black dress was around my stomach. It still clung to one shoulder, but drooped lower on the other side around my elbow, revealing one taut breast. One of my hands was draped over my waist, and the other was lazily flung over my head. My hair was pretty much everywhere. The silver-gray covers were bunched up around me. But he seemed to be seeing so much more than all that, and that's what made me emotional.

I swallowed it down and lay very still, letting this strange, confusing, alluring man paint me.

CHAPTER TWENTY-TWO

Colin

She was fucking extraordinary.

Colin hadn't come to the villa seeking a muse, although that had been the ruse. He hadn't expected to experience any true inspiration. It was a fucking job. But every moment there, every moment with this girl, was a surprise. This place dug into his depths and unearthed urges and emotions he never allowed to surface. He felt it all here. With her.

His hand stilled on the canvas as he watched her eyes flutter closed, and with a jolt she opened them again. Shite...how long had he been at it? Hours?

"Close your eyes," he ordered her. "Rest."

She complied, immediately falling into a deep breathing pattern. Awhile later she shifted in her sleep, but that was okay, because every detail was engrained in his mind. Every curve, angle, shadow, and color. At some point during the night he finished. His eyes were drooping as he climbed into the bed. When he pushed back the covers Angela must have felt the movement because she wiggled and burrowed under as well. Colin flicked off the light and they both slept soundly with a sliver of moonlight spilling over them through the balcony door.

It wasn't the sun that woke Colin the next morning. It was Angela's soft, perfect arse nuzzling against his morning wood under the soft sheets. His sleepy eyes cracked open to find the girl still half-asleep, her eyes closed. She moaned, feeling for his hand, finding it, and pulling it over her breast. When he squeezed it must have fully woken her because she gasped in alarm and tried to turn, saying, "Lo siento, Señor!" What the hell was she apologizing for? Her forwardness? Colin felt a stab of anger at anyone who'd be such a prick.

"Shh, lassie, I don't mind."

The look of fear subsided from her face and he pulled her back against his chest again. Now it was his turn to moan, rocking his hips against her crack as they spooned. He kneaded her breast in his palm and felt her nipple harden inside his hand. She reached back and found his cock, making him hiss.

When she moved her hips so as to take him inside her, Colin panicked.

"Fuck," he groaned. He let her keep stroking him, but he pulled her arse against his balls and reached around, finding her soaking wet center. *"Fuuuck,"* he moaned again. She moved against his hand and he knew she needed him. But he couldn't. He just *couldn't*. Not under these circumstances. Not unless there was no other way.

He pushed two fingers inside her and felt her whole body constrict around him at the contact. She let out a guttural cry of ecstasy and he adjusted his body to have better access. Pushing his fingers even deeper, he curled them against her tight walls, stroking in and out, rubbing her pulsing button with his thumb. Her hand tightened over his cock, squeezing him to the point of fucking pain. He growled, loving it, and Angela gave a shout that morphed into a long moan. Her body bucked and shook with the waves of her orgasm.

Bloody fucking gorgeous.

But she wasn't about to leave him unsatisfied. As soon as he released her she rolled and straddled him. Her drooping silk dress and the sheets tangled around them hid their actions from view. Angela made a reach for his dick and he grabbed her wrists, locking them at her sides. He shifted himself so she was comfortably seated atop the length of his erection. A split second of something like hurt or confusion passed across the girl's face before Colin growled, "Ride me."

They moved together, her arms still not allowed to participate. She looked so beautiful, her hair disheveled from sleep. Wild. Lines from the sheets still creased her chest. Colin pulled both her wrists into one of his hands so he could reach up and cup her exposed breast. He tweaked her nipple, adoring how she reacted positively and erotically to every action.

Because she has to, ya fuckwad, his conscience corrected him.

Could she really be faking it? Was she trained that well? Or did she truly take her pleasure every time she was with a man? The thought made him squeeze her breast harder than he meant and she cried out in pain, the sound whimpering into a moan.

How similar the sounds of pain and pleasure, Colin thought.

She began to move like crazy on top of him, sliding up and down the length of him, squeezing with her thighs.

Ah, fuck me, Colin thought. She looked like she was going to come again. So beautiful, the way her eyebrows came together and her lips parted with the effort of breathing. And sure enough, her panting turned to gasps and she pressed harder against his shaft, vocalizing every sensation as it rocked through her small body. Colin wished like fuck he was deep inside her to feel those throbs surrounding his cock.

He'd never come close to wanting to fuck anyone as badly as he wanted Angela at that moment.

The second she was done he bucked his hips, lifting her, and giving her body a gentle shove downward. She took his cue like a pro and went down, engulfing his thick head in her mouth and swallowing every drop.

When she was done she slid off the bed and went into that fucking kneeling position. But then her eyes caught sight of the canvas and she did a double take, staring at it. Colin watched as her eyes widened, sliding over the image, her mouth slightly agape. He held his breath, wondering what she thought of the way he'd depicted her.

He was nervous all of a sudden. Colin Douglas, who never gave a flying shite what anyone thought, was practically breaking a sweat. Her eyes seemed to drink it in, and he envisioned the scene of the portrait as she gazed.

He'd painted her skin a creamy richness with golden hues. Her face had been at an angle which thwarted any facial features that would have made her recognizable in the picture. Everything about her in the painting was supple. Glowing. Sensual. And then there were her surroundings. The dark bedding was painted in slashes of grays and black. Dangerous. The headboard was a dark, ominous thing looming over her. The bedposts were like sharp daggers. Every rough thing surrounding her glorious image was at odds with her softness. Like an angel caught in hell.

As he stared at her, staring at the painting, a crimson blush rose up her chest and throat, coloring her cheeks. Her eyes moved to his with something akin to shock, and she dropped her head when she caught him looking.

"Puedo ser excusada para ir a limpiarme, Señor?" she asked in a small voice.

"Um..." Damn it. He wished she'd speak English because his Spanish wasn't the best. He thought she was asking to be excused. So she could wash up? "Yes."

She stood, adjusting the dress's fabric down over her arse and up to her shoulders, then left him with her head still lowered.

The second she was gone a heaviness settled on his chest. He missed her. He didn't like not having her in his sight.

Colin lay back heavily, running his palm roughly over his short hair. He was exhausted, both physically and mentally. That painting had taken a lot out of him, and then this morning...the way she'd seemed to need him inside her.

He couldn't do this much longer. And if he was being honest with himself, the things he was doing with her made him just as guilty as sex would have, but he just couldn't bring himself to take full advantage of her. At this point he didn't know if it was for her future benefit or his own. Her parents had basically hired him to save her, and here he was enjoying the fuck out of their enslaved daughter. Wishing he could have more.

The thought made him want to vomit.

He rolled out of bed and took a scalding shower. Then fell back into the sheets and slept restlessly until after lunch. He woke with Angela's sweet, feminine scent around him.

Immediately, he became hard.

And his stomach growled.

Hungry and horny. Fucking fantastic.

It was one thing to be turned on by the girl when she was right in front of him, but craving her when she was out of sight was not acceptable.

Still, he wondered where she was now. Marco knew he preferred her. He wouldn't have leant her to that Italian bastard before he had to leave today, would he? Colin sat straight up in bed, his heart hammering at the thought of that arsehole touching her.

Easy, laddie, he told himself, but he couldn't seem to calm. His chest constricted and his skin flushed as something shifted and changed inside him. Marco had no right to give her to another man.

No right? Ha. Colin scrubbed his face with his hand and fought back an ironic laugh as reality hit him.

Somewhere along the line in these few short days he'd stopped thinking of Angela as Marco's, and started thinking of the girl as *his*. His to protect. His to save. His to...pleasure. The very idea that another man could have his hands on her at that moment had him climbing out of bed and throwing on clothes, pissed off and ready to beat some serious arse into the ground.

Christ Almighty. Colin was right fucked.

CHAPTER TWENTY-THREE

Angel

———◆◆◆———

That painting...

Oh, God, that painting. It was all I could think of as I lay on my small bed listening to Mia hum a European folk song as she played solitaire at the table.

Mr. Douglas's image had detonated some kind of bomb inside me, hitting every nerve and conjuring every emotion. I was a mess. The painting was like a nightmare—vivid in its terror, and in the midst of it all had been me. Beautiful.

He thought I was beautiful. Not just a sex object or toy. Nobody at the villa had ever made me feel that way except Josef, but he was my friend. Mr. Douglas had depicted me as soulful. Alive.

And I felt it.

It'd been so long since I felt alive. It almost hurt to feel that way in a place like this, where I had no chance of acting on it. I was a caged animal with a will to live fully. I'd worked hard to kill that will, because it did nothing but hurt me to feel that way in here.

Why was he doing this to me? Part of me felt angry at his insensitivity. How dare he paint me like that, drudging up old hopes and wishes, when it was only a short matter of time before he'd leave me and possibly never return?

Stop! There I went again, thinking as if Mr. Douglas saw me as anything other than a slave. Less than human. Which he couldn't possibly. He was only seeing me with his artist's eye. I was over-thinking the whole painting.

My feelings were all over the place.

Josef came in the room, his hair a mess. Must've been an active morning for him. He grinned at me and stripped naked. He was so cute. Marco kept him lean by not feeding him enough and not letting him work out with weights, which made Josef appear younger. He looked like a teen when he was actually in his mid-twenties. He came over and squatted next to me, running a hand over my forehead.

"You feeling okay?" he asked in Spanish.

I nodded. He frowned, obviously able to tell I was lying. The press of his lips together showed me he wanted to say something—ask something, but he couldn't.

"Patrons..." he said, searching for the words. "They come and go. Our time with some is more significant than others. We enjoy the better ones while we can, and then we must let them go."

"I know," I whispered. He was right, and I could always count on Josef. But his words stung my eyes.

He ran a hand through my hair, which appeared bright yellow-gold against his tanned skin.

"You are to put on a bathing suit, sunhat, and sunglasses and be at the ready in case Señor Douglas asks for you. He is at the pool. You are being permitted in the lounging area. We will go together once I'm showered."

My heart soared, but I held back any response other than a nod before he stood and strolled to the bathroom.

The lounging area was a screened in porch, of sorts, overlooking the pool. It was full of Marco's imported flowers from around the world. It was the closest I was ever allowed to being outside, because by standing at the back of the lounging area I couldn't see the ocean, therefore people on the ocean couldn't see me.

I went to the closet and put on my red and gold bikini. I swiped red lipstick on, then divided my hair into two low pigtails that lay over the front of my shoulders. A floppy, black sunhat and Hollywood sunglasses finished me off. Josef came over with his hair dripping. I grabbed a towel and patted it dry. He liked allowing us girls to take care of him. He stood still, even closed his eyes, while I ran the brush through his silky black hair. He thanked me with a kiss to the cheek, then put on a tiny black speedo, his package filling it to the max. And we were ready to go. Mia blew us both a kiss.

Luis was waiting to escort us. When we entered the lounging room he directed me straight back to the cushioned swing, and I sat obediently. The *twang* of a Spanish guitar and *swish* of maracas sailed up to us from the live music playing poolside. Josef went to the screened door and looked at Luis, who nodded for him to go. Josef disappeared through the door and down the set of stone steps to the pool. I had a perfect view of the pool from where I sat.

My eyes immediately found Mr. Douglas sipping something brown on ice—probably scotch—under an umbrella with Marco. My heart warmed at the sight of him in his sunglasses, and I had to scold myself.

A cloud moved and a streak of sunlight filtered into the lounging area. It was muted from the screens, but still so lovely. I needed it on my skin. I kicked off my high heels and stretched my legs out, letting the warm streak of light fall across my feet. I smiled to myself. *Hello sunshine, old friend.* I felt like I was doing something forbidden, stealing this moment with the sun. I looked up at Luis who gave me an uninterested glance. I turned my attention back to my feet, wiggling my toes.

Down by the pool Marco called Perla over as a salsa tune began. She was an excellent salsa dancer, and Marco loved to show her off. He must have told her to dance, because she began to move, smiling at Marco and Mr. Douglas in turn. Marco watched her with adoring ownership. Mr. Douglas was harder to read whenever he was in a group setting like this. His lips were tilted up, kind of like a smile, but not. He didn't come across as rude, necessarily, but contemplative, as if his mind were always elsewhere. His surroundings seemed to only mildly amuse him.

As the song ended Mr. Douglas and the surrounding patrons clapped for Perla, who shyly took her place kneeling at Marco's side. Someone must have come in through the veranda entrance because Marco smiled and stood. A short, thin man with a black ponytail came in and was greeted warmly by Marco. A blonde slave in a white minidress went to her knees and assumed the kneeling position when her master stopped to talk. She was as tall as her master. Probably European. Her hair nearly touched her ass. I felt kind of jealous of that hair. I liked mine, but I'd never been able to grow it out like that.

Marco motioned to the girl and they seemed to be talking about her. Maybe she was new. I didn't recognize the patron. And then Marco was adding Mr. Douglas to the conversation. All three men laughed. I wished I could hear what they were saying.

Another of Marco's men came into the sunroom, Paulo. He was usually in charge of me when Luis wasn't around. The two of them started talking and I wished they'd be quiet so I could concentrate, not that I could hear anything anyway. Luis asked Paulo how newlywed life was, and then made a comment about Paulo's fine young piece of ass wife and her sassy mouth. I held back an eye roll when Paulo started talking about how he pounded her into submission every night, and blah, blah, blah. Both men were cracking up laughing, being as vulgar as possible to impress one another.

I turned my attention back to Mr. Douglas, scooting to the far edge of the padded swing to get the best view possible. And then my stomach turned. The blonde slave was standing now, and moving between Mr. Douglas's legs. He looked her over, giving a series of slow nods while Marco talked, I assumed asking him questions of what he thought of the girl.

I sat up taller.

No.

The girl was moving to sit on his lap.

No!

A frantic, nauseating jealousy rose up, choking me. She was sitting on his lap, looking far too pleased at the close-up of his handsome face. One of her lithe hands was around his shoulder and the other trailed up and down the middle of his chest.

I stood, moving closer.

When Mr. Douglas moved her mane of hair over her shoulder as if to get a better look, I reached for the screen door handle. My heart was pounding a distraught rhythm and my skin felt feverish. I became possessed by an impulsive urge to go down there and remind them that I was supposed to be the one taking care of him. I was here, ready to be called on, just as my master had asked of me. Had Marco forgotten? I could just remind him.

I wasn't in my right mind when I peeked behind me and found the two bodyguards in their own conversational world, clueless that I'd ever do anything as foolish as I was about to do. But in my desperate mind at that moment it made sense. I pulled open the door and rushed down the steps on my bare feet.

The sun hit my face. A strong ocean breeze blew my hat off, over the rocks and down the cliffside. I didn't care.

"Maestro!" I called out to Marco. "Estoy aquí!" *Master,*

I'm here.

The shouts of Luis and Paulo sounded behind me, and for one moment I felt elated when Marco and Mr. Douglas turned and saw me. Now they remembered! But Marco's look of confusion quickly turned to anger, and Mr. Douglas's look of shock quickly turned to apprehension. He stood, practically tossing the slave girl off his lap.

Luis barreled into me from behind, lifting me off my feet and running with me toward the house. I struggled against him at first, wanting him to put me down so I could explain. But by the time we hit the cool shade of the indoors my madness had cleared, swiftly replaced by a shameful horror at what I'd done.

Luis dropped me to the floor where I banged my knee and cowered backward against the wall. Trembling began as multiple pairs of feet rushed in, voices raised, Marco asking Luis what the hell was going on. Everyone from the pool seemed to cram into the room to witness the spectacle I'd caused.

I was shaking so hard. What had I done? What had I *done?* I wanted to bury myself in the floor as the shouts rang out above me. I flattened myself in a ball, pressing my face between my knees. And then someone had a handful of my hair and was yanking my head upward. Luis.

"Answer him!" he shouted.

Marco stood in front of me, his hands behind his back, that woeful look of disappointment on his face. I could only whimper because I hadn't heard the question.

"Lo siento," I whispered.

"My Angel." His voice was calm, so calm. "I don't know what you were thinking, but this is your gravest disobedience to me yet."

I swallowed hard and my eyes slipped to Mr. Douglas next to him. His jaw was set as if he were the one angered and scared. Did he think I was a bad girl now? I didn't want him to think that. I was good. I'd been good so long.

I found Josef in the door's entrance. The sheer fear and sadness on his face made a single sob bubble up from my chest and a tear spilled over.

Marco stepped forward and smacked me across the face.

I gasped. He hadn't hit me very hard, but a scorching flare of pain reverberated from my cheek and through my whole body. It was guilt. I had let him down.

"You will be whipped."

I nodded, fighting back tears. It'd been so long since I had the urge to cry, and it was hard to hold back.

"Your actions have also forfeited your prized possession," he said coldly.

My prized...? Oh, no.

"No, Maestro," I whispered. "Por favor, no." Luis yanked my head again to shush me. My chin quivered.

"Sí, Angel, sí," Marco said in a low voice. "I was hoping it would not come to this, but you have pushed me too far this time."

Who would do it?

The air was buzzing with excitement. All around us were hungry eyes.

"What is her prized possession, Señor?" the wiry, short man asked with far too much enthusiasm.

Marco stared at me for what felt like forever, building the tension in the room.

"Her anal virginity."

Oohs and *ahs* and sniggers of enthusiasm rose up throughout the room. I shut my eyes, placing my palms on the floor to steady myself as dizziness took over. My insides quaked with icy fear, spreading to outward tremors.

And then a low, clear, Scottish voice rang out above the

din of whispers.

"I'll do it, Señor." The room hushed and every set of eyes turned toward Mr. Douglas's serious face as he addressed Marco. "Allow me to punish her."

CHAPTER TWENTY-FOUR

He didn't know what the hell'd gotten into him, but there was no way he was allowing any of these idiots to beat Angela on his watch, or let them get their dicks anywhere near her arse. He stared at Marco, waiting for his response, ready and more than willing to fight if it came to that. His muscles were tense and his neck was tight.

He could see Marco was unsure. Contemplating.

"I'll pay," Colin said. Fuck, he was desperate not to let anyone hurt her. Even if it meant he would have to hurt her himself. He knew he'd be a hell of a lot gentler than these shitebags.

Finally, Marco nodded and said, "Very well. Perla, take the girl and prepare her. Mr. Douglas, follow me."

Colin felt the tension deflate from his body, only to return when he realized what the fuck he'd just volunteered for. He forced himself to follow Marco and not look back at Angela.

What had happened to make her come running down the stairs like that? Colin replayed the events, but came up confused.

He and Marco had been discussing his most recent

painting. And then that wee man showed up with his Russian slave girl, and Marco thought it'd be "interesting" to experiment. Marco wondered if it was his Angel who was truly inspiring Colin, or if any beautiful blonde would do the trick. Colin played along, allowing the Russian to sit on his lap. And then Angela was running at them like mad. In fucking pigtails. At first he'd thought she was running *from* the guard Luis, but then it seemed as if she were running to Marco. Or maybe himself.

What could possibly be so important that she'd break an enormous rule and put herself in a punishable position?

Marco opened the solid doors to a darkened room. Not just dark from lack of light, but dark from every wall and the ceiling being black, and...holy Mary...

Colin was no prude, but this room gave him a bit of the fucking creeps, followed closely by the swelling of his cock. Like everything else in this villa, he had dueling feelings—pushing and pulling inside him. Repulsion and curiosity.

He stepped in and watched as Marco moved around the space, running his hand over a hanging whip, then a cane. He stopped next to a rounded *thing* Colin could only imagine someone being bent over, and he turned to face him.

"Have you ever punished a female, Señor Douglas?"

"Ah." Colin cleared his throat. "No, Señor Ruiz. I have not."

Marco's lip quirked up and he cocked his head. "Which of these fine instruments can you envision yourself using?"

"Actually...I was thinking more along the lines of a good old fashioned hard spanking." He held up his hand.

Marco paused, then began chuckling, which quickly turned to an infectious laughter. Even the two stone faced bodyguards behind them laughed. Colin smirked, wondering how much of a fool he was making of himself, but Marco came over and patted his shoulder, giving it a hard squeeze and pointing at him.

"I like you, Señor Douglas. You are what they call a breath of fresh air around here."

Colin grinned, but kept himself guarded as Marco continued.

"You never did get to tell me if my amigo's lovely Russian girl could provide inspiration for you?"

Colin thought about lying, but his candid truths are what seemed to have earned Marco's trust thus far. Marco was the type of man who could probably smell bullshit the second it left someone's mouth. Slowly, with care, Colin shook his head. "Your Angel is the only female who has been able to do that for quite some time."

Marco's voice was soft, contemplative. "So, she's your muse, then?"

"It seems so."

"And you're willing to punish her?"

"I am if she needs to learn a lesson that will keep her safe." Colin felt a nudge of intuition, urging him forward. "Although I'm curious...as to why she is the only slave not permitted outdoors."

Marco pursed his lips, looked to the side, and was silent for a few moments. Colin wondered if he'd pushed too far, but he needed to appear as if he didn't know the truth.

"My Angel," Marco began, "is special. She came to me in a rather unexpected way, and I've had to keep her protected from those who would threaten to steal her. No one can know she's here."

Colin's blood pumped harder with the heat of indignation, but he continued to play his part. "I see."

"Do you? Because it's often difficult for *me* to see when it comes to Angel."

Was that guilt Colin heard in Marco's voice? Well, his

guilt was a worthless commodity seeing as Angela was still held captive, so Colin wasn't about to soften his stance against the bastard.

Marco cleared his throat as if he'd said too much. "Are you certain you won't use an instrument? As far as our punishments go, hand spankings are not...conventional."

Shite. "Unless you're opposed, I'm quite certain. If it's all the same to you."

"Your hand," Marco said with a chuckle. "Twenty strikes should be enough. I trust you to teach her a lesson she'll never forget."

"One I'll never forget, as well, I'm sure," Colin said with reluctance, but Marco laughed and cupped his shoulder again.

"The first punishment is always one to be remembered. And if you enjoy dominating in such a way, you'll crave that feeling the rest of your days."

Trepidation and ecstasy intertwined up Colin's spine. He cleared his throat.

"Where is the punishment to take place?"

Marco opened a hand toward the room. "In here." Then he looked at Colin and chuckled once again. "Ah, Señor, you have a romantic artist's heart. Would you prefer your room?"

Colin knew Marco would be watching no matter which room of the villa they were in, so if he was offering a more comfortable place than this cold torture chamber, Colin would accept. "Yes. The room would suite me better, I think."

Marco nodded.

"I'll have the girl delivered to you once she's been prepared. As I said, this will be her first true anal experience. She's quite frightened by the prospect, so you may meet some resistance." Marco paused, holding Colin's eyes.

"Take her by force, if you must."

A dark thrill shot straight to Colin's crotch and he was so angry at himself for feeling it that he couldn't speak.

Good God...could he really go through with this? Then again, he didn't have any options for getting out of it. Anal sex would not be easy to fake.

Marco kept going. "Although I hardly doubt it will come to that. She seems more than willing to enjoy every moment she can with you." Half of Marco's mouth lifted.

"Is that...out of the ordinary?"

Marco chuckled. "It is, indeed. Angel is good at what she does, but she has not warmed to it the way I'd hoped. Until you showed."

When Marco cocked a complimentary eyebrow, Colin responded with a grin, because that's how a stupid cunt should react. But inside he was overheating. He was good at calling bluffs, and Marco seemed to be telling the truth. The thought of Angela hating every second of her life here, but putting on a show for these men...and then the idea that she had warmed to him. That she enjoyed him. He liked that thought.

"Thank you," Colin said, sticking out his hand. Marco clasped it and they shook.

"Thank *you,* Señor Douglas. This works out well. If anyone can open her eyes to the wonders of her own body, it's you." They released hands. "It would be helpful if you could get her to tell you why she behaved as she did."

Colin nodded. He intended to find out.

"Oh, and one more thing...don't let her come."

Colin froze at that. He couldn't imagine that the girl would be aroused considering she feared what was to come, but he nodded again.

He left Marco and headed to his room, feeling partly nervous like a virginal fucking laddie, and partly ill with dread. Under normal circumstances he'd be thrilled at the prospect of anal sex. This, however, was anything but normal. She fucking cried when Marco told her what was happening. And then he'd hit her. Only a small cuff to the cheek for effect, but it still made Colin want to come out of his skin and strangle the fuckface.

Who used anal sex as a punishment? Had he been holding her anal virginity over her head the whole time she'd been here? Sick fucking bastard.

By the time Colin got to his room he was pacing with anger at the entire situation. He rubbed a hand over his face, then over his head. What the fuck was he going to do? He was in far over his head here. He'd never planned to touch the girl, much less be her first sexual anything. And was he really going to whip her? With his own hand? Bloody hell!

The worst part—the part that made him want to die a painful death—was that he couldn't deny the excitement he felt underneath all the anger and apprehension and guilt. He wanted to touch her again, in any form. And he couldn't get it out of his head that she might like it, as well.

As if that excused any of it. Yes, it would fucking blow if she was appalled by him—if she hadn't "warmed" to him. But it was still wrong, no matter how he tried to spin it. Colin feared he'd go to his grave with the sins of this week staining his soul. And the worst had yet to pass.

A knock on the door signaled the worst was about to begin.

When he opened the door Angela was naked with her head down, her arm being held by Luis. She was still in those damned sexy pigtails, and her hands were tied at the wrist in front of herself. She was trembling and pale. Luis released her and gave Colin a nod.

"Go in," Colin told the girl. She shuffled past him and he closed the door. Angela went to the middle of the room and gingerly lowered to her knees. He had a perfect view of her from behind, and his eyes went straight to her rounded arse and the sparkling, large crystal nestled between those perfect cheeks.

What the fuck?

It took him a moment to realize she'd been plugged. And ah, God, if that didn't go straight to his cock. He supposed that's what they meant by "preparing" her. Probably gave her an enema too, knowing how thorough Marco was about the cleanliness of his people. Colin slowly walked around her. He propped one hip on the side of the small bed and looked down at her.

"Tell me what happened outside today."

Angela jumped when he spoke, but she didn't look up at him. She most likely wouldn't unless he told her to.

When she opened her mouth she spoke in Spanish. "My master called on me to be ready, and so I was. I was waiting to be of service…and then…"

A shudder passed over her and she seemed to shrink herself smaller. The sight squeezed at his chest. He didn't want her to be afraid of him. He knew it was necessary to the moment, but it fucking killed him.

"And then what?" he prompted.

"And then…I saw…" her voice went a little raspy with fear. "I saw another servant girl with you." Colin struggled to understand each word she said as she went on quickly, her voice quaking in Spanish. "And I wanted to be sure my Master knew I was there…if I was needed."

Heat poured over Colin and his mouth opened, but no sound came out.

She'd seen him with another girl and been jealous.

Holy fucking shite. He hadn't seen that coming. Something overcame him then—a softness like feathers falling in his chest. He refused to open himself to it. He couldn't afford to be soft for anyone in his life. Especially not now.

He rubbed his face and then cleared his throat.

"You knew you shouldn't have come down there. You knew you were breaking your master's rule."

Her jaw trembled and she nodded. Part of him was pissed off that she'd been so impulsive, putting them both in this situation. He felt like a right arse for being frustrated at her actions. She'd been driven by emotion, and emotions were dangerous, flimsy things. Look where it had landed them. For that moment, he allowed himself to give in to that feeling of frustration. He would need that mood to get him through what was to come next.

"Stand up and come to me."

His heart pounded as she stood on shaking legs and walked forward. She still hadn't lifted her head. With two fingers, Colin motioned her closer until she stood directly between his legs.

"Look at me," he said on impulse.

When she lifted her eyes and their gazes met he wanted to backpedal, tell her to look away again. It was too intimate. She was too real, too full of emotion. Too close.

"You understand why you're being punished?" His voice was low.

"Sí, Señor," she whispered.

He motioned with his chin toward his leg that was resting partially on the bed.

"Bend over."

He heard her light breathing go ragged as she reached out and placed her bound hands on the bed, nestling her lower stomach against his thigh. In truth, he was struggling to contain his own breathing. Seeing her splayed out at his mercy sent fucking endorphins marathoning through his body and straight to his head.

She sucked in a breath and tensed when one of his hands rested on her lower back to hold her in place, and the other hand circled the soft, creamy skin at the bottom of one arse cheek. He raised his hand and brought it down with a loud *smack*. Angela gasped and tensed again. His second slap landed in the same spot on the other side. He methodically worked his way from the bottom up, one side after the other, trying not to hit the same direct spot more than once.

Colin couldn't deny the primal sense of power he felt dispersing punishment to someone at his mercy. Someone meek and gorgeous who knew he had control and didn't try to fight it.

Angela was a good, quiet girl for the first ten strikes. She panted and shut her eyes. Her forehead creased in discomfort, but she made no noise.

When the eleventh *smack* sounded she let out her first whimper. Colin knew it must have hurt, because his hand was stinging. The skin on her arse had blossomed red in response to each strike, and Colin found the series of marks strangely beautiful. But what was even more surprising was the way the twelfth slap elicited a pained moan, and he could have sworn her hips arched against his thigh. As if she were turned on.

He'd been at half-mast the entire spanking, but the feel of her rubbing herself nearly made his cock punch through his shorts. He stretched his hand, flexing his fingers and making a fist several times. And then raised it again.

CHAPTER TWENTY-FIVE

Angel

Smack.

Ah, shit, shit, shit, that hurt!

I was done holding back. I let myself vocalize the pain. Breathing through my teeth like an animal. There just comes a certain point where the body takes over the mind, and I was there. In so many ways.

I was still in blissful shock that Mr. Douglas had stepped up to punish me. Maybe that made him the biggest, dirtiest creeper of all—that he'd volunteered so quickly and eagerly with a possessive passion in his eyes, but I couldn't bring myself to care. I was so thankful it was him. And even though I was in pain, it was nothing like the belt beating. Being across Mr. Douglas's strong lap...knowing it was his hand causing the sensations across my ass...feeling him hardening against my hip...

So grateful.

I'd stopped wondering what it was about this man that made me so crazy. I'd stopped trying to fight all the insane feelings I had, and gave myself permission to just fucking let go and enjoy it. Every second. He could be gone tomorrow, but for now, he was with me. And now that I'd finally let go of my thoughts I was able to enjoy not just this unconventional closeness with him, but also what he was doing to me. The feel of his hand meeting my skin.

Spanking me.

Smack.

Another holler rang from my throat, turning into a moan, because damn it...every time he hit me, the plug would sort of vibrate inside of me. It was pressing against sensitive places. I was getting wet from being beaten.

The idea was enough to make me laugh. Until the fourteenth *smack* sang against my sensitized cheek. The fifteenth was the hardest yet, and I yelled from the sheer pain as my eyes stung with tears I refused to shed.

Sixteen and seventeen came in quick, simultaneous strikes. He was so hard against my hip. I rubbed myself shamelessly against him now, caught between pain and a build up to pleasure. He groaned, and the sound reverberated through me, stilling me. I think maybe I pissed him off or something because the last three smacks rained down hard, right in the middle of my ass above the plug. I threw back my head and yelled from the shocking, blissful pain of it, and then I collapsed over his thigh, my head falling to my joined hands, breathing hard.

My ass was absolutely on fire. My crotch was wet and throbbing. My eyes burned. My head was a messy fog.

And then I felt his fingers at the plug, slowly twisting it. I moaned, too spent to move yet. My breathing quickened when he began to gently pull and the thick part popped out. The rest slid out easily and he tossed it to the floor. In my peripheral I could see him looking at my ass. He could probably see my swollen pussy, as well. What would he think of me? I felt suddenly ashamed, like I shouldn't have been turned on.

"Fuck me," he whispered in that low voice. "You are so wet." He sounded amazed, in a good way. Relief chased away my shame. I was glad he noticed, and I hoped he'd take care of me like he always did. But his hand never ventured down there. Instead, they focused solely on my ass.

"On the bed," he said, lifting my hips to help me. I crawled up. Mr. Douglas stripped himself of his clothes, and once again I was struck hard at the overall sight of him.

He pulled back the heavy comforter and lifted the sheet for me to climb under. His face looked tense. I didn't know him well enough to read him, but I swore I saw something like worry there. Sudden fear jolted through me. He wanted to keep a sheet over us.

Somehow, I just knew he wasn't going to fuck me. He wouldn't force me to have anal sex. The thought should have made me happy, but it didn't. Not at all. It made me panic.

After today, I knew without a doubt I'd be expected to do this on a regular basis. That meant whatever disgusting douchebag wanted to bang my ass next would actually end up being my first.

Ah, hell no. If anyone was going to be my first, it would be Mr. Douglas.

I reached for the sheet in his hand and threw it back alongside the comforter at the bottom of the bed. Mr. Douglas's shocked look was almost comical...until it suddenly wasn't. Because now he looked just plain angry, and it scared me. The thing was, he knew that I knew what he'd been trying to do. He knew that I was attempting to thwart his plan not to fuck me.

He knew I wanted him.

I shrunk back with my bound hands in my lap, lowering my eyes in shame and fear.

"Lo siento, Señor..." I mumbled to him that I was hot, but that if he wanted the sheet I would pull it back up. I braced myself for a smack to the face, the common punishment for doing something that displeased a patron, but it never came.

Instead he said something completely unexpected.

"To start, I want you on top."

A thrill shot through me as he sat against the headboard and motioned me toward him. His face was not happy. Again, I couldn't read him, but I knew instinctually that he didn't want this. You'd never know it from the size of his rock hard cock. But his manhood and his face were telling conflicting stories.

Still, I scooted forward until I was close enough to swing a leg over his lap. Nerves began to set in. This was really happening. He grabbed lube from the bedside table and put it on himself. He was beautiful to watch, even with that pinched expression that looked like he could punch a hole through the wall at any minute.

Or fuck a woman really hard.

He reached around me to rub lube around the bud of my anus and my ass cheeks. I closed my eyes as he pushed two fingers in, circling them, trying to gently stretch me. It didn't hurt too bad after having the plug in. When he pulled his fingers out I opened my eyes. Our faces were close and our eyes met. His expression softened and he lifted my hips, pulling me nearer. I came up on my knees and positioned myself over top of him. He held himself at the base. I let the sides of my bound hands rest against his chest, wishing I was untied so I could hold his shoulders.

My heart rate rocketed when I felt the head of his penis at my entrance. Maybe it wouldn't be too bad. The butt plug only stung a little. But the second he gave my hips a tug downward over the head of his cock I screamed.

Oh, my God! It hurt so bad. How did people do this? He was *way* bigger than the plug. I closed my eyes, feeling scared now and breathing too hard.

"Shh." Colin was holding my hips tightly. I opened my eyes and found him watching me. In those blue depths I thought I saw an understanding. He wasn't going to force himself in. Maybe that's why he'd chosen for me to be on top. So I could control the pace.

I pushed myself down a tiny bit further and cried out again, panting. Every millimeter felt like a fucking inch. But I found that my body adjusted quickly, the pain waning into a comfortable throb. On my next downward push his head slid into my ass with a *snap* and we both moaned.

"Christ alive, woman, that is fucking tight." His eyebrows were knit together.

I pushed a little more. Slowly, very slowly, I worked my way down until his entire cock was in my ass, impaling me in the most painfully delicious way possible. I sat on the base of him, and as my body adjusted, the heat returned. I lifted myself and the sensation of sliding up his shaft was like nothing I'd ever experienced. It was as if I could feel every tiny ounce of his hardness against the tight ring of my ass. Nerve endings that had never had the pleasure of being rubbed were massaged by his thick length inside me.

I was wet all over again, and desperate to really ride him. Mr. Douglas stilled my hips when I tried to move against him. He slipped a hand behind my neck and pulled my face to his, kissing me hard and deep. I kissed him back, overcome by it all. Then he broke away, his eyes boring into me.

"Little Angel..." he breathed. "I'm going to fuck you now."

My heart about stopped.

All at once I was crying out as he lifted me off him and flipped me onto my hands and knees, positioning himself behind me. He thrust his entire cock into my ass, making me scream with the pleasure and pain of our rejoined bodies. It hurt in the best way. Then he proceeded to pound me, growling words in his Scottish accent that didn't even sound like English, but I made out a lot of "fucks." I could hardly keep myself upright from the force of his thrusts. Oh, God, it felt so good. I never expected this to feel like this. I was so close to coming. If he were to touch my clit even the slightest bit I'd see stars.

But he never touched me. When my arms began to give out, he pushed my head down to the bed to rest on my hands. Moments later his groaning lowered and he grasped my hips harder, pushing as deep as he could.

"Ah, fuck yes, lassie, that's it..." He stilled, his hands tightening on me, and I knew he was about to come as his words stretched into a low, primal rumble from the back of his throat. I moaned at the glorious feeling of his orgasm inside me. I could feel every pump of him.

When he was done he slowly pulled out and moved to sit on the edge of the bed. We were both out of breath, damp with sweat. My body tingled with a need that verged on painful. I waited for him to turn to me, touch me. But he didn't.

Staring at the wall, he said in a deadened voice, "You may go."

For one second I was stunned. Then I got my act together and silently climbed from the bed. It took all my willpower not to look back as I went to the door. Shit, I couldn't even walk right after all that'd just happened.

I'd been a fool to think he was anything more than an average patron wanting to use me. I'd never been used quite so well. Or left feeling quite so dirty.

Luis was waiting for me in the hall. I was surprised when he led me toward the hallway with the video monitoring room. He opened the door and ushered me inside. Marco was sitting alone at the monitor, running a hand over his mustache with a contemplative look. I raised my eyes to the screen he watched. Mr. Douglas was laying naked on his bed with a forearm across his eyes. Without looking at me, Marco spoke in Spanish.

"Was your punishment satisfactory?"

What kind of question was that? One I could only answer in one way.

"Yes, Master."

"Are you in pain?"

My ass cheeks stung like hell and my asshole was thrumming from its beating.

"Yes, Master."

"Good."

He stood now, and stalked over to me, walking me backward until I hit the wall. He turned me around and ran a gentle hand over my ass. Then he turned me to face him and pulled out both of my ponytail holders. He shoved one of his hands deep into my loose hair and fisted it, forcing my face up to his.

"Who is your master, Angel?"

"You are," I breathed.

Holding my hair tighter, his other hand cupped my sex and I moaned.

"You were jealous? Of a patron?"

I was too terrified to make a sound.

"Answer me!"

"Yes! I'm sorry, Master."

"I'm not sure your punishment was enough. I think you enjoyed it too much."

"No. No, Master. Please."

"Did you come for him? This man you broke my rule for? Eh?"

"No!"

His fingers worked me in a fast circle, pressing upward with hard pressure.

"Come for me now, Angel, if you want to spare yourself."

His anger frightened me and excited me, because he rarely displayed his full power over me. I embraced that excitement and leftover lust, and focused on the contrast of his rough hand against my softness. I came hard, bucking into his hand, still feeling the effects of Mr. Douglas inside my ass as my muscles clenched. But I wasn't allowed to imagine him right now. Marco made sure of that. He kept his face close to mine, forcing my eyes to stay on him as he milked my body for every tremor until I finally stilled.

"Never disobey me again, Angel."

"Never again, Master."

"Never allow your emotions to get in the way of my rules and your role."

"I won't, Master. I swear."

He kissed my forehead and released me to leave.

CHAPTER TWENTY-SIX

Colin sent Angela away unsatisfied, just as Marco had requested. It had gutted him. Colin disliked Marco before, but now he hated that manipulative bastard with a murderous intensity.

He knew it'd be dangerous to try and fake it, but after being told she was terrified of anal sex, it tore at his fucking heart. And taking her by force? Fuck that. However, what he'd seen in Angela's eyes when she'd thrown back the sheet was not what he'd expected at all. For a second she'd looked like a little vixen, daring him to fuck her, and that deep, dark part of himself connected with that naughty girl— wanted to say to her, "Thank you, I think I will."

Marco hadn't forced him. Nobody had forced Colin. He could have fought Luis for his weapon when he'd shown up, grabbed the girl, and made a run for it, guns blazing.

And then end up dead, along with Angela.

No, he'd had to take her up on her silent dare at that point. And for whatever reason, she'd wanted him to give it to her. He couldn't deny he'd wanted that as well. What made him hate Marco was that he instinctually felt the man knew things. It's like he saw into Colin's soul and wound his dirty finger around his darkest threads, tugging those lude deSires forward.

Almost like Marco was training Colin to be like himself. The master he wanted to be, deep down. To have power and control over a delicate piece of flesh like Angela—to use her however he wanted, whenever he wanted...

Fuck, man, get ahold of your bloody thoughts, he scolded himself.

An image of his brother Graham flitted into his mind. The true image of slavery. Graham had been an outward visualization of how slavery rotted a person's central being. Everything at the villa was gorgeous, but underneath Angela's healthy demeanor, was she as broken as Graham?

Colin felt like he was suffocating. He needed to move—breathe fresh air. He stood and dressed, then headed from his room to wander the estate. It was time to formalize a plan to escape from this paradise. He couldn't stand to be there a minute more. Voices filtered down the hall from the direction of the dining area, but Colin wasn't feeling sociable.

He went out to the veranda and lit a cigarette, surveying the entire area with care. Two boats were docked at the end of the steps. Colin was running different scenarios through his mind when he heard footsteps behind him. He turned his head to see Marco approaching, one of his henchmen watching them from the rounded doorway.

Marco stopped a few feet away with his hands behind his back.

"And how did it go, Señor?"

As if you don't know, Colin thought.

"It went well, I think." Yeah, Colin was not in the mood for small talk. He was in the mood for face punching.

"Good. Very good. I spoke to her and she was appropriately contrite." Marco joined him at the stone wall, and they stood together staring out at the magnificent sea.

"You seem lost in your thoughts this evening. That is understandable, considering all of your new experiences this week."

Colin gave a slow nod. "It has been a week of firsts, that's for certain."

An idea had begun to form. What he needed was to get Marco alone, away from the villa. It was time to work this man.

Colin inclined his head toward the large and small yachts. "Fine boats you have there."

"Ever been yachting, Señor Douglas?"

"No," Colin lied. "But I imagine fucking at sea is a pleasure."

"That it is." Marco looked up at the darkening sky. "How much longer do you plan to stay with us?"

"Only a day more, unfortunately. I need to get back to the gallery." Colin's pulse was thumping wildly under his skin as he waited, hoping for an opening of some sort.

Marco turned his back to the ledge and crossed his arms. "How about a boat ride in the morning? You, me, two of the girls—Angel of course."

Colin held back a celebratory grin. "Sounds fantastic."

A small smile lifted the edges of Marco's mustache. Colin realized the man probably had an ulterior motive, just like he did. Something was on his mind, though Colin couldn't figure out what. He'd have to be on his guard. He held out his hand and Marco shook it.

"You are a generous man, Señor Ruiz. I cannot thank you enough."

"I assure you, the pleasure has been mine."

Hm. What was this sneaky fucker up to?

Marco left Colin as he stubbed out his cigarette in a nearby tall ashtray, and lit another. His brain went on overdrive, playing out possible situations for tomorrow. He wondered how many men Marco would bring for protection. Every detail was important.

He spent the rest of the evening devising multiple plans based on the many possibilities, until he felt a surge of confidence.

Tomorrow was the day.

◆·┃·◆·┃·◆

The bodyguard Luis was waiting for Colin outside his door the next morning, ready to escort him to the smaller boat. It was a bright morning. Colin slid his sunglasses into place and ran a hand over his freshly shaven jaw as they boarded. Marco was waiting for him at a table under a shaded overhang at the boat's rear. Colin's heart banged when he spotted the two slave girls kneeling at his sides in bathing suits and oversized sun hats. It took him a moment to recognize Angela, and he had to smile as he walked over.

Her blonde hair was hidden under a shoulder-length black wig. It was high quality, and paired with the hat, she was quite stunning. Her skin was pale and creamy, contrasting with the bronzed glow of Perla's. Though Angela's head was down, Colin caught the look of complete contentment on her face. It made his breath catch, and his chest swell. He wondered how a girl in her predicament could find that kind of peace when he never could.

He sat across from Marco and admired the breakfast spread.

"Coffee?" Marco asked.

"Please."

Marco nodded down at Angela, who came up on her knees to pour both men steaming black coffee from a porcelain carafe before returning to a kneeling position.

As the boat pushed off, the men ate in comfort,

occasionally feeding their women bites of fresh berries and pineapple. Colin lounged, but his eyes took in everything. As far as he could see, only one bodyguard was with them. Luis stood to the side with his arms crossed. And then there was the captain driving the boat. He waited for others to appear from below, but none did. Was it possible that he'd earned this suspicious man's trust?

Marco didn't appear to be armed. Luis had two visible guns at his waist. He spied ropes for various uses on the vessel, and an emergency ax in a glass compartment. All things he could use if needed.

When they finished eating, Perla and Angela cleared the table. The boat moved at a pleasant speed, causing just enough warm wind to encompass them.

Marco stood and led them to the bough of the boat, overlooking the glimmering blue-green waters. Colin watched him sit on the white cushions and pull Perla to his lap. Her hands ran through the back of his hair and down over his shoulders. Colin pointed to the corner seat of the cushions and Angela obediently sat. He nestled himself between her legs with his back to her chest, and was rewarded with the feel of her calves as they wrapped around his hips. He leaned lazily back against her as if he owned her.

As if she were his.

That thought went straight to his cock and he swallowed hard. He needed to concentrate on the task at hand, but she addled his fucking brain. Because if he was being honest with himself, he wanted her. He wanted every day with her, to learn her, to feel her, to make her happy.

Fuck.

He'd never felt that for a woman, and this was definitely not the time to start. She wasn't his and she never would be. This was a game. A job.

When Colin turned his head, he caught that same look of ease on Angela's face as she held the top of her hat one with one hand and stroked up and down his shoulder and bicep with the other. She stared out at the Mediterranean. Colin tried to memorize her like that so he could paint this image someday—her black hair and all.

Marco rested his hands behind his head and leaned back, eyeing Colin as if he had something to say. Colin waited patiently, and it paid off.

"What will you do without your muse when you return to work, Señor Douglas?"

Colin stared off, pretending to contemplate.

"Be miserable and uninspired, I suppose." He grinned, and Marco returned the expression. "This week has been enlightening, Mr. Ruiz. With your permission, I wish to be frank with you."

Marco nodded, his eyes gleaming with interest.

"If I may be so bold…" Colin hesitated, mostly for show, but his gut was jittery as hell. "How does one go about obtaining a slave?" At this, Marco raised his brow. Colin continued, unfazed. "If you cannot say, I understand. I'm certain such a purchase would be quite expensive, but I've learned that some things are worth the money."

"Indeed." He steepled his fingers over his chest. "Taking a slave is a lot of work, Señor. Great care and maintenance of their bodies and minds. They must be kept busy. An idle slave brings trouble. You must be willing to punish and train them diligently to earn their loyalty." Colin nodded, and Marco went on. "You would need to find a network of other slave owners wherever you decide to settle. It's best if you're not the only one using your slave, because the females tend to grow jealousies, which lead to problems. In my early days when I was too green to know how to properly train, I had to trade and sell slaves who couldn't control their emotions."

Slaves had human emotions. Imagine that.

Colin watched the slave on Marco's lap, Perla, as she stared sadly down at the water.

"Mr. Ruiz." Colin chose each word carefully. "I'm at a time of my life where I have the means to obtain anything I want, except a woman who will meet my expectations. I didn't think such a thing was possible until now. After spending time in your company, I realize I'm more than willing to make the necessary changes to have the lifestyle I want."

"The lifestyle you *deserve*," Marco crooned.

"Yes." Colin's skin buzzed, making him hyper aware of everything around him. The sunshine on his skin. The way Angela had gone rigid behind him, as if listening intently. Marco's fierce stare, as if figuring out if Colin had what it took to be a slave owner. The way Luis had inched closer. In that moment, Colin was ready to do this. The man was humoring him, and it was time to move this forward.

"What do I need to do to make this happen?"

"I can put you in contact with my people," Marco said carefully.

This was happening. It was almost too simple. Colin had learned that if something seemed too good to be true, it was. How far could he push this?

Colin sat forward on the edge of his seat, forcing Angel's beautiful legs from around him. He rested his elbows on his knees and linked his fingers as he stared straight into Marco's dark eyes. He knew what he was about to do was a long shot, but if it worked it would be fucking brilliant.

"I want to buy your Angel. I will pay any price."

Silence. Even the air seemed to still.

He felt Angela's frame jump ever so slightly. Marco made no move, nor did he change his nonchalant expression.

Without looking away from Colin he said, "Angel, venga aquí."

Angela pulled herself away from Colin and went to Marco, kneeling at his feet with her head down. Marco lifted Angela's chin and spoke to her in English, probably for Colin's benefit.

"Would you like a new master, little one?"

Colin could hardly breathe. He could see her trembling under the weight of Marco's mind game. He clenched and unclenched his fist.

"No se, Maestro," she whispered. *I don't know, Master.*

"Come, come, Angel," Marco crooned. "Be truthful. Can you be loyal to Señor Douglas? Can you love him as a master the way you could never love me?"

Marco stroked her cheek, and she didn't answer. She looked terrified. Colin was itching to intervene—to stop the man's mental torture, but he had to let it play out. If he could complete this mission without raising suspicion, and without bloodshed, it would bring both himself and Angela a measure of safety afterward. Nobody would search for them if they thought he was another legitimate slave owner. He would fall off their radar. It would be worth it.

Marco sat back and gave his attention to Colin again. "One of the most difficult lessons I had to learn as a slave owner was to share my toys. It's the only way to desensitize slaves...and their owners. I learned the hard way that my own actions and selfish deSires were hindering my slaves from understanding their role. Do you understand what I'm saying, Señor?"

Colin could only nod, because he didn't like the direction this was going.

"I've not done right by Angel," Marco said, looking down on the girl. "Her role, in relation to me, was not made clear enough. I had my own issues and regrets when it came to her, and my softness hindered her loyalty. Confused her."

What the fuck was he going on about?

"Would you believe me, Señor Douglas, if I told you I've never even fucked the girl myself?"

Actually, this did surprise Colin, but his insides heated with hatred at the man's attitude of goodwill. Marco Ruiz was the devil underneath. The tempter and tester. A bejeweled serpent. But that wasn't how he saw himself at all, was it?

"Is that so?" Colin forced himself to ask. "You've been missing out, Mr. Ruiz."

The words were sour on his tongue. As was Marco's saintly expression. Colin sensed an obstacle coming. If he could keep his emotions and anger in check, he could pass this last fucking test, exchange money, and get Angela out of Spain by nightfall.

"Angel," Marco said. "Kneel beside Señor Douglas."

Colin's blood pounded hot and hard as Angela moved to his side, never looking up.

"Perla." Marco moved the girl from his lap to stand, and spoke to her in Spanish. "Pleasure the Señor for Angel to see."

It took Colin a few seconds for the words to crash down. *Ah, fuck me.* Fuck, fuck, fuck.

Colin felt heavy. He didn't want to fucking do this. And yet, he made no move to stop the latin beauty as she unbuttoned his cargo shorts.

"Watch, Angel," Marco commanded, and her head snapped up.

Perla worked his semi-hard cock in her hand until he was fully erect. When her mouth came down over him and Colin moaned, Angela's eyes flicked up to his face long enough for their eyes to briefly meet.

What he saw there made him groan with lust. Angela's eyes were filled with the fire of jealousy.

Colin pulled Perla's head down further onto his shaft, signaling her to move faster and deeper. All the while he watched Angela's eyes on them, and he imagined it was her mouth around him. The way her small nostrils flared with anger was fucking hot. Colin couldn't hold back from touching her, but he knew he couldn't be gentle, so he let out his beast, embracing it one last time.

His hand gripped the back of Angela's neck, forcing her face up to his.

"Do you wish it was your mouth I was fucking?" Colin asked.

Angela whimpered and closed her eyes.

His hand tightened, forcing her to cry out, "Sí!"

"Do you wish to be owned by me, Angel?"

Her eyes opened now, hitting him in a hot wave before she dropped them to the sight of his blow job. In a quieter voice she answered, "Sí, Señor."

Marco chuckled, enjoying the fucking show, no doubt.

Colin released Angela to focus on the ministrations of Perla, and soon he was arching his back and blowing his load into the woman's throat. He felt satiated and perverted as hell. Guilt kept him from looking at Angela as he tucked himself back into his shorts.

And then Marco spoke. "Angel, Perla. Aquí."

In that moment the world seemed to slow and stop as Marco motioned Perla to his side, and Angela between his legs. Colin could feel Marco's eyes on him as Angela's sweet hands were pulling out the man's stiff, sad excuse for a cock.

He wanted to vomit when her lips wrapped around the other man's purpled head. Colin's orgasm should have calmed him, but he wanted to break shit and wrap his bare hands around Marco's neck. Then pound his stupid, smug fucking face. Colin must have appeared enraged because he saw Luis's hand move to rest on his gun. The bodyguard was watching him closely.

"It is hard to share, Señor, is it not?" Marco said lazily, his hands rubbing Angela's shoulders, while he eyed Colin with interest. "Try to remember it is for her benefit, to keep her in line and remind her of her place."

Marco hissed and closed his eyes as Angela picked up the pace. Colin envisioned himself tearing Angela away and killing Marco a hundred different ways. Violent and bloody.

Just as his entire body was twitching to jump up and rip his fucking head off, Marco's hips jutted upward and he let out a series of short moans. Angela finished him off and sat back on her heels. Marco put his puny shit away, then he got serious.

"Perla, take Angel below deck."

Colin braced himself, senses alert. The girls hurried away with their heads down, and Luis moved closer. Marco's eyes bore into Colin and he rubbed his palms together. The man appeared almost nervous now.

"Señor Douglas, you should be warned that Angel has been a difficult acquisition. She has never lost her sense of self the way a proper slave should. You see…" He cleared his throat, upping the dramatic effect. "Angel is from the U.S., and people are actively searching for her, even now."

Marco raised an eyebrow and Colin forced his face to slacken in surprise as he said, "I can see how that would make things difficult."

"Yes. Worst of all, she is still a willful American at heart. We keep her under tight supervision because I would not put it past her to try and escape or make herself known. I'm not sure I would entrust such a liability to a first time owner…especially if she can be tracked back to me."

And there's the fucking rub.

"That's a valid concern," Colin said, running his hand back and forth over his jaw in thought. "However, secrecy is of the upmost importance to me, Mr. Ruiz. The vast majority of my culture would come after me with pitchforks if they found out I was keeping a slave. I would need to have a room of my home outfitted for her safekeeping. I'm prepared to discipline her."

"If anyone were to ever find out," Marco said. "I don't know you. We have never met."

Colin gave the man a slow, understanding nod.

Was this really happening? Was Marco considering selling her? Fuck, maybe that'd been his plan all along when he found out she was Colin's "muse." Did he hope to rid himself of the burden of the American girl? After all he'd been through that week, he wanted to laugh.

"I will take our association to the grave, Mr. Ruiz."

Marco nodded. "I believe that about you."

"Name your price," Colin said. "A muse like Angela will cause my business to boom..."

Marco tensed and his eyes went hard. Colin was slow to realize his mistake.

He'd called her Angela. Marco had never referred to her as anything but Angel.

From the corner of his eye he saw Luis going for his gun. Colin embraced the burst of adrenaline that came with the following moments of chaos. Colin launched himself from his seat toward the bodyguard, shoving him against the stern of the boat. He heard Marco shout, maybe calling for the captain. Momentarily distracted, Colin took a jab to the abdomen before head-butting the bodyguard, kneeing him in the gut, and hearing his gun clatter to their feet and slide across the deck.

Colin blocked Luis's sloppy throws, relishing the sound

of the man's pained grunts each time his fists landed, quick and hard, pushing him toward the stern. From the corner of his eye he saw Marco reaching for the fallen gun at their feet. Colin kicked him in the jaw and watched the fucker fly back. It landed him a punch to the skull, but it was worth it.

Luis's knuckle split, gaping, from his punch, and he howled. Stupid fuck. Never hit a man's head with your bare knuckles. Colin ran at him, ramming his shoulder upward into Luis's gut and lifting him off his feet. In a clean sweep, the bodyguard flew over the stern, grasping at the rail and yelling as he looked down at the wash of water caused by the giant propellers. Colin leaned over and snatched the second gun from the man's waist, and then slammed the butt down on Luis's fingers.

The man fell, his garbled holler swallowed up as the rush of water sucked him in with a series of sickening thuds.

Colin turned to take care of Marco and found himself too late. The other man had managed to get his hands on the gun, and he was scrambling backward, trying to point the thing at him.

Colin dove into the near hallway, hearing the bang and whir of a shot fired past him. From the ground, he took aim and fired, celebrating internally when he heard Marco yell, throwing his head back and grabbing his shattered knee with one hand.

"Drop the fucking gun or you're dead," Colin said.

The bloody bastard shot again, clipping Colin's shoulder. Fuck, that stung, and now he was livid. He pumped two more rounds from his awkward angle, shooting Marco in the shoulder and arm.

Marco dropped the gun and fumbled to hold his shoulder and leg. Colin jumped to his feet and stood over the man, kicking the second gun away.

"Señor Ruiz?" called a male voice over a speaker.

Shite. The captain.

"Tell him you're okay!" Colin whisper-hissed to Marco, the gun barrel at his temple. "In English."

Through panting breaths, Marco called out, "I am fine."

A sense of calming resolve seemed to have settled over the man as he stared up at Colin. "FBI?"

"I work alone." Colin's gun never wavered from Marco's face.

"It's not too late," Marco said. "Whoever sent you...whoever paid you...they never have to know. They can think you died, and the girl can be yours."

For the briefest moment Colin allowed himself to imagine it. Marco's eyes were shining with the knowledge that he was calling forth another man's demons.

Colin punched him in the jaw, throwing the man's head to the side and causing him to go even more limp.

"Don't you fucking look at me like that."

Even with all Colin had been through, he'd never been much for murder—he'd injured many, but only killed when the only other option was to be killed himself. He hadn't wished for a person's death and suffering this badly since he'd hunted his family's murderers and Graham's kidnappers. His finger tightened on the trigger just as a shrill scream pierced the air.

Colin turned his head to see Perla at the top of the steps, covering her mouth with a shaking hand. Angela peeked around her side with gaping eyes.

"Master!" A choking sob tumbled from Perla as she took in the sight of Marco's bloodied body and Colin's gun. Her eyes darted around, probably searching for Luis, and when she didn't find him she yelled in panic again. Colin looked back at the man at his feet.

"Tell her to shut her fucking mouth," he said through gritted teeth.

"Silencio, Perla," Marco commanded, his breaths coming short.

She continued to cry, she and Angela gripping one another by the arms.

Colin ignored them and spoke quietly. "I'm here to take back what was never yours to begin with. The girl is going to disappear. And so am I."

Marco's voice was a weak, but wicked rasp. "My people...will hunt you."

Colin's shoved the barrel against Marco's forehead. "If any of your fucking goons come near her, I will be the one hunting *them* and slicing off their worthless balls while they sleep. Then I'll burn your palace to the fucking ground. Your reign is over."

"Don't kill him!" Perla wailed. "Por favor! No, no, no."

"Shh," Angela pulled her close, staring at Colin in fearful confusion.

Ah, fuck. He had no time for crying women.

Marco chuckled at Colin's hesitation to finish him off, or perhaps it was simply madness from blood loss since there was a nice pool of crimson around him. But his laughter turned into a choking sound as the man fought to breathe.

It was time to end this.

CHAPTER TWENTY-SEVEN

When Marco had first sent us away to talk business with Mr. Douglas, I thought I'd tumble down the stairs, but Perla grasped my shaking hand. I was near tears by the time she pulled me into a bedroom and took my face.

"Will he let him buy me?" I whispered in Spanish. I couldn't help the way a sound of hope rose in my voice.

"Listen to me," Perla said, more serious than I'd ever heard her. "And listen well. It is good and acceptable for a slave to love their master, but you must know, Angel. Your master will never love you in the same way. Never. You heard what Master said. Señor Douglas will share you with other men, just as he did today. He will take other slaves and women in front of you, just as he did today. You must prepare your heart and mind for all of this. There will come a day when you are aging, and he replaces you with another. Do you understand?"

Her words hit me like a steamroller as I imagined it. Was that how Perla felt every day of her life?

"Do you love Master?" I whispered.

Her eyes flitted closed and her words were a breath of fervent emotion. "He is my first and only love. Everything I do is to please him. And each day he takes me to his bed I am thankful."

My heart hurt. Could I be like Perla? A loving, loyal slave who took each day, moment by moment, knowing it could never last? Could I take her advice and not become bitter in the process? I didn't know if I could. I wasn't wired that way.

A banging sound like something hitting the side of the boat and yells came from above. Perla grabbed my arm and we watched each other, becoming still.

What the hell was going on up there?

Another yell, sounded like Luis. I sucked in a breath and felt my eyes widen with the rush of fear coursing through me. A feeling of danger punctuated the air.

Oh, my God...was this turning into a business deal gone bad? Were they going to kill Mr. Douglas? A panicked dread spread its fingers through me, and like a lovesick fool I made a move for the stairs. Perla's fingers dug into my arm, holding me in a vise grip.

"You cannot interrupt!"

And then a gunshot rang out, making us both jump. More shots followed, and I heard Marco yell in anguish. Now it was Perla's turn to gasp and run to the stairs. I took off after her, my heart banging in my throat.

What I saw at the top made the world seem to stop. Marco, shot and bleeding on the white deck, his blood a crimson shock to my eyes. Mr. Douglas standing over him with a gun pointed at his head. Luis nowhere in sight.

Holy fucking shit. He was really going to kill him.

I didn't know how to feel. Mr. Douglas could be a psychopath for all I knew, though deep down I didn't really believe that, but it was hard to know what feelings to trust. When Perla cried out, begging for Marco's life, the indecisive look of regret in Mr. Douglas's eyes made all of my distrust for him fall away.

And still, for some reason, the thought of watching Marco be killed sickened me. I thought about how angry he'd been at his son for raping me and kidnapping me. How he'd pampered me and only punished me when I broke serious rules. How he'd protected me in many ways, never forcing me to be his lover until today, and only as a way to "teach" Mr. Douglas.

"No." It left me as a whimper.

Mr. Douglas swung his head toward me, a look of astonished surprise on his face. "After all he's done, you don't want to see him dead?"

"I..." *Do I?* "No." *But he made you a slave.* "I don't know!"

"No, no!" Perla begged. "Por favor, tell him no!" She fell into my arms and hid her face.

Marco would die. Even now his eyes were rolling back, and his hold against his wound was loosening. If left unattended he would bleed to death like an animal. I couldn't help the pity I felt at seeing this man of power brought so low.

Mr. Douglas raised his arm and slammed the butt of the gun against the side of Marco's head, knocking him out cold. Perla and I jumped, and she wailed.

Mr. Douglas grabbed Marco by the ankles, dragging him across the deck and down the stairs. Perla wouldn't leave his side, so she ended up cuffed to a bed next to Marco, gagged.

Mr. Douglas turned to me and I shrunk back, shaking my head. I didn't want to be handcuffed or tied up and locked away. He gave me a shake of his head and gripped my arm, pulling me out of the room.

"I'm not going to hurt you, little lassie. Come on."

He sounded genuine enough, but my insides still

slithered with fear as he pulled me up the stairs and commanded me to sit. I was too scared to ask questions. He worked fast. I watched as he grabbed rope, keeping a gun in one hand. He made his way down the small hall to the navigational area. The captain threw his hands up, backing away.

"Take us to the nearest port," Mr. Douglas said. "Now. You will not use your radio for any reason. When we arrive you will be tied. I won't kill you unless I have to. One wrong move and you're dead. Comprende?"

The frightened man nodded his head. Mr. Douglas motioned to the panel, telling the man to hurry. I sat against the wall, my legs pulled up to my chest.

"Do you have clothes to change into?" Mr. Douglas called to me.

"N-no, Señor."

He cursed.

He watched the captain closely as he navigated us to land, and I sat there bombarded with thoughts.

How quickly life could change.

That morning I'd been beyond thrilled when Perla told me we were going out to sea with Marco and Mr. Douglas. It'd been years since I was allowed to enjoy the sun and fresh air. All of my anger and negativity from the night before had shed from me like a heavy coat. I'd wanted to hug Marco and thank him.

The sun had felt glorious on my skin. After everything I'd been through the past two years, it was ridiculous to think of a boat ride as a vacation, but that's how it felt. Being fed fruit at the hand of Mr. Douglas had been a wonderful start. Without looking up, I'd caught glances of his legs and hips, his forearms and fingers. And I imagined how well he'd used all of them on me last night.

Only he'd sent me away, hadn't he?

I didn't want to think about that. I didn't want to think at all. All I wanted to was to enjoy the moments of pleasure as they presented themselves. In that moment on the boat, with the bright sun and warm wind, I hadn't a single worry or complaint.

I was usually good at drowning out business conversations. They were a bore. But I found myself paying attention to everything where Mr. Douglas was concerned. When he brought up buying a slave I was consumed with jealousy. On the verge of throwing-up. Then the way Marco talked about us, like training dogs or circus animals. That was what I'd become. An entertaining animal. The conversation rolled through me, churning my stomach with sadness and regret for all that was lost.

That quickly, all of my happy feelings disappeared as I realized how easily replaceable I was to men like Marco and Mr. Douglas. My life would have been so much easier if I could get rid of that deep nagging voice that told me I could be special to someone.

I wasn't special.

That's something mothers and fathers told their children when they thought they were safe. When they had free will and open futures. Just another fairy tale from a previous life.

And then. I couldn't believe my ears. My heart had rammed so hard in my chest I could hardly hear the rest over the whooshing in my ears.

He wanted to buy me.

He wanted me.

Me.

That desperation to be needed and wanted sprouted and grew vibrant petals. I should have felt pathetic for my gratefulness in that moment—disgusted at the way these men discussed my life like a transaction—but I couldn't help it. I was so happy. A life as Mr. Douglas's slave would be different. I wanted to please him in a way I'd never cared about pleasing anyone at the villa. For the first time since I'd been taken captive, I felt a desire to embrace my role because I wanted to, not out of fear. Was this how Perla and the others felt?

And once again, Marco's ability to shock was like a sting across my chest when he told Perla to pleasure Mr. Douglas, and for me to watch.

I wanted to grab Perla by the hair and tear her away. I wanted to rain down a series of vicious slaps upon Marco for making this happen. And I wanted to cry that Mr. Douglas was able to get it up for her.

I know. Stupid. I was so stupid to feel any of those things. I wished so badly that I could be a proper slave. But I was a bad slave. Life would be so much easier if I just didn't care. If I could be numb.

I was lost to these thoughts when Mr. Douglas had taken me by the neck and made me look at him. He was so strong—intense and sexy. My body reacted for him, softening, though the explosion of emotion in my chest was far from soft.

"Do you wish for me to own you, Angel?" he'd asked.

Yes. God, yes. I wanted him to own me in every way. But only me.

And then, when I thought the torture was finally over, Marco called me over to service him, talking about "sharing." I'd never touched him intimately before. For some reason the prospect upset me on multi-levels, and once I began to tremble I couldn't stop. *It's just oral sex,* I tried to tell myself, but it felt like so much more than that. Marco's hold over me—his role in my life—had become skewed and complicated. I felt as nervous and sick as I would if I had to blow my own uncle or the Texas senator. It just felt *wrong*. The moment my shaking hand went around him, and my mouth touched his flesh, his ownership over me became complete. I was not my own, or even Mr. Douglas's, unless Marco wanted me to be.

And now he was below deck, dying. Maybe dead by now. I should have been far happier about that.

When we got to the port and docked the boat, Mr. Douglas gagged the captain and tied him on the floor. The knots looked tight enough to hurt. He then reached his hand into the man's pocket and removed a cell phone, slipping it into his own pocket.

He reached toward me and I flinched in fear as his hands wrapped around my neck, then I stared in astonishment as he tossed my collar over the side of the boat into the water. I stood at his impatient motioning, my nerves completely shot, knees trembling.

This was it. He was going to take me. I was scared of my unknown future with him, but I didn't want to look back at my wretched past, either. My life was in Mr. Douglas's hands now, for better or for worse.

Together, we hurried off the yacht.

Mr. Douglas took my hand, twining our fingers together and holding tight.

"Pretend we're a couple."

His strides were long, and I walked briskly in my high heels, still trembling on the inside. I was sweating under the stupid wig and hat. I wished I could rip them off. People on the small port street were starting to look. Did they recognize us or something?

"Nos están mirando," I said under my breath.

He gave me a funny look, and I remembered he wasn't great with Spanish.

"They're staring," I whispered. It felt strange to speak English.

"Of course they are," he said through gritted teeth. "You're a beautiful woman walking down the street in a fucking bathing suit and spike heels."

Oh. I'd forgotten that kind of thing wasn't normal.

He pulled out the captain's cell phone and dialed, holding the phone to his ear. We never stopped moving. "I've got the girl. We'll need a plane stat. Contact Graham and tell him we'll all meet at his place temporarily. It's most secure. Begin the process of liquidating my assets and selling the land. I'll sign when I get there."

Who was he talking to? And why was he talking about how he'd gotten me, as if it had been a prearranged thing? He glanced around and gave our location to the person on the phone. I still had no idea what was going on, but that feather of hope that had buried itself deep inside me so long ago seemed to unfurl and spread open like tentative, atrophied wings.

We entered a busy shopping street, and Mr. Douglas steered me into a boutique on the corner.

"Thank fuck," he whispered.

"Hola," said the shop clerk girl in greeting.

"Uh, yes. Hola. We'll take one of these." He ripped a multicolored maxi dress from a hanger and thrust it at me. "Go put it on in the dressing room."

The woman's eyes widened.

On the inside I felt frantic and thoroughly confused, I didn't want any attention drawn that might lead Marco's men to us. I couldn't go back there, and I couldn't watch them kill Mr. Douglas, even if he was just another bad guy. All I wanted was to get far, far away from here.

I cleared my throat and tried to smile at the girl, though I couldn't keep the slight shake from my voice. "Estamos en nuestra luna de miel y vamos tarde para nuestro barco."

"Ahh…" Her eyes softened in understanding, but Mr. Douglas looked alarmed, which ratcheted my pulse. Did he think I would turn on him? I needed him to know I was loyal.

"I told her we're on our honeymoon and we're late for our boat," I whispered. He let out a breath. Maybe it was crazy, because I knew nothing about this man, but there was nobody else I'd rather be with in that moment. Even in my terrified state, I felt more secure at his side than I'd ever felt with Marco. When he touched the small of my back in a gently possessive way, I shivered with peace.

The girl cut the tag from the dress to ring it up while I rushed to the dressing room to slip it on. I discarded the hat, but kept the wig on.

They must have called a cab, too, because when I came out Mr. Douglas grasped my hand once again and we ran from the store, all but diving into the back seat.

"Aeropuerto," Mr. Douglas told the cabbie.

He leaned down and scanned the area around the taxi as it drove through the port town. He still hadn't let go of my hand.

I stared up at him in confusion and wonder. His eyes skipped past my face and came skidding back, blue-gray eyes latching onto mine as his whole body seemed to relax a fraction.

The way he looked at me, searching deep, made my body feel like it was somersaulting. What was it about this man? My new master. I suddenly dropped my eyes, feeling like I'd taken liberties that could get me in trouble. His hand went beneath my chin and lifted my face to his again.

"I'll explain everything soon, Angela," he whispered.

My breath stuck in my lungs as he squeezed my hand in his, and went back to surveying our surroundings.

He'd called me Angela. Not Angel.

Angela...

Was he a good guy?

I was afraid to even think it. Afraid to jinx myself. Was it possible? Had this man been sent for me? Despite my inner urges not to jump to any conclusions, the wings of hope opened inside me and soared off a precarious edge.

Flying. Free.

But I had no idea how terrifying a free fall could be. I didn't know how to land without crashing. My heart flailed, with no sense of direction, and suddenly I no longer wanted this flight of freedom. It was too scary. Oh, God...what was happening to me?

CHAPTER TWENTY-EIGHT

Colin

He didn't know if he'd ever been more relieved in his life than he was when they boarded that small jet and it took to the sky for Scotland. His heart was still beating too hard, and he wished he'd shot Marco Ruiz in the head while he had the chance, to see the man die for himself. Colin was good at disappearing, but it was more than just his own self he had to keep hidden in case Marco's men tried to find him. The Birch family was not his responsibility, and yet, as he looked down at Angela in the seat next to him, he knew he'd never be able to leave her or her parents vulnerable to those kind of powerful, evil men.

He'd make certain they found somewhere safe to rest their heads. He'd watch over them as long as they'd let him. A moment of guilt seized his gut when he thought of all he'd done to Angela at the villa. Colin wouldn't blame the girl if she wanted nothing more to do with him. And if her parents found out, they'd probably want to kill him.

He was certain they wouldn't want him around after he delivered her, and he'd have to respect that.

The problem was, he wanted to stay near her. In fact, the idea of her possible hatred toward him was fucking depressing.

He looked down at Angela again, at her perfectly manicured hands gripping the armrest. Her delicate chin pointed down to her chest. Her closed eyes. Without thought, Colin pulled the black wig from her head, causing her eyes to open wide and look up at him. Her blonde hair was a matted mess underneath, held up by bronze pins. He plucked one out. Angela reached up with trembling hands and helped him. Together they took out all the pins until her hair fell around her shoulders. Her cheeks were still pink from the excitement.

She was beautiful. Colin wanted to say so, but he didn't feel he had the right. Instead he just stared. When her eyes dropped he realized he was probably making her uncomfortable. But fuck, he couldn't seem to help himself. He wanted to say something, but the words were a right fucking jumble in his brain.

She saved him the trouble when she whispered down at her hands in her lap. "Maestro?"

She'd called him master. It made his abdomen tighten with a myriad of emotions because he loved and hated the sound of it.

"No, Angela. I'm not your master. You can look at me. And you may speak in English."

Her head was slow to tilt up, a look of fear and confusion in her eyes.

"But...then, who is my master?"

God, she sounded lost. He reached out and touched her cheek, cupped it in his hand. She didn't pull away as he feared she might.

"You are your own master now."

"I..." She shook her head. "I don't know how."

"It will take time, but you'll learn again."

She didn't seem so sure, but she dropped it and asked, "How do you know my name?"

This was where the shock would set in. For the past week she'd seen Colin as one of Marco's patrons. And now she'd learn the truth. He prayed that someday she might find it in her heart to forgive him.

"I'm an undercover Agent for the MI-6. Your parents sought our help."

"My parents." Colin barely heard the whispered words, spoken through her quivering lips. Her whole body began to shake, and she brought her hands to cover her mouth as the first of the tears began to fall.

Colin reached out to wipe the streaks away, but Angela yelped and jumped back, crouching low in the seat.

"I'm sorry!" she whispered. Her tears had dried as a look of animal fear settled on her face. Colin felt a knot in his chest as he remembered how Marco had slapped her face when she cried.

"Fuck, Angela, I'd never hit you! That is…I know I *did*, and… bloody hell, I'm sorry for that. I'm fucking sorry for it all." He was stuttering like a lad.

She was still shaking, staring at him. Her head slowly cocked to the side as if working out a puzzle in her mind. Colin could see the moment it all hit her, and his heart sank.

"You." She spoke quietly. "You're not…you didn't even want to do those things."

Colin said nothing, because he *had* wanted to do those things. Only not against her will.

She tore her eyes away and a hard shiver ripped through her body.

"I did the only things I could think of to save you." He hated the way he sounded, defending himself like a God damned bastard.

She pulled her knees to her chest and wrapped her arms around her shins, burying her face in her knees and whispering, "Oh, my God." Her breaths came in pants, like she was trying hard not to cry. "I thought you were going to own me."

"Aye. I understand if you hate me," Colin said, his voice thick. "You never have to see me again once I hand you off safely to your family."

Her head snapped up, eyes red and terror-stricken.

"You're leaving me?"

"What?" His heart jolted with hope he shouldn't have allowed himself to feel. He reached out to touch her, and she watched as he changed his mind and pulled his hand back. "No, I—"

"I'm sorry," she blurted. Her eyes filled with moisture and she wouldn't look at him. She buried her face in her knees again. "I'm sorry you had to touch me. I'm sorry you had to be there and go through all of that for me."

Her tears spilled over now and she shrunk away from him, wiping them as quickly as they fell.

"Och…" He had no idea what to fucking say. He was confused as he tried to process her words. "Angela, you've no need to apologize. I took this case willingly, and I'd do it all again to save you. I'm just…" He searched for the words—he'd always been terrible at voicing his feelings, and really he'd never had a need to do so before. "I'm sorry as fuck that I took advantage of you while you were a slave."

Finally she looked at him, her eyes wide.

"You didn't take advantage of me." She sounded surprised that he thought it, the poor wee lassie. She'd been brainwashed at the villa, and it was time to clear her of those notions, no matter how sordid it caused him to appear.

"Aye, I fucking did." Colin ground his teeth together and turned to stare out at the white clouds. He fisted his hands, and his knee bounced.

"Mr. Douglas…"

His whole body stilled when he felt her hand on his

thigh, accompanying that soft whisper of his name. Her hand moved farther in, and lust clutched him, tensing his hips, hardening his cock. He closed his eyes and grasped her slender wrist.

"My name is Colin."

"Colin."

His name in her sweet voice, like she was tasting it, completed the painful erection behind the zipper of his trousers. He shifted, but there was no hiding it.

"Let me take care of you." Her free hand cupped his hardness through the fabric, and Colin groaned, grasping that wrist, as well.

"No, Angela. You don't have to do this anymore."

"I want to."

With her wrists still being held, she swiftly moved to mount his lap, her legs on either side of him, the dress pushing up.

"Ah, fuck." He dropped her wrist and grabbed her hips to still her. When he looked in her eyes, it wasn't lust he saw. It was desperation. Sadness. Fear. Enough to shatter his hard heart.

And then she put her hands on his face and kissed him.

At the feel of her soft, persistent mouth against his, he lost control. His hands fisted in her hair and his mouth took over, owning hers. She moaned and pushed her hips down until her warm pussy was rubbing hard against him.

Her hands went to his pants, unbuttoning, unzipping.

What the fuck was he doing?

"Wait—"

"I want you," she breathed against his mouth. "Fuck me, Mr. Douglas, *please*."

"Angela." It about killed him to do it, but he reached between them and grabbed her hand.

She moved against him with renewed, desperate fervor. "Please, master, fuck me. I need you."

"Ah, shite." With swift moves he took her by the hips and lifted her off his lap, moving to stand. He felt like a sick fucker for letting it go as far as it had. "I'm not your master, Angela."

She fell to her knees and wrapped her arms around his legs, pressing her face to his thigh, and crying. "I need you to be my master. I don't know what I'm supposed to do."

"Angela..." He tried to step back, but her arms bound his legs as she repeated over and over.

"I need you. I don't know what to do."

He stood there dumbfounded and shaken as her sobs filled the cabin, the sound hammering against his heart. At a complete loss, he lowered himself to his knees with her and held her in his arms, letting her cry onto his chest.

"It'll be alright, sweet lassie. I swear to you. You'll be okay."

He had no idea if his words were helping. He was no good at calming distraught women. But she clung to him as she cried, her fingers digging into the fabric at his back, and he let her.

"I'm sorry," she sobbed. "I can't...stop crying."

"You can cry," he said. "You never have to be afraid again. I won't let them near you, I swear it."

After a moment she took a shuddering breath and asked, "Is he dead?"

"He's dead."

"And my mom and dad? They're really...oh my God. I can't believe this is happening."

"It's happening, Angela. You're free."

Another resounding wail of emotion pulled from her chest, and she shook in his arms.

"Don't leave me," she begged. "Please, don't leave."

"I won't."

He held her so tightly he worried he'd crush her, but she didn't complain. After a while the wracking tears subsided, and she breathed heavily against him. He knew she was suffering from shock, and possibly even some hero complex that made her want to keep him near. Perhaps it was selfish of him, but as long as she wanted him by her side, that's where he'd stay. Someday she would come to her senses and feel all the negative things he expected her to feel toward him. When that happened, he would leave. But for now, nobody could tear him way.

CHAPTER TWENTY-NINE

I hadn't cried like that since the day I'd been locked in the cellar at the villa over a year and a half ago. It was cleansing and renewing, but it made me tired. I leaned against Mr. Douglas—*Colin*—with my arms encircling his bicep as we sat there, realizing just how needy I was. In my freak out, I'd made a fool of myself, begging him to have sex with me. It would never happen. He was a man, yes. My touches made him hard, but he didn't want me like that. I was a job to him. He'd had plenty of opportunities and never taken them. Deep down, that fact sliced through me and stung, while also making me begrudgingly admire him.

I was certain he was humoring me now. Being kind. And I was grateful for it, but I knew it couldn't last. He would hand me over to my parents and I'd most likely never see him again.

My hold on his arm tightened and he patted my knee. So comforting.

I thought back to the moments we'd shared at the villa. All along he'd known who I was. It made sense now that he looked at me differently. Part of me wished he hadn't kissed me the way he had, or painted me as if I were beautiful to him. Maybe he'd been trying to win me over, as well as Marco, so that I wouldn't object when it was time to leave with him. Whatever the reason, I kind of wish he hadn't been such a great actor. He'd made me want him too much.

I couldn't think about him leaving me without a feeling of panic threatening. How could I ever feel safe without him? I felt pathetic and weak, wanting to keep him by my side, in my sight.

I used to have an inner-feminist who would bitch slap me at the sound of these "dependence upon a man" thoughts, but she'd been the first aspect of my personality to be murdered at the villa. I didn't know if I'd ever feel her strong, independent presence again.

An image of my mother flitted into my mind and it made my sinuses burn with rising emotion. She was strong—a Texan beauty with her short, coifed blonde hair and sunny smile. She raised me to shoot for my dreams, and to be able to support myself. Would she be ashamed to see how far I'd fallen? And what about my dad? When he found out I'd been a prostitute for drug dealers and murderers, would he be able to stomach my presence?

I wasn't their little girl anymore, and I could never go back to being her again. I would never be good enough. They'd still love me, I knew they would, but it could never be the same. Our love would be tainted by the big, ugly thing that happened to me. The lie I'd told, and my act of disobedience that ruined everything for our family.

A choking sob erupted from my throat and I bit it back, burying my face against Mr. Douglas's shoulder. He reached over and ran a hand down my arm.

"Mentí," I whispered.

He pulled away and looked at me. "What, lass?"

I stared at his chest. "I lied."

"To me?"

"My parents." My voice was thick again. "I wasn't supposed to go to Cancun."

"I'm certain that's the least of their concerns at this point." He took my hand. "Angela. I know this is not going to be easy for you, but I need to know what happened in Cancun. I need to know how you ended up with Marco Ruiz." He lifted my chin and I looked into his serious, compassionate eyes. "Can you tell me?"

I swallowed hard. My stomach squeezed in a fit of residual panic when I thought about that night. But I took a deep breath, nodded, and told Colin Douglas everything that happened. I watched his hands open and close in tight fists as I recapped Fernando's actions.

"Do you have any idea where he is, Angela?"

"Marco said he was sending him to Asia, but that was two years ago, and I haven't heard anything about him since."

His jaw moved from side to side as he stared off in thought.

"What's going to happen?" I asked.

He shook his head. "I don't know. But you don't need to worry, okay? You should try to eat something. They've usually got sandwiches and drinks—"

"No." I couldn't eat.

I shivered and he pulled me into his arms again, where I stayed for the duration of our flight.

——✦·⦙·✦——

The air in Scotland was cool that evening as we were ushered straight from the plane into the back seat of a tinted, black sedan. The driver gave a mustached grin as he stuck out his hand to Mr. Douglas.

"Agent Douglas. Well done, pal. Very well done." He sped us away from the airfield.

258

When we stopped at a light he turned and held his hand out to me. "Angela Birch? Welcome to Scotland. I'm Agent Abernathy."

I looked to Mr. Douglas, who nodded his approval before I took the man's hand, feeling skittish and out of my element at this innocent touch from a man. "Hi," I forced myself to say.

He turned back to the road and spoke as he drove. "The Birch family arrived at Graham's this afternoon. They've taken residence in Scotland for the past four months in hopes that this day would arrive."

Giant butterflies swooped inside of me and my heart slammed in my chest.

My parents. They were here and I was going to see them.

I looked up at Mr. Douglas, trying to get ahold of my breathing with a hand to my chest. He gave me a small smile.

"You'll be alright."

"No. I'm scared," I admitted, my voice sounding small. "Maybe I shouldn't...maybe we should wait. I—I need a shower."

I caught Agent Abernathy shooting Mr. Douglas a look in the rear view mirror, like he was telling him to calm me, and the pressure made my heart beat even faster. Mr. Douglas took my hand, running his thumb back and forth over the top. I wanted to enjoy that touch, but I couldn't when I knew he was only doing it because his partner silently told him to.

"Don't leave me," I said.

The other Agent's quizzical eyes went to Mr. Douglas in the mirror again, but my savior's attention was fully on me.

"I'm right here. I'm not going anywhere. The house we're going to is my brother's."

I nodded, inhaling and exhaling with care.

We ended up on a winding road over gorgeous hills and into the dip of a valley. At a black gate, Agent Abernathy entered a code and the iron gate swung open. The house looked like a grand cottage. Too large to be quaint. Too small to be ritzy. Perfect, really.

As the headlights rounded the curve and landed on the house, the door flung open and two familiar bodies came sprinting out, running at the car before the Agent could come to a stop. My heart swelled gigantic in my chest. Agent Abernathy slammed on the brakes, muttering a curse and I felt a fresh set of tears forming in the back of my eyes. My hand fumbled for the door handle and I shoved it open, stumbling out and into my mother's arms.

Our simultaneous cries rose up and filtered into the night air. I felt my father's arms come around us and his face against mine, kissing my wet cheek countless times, and whispering, *"Thank you, Lord."* Mom's hand felt my back, my arms, and she pulled away enough to look at my face.

"I knew you were alive," she whispered.

She hugged me again, so tightly it was as if our breaths depended on this closeness. She petted my hair and for a second I felt five-years-old-again.

"It's all over now, baby." I wanted to sink into her comfort, to take her every word as the gospel truth, but it wasn't all over now—not in my head, anyway. Her unconditional devotion and affection was overwhelming. I didn't deserve it. How could I have deceived this woman, who only ever wanted the best for me?

"I'm sorry I lied to you, Mama." A fresh sob sounded from my chest. "I'm sorry I went to Cancun. I'm sorry for what I put you through."

She stood straight and took my face in both hands, her voice quaking. "Don't you do that, sweetheart. No matter how you ended up in Mexico, what happened there was not your fault. You hear me?"

My face fell to her soft shoulder again, and I let her hold me, soaking in her unconditional love and forgiveness. Dad's hand smoothed down my hair and my back.

"We're going to have a fresh start now, Angie girl," he said. "We'll work through this thing together."

I nodded. My soul felt fuller than it had in ages, but it was a foreign feeling. I was scared to let myself enjoy it. Afraid it would be snatched away.

I heard Dad's footsteps crunching away and looked up to see him walking toward Mr. Douglas, who stood at the head of the car with his arms crossed. Mom fit my hand into hers and held tight as we watched.

Mr. Douglas uncrossed his arms and took Dad's outstretched hand. Hearing my daddy getting choked-up when he spoke almost made me lose it again.

"Thank you, sir. I can't thank you enough." Dad kept shaking his hand, thanking him, not letting go. Mr. Douglas looked embarrassed by Dad's profuse gratitude.

"It was my honor, Mr. Birch."

Dad then reached around and hugged Mr. Douglas's tall frame, pressing his face to his chest and slapping his back. Mr. Douglas gave him an awkward pat and looked strangely shamefaced.

Mom was next to bombard the man who'd saved me. With a series of sniffles, she released me in order to embrace him. Mr. Douglas still looked uncomfortable, but he was a good sport. Dad was quick to take Mom's place at my side, wrapping his arm around me and kissing the top of my head. I kept my eyes down, a deluge of strange emotions toppling end over end. All of the love and affection was almost too much, like an overload of rich food to my system. I didn't deserve it. I could hardly process being touched in a nonsexual way by people who wanted nothing from me except my love, which I'd tucked away so deep for so long.

I started to feel lightheaded and I tilted to the side, reaching out for the car.

"Whoa, there," Dad said, righting me by the elbow as Mom gasped.

In a flash I felt Mr. Douglas at my other side, his arm around my waist. "She hasn't eaten since this morning."

"I'm not hungry." I felt my eyes flitting closed and my body suddenly scooped up, floating.

"I'll get her inside," Mr. Douglas said.

My head was heavy on his shoulder and I let my eyes close as my body shut down and I passed out.

CHAPTER THIRTY

Colin

Colin barely slept that night. Twice he left Graham's house to walk the sprawling land and look for signs of prying eyes. It felt good to have the weight of his gun back in his hand. He regretted bringing the Birch family to his brother's home, even though nobody knew Colin and Graham were brothers except the authorities. Colin never came around, so he knew it would be safe, yet he didn't feel at ease.

He never felt completely safe in his life before this, but it was different when innocents were in possible danger, as well. He couldn't stop thinking about their reunion. He'd never seen such open, genuine love in his life. His own parents had loved him, but they hadn't been overly affectionate verbally or physically. But what the Birches had...that's how a family should be.

Angela had woken when he placed her in the guest bed, and she absolutely freaked the fuck out when Colin went to leave. It took her parents, Colin, and Abernathy to calm her and make her believe Colin would be just down the hall. Her parents had exchanged a worried look, but they didn't seem to question Angela's clinginess to Colin.

Abernathy, on the other hand, raised an eyebrow at him as they left the room, and whispered, "Got a bit deeper on the case than expected, eh, son? I wondered if it might."

Colin blinked and looked away, but Abernathy stopped him in the hall with a hand to his shoulder.

"Whatever you had to do to get her out, it was right."

Colin swallowed, clenched his jaw. He wasn't certain he'd done right at all.

Abernathy gave his shoulder a solid pat. "You're both safe, and time will heal. We'll meet tomorrow to debrief. I expect every detail." Again his eyebrow went up. He seemed to know Colin had done something at the villa he regretted.

Colin could only nod. He wasn't looking forward to that debriefing.

The night was long, and Colin's thoughts were tangled, prickly vines. Every negative emotion kept going back to Fernando Ruiz. Marco's son. The original fucking bastard who sought out a young woman to hurt her, stealing two years of her life and any sense of normalcy hereafter. He had no doubt Fernando was a serial rapist. And with Daddy's supply of money he could get away with it.

Colin didn't think he'd be able to lay his head to rest again knowing that fucker was out there alive. Probably happy. Especially if an inheritance had been left to him. If Fernando returned to the villa to take his father's place, he would become an untouchable. Colin couldn't allow that. The very thought made his muscles tense. At two AM he texted Abernathy.

See what you can dig up on Fernando Ruiz in Asia before we meet.

There was no response, but Abernathy would be on it.

At three AM Graham's stupid arse stumbled in, wasted.

"Holy fuck," he said when he saw Colin standing there. "Thought you was a fuckin' ghost, I did."

Colin glared at his brother, too thin for his tall body, hair a mop of curls, lip ring and stretched earlobes. "Do look fucking transparent?"

Graham steadied himself and tilted up his chin to peer through his hair. "Nae. S'pose not. More like a pissed off ring fighter or some shite. What you so mad about? Why're you lot usin' my place anyhow?" He stumbled past Colin to the bathroom and took a piss with the door wide open.

"I'll explain everything in the morning when you're sober. Just try to be polite to your guests. They'll only be here a few days."

Graham grunted and bumped backward into the wall.

Colin forced him to drink a tall glass of water and brush his teeth before crashing onto his bed. He allowed himself to peer down at his sleeping brother for one moment before sighing. It never got easier seeing the wreck of his younger brother's life. For years he'd tried to get his brother to dig himself out of this bottomless pit, but Graham didn't give a fuck about anything. Or so he made it seem. He didn't want this kind of future for Angela. He hoped to God she would rise up through these ashes, not fall into them.

Colin left his brother to sleep. He wasn't too worried about Graham bothering the Birches while they were here. His brother would sleep during the day and be gone during the night.

By the time everyone woke the next morning, Colin had buzzed his hair and shaved his face. He gave himself a good long stare in the mirror and swore he'd do the right thing by Angela, whatever that may be. It physically hurt in his gut to think about being without her, but he would never force himself on her or her family. He didn't think he could ever fit into a unit like that, anyhow. Although it might be...nice.

He shook his head. He needed to erase that thought from his fucking mind.

At six AM a light knock at the front door caused Colin's heart to pound. Who'd gotten through the security gate? The house was silent as he slipped from his room. He held his gun close and pulled back the edge of the curtain enough to see a tall brunette in business attire.

The head shrink. Fuck, he didn't even have a shirt on. He'd forgotten Abernathy said he was sending someone.

Colin opened the door. The woman's bland expression morphed into one of interest as she took in Colin's face and bare chest, all the way down to the gun in his hand. She spoke in a pleasant Scottish accent.

"You must be Agent Douglas? I'm Agent Deena MacDonald, the psychologist."

She stuck out a slender hand, her eyes perusing him once more. He shook her hand and asked, "Bit early, isn't it?"

"Agent Abernathy and I agreed it would be best to speak with the girl first thing when she wakes."

He nodded and let her in, his gaze scouting the grounds once before closing the door and locking it. He stuffed his gun into the waistband of his jeans.

"Everyone is still asleep," he said.

"That's fine. I can speak with you first." She looked professional enough, but Colin could hear the hint of something in her voice—that flirtatious vibe some women gave off.

"Let me get a shirt on."

Her near smile fell as he left her to put on the wrinkled shirt from the day before. He'd have to ask Abernathy to bring something for him to change into when they met later.

Agent MacDonald was sitting at Graham's dining table—probably the only person to ever sit in that proper room—with her long legs crossed, skirt landing just above her knees, and a notebook in hand. She slid on a pair of wire rimmed glasses and watched him with that same interest as he sat across from her.

She was attractive, he admitted in a fleeting thought, and that's where it ended for him. Because while this woman's stealthy gaze roamed his body, all he could think about was Angela. Agent MacDonald's bit of cleavage, and the shadow leading up her legs into her skirt didn't quite have the appeal they might've over a week ago.

Fuck me, he thought. Maybe he was the one who needed a head shrink.

"Agent Abernathy tells me the girl was held captive as a sexual slave for two years. Is that correct?"

"Angela," Colin said. He cleared his throat, crossed his hands on the table in front of him. "Yes, that's correct."

"You may not have all the answers I'm seeking, but every bit helps. Do you know if they drugged her regularly?"

He shook his head. "Not that I know of. I never saw her drugged." He remembered what Graham had been like, and it was nothing like that at the villa. The other Agent took note.

"How about physical abuse? Was she beaten?"

Yes, by me. Colin dropped his eyes and his knee began to bounce. "Uh." Again he cleared his throat. He suddenly wasn't in the fucking mood to talk about this. "Not regularly. There were mentions of previous punishments."

"Mm." Agent MacDonald watched him a bit too carefully for his liking. She tapped the pen on the paper until his steely gaze hit hers and she sucked in a small breath. She touched her fingers to her chest before continuing.

"How would you describe the overall conditions where she was held captive?"

"It was a fucking seaside mansion." Her mouth quirked at his language, but he was certain she was a big girl, so he kept going. "She and all the slaves were kept very clean. I never saw the slave quarters, but I imagine they were pristine like the rest of the place. She wasn't fed enough from what I saw, but—"

A shriek sounded from down the hall.

Colin ran, barely hearing the crash of his chair as it fell backward into the wall. Angela called his name, sounding panicked. He flew down the hall, narrowly avoiding a collision with her parents as they rushed from their room.

Colin swung open her door and she stood there in the middle of the room grasping at the printed dress he'd bought as they fled Spain. Her eyes were wild and confused.

"Mr. Douglas!" She stretched her arms out to him.

He went to her and she leaned her forehead against his chest, shaking, still clutching her dress. Colin took her by the shoulders. "It's okay, Angela. You're safe."

Her parents came in and Colin stepped back to let them embrace her. His hand and arms ached.

"You fainted, honey," her mom said. "And slept right through the night. You needed the rest."

Colin felt another presence and looked to find Agent MacDonald watching the scene from the doorway, that bloody notebook in her hands. Once Angela calmed they all turned and saw her, as well.

She boldly stepped into the room.

"I'm Agent Deena MacDonald, a psychologist. I hope you don't mind, but I'm here to speak with Angela and help with her transition. You must all be thrilled and relieved to have her back." She smiled warmly at Angela's parents, who both nodded and got teary-eyed, rubbing their daughter's back.

Angela kept her eyes down. "May I take a shower?"

"Of course, baby," her mom said. "We brought some of your clothes, too. We'll go get the bags."

Her parents bustled out, and Agent MacDonald stepped closer to Angela. The woman seemed to make her nervous.

Fuck, she was starting to shake. Colin probably should have left the room long ago, but instead he found himself pushing past the other Agent to get to Angela and lead her back to the bed.

"You need to eat. Before you even shower."

"I..." She sat and pulled her knees up, shivering.

"Don't move. I'll be back." He left the room and cursed when he got to the kitchen. The cupboards were bare. He grabbed a package of opened butter biscuits and ran back to the room, hoping they weren't too stale. "Here." He placed them in her lap, but she made no move.

"Angela, you need to eat."

She stared at them.

"Fuck." Colin ran a hand over his hair, then dug his fingers into the package and pulled out a flaky biscuit. He brought it to her lips and she opened her mouth for him without hesitation. His chest swelled with an overwhelming gratitude and something else. Something he couldn't name or understand. He shouldn't have felt this way, but Christ, she was so obedient to him. It appealed to the very core of his nature, like she was giving him a gift, and he wanted to reward her.

She took dainty bites, being careful not to make crumbs. After the second was finished Colin caught movement in his peripheral and turned to see Agent MacDonald watching agape, and her parents in the doorway holding luggage. He dropped his hand and realized he was a right fucking mess. They both were.

"She's..." He started to explain that she wasn't accustomed to feeding herself in front of others, but he didn't want to talk about her like she wasn't in the room. Instead he turned his attention back to Angela. He pulled another biscuit from the package and put it in her hand, closing her fingers around it. Her eyes met his with hesitation and he nodded. Slowly, she brought the food to her mouth and ate.

"Darling," Angela's mother said to her father. "Can you bring a glass of water?"

Her father ran off and returned moments later, placing the glass in Angela's shaking hand. She took a big drink and gave her parents a shy smile as they beamed in return. It was then that Colin stood to take his leave.

"Wait!" Angela pushed the biscuits aside and scrambled to stand as Colin stopped in the middle of the room, his heart working overtime. When she got to him she began to kneel, then caught herself midway and made an awkward movement to stand again. Her head stayed down and she wrung her hands.

"I'm not leaving," Colin gently told her.

"I don't know what to do," she whispered.

Colin wanted to touch her. To hold her. But they were in a bedroom with her parents and a therapist. "There's no pressure to do anything. Take your shower and relax. You can talk with Agent MacDonald if you like—"

"Yes," the Agent stepped forward, and Colin bit back a feeling of annoyance as he stepped back. "Angela, I'm sure Agent Douglas has work to attend, and a debriefing to give. Your parents and I will be here—"

"Mr. Douglas," Angela called. He'd already begun making his way to the door, but he turned at the sound of her voice. "You'll be back?" So much hope and fear in those words. It stabbed at him. He knew this thing between them, whatever it was, was not healthy, but he couldn't tear himself away.

"I'll be back," he promised. "You're safe here."

Agent MacDonald pursed her lips at him and made a motion toward the door, like he was a parent reluctant to leave their child and dragging out the separation anxiety. He shot her a glare in return. He'd let himself be pushed away by Angela or her parents, but not this woman. With one last nod to Angela and her frightened, lost eyes, he turned to go. On the way out, Angela's mother touched his forearm and gave him a tender look of appreciation before returning her attention to her daughter.

Nobody should have to go through what this family was experiencing. Vengeance rose like a thick bramble through his torso and limbs, scraping his flesh from the inside. He needed to do something. Stop others from this kind of suffering.

He needed to kill Fernando.

CHAPTER THIRTY-ONE

Everything felt wrong. Like a strange dream. My parents—
my parents!—wore constant smiles, expressions which were
at odds with the turmoil I felt every minute. I so wanted to
be happy, too. In the far reaches of my mind I knew how I
should be feeling, but I wasn't quite capable of reaching it.

Especially when Mr. Douglas was out of my sight.

Mom showed me to the restroom to shower and closed
the door for me. A flare of panic, like I was going to get in
trouble, burned across my skin as I stared at the closed door
and then swung my head around at the bathroom.

Alone. Private.

I began to shake as I backed into the wall and slid down,
holding myself at the middle. Overwhelming gratitude for
this moment of privacy shook my body.

I was allowed to be alone. There were probably no
cameras, and I could do whatever I wanted! Not that I
wanted to do anything, but still! God, I'd never wanted to
kiss a bathroom floor before that moment.

Through the entire shower, I trembled, peeking now and
then around the curtain to see the door still closed. Afterward
I dressed in a pair of jeans and a soft cotton shirt. They were

too big, but I remembered them from my old life. Another tsunami of nostalgia rushed me, threatening tears in its wake. How long had it been since I wore jeans? Or a shirt that was solely for the purpose of comfort? Or underwear that actually covered my ass?

Mom was waiting for me, watching from a nearby room. I knew she was trying not to suffocate me, but she couldn't help herself. She looked hesitant and timid, so I held out my hand and the doubt left her face.

I found myself constantly looking for Mr. Douglas, and feeling a heady flood of relief and excitement whenever I heard the rumble of his voice from a nearby room, or when I caught a glance of him walking past. Each time I had to restrain myself from calling out for him or running to him.

And we were only two hours into the first morning.

I'd put off talking to Agent MacDonald as long as I could. She'd been a force looming over me all morning, watching from doorways with those inspector eyes, silently rushing me. Mom had taken to glaring at the woman over her shoulder, but the Agent was unperturbed. Clearly, she'd wait all day. As much as I didn't want to talk to her, I also wanted to get it over with so she could leave.

When I finally approached she said, "Aye, good. Let's talk in the office."

The office wasn't much more than a desk with a lamp, and some miscellaneous boxes, as if the man who lived here had never fully settled in.

Agent MacDonald motioned for me to sit across from her at the desk, and I stiffened as her eyes bore into me. I wished she wasn't so beautiful and intimidating. I felt like a filthy little creature in baggy clothes. She set a tape recorder on the desk and hit record. I thought people were supposed to ask permission to do that. But maybe that was only in movies. I probably would have just told her yes anyway.

She twined her fingers and placed them on the notepad in front of her. "How are you feeling this morning, Angela?"

How to explain? I felt a little of everything. Every minute a different strong emotion would hit.

"I'm...I don't know. Okay."

"Okay," she repeated. "I imagine the abrupt change of lifestyle would be quite confusing to the system, aye?"

"Yes," I whispered.

She gave me a small, therapist smile. "Your parents love you very much. I'm sure you missed them." Her comments were leading, even demanding, and it made me want to pull back, be more careful.

"I did..." My voice trailed off and she cocked her head to the side, eyeing me. My heart rate kicked up at the dominance of her personality, and I found myself spilling information I had no intention of telling anyone. My voice broke. "I missed them at first, but after a while I had to stop thinking about them. It hurt too much, and I never thought I'd see them again."

This revelation seemed to please her and she relaxed a little. I thought therapists were supposed to be gentle and kind. This lady seemed like she was not above using torture techniques to get people to talk.

"Does that make you feel a bit guilty seeing them?"

I dropped my eyes. "Yes."

"And perhaps a bit undeserving and inadequate?" she asked.

"Yes," I whispered. I couldn't look up.

"That's all normal to feel. I assure you. And it will pass, Angela. There may be times in your life where you still feel remnants of those emotions, but they will not always have the power they do at this moment."

I chewed my lip and nodded. I wished I could skip right

over all these emotions. I didn't believe they'd ever leave me. How could I be good enough for anyone again? They'd never know me, the real me, because I'd never tell them all I'd done and seen. I felt like I could never be close to someone again.

"Was there anyone who you came to care for during your time of captivity? Anyone who, perhaps, befriended you?"

My sweet Josef. Oh, no. What would happen to him? And Perla and the other girls? Tears slid down each of my cheeks and I quickly swiped them, the familiar feeling of paranoia rising enough to dry my ducts.

"The other slaves. There were five of us. We couldn't talk...I mean, not really. Not about anything important. But they were my friends."

Don't cry anymore, I chanted to myself as Agent MacDonald scratched something on her pad of paper.

"I know this is going to be difficult, Angela, but I need as much information as you can possibly give me about what happened from the moment you were taken to the moment you were rescued. Can you do that for me? This kind of information will aid our organization to help others in similar predicaments."

My abdomen twisted at the thought of regular people knowing these things about me.

"You'll be sharing this?" I hated how small and timid my voice sounded. "I thought there might be some sort of client confidentiality or something."

She smiled at me. "That's the case for regular private psychologists, but since I work for the government I'm here to help you, and to also help us. In the end it's a win-win for all. Will you help us?"

I nodded. "I...yes. Okay."

I felt like I was in that room with her forever. I tried to

tell the facts like they weren't raw and real. I skimmed over the sexual acts, even when she pressed for more information. I didn't want to tell those details to anyone. Ever. I gave her the information I thought would be useful to them—the stuff about how and where I was held. How they controlled me. The names of people who came in and out. She dug for every detail of my first days, wanting to know exactly how they'd broken me down. I started to feel faint by the end of our time, and I'd only skimmed the surface.

She was an avid listener, eating up the details with rapt interest, every now and then throwing in a compassionate expression.

I jumped at a knock on the door and turned to see Mr. Douglas peek his head in. A spasm of joy zipped through me. His cool eyes met mine and for that moment my breath caught as he held my gaze before blinking and looking at the other Agent.

"You've been in here awhile."

Her lips pursed, displeased. "We're making good progress, but we're not finished, so if you don't mind—"

"Agent Abernathy brought dinner. I suggest you stop for a bit and eat."

The woman looked at her watch and her eyes widened in surprise. She glanced at me and reluctantly nodded. "We'll continue this later. Thank you, Angela."

I quickly stood, and went to the door he held open. I watched as he took in the full sight of me dressed as a regular American girl with no make-up, and a smile skimmed his lips. It disappeared when Agent MacDonald cleared her throat, coming to stand near us. She gave him a sharp look.

"I won't be staying for dinner, but I'll return first thing in the morning. I'll need to speak with you, as well, Agent Douglas—"

"I don't think that'll be necessary."

Her eyes narrowed as he cut her off yet again. "Aye, I do believe it is necessary after the lengthy undercover operation you pulled. Just because you're a man doesn't mean nothing can get in your head and screw with it. I'm certain your time in Spain has affected you in various ways, Agent."

He seemed to go to stone as she punctuated her statement with a pointed look. I shouldn't have stood there watching, but nobody asked me to leave, and I was riveted. For the first time I wondered about what Mr. Douglas had been through. How long had he been on this mission?

His steel eyes were hard, and I don't think he cared for the other agent much. "I'm not available to speak for a few days. I've got a quick turn-around trip to attend to."

That jolted me and I stepped closer. "Where are you going?"

Agent MacDonald's head swung toward me as if she'd forgotten I was there.

"I'm not inclined to say—"

Before he could finish I panicked, grabbing his arm, because I just knew he was going to go off and do something dangerous. "Please, don't go. Stay here."

His jaw locked for a second. "I need to do this one last thing. I'll be back."

"No!" I had his shirt in both fists. *Oh God, oh God, oh God,* he was going to get himself hurt or killed. What would I do without him?

He put his hands on my wrists, trying to gently unpry me. "Angela—"

"Where are you going?" And then it hit me with acrid clarity. "You're going to try and find Fernando, aren't you?" His pale look of surprise told me I'd hit the mark. "Take me with you!"

By now I could hear others coming down the hall, convening behind us.

"Please," I begged. I felt his hands rubbing up and down my shoulders and arms in a way that was supposed to be calming, but had the opposite effect. "Take me. Don't leave me. You don't have to do this."

"Aye, I do," he said in a fierce voice. "I really do."

"Angela," Agent MacDonald said in a frigid tone. "Step away from Agent Douglas."

"It's fine," he told her. "She'll calm in a moment."

I couldn't take my eyes off his face, which was turned to the side. He was trying not to look at me. In that moment I knew, instinctually, that somewhere along the way we'd bonded. I believed he had a weakness for me. Maybe it stemmed from pity, or maybe it was a compulsion to care for something you've saved, but whatever it was that he felt for me, I would use it. I couldn't let him leave.

"I can't lose you! Don't go, please don't go!"

"What's going on?" I heard Dad ask from behind me.

"Everything is fine, Mr. Birch," Colin said. "I have some business to attend to, and I'll be back shortly. Angela's a wee upset, is all."

"It's time to let Agent Douglas go," Agent MacDonald said, and then she put her hands on me. Her grip on my arm was tight as she tried to separate us. It reminded me of the grip Luis used to take.

Yeah. I flipped out.

My arms swung toward her and shoved her away as I screamed. I heard shouts. Mr. Douglas pulled me back, but Agent MacDonald's claws surrounded my arms again and a shriek ripped from my throat. I couldn't see straight. Mom's sweet voice calling my name barely registered. I began thrashing, kicking my legs since they were the only part of me free. I felt my feet connect to soft tissue and heard the

Agent's angry yell.

"Just back away!" Mr. Douglas said to her.

He made a move to turn me and I heard Agent MacDonald say, "Hold her still."

"No!" he yelled, and then I felt a sharp pinch in my upper arm. I looked up to see the fire of anger on his face, aimed at Agent MacDonald, who stood with a small syringe in her hand.

Mom rushed over and brushed the hair back from my face as I felt myself going limp in Mr. Douglas's arms.

"You didn't have to bloody drug her," was the last thing I heard through his clenched teeth before the world went black.

CHAPTER THIRTY-TWO

Colin

He hated leaving for Thailand without even saying a proper good-bye to Angela. He also hated that the impulsive, power-hungry psych Agent had resorted to drugs when the girl hadn't even had a decent meal that day. She'd probably wake up feeling ill. And he didn't appreciate the knowing looks Agent MacDonald kept giving him, as if she couldn't wait to dig around in his mind and fix him.

That shite wasn't happening. Colin was right fucked up, but that bitch wasn't the cure.

This trip would be the beginning of his cure.

One of the downfalls of being a secret payroll Agent was that he couldn't carry a badge, which meant no weapons while flying.

It would be his first time in Thailand. Colin crammed as many Thai words and phrases into his mind as he could during the long flight. It helped keep his mind off Angela. As they neared their destination, Colin stared down at the thick green jungles and crystal blue waters. His fingers itched to paint it.

When he landed in Bangkok, he headed for the red light district, navigating his way through the busy streets to the arms dealer Abernathy had dug up. Despite the smog in the city, an aroma of spices made it smell like an exotic heaven, matching the rich culture all around him. But he wasn't there for tourism and pleasure. He pulled a ball cap low over his forehead to hide his face and entered the side door of a bustling street market.

To an older woman with suspicious eyes, he said in Thai, "I need to see Daw." He probably slaughtered the pronunciation, but she gave a jut of her chin toward a man handling an icy vat of fish.

The man stood when Colin approached, and without a word wiped his hands on his apron and motioned for Colin to follow him into a back room.

"You have money?" Daw asked when the door closed behind them.

Colin pulled out the wad and Daw snatched it with greedy hands, counting.

"What you want?" the man asked.

"A handgun."

He pulled out three handguns of different calibers for Colin to choose from. He took the 9mm semi-automatic and disassembled it to be sure everything was in good condition before nodding and reassembling, stowing the gun at the back of his pants under his shirt. He bought a couple of clips, loaded.

"If it doesn't work, I'm coming back for you," Colin warned.

"It work. I try myself."

Colin pulled a picture of Fernando from his pocket, but Daw turned his head and held up his hands, saying, "I do not involve myself in your business."

Fair enough. Colin slid the picture back into his pocket and asked, "Where can I find a whore house?"

Daw didn't blink an eye at this. He rattled off an address and opened the door for Colin to leave. It was the quickest, easiest acquisition he'd ever encountered, and he could only hope the rest of his stay in Thailand followed that pattern.

The tiny middle-aged woman who greeted him at the address he'd been given wore a large, fake smile. She bowed her head to him and waved a hand toward the scantily clad girls lined against the wall. Some eyed him coyly, others brazenly.

Colin pulled out the picture and the woman froze as she peered down at it, the smile disappearing.

"You looking for friend?" she asked in broken English.

"No," Colin said. "Not a friend. Do you know where I can find him?"

She shook her head tightly and clasped her hands in front of herself. "I am business woman."

Of course. Colin knew all too well that it was often difficult to get "business people" to talk. He pulled another wad of Thai bills from his pocket.

"May I speak to a few of your ladies?" He inclined his head toward the women against the wall.

The woman grabbed for the money and stuffed it away. "Be fast."

Colin approached the girls, feeling a natural tingle of arousal when the first put a hand on his chest and cocked a knee to rub his leg. He held Fernando's picture out to her and she stepped back, shaking her head.

"Do you know this man?"

Again she shook her head, dropping her eyes. He held the picture out for all the girls to see. The fear and loathing in their eyes showed they all knew of him.

"Tell me where to find him and you'll never see him again."

They exchanged looks of hope and suspicion, a silent conversation. Finally, the meekest stepped forward and blurted in a tiny voice, "He take the girls to rooms by the parks next to Royal Palace." Her eyes got big, as if she couldn't believe she'd said it.

"By Wat Po," another added. The small girl gave her a grateful look.

"Rooms?" Colin asked. "Like a hotel?"

The two of them nodded. Then they all dropped their eyes nervously.

"Thank you," Colin said, feeling right fucking chipper. "Have a lovely day."

He tipped his head to the mistress and left. *Here I come, motherfucker.*

Colin scouted the Royal Palace area looking for possible hotels or rooms where Fernando might take girls. He found three possible alleyways—shady places. It was a large, busy area, so he'd have to keep a keen eye out. He bided his time until nightfall.

By midnight, when he still hadn't seen Fernando, he had to be proactive. He received hostile looks from a set of drug dealers at a corner, but paid them no mind, heading straight for a prostitute in a black mini skirt. He stood close enough to her to hide the fact that he was pulling out a picture between the two of them. In his other hand he held out money.

"Where is this man?" Colin asked.

She swallowed and swayed on her heels, turning her bloodshot eyes away with a tight shrug. Fine. Colin moved to the next.

This girl bit her lip and shot a glance past him to the two dealers who were inching closer.

Fuck.

He turned from the girl and strode to the two men, needing to get them off his tail.

"What can I get for this?" Colin asked, flashing cash between his fingers. The men seemed to relax at the sight of the money. One pulled out a rather large bag of marijuana and a smaller pouch of cocaine. Colin took the coke and handed over the money. "Thank you. Now I just need a woman and I'm all set. I'm quite enjoying my time in Thailand."

One of them grinned with blackened teeth, probably relieved to think Colin was just a stupid tourist looking for a good time, and not a threat after all. They turned and left him alone. He'd flush the cocaine later.

Going back to the girl, he held out the money and picture. She stared down at them for a moment before slowly reaching for the money and whispering a street name.

"Kop kun," he said. *Thank you.*

She quickly turned away and he walked the two blocks to the street she'd given. He followed the sound of voices down an alley. He wished he could read the Thai signs hanging. When he came to the first doorway where a drunken man and woman stood, he asked, "Suorsdei?" He was fairly certain that meant "hotel."

The man pointed to the next entrance and Colin nodded. He walked to the open doorway and pushed a thick curtain aside. A thin man stood inside behind a desk, alert.

Colin pulled out his cash, a universal sign of fucking peace, and said, "One room."

"How long?" the man asked.

"One hour." He nodded and they exchanged the money. The man gave him a room number, but no key, which Colin assumed meant no locks on the doors. Fan-fucking-tastic for him. He took his time down the hall, listening to the squeaking of beds and panting grunts sounding from inside. Two people fucked so hard in one room that the wall shook. The woman screamed. Colin tried the doorknob, peeking into the crack, but it was a Thai couple who didn't even notice him. He closed the door and kept going.

At the end of the hall he heard the muffled protests of a girl and low voice of a man without a Thai accent. He stepped closer to the door and his heart clenched at the sound of the girl's crying followed by another stifled shout of her pain and his moan of ecstasy.

With a glance down the hall, Colin pulled out his gun and cracked the door.

Fuck, yes.

There was that handsome face used to lure women, rutting against a girl from behind, shoving her face hard into the mattress to quiet her pleas. When Colin stepped in and closed the door with a kick of his heel, Fernando sat up on his knees with a look of shock. There was blood on his hands and stomach—on the girl's back and ass. It turned Colin's stomach and he pointed the gun at the bastard's face. The girl flipped over and scuttled back.

Fernando's hands flew up and his eyes darted around the room. "Qué chingado! Quién es usted?" *What the hell! Who are you?*

That, Colin could understand. "I'm the man who killed your father. And the man who's going to kill you."

Fernando went deathly still for a moment, and then his wicked eyes lit up and he chuckled.

"My papa lives."

Colin's gut slickened with doubt. *No.* Was Marco alive? He couldn't be. Fernando simply hadn't heard the news yet.

"He's dead, and so are you."

Colin pulled the trigger and a light click sounded. He cursed. The fucking gun was faulty!

Fernando took that opportunity to launch himself from the bed at Colin, making him drop the useless gun. Fernando may have gotten in the first punch to Colin's jaw, but that was all he'd get. Colin's fists met Fernando's torso in a rapid succession of hits, making the man fall back with an *oomph*. In the next breath Colin was straddling his chest, beating that pretty face to a bloody pulp as Fernando struggled uselessly to get out from under him.

All he could see was Angela's face and all the other faceless women and families this man had haunted. He was glad the gun was broken. Killing him with his bare hands was far more satisfying.

Colin stopped long enough to take Fernando by the throat and lean close. "How's it feel to be on the receiving end of a beating?"

The man arched his back and let out a pathetic, gurgled cry.

"Please, please, por favor..."

"Do you let women go when they beg you?" He squeezed tighter. "Do you? Because I know you didn't give a fuck when Angela pleaded for you to get the fuck off her!"

Fernando's wild eyes cleared and he gripped Colin's wrists. "Angela? The American whore?" He slowly smiled. "She wanted it, Señor. Trust me."

Colin punched the fucker's mouth so hard he had to fling his hand to clear the sting. Fernando spit blood and a chipped tooth through his swollen lips, groaning pitifully.

A gleam from the corner of Colin's eye caused him to pull back and release Fernando's neck. The Thai woman stood over her attacker, naked, bloodied, and shaking, with Colin's gun in her hands. She pointed the gun, down, down, right at Fernando's crotch. Colin leapt away.

"No!" Fernando yelled, but this time, when the trigger was pulled the gun went off. She stumbled back with the light kick and Colin stared. Fernando's mouth was wide and he gasped unsuccessfully for air. A primal keening wail was rising from the man's throat.

"Bloody hell," Colin whispered. The woman whimpered, lowering her arms. He grabbed the gun from the her hand and shot Fernando in the forehead. He felt back with a *thunk*.

Shouts rang out from down the hall. Colin slipped the gun into the back of his jeans, then pushed the bed in front of the door. He ran to the window and forced the creaky thing open.

"Go," he told her. "Go!"

He helped the girl clamber out as fast as she could, and then followed. She ran into the maze of back alleyways, stark naked, and he ran for the open streets, ready to get the hell out of Thailand and back to Angela.

CHAPTER THIRTY-THREE

I woke in the middle of the night with a splitting headache and rolling stomach. Mom was at my side the moment I sat up, thrusting a small bin under my face when the wracking dry heaves began. She rubbed my back. The combined tenderness of her care for me and the painful convulsing of my body forced moisture from my eyes. Just when I thought I was finished I remembered Mr. Douglas going to Asia to look for Fernando.

"Is Mr. Douglas gone?"

"Yes, dear. He left last night."

I covered my mouth and shut my eyes as the illness threatened again.

"Poor, sweet thing," Mom cooed, handing me a tissue which I used to wipe my face. "God forgive me, but I wanted to punch that woman in the face when she came at you with a needle."

I chuckled. The sound of it and the feel of it in my chest was shocking. Mom and I made eye contact and I chuckled again. Then she giggled, and we broke into a fit of laughter that had us gasping for breaths. Nothing was really funny. Nothing at all. But it was glorious to be able to just let loose again, and by the end we were hugging.

"Oh, Angela. I've missed that sound. Your laugh. I missed you, baby."

"I'm sorry," I said.

"No." She pulled back. "No more apologies. You have nothing to be sorry for."

When she released me by body trembled.

"My friends," I said. "The ones I was in Mexico with…"

"Yes?" Her voice and eyes were heavy.

"Are they okay?"

It took her a moment to answer. "They were upset, Angie. Very upset. All of their parents flew down with Daddy and I when we went. But they're okay. I'm sure they're okay."

"I wish I could tell them it wasn't their fault," I said.

"Me too. But you can't contact them. If the media finds out…"

"I know."

"Maybe someday," she whispered.

"Maybe someday," I repeated.

Over the past two years I'd become so accustomed to being hungry that I stopped feeling any kind of pang. But at that moment, I could feel the painful twist of emptiness. My body needed food.

I looked at Mom with those big, tired bags under her eyes. "You can go back to sleep, Mama. I'll be okay now. I promise. I'm gonna grab some crackers and sleep the rest of the night."

"Are you sure? I can make you something."

I shook my head and she patted my hand. "Okay, then. Night, sweetie. I'll see you in the morning. Let's hope I don't have to punch anyone."

I smiled as she left me.

When Mom was back in her room I slipped out of bed and walked on weak legs to the kitchen. Just outside the entrance I heard a clatter that sounded like glass in a sink, followed by an unfamiliar male Scottish voice saying, "Bloody fucking hell!"

I froze, all sorts of horrid scenarios running through my mind, certain someone had broken in.

Then he grumbled, "Fucking Colin hiding my fucking alcohol."

Oh. It was the guy who lived here…Colin's brother. I hadn't met him yet, and I thought maybe he wasn't even staying here at the moment. Curiosity urged me forward, and I peeked around the corner.

He was tall like Colin, but thinner. His hair was longish, curly and brown. His clothes were black and loose, in a goth sort of way, and he wore black leather bands around his wrist. He must have felt me watching because his head snapped up and he jumped back, spilling the soda he'd been trying to pour.

"Ah, fuck me," he yelled, flinging his wet hand toward the sink.

I slunk back into the doorway, whispering, "Sorry." My heart was beating too fast.

He's not going to punish you. You're not in trouble.

I turned to leave but his voice called me back. "Nae, it's all right then, lassie. Come back."

I moved slowly into the kitchen, feeling my body tucking inward as I stared at the floor.

"Sorry," I said again. "I…I was just looking for crackers or something. But I can go—"

"Here." He moved to a cupboard behind him and

rummaged for a box, which he held out to me. "I was just making myself something, as well. We can share if you like."

"Okay," I said. I didn't know what to do with myself. I stood there in the middle of the kitchen holding the box, knowing I should choose to do something. Lean against the counter. Sit at the dinette. Something. Anything.

The guy stopped and looked at me. His body seemed to go slack, arms falling to his side.

"Aye. You must be Angela then."

My breathing skidded to a halt and picked back up in quick time. Had Colin told him about me? What had he said?

I nodded, still not looking up.

"Someone bought food. Sit here with me." He led me to a chair and I sat obediently.

He cut slices of sharp cheese and some sort of sausage and put them on a plate between us, then dumped crackers on the side.

"Help yourself," he said.

After he'd taken, some I gingerly took one cracker with cheese and nibbled it. My stomach let out an obnoxious, embarrassing gurgle of happiness.

"Eat up. Don't be shy. I'm Graham, by the way."

My eyes flicked up and found him watching me. He was like a younger, punked out version of Colin, and I couldn't help but stare as he shoved as cracker sandwich in his mouth. He seemed just as intense as his brother, never smiling, and it made me wonder what they'd been through.

When we'd cleared the plate he slouched down and crossed his arms, bringing a thumb up to touch his lip ring. He stared at the shuttered window.

"It's strange isn't it?" he asked. "Afterward? You know you should feel safe, but you don't. You know you should be happy, but you aren't."

I stared at him. How did he know? The way he sounded—the certainty and understanding in his voice made something vulnerable inside me crack open in a way that psych lady couldn't dream of achieving.

"Yes," I whispered. "And I know I should want to be free, but…"

"But you don't know how anymore."

He looked at me now, and I felt a camaraderie like I felt with Josef. It made me miss him terribly.

"How do you know?" I asked.

"Colin didn't tell you?"

My pulse sprinted and I shook my head.

"He may not want you to know. He's a secretive shit, but fuck it. I feel like, maybe…I dunno, maybe it might help or something."

He looked nervous and unsure now.

"You can tell me," I said, and not just because I was dying to know their story, but because it seemed like he needed to get it out, whatever it was. For himself and for me.

He took a deep breath, and his hand shook as he raked it through his hair.

"When I was a wee lad, only ten, and Colin was sixteen, our Mam and Dad were killed. I was kidnapped and sold into slavery. Colin wasn't home."

Holy shit. My heart stalled. I couldn't breathe. I covered my mouth to hold back the sounds of shock and mourning my body wanted to release.

"Seven years later he found me. Colin saved me, but I was a fucking disaster. Still am." Graham grabbed his earlobe. "Fuck, I need a drink."

I don't know what made me do it, but I reached across the table and took his hand. We both stilled, and then he gave my hand a squeeze.

"Ever play video games?" he asked.

"No." I almost giggled.

"How old are you?"

"Twenty-two."

"Same as me," he said. That would make Mr. Douglas twenty-eight. I felt myself warming all over at the thought of the older, rugged man.

"If you're having trouble sleeping you can hang with me," Graham said.

"Okay."

He had the master suite at the far end of the house. He brought us both sodas and we sat on funny gamer seats in front of the television. What I found was that Graham wanted to talk, but needed a distraction to cushion the intimacy it would require. While he killed zombies, he asked questions and I answered. Then he answered in return.

How many masters did you have?

What was your master like?

Did he beat you? Drug you? Fuck you?

Our question and answer session, with both our sets of eyes on the screen, felt oddly normal, though it was anything but. It wasn't like talking to the psychologist. It was like talking to my friends from the villa because they'd lived the same life. Graham understood. The pain and fear that could have arisen from discussing it was tampered by the click of his fingers and thumbs across the controls, and the sounds of the *bangs* and *pows* coming from the game.

After nearly two hours I must have fallen asleep because the silence of the game being turned off startled me and I jumped.

"Sorry," he said.

I gave him a small smile. He searched my face before

looking away.

"Thank you, Graham."

He nodded.

"I'll see you later, right?"

"Aye." He pushed a hand through his locks, seeming nervous.

"I won't tell anyone what we talked about," I promised. "I don't really want everyone to know those things about me either."

This seemed to calm him. As I left the room and closed the door behind me, I heard some sort of heavy metal Celtic music being turned on. I didn't even know there was such a thing.

It took me forever to fall back asleep as puzzle pieces about Colin Douglas clicked into place. His roles of new master, savior, and now slavery-hater clashed like a total mind fuck in my foggy brain. I thought of all the things he'd had to do—the way he'd looked at me with a mixture of lust and something I couldn't identify when I gave him that first blowjob. I knew now that the unfamiliar expression was regret—something nobody else felt at the villa. Deep down he hadn't really wanted me to do that. Just like he hadn't really wanted to have anal sex, but I'd torn the covers away. Had he been thinking about his brother, and all he'd been through, comparing us and feeling guilty? A torrent of blame soaked me now. Was he ashamed?

I wanted to talk to him. To tell him it was okay. He did what he had to do, and I was grateful. I wanted to properly thank him.

I thought about how he'd punished me with his bare hand. And...yeah...that memory surged like a heatwave straight between my thighs. Lying in bed, in the dark, feeling aroused, brought back helpless feelings of fear. I wasn't allowed to feel this way.

Or was I?

My heart thrummed faster. Nobody was watching. No video cameras. No one would come to punish me. Nobody would even know. I could do it. I could take back this small piece of my old life and make it mine again.

I slipped a trembling, tentative hand into my underwear and found myself swollen, begging for attention. My breaths quickened as my fingers moved between my legs, rubbing all around that little sensitive spot. Faster and harder my fingers circled, kindling a fire deep in my belly.

I moaned, too loudly. My free hand grabbled the pillow and pressed it over my face as my other hand worked between my thighs. I felt reckless and rebellious. A spark caught and my hips flew up, grinding against my hand as an explosion rocked my core and I panted into the pillow, barely containing the scream I wanted to make as my clit convulsed in rhythmic bliss.

While my body came back down, pulsing with its residual release, I bit my lip and smiled, even let out a breathy laugh of triumph.

Take that, Marco.

Maybe I could do this. Maybe I could take back my life, one rebellious moment at a time.

—◆·◆—

I woke the next morning to the sound of mom's voice, stern. I poked my head out the door and heard her conversing with Agent MacDonald at the entrance of the house.

"Yes, I understand and I agree it's important, but she hasn't even had a single day to rest and try to be normal."

"There is no normal for her right now, Mrs. Birch, with all due respect—"

"With all due respect, of course there's no normal when you're stuck in a room with a shrink all day. I will not allow her to be questioned today."

"I'm simply doing my job."

"When your job interferes in my daughter's healing and well-being, I take issue. We're only talking about one day. You can come back tomorrow when Agent Douglas is back."

God, I loved the sound of that tough Texan accent. It filled my chest with pride.

Agent MacDonald clearly wasn't happy, but she left nonetheless and I wanted to clap.

Mom's face was pinched and angry when she rounded the corner, but she relaxed when she saw me. "Mornin', baby."

"Mornin'," I said.

"I got stuff to make your favorite meals today." She beamed. "Oven fried chicken. Mac and cheese. Sweet tea. We're gonna have us a good day."

My mouth watered. I tried to smile, but I still felt like I didn't deserve any of this. Mom took my hand, unperturbed by my wary attitude.

"Come on. You can help me. I'll even let you shred the cheese."

—⋅✦⋅—

When our big, late lunch was ready I thought about Graham as Mom, Dad, and I prepared to sit.

"Can I invite Mr. Douglas's little brother?"

"Of course," Dad said, looking around. "Is he here?"

"Yes. I think he sleeps during the day, but I'll wake him up."

They looked like they didn't know if that was a good idea, but I left to get him. When I hit the hall I had the urge to crawl, and I had to shake the thought away.

No more crawling.

I dragged Graham out of bed and presented the disheveled punk to my parents. To their credit they only batted surprised eyes for a second at his appearance before falling into hospitable mode, welcoming him to the table and asking him to eat as much as he could.

"Sorry 'bout my hair," he said, trying to press it down with his palm.

Mom waved off the comment and filled a plate for him.

I stared around the table at everyone else beginning to eat. Mom smiled at me, and I picked up my fork, knowing that's what she wanted.

It was too much food. And so rich. I'd only cleared a quarter of my plate before I had to stop and clutch my stomach. Mom put a hand to my forearm.

"It's okay. Take your time, Angie. I gave you too much, but I couldn't help myself. You're just so thin."

My gut settled after a few minutes of not eating, and I was content to hear my parents chatting, and watch Graham finish his entire plate. This made Mom happy.

"You can have mine if you want," I told him, pushing it forward.

He glanced at my parents, who both nodded, so he pulled my plate up and dug in. I wondered how long it'd been since he had a decent meal. Afterward he holed himself back in his room, and I had a strangely normal day with my parents. The three of us walked around the land behind the house, holding hands, then watched a movie. Then I beat Dad at a game of Gin-Rummy, though I'm certain he let me win.

Agent Abernathy showed up for an hour to scout the property and check on us, a reminder that were not just some regular family on vacay in Scotland.

I felt myself holding back, afraid to be happy. I didn't

laugh or smile as much as the wonderful day warranted. I was so scared of my parents learning of the things I'd done and being disgusted with me, though they'd never admit it. And I couldn't stop worrying about Mr. Douglas, and wondering about Josef and Perla.

—٠✦٠—

That night when everyone went to bed and the house was quiet, I tossed and turned for hours. When I heard footsteps going down the hall, I got up and tip-toed after them. I knocked on Graham's door, and he opened it right away, still holding a brown paper sack in his hand. He looked refreshed, wearing a skull T-shirt.

"Are you going out?" I asked.

"Nae, coming in for the night. Join me if you'd like."

I did, and he closed the door behind me. He took a bottle of vodka out of the bag and drank directly from the open neck. When he held it out to me I shook my head.

We sat on the gamer chairs, and talked. I watched as he progressed into a more relaxed version of himself with the drink in his system. He even smiled, which made him incredibly good-looking. Was Mr. Douglas that breathtaking when he smiled?

"Come on," Graham said. "Have a drink with me. Just one."

I chewed my lip. "I can't drink a lot. And not straight like you're doing."

He stood and went to a mini-fridge, pulling out a carton of orange juice and bottle of cranberry juice. In seconds he had a drink in my hand. I sipped it and let it warm my chest. It wasn't too strong. I thanked him and he sat next to me again.

We talked and talked. I asked him about Colin as a boy, and heard how Colin had always been the painter and partier while Graham was the drawer and gamer.

"Do you still draw?" I asked.

He shrugged, hiding his face behind his hair. "I mostly dick around with computer graphics and shite."

"Have you ever taken a class?"

"Nae. Can't keep much of a schedule. Though I sometimes dream of going to New York City and attending graphic design school."

My eyes widened. "You should! Graham, that would be wonderful for you!"

He shook his head. "Nae, nae. Shouldn't ha' told you that. I could never do it. Be a responsible student and citizen and all that shite."

I disagreed, but the way he curled inward and chugged from the bottle told me he was finished with that aspect of the conversation.

As the night progressed and tiredom set in, I drank through it, accepting my third. My tongue was loose. We shared disturbing things—the stuff that haunted us at nights and made us hate ourselves. Graham's stories were so much more awful than mine. While I was often revered by men at the villa like a goddess, Graham's experience was the opposite. He'd had four owners, each worse than the previous. He was reminded daily that he was despicable trash, a body barely worthy of their use. And he'd been so young.

His eyes were red when I pushed the hair from his face and made him look at me. He reminded me so much of Josef, his thin frame and pained past.

"You're a good person, Graham. They were monsters."

"Your master was a monster, as well, Angela. Though you speak of him fondly…"

An image of Marco filled my mind. Was he a monster?

Yes.

I shuddered. Without a doubt Fernando was a beast of nightmares. A wolf in sheep's clothing. And right now Colin Douglas was out there chasing my monster.

My thoughts of fear and gratitude were interrupted when Graham moved closer, on his knees in front of me. I smelled the warmth of alcohol on his breath, and saw the way his tentative gray eyes searched me for something. With an impulsive move he took my face and pressed his firm lips to mine. His lip ring was cool in contrast to the heat of his mouth.

Never tell a patron no. Allow him to do whatever he wishes...

Unease ratcheted through me.

No. *No.* Not a patron. This was Mr. Douglas's brother. He was only trying to thank me in the only way he knew how. To reward my kindness physically. I couldn't let this happen.

Going against every instinct I'd learned at the villa, I pulled back, turning my head to the side. He stayed close and I felt his breaths on my cheek.

"Jaysus..." Graham thrust his fingers into his hair. "I'm sorry."

"It's okay," I whispered, not wanting him to feel bad.

A shuffle sounded by the door and a deep voice rang out. "What...the *fuck?*"

I didn't even have to look up. At the sound of my master's voice I fell to my knees. His footsteps pounded toward us and Graham curled into a ball on the floor as Mr. Douglas reached over him, grabbing the bottle.

"You're giving her alcohol? Of all the stupid shit, Graham! What the fuck are you thinking?" He launched the nearly empty bottle toward the trash can across the room and it hit the wall with a *bang* before falling into the canister.

"Angela…please. For the love of God, don't kneel. Graham, Christ, I'm not going to hit you. Fuck!" He stood and kicked one of the gamer chairs. It flew into the bed and I started to shake.

"Come on, lassie." Mr. Douglas's voice lowered, as if he were forcing himself not to be angry, and he helped me to my feet. Then he grasped Graham by the arm and lifted him, leading him to the bed where he fell in a drunken heap.

Graham quietly murmured, "I'm sorry, I'm sorry, I'm sorry…"

Mr. Douglas took his brother's face in his hand, making him look at him. "I shouldn't have yelled. All right? Sleep it off. We'll talk in the morning."

His face was stern and full of regret when he placed his wide palm on my back and led me out of the room, down the hall to my own room. Inside, I climbed into bed, but grabbed his arm when he turned to leave.

"Stay with me," I pleaded.

He froze, half turned, and shut his eyes.

"Don't ask that of me."

"I know you only did what you had to do in Spain, Mr. Douglas—"

"Please—"

"No, I understand. I do. I'm not mad at you. I'm grateful."

"You're drunk."

"I'm…" Okay, the room was spinning a little, but slowly. I wasn't plastered, just nicely buzzed. I let him go and looked up at him. "I know what I'm saying right now. You don't owe me anything."

"Nor do you."

"Yes, I do. I owe you so much. I want to give you everything."

He turned from me. "Well, I can't accept it. I've been given all I'm owed. You're free now, and…that in itself is reward enough."

My insides shivered at the sweetness of those words.

"Is…is Fernando dead?"

"Yes."

My insides galloped at that single word. I didn't realize just how much old fear and angst had attached itself to the idea of Fernando until I could feel it dissipating and releasing. He'd never hurt another girl again. "Thank you," I whispered.

"Believe me, it was my pleasure. Now, get some sleep."

I reached for his arm again as he moved away, but I was too slow this time.

He was almost at the door when I whispered, "I love you."

The moment the truth slipped out, I felt lighter, and the room spun faster.

He stopped, tense, never turning. "You're drunk," he said again. "And I wish you'd call me Colin."

With my sentiment ignored, he left me.

CHAPTER THIRTY-FOUR

I love you.

Fucking Graham and his fucking vodka. He wanted to strangle his idiot of a brother. Colin's chest constricted, like he couldn't breathe when he remembered what he'd seen in that room—the two of them so close, their faces mere inches apart. And the bottle next to them.

He wasn't opposed to them talking. In fact, if they could help each other, he'd be fucking grateful, but how had they gotten so close in the couple days he'd been gone? He didn't want them *that* close. And he sure as fuck didn't want Angela turning to drugs and alcohol the way Graham had.

I love you.

He scraped at his scalp with his fingertips, pacing his room. God damn it!

Some people said alcohol made the truth come out. But Colin knew from his own drunken stupors that alcohol also made you do and say things you'd never want to do or say in a sober state—things you didn't mean at all. She'd been through so much. She was confused.

She couldn't have meant it, but it affected him just the same. He'd wanted to turn around and take himself back to her bed, to cover her skin with his, to bury himself deeper inside her than anyone ever had, and listen to her say those words over and over. To him.

The best thing Colin could do for both of them would be to leave. He'd allowed things to go too far. But the selfish, masochistic part of him wanted to stay, wanted to see how things would play out, good or bad.

Dawn broke, spreading a buttery light through his room. He wasn't tired, having slept a bit on the plane. In fact, he felt wired as Angela's words resounded in his head on replay.

Soon, he could hear the Birches moving around in the kitchen and smell coffee brewing. It lured Colin from his room. Mrs. Birch brightened, beaming at him when he entered.

"Coffee?" she asked, already grabbing a mug and pouring.

"Please. Just black."

She handed it to him and picked up her own. They stood there staring at one another for an awkward moment before Colin said, "Thank you."

She held his eyes, all seriousness, and then verbally knocked him on his arse when she said quietly, "You're in love with her, aren't you?"

Mr. Birch took that prime moment to bustle into the kitchen, sweeping a kiss across his wife's cheek, and holding out a hand to Colin.

"Ah, Agent Douglas. Good to see you back!" They shook hands, and Colin made one last moment of eye-contact with Mrs. Birch, whose gaze was soft and understanding.

Colin sat at the table, rattled, while Mrs. Birch buttered toast and fried eggs, and her husband sat across from him wanting to discuss all things Scotland. Within minutes they were both devouring platefuls of breakfast. When they were finished Colin took the dishes up and rinsed them, despite Mrs. Birch's attempts to do it.

He heard a shuffle at the door, and he felt Angela's presence before he saw her.

"There's my girl," Mr. Birch said.

"Mornin' Daddy." She sounded tired and wary, the second part Colin knew was probably because of him. "It smells good."

Mrs. Birch moved back to the stove. "Sit down, honey, and let me make you an egg." She patted Colin's arm and said, "You sit, too." She inclined her head back to the table where Angela was pulling out a chair next to her dad.

Colin's instinct had been to leave and let the family have their time together, but he didn't want to be rude. He took a seat across from Angela, who stared down at her hands in her lap. Her hair was pulled up in a high ponytail, which Colin thought was incredibly cute, along with the pillow lines on her face from the couple hours of sleep she'd gotten.

Mrs. Birch put a cup of coffee in front of her daughter. "Cream and sugar, just the way you like it."

"Thanks," Angela whispered. She and Colin sipped their coffee, never making eye-contact, while her father rustled a newspaper. After a few minutes Mrs. Birch set a plate in front of Angela, and then sat next to Colin, sighing happily.

Angela made no move for her fork. No move to eat, at all.

"Aren't you hungry, sweetie?" her mom asked.

"Um." She fingered the fork next to her plate. "Not really."

Her mom looked sad. "You should try to take a couple bites. Just to have something in your stomach. You did so well last night..."

Angela sucked her bottom lip into her mouth, and Colin

realized it was probably his presence hindering her from feeding herself. Part of him wanted to get up and leave, while another part of him wanted her to get past this hurdle, and be able to feel comfortable eating in front of him.

"Angela," he said quietly. "You can eat."

A breath left her, and she seemed to roll her shoulders inward, balling herself. Both her parents were watching her now, their eyes darting to Colin, as if trying to figure out the problem. He didn't want to take drastic measures and be domineering, but he desperately wanted to see some sort of positive progress with her.

"Look at me," he whispered, his voice low.

Her eyes lifted with hesitation.

"It's okay. Eat. Anytime you're hungry, you can eat."

Finally, she picked up her toast with a shaking hand and took a tiny bite. Colin and her parents deflated of their tension, relaxing back into their seats. The Birches chatted about weather, while Colin watched Angela eating, wanting so damn badly to reward her for being a good girl. He could think of several ways.

He cleared his throat and stood. Thoughts like that were inappropriate as it was, but even more so in front of her parents. As he rinsed his coffee mug he heard a knock at the front door. He pulled out his gun from habit, although no criminal worth their salt would knock on the door.

"Stay here," he told the Birches, who watched him.

At the door, he frowned when he saw Agent MacDonald, and begrudgingly let her in.

"Agent Douglas," she said, smiling. "You're back. Good to see you."

"Mmhm." He stowed his gun, then closed and locked the door.

MacDonald stepped in his path, moving her chestnut waves from her shoulder. "We should really have our talk

306

today."

"Sure. Later." He moved around her, heading toward the kitchen with the other Agent on his heels. None of the Birches looked thrilled at the sight of her.

"Good morning," Agent MacDonald said with false cheeriness.

Mrs. Birch offered her coffee without a smile.

"No, thank you. I've had mine already."

"Well," Mr. Birch said. "Before everyone gets started today, my wife, Lanie, and I would like to tell you our plan. We know we can't stay here forever. We've discussed places in the world where we can start over with our new identities, and we've decided on The Netherlands. Angela knows a little of the Dutch language already."

Colin's gut twisted. The thought of Angela moving far away grew a protective beast inside him. He would follow her wherever she went, unless the Birches requested otherwise. He wasn't ready to let her go. He had to keep her safe.

"That sounds like a good choice," Agent MacDonald said. "Do you have your new identity paperwork yet?"

"Yes," Mr. Birch answered. "We received everything yesterday. We'd really prefer not to take Angela there until we've secured a place to live, so Lanie and I are leaving this afternoon to look for a home out there and get everything squared away. We'll be back in a few days for Angela. Hopefully no longer than a week."

He reached down for his daughter's hand and she smiled shyly up at him. "This okay with you, pumpkin?"

"Yes," she said. Her eyes briefly met Colin's, making his pulse sprint.

Mrs. Birch caught the direction her daughter's eyes had gone, and she looked up at Colin.

"And what are your plans, Agent Douglas, if you don't

mind me asking?"

"Nae, I don't mind. But I haven't yet decided where I'll go when I leave Scotland."

"Of course," said Lanie. "Well, we hope you'll consider making your home in The Netherlands, too. It'd be an honor and a comfort to have you close by."

He held back his grin. Agent MacDonald's eyes nearly popped out, and as she opened her mouth to say something, Colin blurted, "You're very kind. I will consider it." This shut the psychologist up long enough to allow the Birches to rise and say their temporary good-byes.

Mrs. Birch took Colin's hands and reached up on her tip-toes to kiss his cheek. "We'll be back soon. Thank you again, for everything."

"You're welcome, Mrs. Birch. Angela will be safe here."

"Lanie, please. And I know she will be." She gave him a wink and squeezed his hands before leaving.

He liked that woman, though he knew she might not be as kind if she knew all he'd done and the thoughts he still had toward her daughter.

The afternoon was filled with packing and bustling. Colin could see Angela was stressed about her parents leaving. And Agent MacDonald was stressed about not being able to begin her question session with Angela straight away, which amused him, because Lanie Birch wouldn't allow the Agent anywhere near her daughter. She and Mr. Birch probably kissed and hugged Angela a thousand times before they made it to the door.

The second Angela's parents were gone, Agent MacDonald pounced.

"I trust you had a lovely day yesterday," she said to Angela. "Follow me, and we'll pick-up where we left off."

Angela followed with her head down, and Colin

frowned. He didn't understand why the agency was forcing this woman down their throat. It didn't seem like the best thing for Angela at the moment. He decided to stay near, in case there were any more incidences where Agent MacDonald felt the need to wield a needle.

He stationed a chair right outside the fucking door and opened the newspaper. At the sound of the rustling the door swung open and Agent MacDonald peered down at him.

"Exactly what do you think you're doing out here?" she asked.

He leaned back, unruffled by her tone. "I promised her parents she'd be safe."

"I've got a gun to protect her, as well, in case you've forgotten."

"Double the protection. Excellent." Colin went back to reading the paper.

"Let me do my job."

"Nobody's stopping you. I'm only sitting here."

She *hmphed* and shut the door.

Colin grinned. Truly, he just didn't want this woman's personality to overpower Angela while her mindset was already of a submissive nature. Agent MacDonald was likely to push for the information she wanted, despite how it would affect Angela. He knew her type. She was more of an agency bully than a helpful shrink. Colin had dealt with many of her types when it came to Graham over the years. The difference was, Graham would shut down and clam up, giving no information whatsoever, while Angela would allow it to be painfully extracted.

He wouldn't hesitate to put MacDonald out on her fancy arse.

Their voices inside were low, lulling. Colin didn't try to make out what they were saying, though he would have loved to be a fly on the wall. Just to know Angela better and hear her thoughts and feelings.

Noontime came and went. Colin looked at his watch and shook his head. They should be stopping to eat. He'd give them one more hour before interrupting and demanding they take a break. His intervention ended up not being necessary, as forty-five minutes later the door opened and Angela slipped out, heading for the restroom without looking his way.

Agent MacDonald watched from the door, a look of awe in her eyes. "Her story is fascinating," she whispered. "The meticulous way they broke her down and actually got her to care for him. She doesn't even realize…"

Colin bit down hard, grinding his teeth. "Her story is tragic and unfortunate. Not fascinating."

The woman blinked at him. "Well, I assure you from a psychological perspective it's quite riveting. I'd love to know what you experienced in there."

He wouldn't be telling her a fucking thing about his time at the villa.

Angela returned and Colin stood, blocking her entrance to the office, looking at Agent MacDonald.

"You need to stop for lunch."

She sighed. "Fine. But make it quick."

Colin led Angela to the kitchen and opened the refrigerator, which had been fully stocked by the Birches. He pulled out the makings for sandwiches and got to work.

"You like turkey sandwiches?" he asked.

She gave a small nod. "I can make them."

"No, I've got it. Have a seat."

She slid into a chair and pulled her knees up, resting her chin on them.

Colin sat across from her, placing the napkin with her lunch in front of her. He'd even cut it in half. But once again

Angela only stared at it. He glanced toward the kitchen door and hall, but they were alone. An urge rose up in Colin, and he wanted to smack it down, but he found himself following it, with a hammering in his chest. He lifted Angela's sandwich to her mouth and she opened her lips, taking in the offering and biting.

She would do anything he wanted, Colin realized. She was still his. He could demand her on her knees under the table right that moment and she'd obey. His cock sprung to life like an erotic kick and he wanted her—wanted to command her actions and feel the hum of satisfaction as he watched her obey.

Her eyes lifted to his, scorching him with their heat, and he wondered if she was thinking the same.

"Fuck." He dropped the sandwich, glad the table was keeping his erection hidden. "Angela...I need you to feed yourself. *Please.* I can't keep doing this. It's not good for you."

Or me.

She swallowed her bite and started to tremble. "I can't."

Colin felt frustrated. He didn't know the right or wrong of it anymore.

"Look at me." His voice was harsher than intended, but it did the trick. Her wide brown eyes looked up. "Pick up your sandwich and take a bite. Continue looking at me as you eat."

With shaking hands, she did exactly as he'd ordered, and it was fucking beautiful. To reward her he reached down and ran his hand up the length of her soft forearm. "Very good. From now on, I want you to do this on your own. I will no longer feed you. I like to see your independence. Do you understand?"

She swallowed and nodded. His hand lingered against her skin, and he watched the rise and fall of her chest quicken.

"Ahem."

He pulled his hand back and looked at Agent MacDonald in the doorway. Nobody usually got the drop on Colin, but he'd been too wrapped up in Angela to hear her approach. Now he inwardly cursed himself.

Agent MacDonald crossed her arms and moved closer. "I think this thing between the two of you needs to be addressed right away."

Every muscle in Colin tightened and Angela dropped her sandwich.

"I was going to speak to you each individually, but it might be beneficial to discuss this with both of you at once." She took a chair and pulled it to the end of the table. "What happened between the two of you in Spain?"

Straight for the balls. Neither of them replied.

"Did you have sex?"

"Agent—" Colin began, but Angela cut him off.

"No. He...wouldn't."

Agent MacDonald's eyebrows went up. "Interesting. Then what? Kissing? Touching? Oral sex, maybe?"

"Where the fuck are you going with this, Agent?"

She *tsked.* "Language, please. There is an obvious link between the two of you, brought on by the trauma you shared. Angela treats you as a savior while you seem to feel a constant need to continue serving her, even while your job is technically over."

"She is still under my protection while in Scotland."

"Nobody knows where she is—"

"That we're aware of."

"Agent Douglas." The woman's condescending tone was grating. "You witnessed Angela in an openly sexual environment, and I can only assume the two of you had sexual contact of some sort, which further muddied the waters. You both did what you had to to pursue freedom, and I commend you, but it is time to move forward. Agent Douglas, the longer you linger in Angela's life, the longer you're prolonging her mental instability."

Angela's head lifted abruptly. "No."

"Yes," Agent MacDonald crooed to her. "It is difficult to heal while someone from your past is in the picture as a constant reminder of all you experienced. Every time you look at him you must see the enslaved girl you once were."

"Every time I look at him I see the goodness in humanity!" Angela slapped a hand over her mouth, as if dumbfounded by her shout.

Something inside Colin fluttered, both at her words and her outburst that showed renewed strength. Was that really how she saw him?

Agent MacDonald couldn't accept this, as proven by her pursed lips. "Let me ask you this, then," the woman said to Angela. "What do you want from him?"

Angela said nothing, only stared at the table, taking steady breaths.

Agent MacDonald prompted her. "Do you just want him to be near you, forever? To keep you safe? Do you want to spend your life thanking him? Perhaps with your body?"

Colin tensed. The way she said that, as if accusing and judging Angela made him see red with rage.

"That's enough," he said.

"I'm only just beginning," she said. "The two of you need a serious reality check."

"Not like this." Colin stood. "It's time for you to leave."

"Excuse me?" Agent MacDonald stood, as well, a challenging look on her face.

"You heard me. You're not helping the situation. Only

making things worse. I want you to leave."

"You are making a grave mistake."

"Now."

Colin could tell by her puffed up chest and clenched fists that she wasn't accustomed to taking orders. But she could likely tell by the unflinching glare of his eyes that he would not back down.

"Abernathy will be hearing about this." She clinked her heels from the room, and Colin followed to show her out. She turned at the door and pointed a finger at his chest. "That girl believes she's in love with you! It's completely irresponsible for you to allow this to continue."

He wanted to argue with her, but the problem was he knew she was right. He felt like a gobshite at any given moment for not wanting to let her go, but he couldn't.

"I know what you're thinking," she continued. "That you can have a future of some sort together, but it will be a mockery of a relationship. What kind of man pursues a traumatized woman who's been so poorly used that she can never hope for a normal life?"

Colin stepped closer, keeping his voice low, and watched the Agent's breathing quicken.

"The kind of man who cares for said woman, and wants to help her find that 'normal life' you believe she can never have."

"You're just as emotionally disturbed as she is!"

"Well then we make a nice pair."

Agent MacDonald looked him square in the eye with a malicious gleam. "Are you intimidated by strong women, Agent Douglas? Afraid you can't handle one like me who's actually got her act together? You want the weak ones who will cave to your will?"

Colin briefly allowed himself to envision taking this woman over his knee. It would do her some good. Instead he said, "Angela Birch *is* the strongest woman I know. And yes. She intimidates the fuck out of me."

He opened the door and gestured for her to exit. Angry fire lit Agent MacDonald's face as she stomped past him. He shut the door, locking it behind her with relish.

When he turned he caught sight of Angela standing at the edge of the hall, watching him. How much had she heard? He started to call her name, but she turned and rushed away.

Colin cursed, and ran to catch her, but she was down the hall, closing the door to her room. He went to her door, placing his palms and forehead against it.

"Angela...can we talk, lass?" He had no idea what to say. No idea what to do. What did he expect from her? What did he want for the future? Was the psych Agent correct in her assessment of his complete fucked-up-ness for having all of these feelings he couldn't understand for the girl he'd saved?

The door slowly and quietly opened, making his blood pump and nerves dance.

Angela's eyes were down as he came in and closed the door.

"Will you talk to me?" he asked.

She gave a small shrug. "What do you want me to say? Nobody takes me seriously."

All lines of right and wrong had been blurred and gray since he met Angela, and he still didn't know what to believe or think. All he knew was that she'd gotten to a place inside him that nobody else ever had. A place he hadn't even known he had.

"I...fuck. I want to know you. To know what you're feeling."

"I already told you."

I love you.

"Look at me," Colin whispered. Her pretty eyes raised to his. "Please understand that I'm questioning every single thing in my life right now. All that I did to rescue you—I'd do it all again to save you, but I can't help but wonder if I could have done things differently."

"You couldn't have." A tremble of emotion was in her voice. "It was dangerous for you not to have sex with me—real sex. You don't have to question that anymore."

"Even so. I now question everything I feel. Everything you feel. I want to do right by you, but what if Agent MacDonald is right? What if I'm only holding you back?"

"She's wrong!" Angela's eyes filled with righteous tears that didn't spill. Her voice was strong as her little hands fisted with indignation. "I don't want to hear you or her say my feelings aren't real because of what I've been through. My mind and my heart might be hurting, but they're not *broken*. They're working just fine! I know what I want!"

She was shaking, as if the force of her words conjured fear after so long of not being able to speak her mind. The strength in her voice did crazy things to Colin.

"What do you want?" he asked her.

She closed her eyes. "I want you."

So many things flitted through Colin's mind at top speed. Did she want him for good? Or temporarily? Did she need to fuck him to get closure from him? So many reasons cropped up for him to tell her no. It'd only been a handful of days since she'd found freedom. He could still be taking advantage of her.

She stood there before him, head down, fists clenched in frustration, and Colin had never wanted to touch a woman so badly. The absolute certainty and exasperation in her voice made him push all doubt aside. As he made his decision, he felt desire working its way through him, spinning like a maelstrom. And he embraced it.

He stepped closer, nearly growling. "You want me?"

She sucked in a breath, and Colin knew she could surely see the arousal growing in his pants. "Yes, Mr. Douglas."

Even the sound of her formal name for him made him feel wild. Unfettered.

"On your knees."

She dropped to her knees without hesitation, sending a thrill through his nerve endings strong enough to push his guilt aside. Maybe she really wanted this, or maybe she only thought she did. Either way, he was going to give it to her.

"Tell me exactly what you want, Angela."

Her eyes stared down at her hands on her thighs. "I want…"

He stepped forward, placing a hand on her head, digging his fingers lightly into her hair. "Yes?"

"I want you to own me. Right now. To be my master in the bedroom."

Colin had never been so hard in his life. He struggled to take even breaths.

"Stand up, Angela. Take off your clothes."

She did as he asked, letting the clothes fall to the floor at his feet. Her body was as gorgeous as he recalled, taut valleys and soft curves begging for his touch. Her apparent nervousness only added to the lust factor for him.

He stepped closer until he was inches from her, and she kept her head down, never moving.

Colin reached behind her and pulled out the ponytail holder, then thrust his fingers into the hair at her neck, tugging lightly to lift her head.

"Look at me."

She did. Their mingled gazes were almost too intimate to handle.

"Tell me what else you want," he demanded.

"I want you inside me. In every part of me. From every angle. I want you to use me." She paused for breath and it took every ounce of self control for Colin not to attack yet. Then she said, "I want to be your slave. Your whore."

He leaned his face closer to hers, feeling fierce. "You are neither of those things to me, Angela. You are my woman. My beautiful, submissive woman. Do you understand?"

She gave a tiny nod and then gasped as his grip in her hair tightened.

"Words."

"Yes," she breathed.

"I want to hear you say it. You are not a whore."

She closed her eyes and he held her hair tighter, forcing them open.

"I'm not a whore."

"You're not a slave."

Her voice cracked when she whispered, "I'm not a slave," and Colin felt that place inside of him that she owned crack open as well.

"You are my woman."

A tear slipped down her cheek and he made no move to wipe it away. It was a part of her. It could stay.

"I'm your woman, Mr. Douglas. Yours."

He crushed his mouth to hers, using his hands to pull her tiny, naked body against him. He felt her fingers at the button of his trousers and he grabbed his shirt, ripping it over his head.

Colin let go of every fear. Every doubt. Every worry.

He let it all go, and embraced his instincts. He would own this wee lass. Completely.

CHAPTER THIRTY-FIVE

Angela

I'd never wanted to cry of happiness from a single touch until that moment. But each fingertip that met my skin, each hungry tug and pull, each press of his palms and crush of his lips made me want to weep with joy. These were touches born of true desire. These were touches I'd chosen, and he'd chosen, despite how difficult I know it'd been for him.

He was too noble for his own good, and to see him let loose lit me on fire.

This is what I wanted and needed. This man and his firm grip of ownership on my body. Maybe in the eyes of Agent MacDonald our relationship wasn't healthy, but I didn't care. Nothing had ever felt more right.

He walked me backward to the bed, pushing me down and standing over me. I grabbed the waistband of his underwear and pulled them out and down, reaching for his thick shaft with greedy urgency. He moaned as my fingers curled around him. His own hand dipped down and cursed with lust when his fingers found my wetness. I pushed my hips toward his hand, and he shoved me back on the bed, covering my body with his, kissing me hard.

His lips were firm and his tongue was soft as it flicked

mine, then rubbed it in a smooth, methodical way that sent a zap down through my belly. God, I wanted that tongue all over me. But mostly I needed to feel that perfect cock inside me. I reached down and took him in my hand again, loving how his whole body tightened and he hissed in response.

He reached for both my hands, grasping my wrists and thrusting them over my head. "Not yet," he said, moving his mouth down the dip of my throat to my chest. "You're gunna make me come too fast, like a lad."

I arched my back, loving the light scrape of his five o'clock shadow on my sensitive skin, and when his warm mouth covered my breast I cried out in ecstasy. His tongue circled and flicked, his teeth gently biting as he sucked and pulled, causing just enough mild pain to make me groan wildly. His mouth ventured to the other side and I was panting. My hands tried to tug from his grip, needing to touch him, but he pulled them higher and tighter, pressing my wrists into the mattress.

He leaned on his elbow and reached down to hike my knee, putting his thickness right where I needed him. Then he lifted himself just enough to hover over me, staring deep into my eyes. My breaths were ragged as his hips circled, his head at my entrance. I expected a plunge, but he pushed himself slowly into me, forcing me to feel each inch of his hardness as it filled me, stretching me to a glorious fullness until his pelvis was against mine and we were both fighting for breaths.

"Yes," I whispered. I was so primed for this. Any amount of friction would put me over the edge.

I waited for him to begin fucking me with fast abandon, but he was full of surprises. He pushed his hips harder, pressing me into the bed and forcing me to feel him deeper. I moaned loudly. He never pulled out an inch, only began rocking his hips in hard motions, pressing my clit against his pelvis with jarring firmness.

"Yes, oh God, Mr. Douglas, I'm gonna come."

"Aye, come for me. I want to hear you call me Colin."

His hips rocked into me again, harder, detonating an explosion in my clitoris that shot outward, making my whole body convulse. I pressed my hips up, rubbing against him and screamed.

"Colin! *Yeah*...oh, God, *yes...*"

As my crotch continued to constrict and pulse around him, he brought his mouth down on mine, tasting the last of my moans.

I sucked in a shuddering breath as he released my wrists and pulled out of me. He took me by the hips and flipped me to my stomach, positioning me on my hands and knees before him. He gripped both of my ass cheeks in a tight squeeze and buried his face between my legs. My clit was still so sensitive that I nearly flew out of my skin. He steadied me, ignoring my whimpers as he suckled and rubbed until my nerve-endings were worked into another frenzy. Just as I thought I might come again, he sat up.

In a swift plunge he was inside of me, and the pounding I'd been waiting for began. I didn't try to be quiet. I vocalized with each thrust—each smack of his hips against my ass—each swing of his tight balls against me. I turned my head and watched as this beautiful man pulled back my hips with each forward movement of his own. His eyes met mine and I wanted to melt at the intensity in them.

"Is this what you want?" he ground out. "You want more?"

"Yes. I want it." I used my knees and palms to rock myself back into him, meeting his rhythm, slamming our bodies together as hard as possible. I felt one of his hands release my hip, and seconds later a wet thumbtip was at the entrance of my ass, gently pressing in. I groaned as he pressed it all the way in and began to fuck me with smooth swipes in and out, his thumb matching the strokes.

So good.

His free hand reached around and slipped up and down my still-wet slit.

"Yes, Colin," I breathed. I loved saying his name.

Pushing with all his hard weight, he pressed my body flat against the bed and brought my arms up, holding them in place tightly above me as my cheek hit the sheets. I lifted my ass as high as it would go, to take him as deep as I could, and we rocked back and forth together. Usually I was not able to come from behind, but I was so worked up, and the tightness of the position was enough to arouse an orgasm when I squeezed my thighs together.

Colin lightly bit my shoulder, his pace and breaths quickening.

"Give it to me, Colin."

"Och, lass, *fuck*..."

He shoved deeper and held himself there, grunting a masculine shout that sparked against my clitoris and lit up my world. Together our bodies found their pleasure, and earthquake of joined throbbing that had us both sucking air and moaning for minutes.

He lay on top of me, placing kisses across my upper back and shoulders as we caught our breath. I felt bold and alive.

"Come with me to The Netherlands," I whispered.

I thought I heard a grin in his voice when he responded, "Aye, then. You couldn't keep me away."

I smiled, keeping it partially hidden by my arm, but he took me by the shoulder and turned me to face him.

"I saw that," he said. His thumb brushed over my lips. "You smiled."

Feeling shy, but unbelievably happy, I let the smile

return. He stared down at me, his eyes lighting, and then a grin graced his own lips, making mine stretch wider.

The smile transformed his face, turning him into a handsome younger man without a care. It made my soul take flight. I reached up and touched his face. I felt so many things. I couldn't put it all into words, but I needed him to know.

"There was always something different about you," I said. "I never understood why, but I couldn't think of you as one of them. I think I felt you, the real you, all along."

He closed his eyes and leaned into my hand. After a moment he leaned down, resting his elbows above my shoulders and his forehead against mine.

"I love you, Angela. And until you tell me to leave, I will be at your side."

"Then you'll be there forever."

He kissed me, tender and sweet.

This is what Marco could never offer to his patrons. True paradise.

As he held me, I traced my fingers over the tattoo inside his left arm—a Celtic knot in the shape of a wicked tree, the roots branching out just below his elbow. The jagged lines curved and weaved, but all were connected—no beginning and no end. Then I looked at the beautiful Gaelic script up the inside of his right arm.

"It is better to try than to hope," he whispered.

For some reason that phrase made me sad. "It's okay to hope, though," I said. "Hope is necessary. Without it, you feel dead."

His eyes met mine, and my words seemed to cause him pain, as if he were imagining me without hope. I kissed the words inside his arm, and he kissed my bare shoulder.

"What about the one on your back?" I asked.

"Freedom."

I smiled up at him and he grinned in return, making my tummy flop. "Now that one, I like."

We lay together well into the night until an alarm blared, followed by the sound of an engine revving and gravel kicking up outside by the gate. Colin moved so fast. He leapt from the bed, tugging on his pants and shirt with serious eyes. My heart pounded. He held his gun in a trained arm by his side.

"Stay here," he said.

I jumped down as he left and quickly got dressed. I pressed my ear to the door, listening to the sounds of Colin opening the door, then closing it again, the rustling of paper followed by a low curse. I couldn't take the worry and suspense anymore. I slipped out of the room and tiptoed down the hall to the corner. What I saw made my stomach plummet as if I'd fallen from a cliff.

My world spun.

Ripped paper was on the floor, and in Colin's hand was a painting of a girl bathed in gold, surrounded by hellish surroundings. The painting he'd done of me at the villa.

"Oh, my God," I said. Colin's head snapped up, terror swimming in his steel eyes.

"He's alive," Colin hissed, disbelief coloring each word.

I went to his side, shaking. The front of the painting had a loose paper taped on that simply said: *You left something.* ~M.

Fight or flight instincts kicked in. I wanted to run like hell.

"We have to get out of here!" I said.

Colin turned the painting over and there was an envelope. He ripped it off and set the painting down. Inside was a photograph, but I could only see the back. Colin's face drained of blood. I'd never seen him look like that—

defeated, at a total loss.

"What is it?" I asked, but a horrible sinking feeling had already set in. Somehow, I knew.

He pulled off the note from the front of the picture and crumpled the photo in his hand. The note said: Now we are even.

Shit. What had Marco done? Dread ripped at me, shredding my soul.

Colin's hand went to his head.

"Your parents," he whispered, pain obvious in each word. "They're gone, Angela."

"No," I whispered. His words cascaded over me like blazing acid, each word punctuating with a sickening burn. *"No!"*

I slid to the floor, swallowed by a fire of anguish.

CHAPTER THIRTY-SIX

He should have killed Marco Ruiz when he had the chance. He should have watched him take his last breath—made certain he was dead, as Colin had done with Fernando.

He bent and grasped Angela by the shoulders. "We have to go! Now!" But she was an inconsolable puddle of grief. He scooped her into his arms and ran with her to Graham's room, kicking the door with his foot until his brother opened the door, disheveled and wide-eyed.

"What the fuck?" Graham grumbled.

Colin ran in and lay his sobbing Angela on the bed, where she curled up in a ball and moaned, "Mama, I'm sorry." Colin felt his own eyes prick with emotion, but there was no time for it.

He pulled out his phone and dialed Abernathy while speaking to Graham. "You have one minute to pack your shite. The man who held Angela killed her parents. We're getting the fuck out of here."

Graham's stricken eyes went to Angela as her keening wail rose up and filled the room.

Abernathy answered and Colin rattled off their information, telling him to meet them in the field behind the forest of Graham's house.

Colin didn't bother packing anything for himself or Angela. He took her by the hand and made her sit up. Her chest heaved and her eyes were far away. Lost. He took her face in his hands.

"You need to run with me. I can't carry you in case I need to fight. Here."

He pressed a small handgun into her palm and though her whole body shook uncontrollably, her fingers curled around it.

"Good girl," Colin whispered, relieved.

The three of them moved to the back of the house, where Colin peered through the windows. He saw nothing, so he ushered them outside, and they sprinted through the lush yard and into the forest, dodging trees and underbrush. Graham and Angela kept up, both breathing hard. It was a quarter mile of land before they hit the open clearing where Abernathy pulled up moments later, tires uprooting a line of grass.

Colin yanked the backdoor open, pushed the other two in, and Abernathy was laying on the gas before Colin's legs were even in the door.

"They're gassing up a plane," the Agent said. "Decide where to go, pal."

"Fuck." Colin scrubbed his palms over his face and looked to Angela, who sat like a pale stone next to him, her arms circling her waist and holding tight. "What languages do you know?" he asked her.

She looked at him blankly for a moment before her eyes semi-cleared. "Russian. Spanish. German. French. A little Dutch."

Colin nodded. They'd go to Russia. He'd been on several missions, and knew which areas to avoid.

"I want to see the picture," she said.

Colin hesitated. "I dropped it back at the house." He'd

tossed it on purpose. He would have never, ever let her see that picture. No matter how much she begged and how much closure it might have brought. It would have also brought nightmares.

"Was it my Mom and Dad?"

"Yes," he whispered.

A sound escaped Angela and she covered her mouth, bending at the waist and hiding her face. "This is my fault. I shouldn't have stopped you. I should have let you kill him!"

"Nae, lassie, nae. It's not your fault. We both thought he was as good as dead."

Colin placed a hand on her back, feeling helpless and wanting to kill Marco ten times over. He couldn't believe the man had survived the fatal injuries. He met Graham's aching gaze, and their eyes stuck as they shared the realization that all three of them were united in similar horror. They'd all lost their parents to the criminal underworld. They'd all been involved in sexual slavery, and would all carry scars on their souls for life.

He couldn't let this cycle continue. Couldn't allow Marco to terrorize them for life. He envisioned himself finding safety for Angela and his brother, then flying to Spain.

Graham shook his head. "Ya can't go after them. Not this time."

Even Abernathy shook his head. "Nae, son."

Angela sat up and looked at Colin, panic in her bloodshot eyes. She grabbed his hand.

"Don't even think about it!"

"Angela—"

"No! If he says we're even, then we are. He always has to have the last word, and I know it sounds crazy, but he has this strange sense of fucked up honor. He means what he says."

Colin's jaw clenched. He didn't want that fucker having the last word this time or ever again. And he hated that Angela knew that bastard well enough to say that.

"Please," Angela begged. The sadness in her thick voice killed him. "He's taken enough from me. I can't lose you too." Her sobbing renewed, but this time her head went to his lap, her tears soaking the fabric at his thighs, and he pulled her up to his chest, holding her tight.

"You can't save the fucking world," Graham said. "You can't fight them all. What's the use if it gets you killed? You've done enough!"

Graham had never vocalized that he wanted Colin to stop what he did for a living. Hearing it took a bit of the angry wind out of Colin's sails.

Angela gripped his shirt. "Swear to me. Say you'll never go back there. Swear you'll never try to get revenge." When he said nothing, she began to punch his chest with fury. *"Swear it!"*

Colin wouldn't lie to her. From what he knew of Marco, he believed what Angela said was true, but it didn't make him feel any better. Still, he took her hands firmly and made the most difficult promise of his life.

"I won't go back. I swear it."

She collapsed into him, and even Graham let his head fall back and his eyes close, as if consoled by the sound of his brother's promise.

It was hard to imagine a life that didn't consist of hunting down criminals and trying to erase them. He'd done a lot, but it didn't feel like enough. It was never enough. He wanted to destroy them all, burn the entire underworld of slavery, but that's not what Angela or Graham would have him do. They were all he had. They were his life now. Could he dedicate himself solely to keeping them safe and happy?

Staring down at Angela's sweet, tear stained face, and

the familiar slope of his little brother's nose, the answer was clear.

Yes. Yes, he could make a life out of being there for them. A life fueled by love instead of hate—hope instead of fear. He would do that for them. For himself. He would attempt to rebuild for them a tiny piece of what'd been stolen.

At the airport Abernathy flashed a badge and sped to the terminals, slamming on the brakes next to the private jet.

"Get in touch someday when you're settled," Abernathy said, turning to hold out his hand.

Colin slapped his hand into the older gentleman's and shook it, holding on longer than normal as they spoke many thanks through their eyes. Abernathy nodded and pulled his hand away.

"Go, and try to find yourself some happiness, aye? Off with ya."

They slid out of the car and up the steps of the plane.

Colin allowed himself one last look over the Scottish landscape before saying good-bye to his homeland, likely forever.

EPILOGUE

Eliska

Three Years Later...

———◆•◆———

People in our Russian community called us Nico and Eliska, but at home we were still Colin and Angela. Graham left us two years ago for New York City to chase his dreams, something that made Colin and I happy despite missing him. He left the day after Colin became my husband.

The doves on the fire escape outside our apartment window were loud that early morning. The sun was barely awake. When I stirred, Colin's hand went around my waist, spooning me from behind and pressing his morning erection against my ass. His warm, steady breaths at the back of my neck signaled he was still half asleep.

He usually woke earlier than me to work out, so we didn't often get to have morning sex. I fully planned to take advantage of it now.

I slid my underwear down, letting my backside wiggle against him. He pushed my hair aside and kissed the back of my neck.

"Is there something you'd like to ask for, my little lassie?"

"Please, Mr. Douglas, may I touch you?"

"Mm, aye, you may. Such a good little girl."

I reached behind me and encircled his cock, both of us moaning as I arched my back and led him inside me. Sex was the only time I could get away with calling him Mr. Douglas. It no longer carried the weight of his time as a pseudo patron. We'd taken back the power of those words. When he owned me now, it was for our pleasure. It was a relationship born of trust.

We rocked against each other, his grip on my hip helping him to push deeper. I squirmed, reaching back over my head to feel the familiar fuzz of his head as my ass circled, driving him crazy.

"You are so fucking incredible," he said into my neck. His hand left my hip, letting me control the pace of the thrusts, and he reached up to palm my swollen breast, squeezing with enough pressure to make me cry out. Then his hand slid down between my thighs and gently pinched my clit. I gasped and pressed my hand over his, making him press harder.

As he worked me faster, both with his hand and from behind I felt an orgasm building. The arm underneath him reached up and his hands tangled in my hair, gripping enough to make me gasp as he pulled back to run his scruff across my jaw. I shouted the pleasure of my release loud enough for the neighbors to hear, just the way he liked. He followed right behind me, coming deep inside me and practically growling, just the way *I* liked.

Afterward we lay there coming down together, him still inside me.

"Well, good morning," he purred against my shoulder.

I smiled. His hand slid up and stopped on my rounded belly, fingers splaying across my taut skin. I placed my hand on top of his.

"How do you feel?" he asked.

"Good," I was happy to admit. The first trimester had been awful. I was physically sick, and emotionally scared out of my mind. We hadn't planned to get pregnant. Ever. It had been too frightening to think of having a tiny innocent to care for and protect. But we'd also lost so much, that the thought of another person to love, no matter how scary, was also exhilarating.

I was disappointed when Colin slowly pulled out and sat up, grabbing a towel to clean my thighs. He tossed it to the hamper and leaned down to kiss my lips, then placed a kiss to my tummy before standing.

"Latch the door behind me," he said, just as he did every single time he left the apartment.

"I will."

The bolt lock clicked into place as he left for his run. I slipped on a robe and slid the chain at the top of the door, then went to our window, watching Colin as he exited our building into the chilled morning and scouted the surroundings before setting off on his jog.

I touched the glass, my chest squeezing at the thought of anything happening to him. Each time he left to run or work odd jobs—construction, painting, uprooting trees, anything to keep his hands busy—I watched him go.

We wouldn't be staying in Russia much longer. We'd already lived in three parts of the country, deciding we would move every year of our lives. Forever. With each fresh start we felt a renewed sense of safety, and we needed that feeling now more than ever. In two weeks we were off to France.

I was excited about the small cottage we'd secured, but I would miss the Russian girls I'd been working with. I moonlighted part time as a counselor to rape victims, and I'd even come across a couple girls who'd been slaves at one time. Abernathy had doctored up fake credentials to allow seeking these kinds of jobs, and I only felt the slightest bit guilty about lying to employers.

If I could use my past to help one girl realize she had self-worth and a future worth living, then I would lie about my education a thousand times to make it happen.

I often wondered about Josef, Perla, Mia, and Jin. I was certain they were still with Marco. I prayed they were safe, and experiencing as much happiness as possible. But I ached at the opportunities of love they were being denied. Perla loved Marco, but to be loved in return was key. I counted my blessings daily.

Marco once said that it was like acquiring me had been "meant to be." I'd hated him for saying it—for making light of something so dark. But now I wondered...was it all meant to be? I would have never met Colin. He was likely to have never stopped seeking justice, only to have his own life taken. And I would have never been able to administer to the hearts and minds of the abused girls I'd come across.

I didn't know what to believe. All I knew was even through the daily grief, I was thankful. I refused to let it all be for nothing. Because even within all the ugliness of the world there was beauty. Some of it needed to be pulled from the dirt and dusted off, given wings.

I had to hope there would be justice—if not in this life, then in the hereafter.

A half hour later my stomach dipped and lifted at the sight of Colin returning, sweat beading at his faint hairline. I listened for the click of the bolt and his secret knock before unlatching the top lock. Inside he secured the locks again and kissed my temple.

"I don't think we should wait two weeks," he said. His brow was furrowed.

"Did something happen?"

"Nae," he admitted. But he worried. Always.

"Okay. Let me say good-bye to the girls, and we can leave tomorrow."

He closed his eyes and nodded before kissing me again. "Thank you."

I absently rubbed my belly and watched him strip down and head for the shower. I wished I could take away his constant fear, but it was part of how he showed his love. The thing was, I knew Marco wasn't coming for us. He might be keeping dibs, just in case we ever crossed him again, but I felt with certainty he would leave us be. Marco had never wanted me dead. And I'd seen the look of disappointment in his eyes when Colin turned on him. He'd thought of him as a protege.

I couldn't think about what he'd done to my parents. If I went down that road I'd be depressed for days. My parents would have willingly given their lives for mine any day, but that doesn't make it okay. The world lost two wonderful people because of one man who thought he could create paradise. The scary thing about Marco was that he believed he was a good guy. He believed he had the right to take lives at his will, to maintain his lifestyle of pseudo perfection. But what he didn't realize was that nothing was perfect.

Nothing except love.

Colin came out of the shower, still wet with a towel over his shoulders. I grinned at him, and he came straight to me, covering my mouth with his, the clean smell of him surrounding us. He pulled away and held both ends of the towel, eyeing me.

"To your knees, woman."

I dropped my eyes and smiled to myself, obeying.

ACKNOWLEDGMENTS

This book was far out of my comfort zone to write, as I had only written Young Adult stories until this point. The idea had plagued me for a while, and I've come to learn as a writer that it's best to get it out or it will take up permanent residence in your mind. It was a freeing experience. I don't know if I'll write more in the dark-adult, but I'm open to the whims of my imagination, wherever it may take me.

Putting story ideas to paper, and actually making them something readable and rich with detail is not a solitary endeavor. I've had the help of many people along the way.

I need to thank my husband for his unflinching support from the beginning, along with his "James Bond-like" expertise, ha.

Thank you to my first reader and wonderful friend, Kelley, for pushing me to write this book, and helping me through the independent publishing process.

Thank you to my second readers and cheerleaders, Carol and Jill.

Thank you, Bren, for proofing my Spanish and always being at the ready to translate. Thank you Elizabeth and Paula for Scottish dialect help.

Thank you E.J. for designing my blog.

Thank you to Miss York for designing the original cover and

jacket, and Jennifer for designing the updated image. Thank you Angel's Indie Formatting for your beautiful work on the manuscript.

Thank you to all the lovely readers and reviewers on Goodreads who spread the word and raised their hands to do early reviews. You guys are incredible, and you help us Indie authors immensely!

Lastly, thank you Lord for it all.

ABOUT THE AUTHOR

Gwendolyn Field hails from the Washington D.C. area of the U.S., where she lives with her husband and two children. *Escape from Paradise* is her first adult romance novel.

Feel free to contact Gwen online.

Email: gwendolynfield@hotmail.com

Gwen on Goodreads:
http://www.goodreads.com/author/show/6996431.Gwendolyn_Field

Gwen on Facebook:
https://www.facebook.com/pages/Gwendolyn-Field/170286603121602

Made in the USA
Charleston, SC
20 May 2016